A Warrior's Path

Volume One: The Castes and the OutCastes

Davis Ashura

A WARRIOR'S PATH

ISBN: 978-0-9911276-1-0
DuSum Publishing, LLC

DEDICATION

To my wonderful wife, Stephanie.
For all the things you do,
especially the ones that I somehow overlook.

Acknowledgments

Like all things of worth, this book would not exist without the help of some wonderful and generous people. First comes my wife, Stephanie, who gave me the time and freedom to actually sit down and write this thing I love but which was simultaneously a pain in the ass. Next, the men and women of the Catawba County Asswhoopin' Writer's Group. They were kind enough to slog through the manuscript when none but the brave or masochistic should have taken a look at it.

To Holly Cook, an amazing and perceptive reader, who read it, liked it enough to finish it, and never seemed to mind too much when I peered over her shoulder to skulk out whatever criticisms she was writing.

Also to my sister with whom I share a brain, and who immediately noticed all the problems I didn't want to look at.

I would be remiss if I did not include my editor and fellow writer: the peripatetic (or is that priapistic?) Kevin Keck. It was only after witnessing his opiated and genitally obsessed ramblings that I realized that if such a delusional person as he could successfully write a book, then hell, I could too.

To all of them, I offer my most humble 'thank you'.

TABLE OF CONTENTS

A Warrior's Path

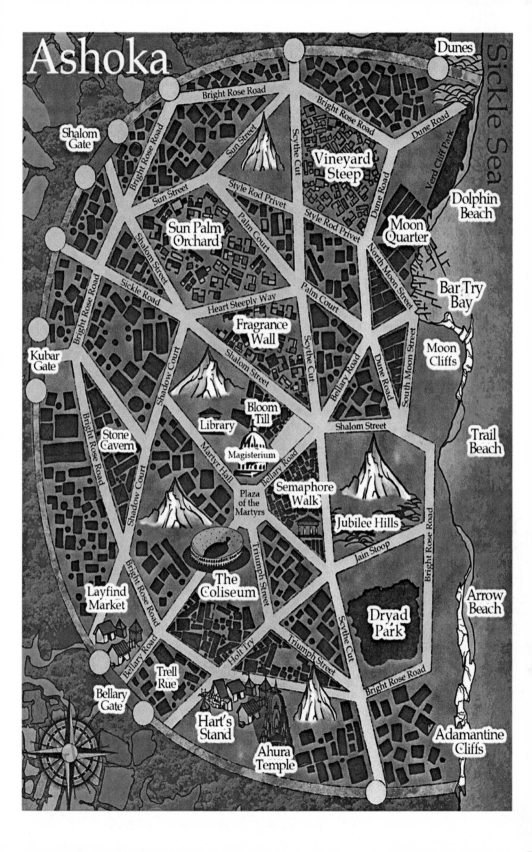

CHAPTER ONE
ENCIRCLED

The Trials are our exegesis, and what we need
to learn from them is all too obvious…
we were meant for so much more.

~The Warrior and the Servant (author unknown)

"**P**ut some ass into it, men" Sergeant Lathe growled. "You pansies might be needing this ditch an hour from now." Lathe took his own advice as he bit into the hard ground with his shovel and flung aside a load of dirt. Nearby, other warriors were preparing the stakes meant to line the trench and slow down the horde of Chimeras heading their way.

Six weeks out from the city of Ashoka, and the caravan to Nestle faced what might be overwhelming odds in its first and possibly last battle. Given the history of Humanity since the birth of Suwraith two millennia earlier, it shouldn't have surprised anyone.

No one knew where She had come from or what drove Her hatred, but upon Her sudden entrance into the world on the Night of Sorrows two millennia ago, She had murdered fully half of all

1

people living at the time. It was a blow from which Humanity had yet to recover because Suwraith's fury continued unabated. She raged on, stalking Humankind and going so far as to create the brutal, beast-like Chimeras to aid in Her destructive ambition. The only safety was found within the narrow confines of the few cities still alive after the Days of Desolation. But beyond and all around them, in the great swatches of untamed land throughout the rest of the world, it was a killing field. It was the Wildness.

Only the brave ventured into those lands, serving as warriors in the Trials, the great trade caravans that maintained a fragile contact and civilization of sorts between the encircled cities. Those who volunteered to leave the sanctuary of a city were faced with an important yet fearful task because to traverse the Wildness was to court death. Between Suwraith and Her armies of Chimeras, the Fan Lor Kum, one out of every four warriors on Trial could expect to die. Those numbers had declined somewhat in the past several centuries, but the Wildness was not a place into which a wise man would freely choose to travel.

Corporal Rukh Shekton, a warrior of Caste Kumma, the Caste seemingly bred for battle, stood near the officers, waiting for orders as he sweated in the late morning sun. He was young, in his early twenties, and unseasoned. This was his first Trial, he was what the veterans named a Virgin, but panic didn't seize his heart. Since he had first held a sword, the possibility of an early demise had been greatly impressed upon him. It was something he no longer feared – much. He had been trained to set aside his dread of dying and to focus on the task at hand. Duty above all, as his Martial Masters taught. At this point, death was merely an unwelcome companion, a shadow looming behind him with a cold, clammy breath, but unable to unman him.

Or at least that's what he told himself. He swallowed, trying to recall the lessons from his Martial Masters as he sought to muzzle his anxiety over whether this day would be his last. For the most part, it worked.

He listened as barked commands had men scurrying about, trying to accomplish the myriad tasks set to them. An outside observer might have thought the Ashokans were all panic-stricken, but most of these men had trained their entire lives for this moment. They had a rational madness. Seeing their calm in the face of disaster helped to settle some of Rukh's nerves.

He'd be alright.

"How the hell did they get so damn close?" Lieutenant Oak Pume demanded of no one in particular. Rukh's lieutenant had ordered Rukh to accompany him to his meeting with Captain Stryed Bosna. Pume looked angry enough to chew nails, spit them out, and go back for seconds.

"Doesn't matter now," Captain Bosna replied. "We've got work…"

His words were interrupted when scouts from the west thundered into camp. Their sergeant in charge, Marag Dwain, dismounted and threw a hasty salute even before his horse had slid to a stop.

Rukh frowned. This couldn't be good.

It wasn't.

"Two, maybe three thousand Chims heading our way," Dwain reported.

"Suwraith's spit," Bosna cursed softly.

Corporal Grate, a Muran and one of Lieutenant Danail Starb's men, stood next to Rukh. He rocked back, his face ashen. "Devesh save us," he prayed. His emerald eyes, which along with his golden-brown skin were the hallmarks of Caste Muran, darted about in fear. While Grate was a veteran and on his second Trial, Rukh could tell the man was terrified. It was a forgivable breach. After all, while Murans were brave enough, they were generally farmers. They couldn't be expected to have the courage of a Kumma.

Rukh listened as Grate murmured a fervent prayer to Devesh. Murans were also known for their piety.

Rukh sometimes wished he could pray, but it was a fleeting wish, gone in the instant of a breath. As best he figured, their God, Devesh, was an uncaring sort. His silence through the centuries as Humanity had slowly slouched its way toward extinction echoed with His utter disregard and callousness. So why would He heed their prayers now, especially from someone with as little faith as Rukh?

Devesh wouldn't. A dog might walk on its legs and talk like a person before Devesh did a single thing for Humanity.

Rukh snorted in derision. Besides, wasn't it true that bad news was hardly ever an orphan? The worst might be yet to come.

Pume glared at the still praying Muran corporal. "Shut up, Grate! Your chanting is making my ears itch." He turned his angry gaze to Rukh. "And why in the unholy hells are you standing around, Corporal?" the lieutenant barked. "Do something useful."

"Waiting for orders, sir," Rukh shouted, coming to attention and hiding his annoyance. Why was the lieutenant yelling at him? Pume had commanded Rukh's presence here, but the lieutenant had never bothered to hand out any further orders.

His answer didn't mollify the lieutenant, whose face was already beet red, from either anger or fear or a combination of the two. "Get over to your unit. Double-time it. Have them ready to move at a moment's notice. And pass the word to the other corporals. This whole situation stinks like three-day-old fish rotting out in the sun," the lieutenant said with a growl.

"Yes sir," Rukh responded.

He saluted and was about to leave, but just then the southern scouts galloped into the encampment. Rukh paused, taking note of the scouts' appearance. Both the warriors and their horses looked done for. They must have ridden hard out.

"Two thousand Chims," their sergeant, Derig Liner, gasped. "No more than two hours before they're on us."

Captain Bosna took the news with an admirable stoic aplomb.

The same couldn't be said for Jared Randall, the caravan master. The skinny Rahail hopped up and down like a bug on hot skillet. He screamed like a panic-stricken child. "East. West. South. The damn Chims are coming from everywhere. Seven Fractures. Son of a bitch. That's almost half a Shatter. What are we going to do?" He looked to Bosna as if the man could magically provide relief from their near-certain ruination. The Captain remained silent as he stared at the caravan master, not bothering to hide his disdain for the Rahail. Randall didn't notice. He'd fallen to the ground and was sobbing like a child. "We're fragged. We're well and truly fragged," he moaned, rocking back and forth.

Rukh pitied the man. Randall was the caravan master, and he'd already survived three Trials in his life. It was a very respectable number, even for a Kumma, and this was to have been Randall's last one before he returned to his home city of Nestle. One last journey, and he would have retired fabulously wealthy with a hard-earned and well-deserved respect from all. Randall probably wasn't a coward, but the shock of learning so many Chimeras were coming after them must have unmanned him. He must have hoped karma would overlook him one last time.

She hadn't.

Of course, Rukh was in the same position as far as the onrushing Chimeras were concerned. A half-smile formed on his lips. How apropos. His first Trial, and it was likely to be his last. Karma was a bitch, and she'd kissed him hard.

He broke from his reverie at the captain's shout. "Attention!" Bosna barked.

Shouts from the lieutenants and sergeants reinforced the captain's order for silence. Within moments, quiet reigned in the foothills northwest of the Hunters Flats.

The captain spoke. "In a little under two hours, this area will be overrun by seven thousand Chims. Seven Fractures. We can't stop them or even slow them down. They'll run over us like an avalanche thundering down a mountain. We only have one choice," he said. He paused briefly, seeming to study the men. "We'll have to break north and leave everything else behind. We have to escape this trap and carry word to Ashoka," he said.

"You want us to run?" Pume asked, frowning in displeasure.

The Captain turned to face him. "Think about it, Lieutenant. When was the last time we ever heard of this many Chims gathered together in one place. They wouldn't all be here just to destroy a single caravan," he said. "Their aim has to be higher. We have to assume they're here for Ashoka."

Murmurs of consternation greeted the Captain's explanation as his words were passed down to those too far away to hear them. Most of the warriors immediately understood what was at stake.

"Suwraith's spit," Pume murmured softly. "I never thought I'd live to see the day."

Captain Bosna turned away from the lieutenant and spoke again to all the warriors. "As of this moment, your pledges to this caravan are hereby rescinded. Your swords must be for Ashoka's defense only. We ride to the northern hills. From there, one of us *must* get to the city. Don't stop and aid anyone you see fall behind if it puts you at risk. Get to the city. That is your only task."

Stunned silence greeted his words. Rukh had guessed the Captain might say something like that, but hearing the words spoken aloud carried home the truth of their dire predicament with the force of a war hammer to the face. His heart pounded out the rhythm of his sudden dread. The reality of the situation came into focus: he truly might die out here in the Wildness today.

The captain gathered the lieutenants and gave them short, terse orders. Bosna called for the maps, and he and the other officers pored over them.

Rukh wasn't sure what he should do. Lieutenant Pume had told him to get his unit and the rest of the company up and ready to move, but what about the wagons? Surely he'd want them to offload the supplies they'd need to get back to Ashoka. Uncertain as to what the lieutenant would want from him, he decided to stay put and wait for the officers' meeting to end.

Pume came striding over. "Shektan. Get to the men. I need you to unload the southern wagons. Gather up anything you think we might need for the trek back to Ashoka: food, medicine, blankets, whatever you can think of. Once the wagons are emptied, fire them. And make sure the Chims don't gain anything of value from this attack. Go!"

Rukh saluted sharply, glad to have something to do, especially something that made sense. He ran to where the horses were picketed. His heart pounded with adrenaline and fear. He quickly gathered together his unit and passed the word to the other corporals and warriors of B Company. He set some of them to unloading the southern wagons of anything they could use while other warriors readied the horses.

He had to saddle his own mount since no one else would go near the unruly stallion. The beast was either vicious, stupid, or had been mistreated sometime in his life – or maybe a combination of the three. How Rukh had gotten stuck with the animal and how no one had decided to geld the stallion was something he still couldn't figure out. As usual, the beast reached back and tried to bite him. Through long practice, Rukh slid aside, and the horse's teeth clacked together, missing his thigh by inches. He tugged the reins until the horse was looking him in the eyes. "We don't have time for this," he told the stallion.

For a wonder, the animal seemed to understand his words, settling down with a snort and a shake of his withers. Maybe the weeks of relatively gentle care had earned Rukh the stallion's trust.

Whatever the reason, the horse waited calmly while Rukh saddled him.

As soon as he was done, he led the horse to where the warriors of B Company were unloading the wagons. They worked quickly and soon had a large pile of food, medicines, and other supplies.

"Get those horses out of their traces. Use them as pack animals," Rukh ordered as some of the warriors began stuffing items into their own saddlebags. There was no way they would be able to save enough supplies for the six week trip back to Ashoka, not just using their own mounts. Rukh watched. Soon enough, the men had the wagon horses unharnessed from their traces and loaded with supplies. The animals whinnied nervously and shifted about, catching the mood of fear and agitation that had swept over the caravan, but eventually they settled down.

Rukh glanced around. B Company was about ready to go. The other companies weren't far behind. They'd be leaving soon.

"Looks like we chose the wrong caravan," Keemo Chalwin said, leading his deep-chested roan mare and surprising Rukh as he appeared next to him.

"We all have to die sometime," Farn Arnicep said, moving up to Rukh's other side while also leading his mount, a gray gelding.

The three men looked to be brothers. Their resemblance wasn't surprising since all members of a Caste shared certain defining physical characteristics. As Kummas, they all had a tall, rangy build, dark hair and eyes, and skin the color of tea touched with milk. But in the case of Rukh, Keemo, and Farn, the ties went even deeper. Farn was a cousin and Keemo a close family friend. The same age, all three men had essentially been raised together. They had even attended the same Martial College, the House of Fire and Mirrors. And now, here they were, together in the Wildness, having joined the same Trial as Virgins. Keemo and Farn were as close to Rukh as his own brother.

Of course, it was said that during a Trial, all men were brothers – a trite, meaningless phrase, but it sounded nice.

Before Rukh could respond to Farn or Keemo, Brand Wall strode toward him. He was a member of B Company and a part of Rukh's unit. He, too, was a Virgin, but unlike Rukh and the other two Kummas, Brand was a Rahail, the only other Caste other than Kumma and Muran who ventured out into the Wildness. And also unlike the other two Castes, whose members were universally darker skinned, Rahails were noted for their fairness and had hair ranging in color from honey-brown to blond. Their eyes were typically lighter in hue, either blue or hazel. A green-eyed Rahail was a rare and striking sight.

During the Trial, Rukh had come to know Brand pretty well. He liked the man and considered him a good friend. They'd shared laughter, food, and the gallows humor that developed between two men on Trial together.

"We've emptied the wagons," Brand said. "There's only a few things left. Nothing we can use."

The ground around the wagons was littered with bolts of fabric, packets of spices, as well as bales of dried spidergrass and cords of roped off ironwood. It wasn't anything they could haul off with them or use on the trip back to Ashoka. "It's too bad we won't have time to toss everything we can't use back *in* the wagons. It would be easier burning it that way." He smiled. "We don't want the Chimeras to get ahold of good spidergrass or ironwood."

"I don't think you have to worry about that," Keemo said with a grin. "They'll be too busy trying to get ahold of us to bother with our supplies. Maybe after we've been corpsified, they'll come back for the wagons and what was in them."

Rukh laughed and even Farn, so often dour and cheerless, grinned.

Brand looked between the three of them, trying and failing to understand the humor. "I have no idea how you Kummas are so easy-going when you're about to die."

Rukh laughed again. "Easy. We were raised to believe we'd die young, so actually doing so doesn't seem all that frightening." His smile left him. "Or at least that's what I tell myself." His words weren't just bravado. He meant what he said, but it didn't mean he was unafraid, but for now, he had control of himself…and his worry. His Martial Masters had trained him well.

Brand glanced back and forth between them once again, appearing perplexed. Eventually, he shrugged. "Kummas are strange," he noted.

"Different," Rukh corrected. "We all have our own way of dealing with this." Just then he noticed Sergeant Folt gesturing for him. "I need to go," he said, nudging his horse forward. "You two also." He motioned to his Farn and Keemo.

"Doesn't the sergeant want all of us?" Brand asked.

Rukh shook his head. "Just the Kummas this time. You'll see why."

Rukh, Farn, and Keemo formed up in a line along with all the others from their Caste in B Company. Lieutenant Pume had arrived as well.

"Step away from the wagons!" the lieutenant yelled at several Murans and Rahails who were still pilfering the supplies or frantically lighting torches and tossing them into the ironwood wagons. Their efforts were unnecessary. When they saw the Kummas lined up and ready, they immediately understood what was about to happen and scrambled out of the way.

"Fire," Pume said.

To a man, the Kummas glowed. An instant later, Fireballs launched from their hands with a dull boom. They crashed into the wagons, which didn't so much catch fire as simply explode. Splinters of wood littered the ground as thick, black smoke curled upward, panicking some of the horses.

Rukh watched the wagons burn. Strange. It was like watching his hopes for the future burn to ash and drift away. Only two months ago, he'd been so sure of his place in the world, and now...this. He remembered the last time he had been certain of anything.

———◦———

The smell of seared meat, falafel, and samosas carried throughout Glory Stadium, briefly reminding Rukh of his hunger. He glanced around, taking in a few last impressions before his upcoming fight. Looming over him from where he stood on the floor of the stadium was the crowd. Over fifty thousand people, and they droned like a nest of angry bees. The weather was cool, but the bowl of the Coliseum was an oven, trapping the day's heat. The last rays of the twilight sun shone like a beacon into the eyes of those in the western-facing stands. Shadows crept long across the arena floor and over much of the high, unadorned, white wall that framed the pitch.

This was the moment Rukh had dreamt of his entire life. He just never thought it would arrive while he was still so young – only twenty-one. In fact, his entry into the Tournament had been nothing more than a lark. He had only wanted to test himself and get an honest assessment of his skills in comparison to those who were counted as Ashoka's finest warriors. The men Rukh had faced thus far were far more accomplished than he was. They had already fought their Trials and their battles. They had years of experience, if not skill, over him. Rukh never reckoned he might actually go as far as he had. He'd merely hoped to win a few matches if he was lucky, gain some experience for the next time, but this result...he could never have imagined it. The Finals.

He was broken from his reverie by a loud call to silence.

"Two warriors have entered the Coliseum of Ashoka. Only one

will leave a champion. Only one will exit a legend," Fol Nacket, the Magistrate of Caste Cherid, and de facto ruler of the city of Ashoka and her surrounding Oasis called into the growing silence. He sat in the west-facing stands and the sun reflected brightly off his white hair and his handsome, almost pretty face. Beside him were the other Magistrates – seven all told, one from each Caste. Behind the assembled rulers sat close family members of the two combatants: mothers, fathers, and siblings. Further back were the high members of Caste Kumma, such as the 'Els – the individual Heads of each House – along with their spouses and children. And scattered throughout the rest of the stadium, claiming most of the best seats were other Kummas. People unrelated to the two combatants. It wasn't unusual for them to be seated so well. After all, for this event it was only right for the warrior Caste to have pride of placement even if some believed that precedence wasn't always earned, but rather assumed.

Rukh chided himself. Now wasn't the time to consider Kumma arrogance.

Magistrate Nacket continued in his deep, resonant baritone made even louder by the power of his *Jivatma*. "For two weeks now, these two magnificent combatants have tested their skill, their strength, their courage, and their will against all opponents. They do so in honor of the greatest warrior, the greatest Kumma to ever grace this fallen world. Thus, every three years in his name do we hold here in Ashoka – and simultaneously in the cities throughout the rest of the world – the Tournament of Hume!"

While the magistrate was talking, Rukh measured his final opponent, Kinsu Makren, the defending Grand Champion. The older Kumma was also a Shektan, and three years earlier, an eighteen year-old Rukh had watched in awe as his kinsman had dismantled one opponent after another with astonishing ease. In *this* tournament, Kinsu had been even more brutally efficient in the destruction of those unlucky enough to come against him.

And now, it fell to Rukh to fight this man. Not only did Rukh have to overcome his hero-worship, but he also had to settle his nerves. Anxiety could sometimes act as an asset for a warrior, providing a burst of adrenaline, but more often than not, it simply distracted – like now. Rukh was a bundle of nervous energy.

He focused on his breathing, trying to will himself to a calm state.

By comparison, Kinsu, who stood thirty feet away, appeared as tranquil and composed as a winter lake. No ripples to mar his perfection. Unexpectedly, Kinsu winked at him, grinning impiously and looking like an indulgent older brother.

Rukh hid a scowl. He knew what Kinsu was doing. The man was trying to get under his skin; put him off balance and make him easier to defeat. He was only doing what Rukh had been taught by the Martial Masters of the House of Fire and Mirrors: take any advantage needed for victory and survival. For a warrior, those were the only two matters of importance, and in that order. In fact, Kinsu had actually been one of Rukh's instructors at the school. He must have remembered how much Rukh hated being patronized.

Rukh closed his eyes and took a deep, cleansing breath, letting out his anger and anxiety. *Focus on something else.* He made himself pay attention as Magistrate Nacket continued his speech.

The man was in full volley. "Even now, across the world in far off cities such as Fearless, Samsoul, and Defiance, even in fabled Mockery, men battle, fighting to win the coveted title of Grand Champion of the Tournament of Hume," he said in a stentorian roar. "So, we must know: who was this Hume that we should offer such glory to his name?" He paused rhetorically as he glanced over the crowd as if he was awaiting an answer.

Before anyone could interrupt or respond, he continued. "Hume Telrest, the greatest son of the lost city of Hammer, was the finest warrior to ever walk the green fields of Arisa. A Kumma of unsurpassable speed and strength, his skill and daring with the sword was said to be the equal of any other three. He was implacable in battle, known to have faced death countless times and yet, never to have tasted defeat. And who are we to say the legends lie, for it is a fact that Hume Telrest faced the Trials with unflinching courage twenty times, an unbelievable feat when no other Kumma in all of history has faced it even nine!"

The crowd cheered, and the magistrate let them, holding up his hands as though the accolade was for him. He let them go on a moment longer before gesturing once more for silence.

He continued in a more somber tone. "But despite his accomplishments, Hume was not overly-proud. He remained a humble man, a servant of his city and, in truth, of all Humanity. He called himself a simple warrior, but we all know he was so much more. He was the embodiment of all we know a Kumma strives to be: a man of courage, honor, decency, and humility. A man who puts the needs of others above of his own. He fought an unyielding battle, but in the end, not even his indomitable will and valor could save his doomed city, storied Hammer.

"For when the city was attacked by hordes of Chimeras, Hume would slay a hundred, but there were always a thousand more to take their place. Three Plagues attacked his proud city, and in the end…" Fol bent his head, and from where Rukh stood, in the bowl of the arena, the Magistrate looked to be holding back tears. Cherids were known for being overly sentimental and emotional. "…in the end, with the city in flames and his family murdered, with Chimeras running amok in the streets, and the Sorrow Bringer Herself, Suwraith, raging with madness in the skies above, Hume Telrest, the last son of heavenly Hammer, was felled. But it was not by the savage, scurrilous hand of some nameless Chimera. No. His body bore no mark nor any wound. Rather, Hume Telrest was ended by his broken heart; shattered in spirit just as his city was in truth."

The crowd remained silent and respectful. They all knew the legends and myths – everything from the *Days of Hume* to the melancholy song *Woe of Hammer* – but still they enjoyed hearing the stories again.

"And today, this very evening," the magistrate intoned, his voice seeming to gain power, "we ourselves will witness history. Two Kummas, both worthy of the title Grand Champion, shall do battle, armed only with a shoke, neither offering quarter, neither conceding any ground. It is the final battle of the Tournament. And there can be only one Champion!"

The crowd roared.

Rukh loosely gripped his shoke, the weapon in question. It was a slender, wooden sword with a slight curve at its tip. Used only for training and tournaments, the blade was the color of black walnut with a blue-purple tint and an oily sheen. Beyond a dull edge, it otherwise perfectly mimicked the single-edged swords favored by Kummas in balance, length, and shape. When struck, a shoke caused a pain and paralysis that was as true a representation as possible of the damage inflicted by an edged weapon without actually causing permanent injury or risking death.

Magistrate Nacket continued. "One of these men is well known to us and is, in fact, the defending Hume Champion. Kinsu Makren!" he said, gesturing imperiously in Kinsu's direction. "Survivor of five Trials. Slayer of five hundred Chims…" The last was a patent exaggeration, but Cherids did love embellishing a good story. "Now, attempting a feat not done in a century: successful defense of the title of Grand Champion. Should he succeed, surely his name must be written alongside those of the other great warriors of history, to be revered for time immemorial!'"

Again, the crowd roared in response and stomped their feet. Some drunken bravo could be heard over the throng, yelling for Kinsu to strike down the arrogant whelp. Kinsu made no motion or indication that he had heard the words. He politely acknowledged the cheers as he waved to the audience.

Rukh flicked a glance at Kinsu, studying his opponent, hoping to find some sign of weakness. His eyes narrowed in speculation. Kinsu's posture and carriage was of a man who was tense. Were those lines of worry around his eyes? Rukh couldn't be sure, but maybe Kinsu was more concerned about the outcome of this match than Rukh suspected. After all, Kinsu was thirty-five, which wasn't old – but maybe it was old enough. Perhaps he was feeling the fatigue that came from fighting fifteen matches in two weeks. And perhaps he was not as strong as Rukh feared.

A smile of pleasure almost broke across Rukh's face, but he quickly schooled his features to stillness, doing his best to hide his sudden hope. Instead, he considered the possibility of victory as he idly scratched at the skin under one of his Constrainers, the leather vambraces worn by all combatants in the Tournament as a means to suppress the expression of their *Jivatma*. Until now, triumphing over Kinsu had only seemed a fantasy, but maybe there was a way. Belief was the first step to achievement, as his nanna liked to say. Nanna had a lot of sayings like that, and they usually turned out to have a grain of truth to them. Another of Nanna's aphorisms was this: show me someone who accepts losing, and I'll show you someone who will lose. Rukh had never considered himself a loser. He hadn't always won, but he'd never given up the fight before it had even begun.

He nodded to himself. There it was. He wouldn't lay down for Kinsu. Win or lose, he'd leave it all on the arena floor. It was the best any man could hope to do.

The magistrate held his hands up again for silence, and the throng quieted to a dull murmur. "And his opponent. Rukh Shektan, the elder son of Dar'El Shektan, Head of House Shektan. Rumors state that he is perhaps the finest warrior to train within the walls of any of the Martial Colleges of Ashoka in a generation. It seems, rumor must be fact, for no one in living memory has entered the Tournament as a Virgin to the Trials. And yet here he stands, in the finale itself, a magnificent achievement and a true testament to his skill, his House, and his Martial Masters of the House of Fire and Mirrors! Should he win or lose, he *will* be heard from again. And most assuredly, will he do well in his Trials and face the evils of the Wildness with unflinching courage!"

The crowd interrupted with cheers once more. This time it was Rukh's turn to smile and wave acknowledgement to the assemblage. His smile faltered when he heard the same bravo who had called for Kinsu to strike him down, now yelling something coarse about his parentage. Rukh ground his teeth. "Jackhole," he muttered under his breath.

Once the throng had settled, Magistrate Nacket continued. "Today, this very evening, Rukh Shektan will attempt the improbable. Perhaps the impossible. Success he has had. Great success. But now he must face Kinsu Makren, the reigning Grand Champion," he pointed dramatically at Rukh's opponent who stared impassively forward. "A man who has never known defeat within the Tournament!"

The crowd seemed bent on cheering themselves hoarse at every mention of Kinsu's name. "Should Rukh Shektan – the elder son of the ruling 'El of House Shektan – succeed, he will be legend, for never has there been a Virgin Grand Champion." The magistrate continued, his voice swelling with power, soaring to every corner of the Coliseum. "Should he succeed, it may be that someday, we will compare his exploits with that of Hume himself!"

The crowd greeted this last statement with initial cheers which trailed off into confused mutterings. A loud guffaw of amazed disbelief broke across the arena and scattered chuckles arose here and there. Fol Nacket glanced around, looking offended. Exaggeration was as natural to a Cherid as water to a fish, but comparing a Virgin, no matter how skilled, to Hume? Ridiculous.

Rukh himself shared the crowd's sentiment and he flushed with embarrassment. He reddened further when Kinsu grinned and bowed melodramatically as if in acknowledgement of Rukh's superiority. The older Kumma's actions set the crowd to laughing and now even Magistrate Nacket chuckled in good humor. The laughter spread and the throng began shouting, "RUKH SAI! RUKH SAI! RUKH SAI!" They gave him the chant reserved for the Grand Champion upon his victory.

Rukh smiled. He chuckled with them, raising his shoke in the air, and throwing his head back as if he were basking in the crowd's adoration. It set off a fresh round of cheers and laughter.

After the assemblage settled down again, the magistrate continued. "And now gentleman," he said speaking specifically to Rukh and Kinsu, "prepare yourselves. Glory awaits one of you tonight!"

Rukh had trouble believing what was about to happen. He conducted his *Jivatma*, his spiritual essence – some would say his soul. His senses heightened, and he twitched, ready to explode into eye-blurring movement. His breathing came easier. His focus narrowed on Kinsu to the exclusion of all else. Rukh tightened his grip on the bamboo hilt of his shoke, lifting it to the ready.

Soon. Get ready. Be strong. Focus.

He noticed Kinsu's grim determination as well.

The roar of the crowd faded, and the last he knew of the outside world was when he heard a single word shouted from the mouth of Magistrate Nacket. "Fight!"

Rukh leaped forward, his jump carrying him seven feet vertically, one-third his normal ability.

A blue Fireball passed below. It exploded against the white wall ringing the arena. Those who had been sitting near where it impacted shouted with fear and reflexively threw their hands up to protect their faces. No one was at risk though. The Constrainers made sure of that. They damped a person's Well so the worst injury anyone hit by a Fireball might have would be a mild sunburn. Of course, for the combatants, to be so struck would be counted a deathblow and signal the end of the fight.

Rukh dimly noted all this as he drew more *Jivatma* from his Well and threw up a Shield. A dull green light glowed about him. Kinsu continued with Fireballs and sparks of red flashed to the ground in an angry counterpoint when they collided with Rukh's Shield.

They were hard blows, and Rukh knew he couldn't take an endless number of them. He dodged a few more, while still in mid air before landing. He paused, swiftly considering his options. He was motionless for less than a split second as Kinsu sprang forward. Rukh watched, waiting for the right moment. When it came, he leaped forward to meet his opponent. They clashed high above the ground, their bodies parallel with the arena floor as they exchanged blistering strokes. Then they swept past one another. Rukh turned in mid-air to keep Kinsu before him. He threw a Fireball. It screamed through the air before colliding in a coruscation of light against Kinsu's Shield. They completed their leaps and landed lightly on their feet, facing one another.

Even with the Constrainers, the two warriors moved at speeds that left most of the crowd breathless. In fact, only the Kummas in the audience were truly able to follow their motions.

Rukh breathed easily. He felt strong and fast. The first pass had gone well. He was confident in the handling of his shoke, even in comparison to Kinsu.

He took a chance. He drew deeply on his Well, and his Shield briefly glowed more brightly. Rukh leapt up, mirroring Kinsu. He released a Fire Shower, an energy wave that raced outward in all directions, potentially killing everything unShielded in its path. Kinsu was knocked further upwards and back by the concussive blast when the Shower impacted his Shield.

Though the Fire Shower left him unShielded, Rukh was prepared to race forward and attack. But Kinsu had already recovered with a controlled somersault. The older Kumma threw a Fireball.

Rukh bent backward at his knees, holding his torso and thighs parallel to the ground as the glowing orb passed above. He twisted to the right and snapped upward, spinning and jumping all in the same motion as he evaded another Fireball. He did a front somersault over another one and landed on his feet, facing Kinsu. He re-ignited his Shield and allowed Kinsu's next Fireball to impact harmlessly against it.

Not bad.

Rukh was somewhat impressed by the maneuvers he'd just pulled off, but an instant later, his eyes widened in consternation.

Kinsu had charged in behind his Fireballs while Rukh had been busy dodging them. He was only five feet away. Rukh didn't have the space or time to bring his shoke to the ready. He needed distance. He leaped straight into the air with Kinsu paralleling his jump, following closely. The slight increase in separation was all Rukh needed. Their shokes hammered against one another. The two of them kept at it even as they landed, attacking and defending in classic Ashokan sword patterns. The final was a particularly bad pass for Rukh. Several of Kinsu's strokes had gotten through his defense and rocked his Shield. They separated once more and stood facing one another.

Suwraith's spit, but Kinsu was strong.

Rukh's palms stung from the heavy blows, and he had difficulty stabilizing his Shield. It wavered, flickering for a moment before he was able to bring it back under control. Kinsu fired several Fireballs upon seeing Rukh's shaky defenses, but again the only result was a brilliant display of sparks.

They paused, assessing one another. Rukh was still fit and breathed easily, but he was worried. He was game for the fight, but he knew he was reaching his limits. His Well, the source of his *Jivatma* was emptying too quickly. Fifteen hard matches in less than two weeks had taken their toll.

By now, the entire arena was cast in shadows, and the sun was barely above the horizon. There wasn't much daylight or time left in this, the final match. Rukh knew he had to go all out, and now, if he wanted to win.

He feinted right, but charged from the left. Kinsu met him in the middle. Again they exchanged heavy, fast blows. Their swords blurred, and even the Kummas in attendance had difficulty keeping track of the strokes. Rukh was the first to disengage and he jumped straight back fifteen feet. He wanted to shake out his stinging hands, but he didn't have the time, and he couldn't afford to show weakness.

He needed a distraction.

He threw three Fireballs in quick succession, charging in behind them, just as Kinsu had done to him earlier. Rukh attacked, and this time it was Kinsu who gave way, leaping backwards. Rukh almost raced forward, but just then he noticed a slight brightening of Kinsu's Shield. He jumped upward and Kinsu's Fire Shower passed underneath. Rukh launched Fireballs at his unShielded opponent, but Kinsu dodged them with ease and closed the distance in a blur.

Now the older Kumma tested him. It was skill with sword alone, and Rukh found himself unable to disengage. Kinsu bull rushed, and Rukh defended but was still pushed back. Every attempt he made to attack or even just hold his ground was anticipated. Kinsu struck hard and fast. His strokes seemed to have more power now than they had at the beginning of the match. Rukh's mouth hung open as he panted for breath. His *Jivatma* was thinning. His stamina was fading. It took all he had just to maintain his Shield and speed.

Kinsu was winning.

Rukh was backed up almost to the arena wall. He tried desperately to gain more room. He feinted left and right but always Kinsu was there to meet him, pounding at his defenses. He even tried leaping over Kinsu, but he was met in mid-air by the older Kumma and shoved back toward the wall. Rukh gasped for air, and so did Kinsu, but his older opponent was obviously the fresher of the two.

Rukh had long since lost any feeling in his hands as a result of Kinsu's heavy blows. His legs trembled, and his arms shook. The end was near, and he prepared to meet it. Nothing he could do would change the outcome. He was defeated, and the tip of his shoke dipped tiredly to the ground.

Kinsu smiled and withheld his attack for a fateful moment. "You've done well, young Master, but you are not yet ready. Perhaps next time." His voice was surprisingly high and reedy, and his eyes reflected his imminent victory. He knew he had won. All he need do was apply the killing stroke.

Rukh's eyes flashed in anger. Kinsu's smile and words ignited one last fire. He wouldn't go down like this. Kinsu would have to earn his victory.

With that, Rukh drew seemingly to the last dregs of his Well. His mind raced as he assessed options. He made his choice.

Kinsu stepped forward, prepared to mete out the final stroke.

Rukh straightened suddenly. He blocked, shoving a surprised Kinsu back a pace. With the small opening, Rukh hopped two short feet into the air and pushed off from the arena wall. His shoke flashed forward like an arrow, aimed directly at Kinsu's throat. Kinsu gasped in shock. Desperately, he adjusted his own shoke, managing to bring it down on Rukh's left shoulder, simultaneous to when Rukh's shoke struck Kinsu across the side of the neck. The older Kumma fell heavily to the ground.

The world slowly came back. The crowd was cheering wildly as horns trumpeted his triumph. They were shouting his name: "RUKH SAI! RUKH SAI! RUKH SAI! RUKH SAI!" But this time, they weren't chanting his name in mockery. This time, they gave him the salute of a true Champion.

He was the Grand Champion! HE WAS THE GRAND CHAMPION! Rukh fell to his knees in disbelief. He should have lost, but somehow he had emerged victorious.

Other observations impinged on Rukh's thoughts. His left arm hung limply at his side – it would hurt like a banshee, but the pain would be worth it.

He heard movement and glanced over. Hastily, he stood and offered a hand up to a groggy and wobbly Kinsu. The older Kumma rose slowly to his feet, rubbing at his throat. A large red welt could already be seen. Rukh winced in sympathy. Even when the pain from the shoke wore off, the bruise might take weeks to heal.

"Fragging rabid wolves, I didn't expect that," Kinsu said hoarsely and with deep disappointment.

Rukh grinned and laughed. Winning had a way of making any man generous. "Yes, but I doubt I'd be able to play that trick on you twice."

Kinsu scowled. "Damn right," he said, his eyes flashing angrily before his shoulders drooped with a dejected sigh. "But once was all you needed. Congratulations, Champion." He extended his hand, and they embraced.

They separated and turned as one to face the Magistrates, Kinsu raising Rukh's right arm. The crowd continued to cheer, and Rukh's spirit soared.

Chapter Two
Run to the Hills

There are many lives a man can lead,
but in the end, they all lead to death.

~*Kumma saying, dating to the Days of Desolation*

Packages, once filled with spices, resin, clothes and books, had been ripped apart, and their contents littered the ground. Salted meat and fish, too much to pack away, burned on bonfires. The slight breeze carried the smoke and soot from the wagons aflame high into the sky. The warriors rushed about, cursing as they stowed away a few last items.

They were just about ready to move out.

"B Company, gather up your gear and line up on your corporals. Make it quick," Lieutenant Pume shouted. "The captain says we leave in five. Move!"

"Suwraith's spit. This can't be happening," Jared Randall shrieked to no one in particular. The caravan master floundered in the midst of the burning wagons, near the lined Kummas. He caught sight of Rukh, a mad gleam in his eyes. "You won the Tournament," he said.

"Protect me. Please. I'll pay you anything," he pleaded. "I don't want to die!"

Rukh stepped away from Randall, confused by the man's panic. Fear he could understand, but right now, the man's behavior was downright cowardly. It was embarrassing to witness, and Rukh wished he could look away; pretend he couldn't see or hear Randall's blubbering.

Randall still shrieked, begging for protection, almost directly in Rukh's ear.

Rukh grimaced.

He wished someone could smack some sense into the caravan master. Tell him to be a man about it.

The thought was brief and fleeting. First of all, hitting a caravan master was absolutely prohibited. The law was quite clear on the matter but vague on the punishment, but well-known to be quite severe. Beyond that: while hitting the man might be momentarily satisfying, it really wouldn't help the situation.

Rukh gathered his patience and sympathy. Maybe he could calm the man down. "We're all afraid," Rukh said in what he hoped was a reasonable tone, "but now is not the time to panic."

"Now is the perfect time for panic, you fragging idiot!" Randall cried. "In case no one's informed you, we're about to get our back passages stuffed with Chimera spears!"

Rukh's patience snapped. "Stop your sobbing, you fragging coward!" Rukh said. "We aren't dead yet."

"How dare you!" Randall shrieked. "When we get back to Ashoka, I'll make you pay. I'll make everyone pay..." he trailed off and licked his lips. "Yes, we must get back to Ashoka. I was promised." He snarled suddenly. "I will have what's mine," he vowed, mounting his horse and heeling it into motion.

"What's wrong with Randall?" Brand asked, riding up just then.

"The man's a coward," Keemo said, as if that answered

everything. In the world of the Kummas, it did. Nothing else was worse.

"Leave him be," Rukh said. "He's not worth our time. We've got more important things to do, like getting our gear and supplies together. As in five minutes ago. We don't want to be left behind or cut off."

"What do you mean?" Brand asked.

Rukh had thought about their situation while overseeing the offloading of the wagons. Three large groups of Chims were rolling toward them. Who was to say there wasn't a fourth? Even now, the caravan might already be encircled. He wasn't sure how the veterans would treat his suspicions. They might tell him he was just jumping at shadows. He was only a Virgin, after all, but with Farn, Keemo, and Brand, he would get a fair hearing.

"I think we're going to find Chims up north as well," Rukh said. "We need to get moving if we're to have a chance of getting out of here."

"Chims to the north," Brand said, surprised. "How do you figure?"

Rukh nodded even as he wondered how they would react to the rest of his reasoning and his fears or whether those fears even had any basis in fact. He suspected they did. "All these Chims coming at us at once and on top of us before we even knew they were there. The only way I see something like that happening is they already knew how our scouts operate," he said.

Brand wore a look of skepticism. "What are you saying? Someone in the caravan told them?"

"I think he's saying Sil Lor Kum," Farn said. "Aren't you?"

Rukh nodded again, not surprised by Farn's correct guess. His taller cousin had always been bright, sometimes even the brightest of the three of them. "The Secret Hand of Justice."

"The Sil Lor Kum are nothing but a legend," Keemo scoffed. "They have to be. I mean, Human agents of Suwraith? Who in their right minds would agree to serve Her? The Chims just got lucky finding us."

"Keemo's right," Brand quickly agreed. "There's no such thing as the Sil Lor Kum. It's all talk and no fight."

Rukh wasn't surprised by Keemo and Brand's disbelief. He had trouble believing it, too. For most people – until now, Rukh included – the Sil Lor Kum *were* a legend. They were a handy means to scare misbehaving children or explain away whatever inexplicable calamity happened to befall someone. And as far as Rukh knew, not a single member of the Sil Lor Kum had ever been discovered in all of Ashoka's existence; nor had even the rumor of membership ever been raised for even the most degenerate of people, but that alone didn't mean the Sil Lor Kum didn't exist. It only meant their existence was somewhat unlikely. But given what was happening to the caravan, Rukh thought his hypothesis made a horrifying kind of sense.

Farn seemed worried about it, also. He was subdued and pensive.

"My Nanna always figured they were real," Rukh said. "I suppose I just closed my eyes to the possibility, and I sure never expected to come across proof of their existence."

"You still haven't," Brand said. "All you have is an answer to a question. But I'm with Keemo. I think he's right: the Chims got lucky."

"But it wasn't just one or two or ten of them who snuck up on us," Farn said. "It was seven *thousand*."

"And also, remember this: these Chims managed to skirt around our scouts from three different directions. When something happens once, maybe it's luck. Twice…maybe real lucky, but three times…three times isn't luck anymore. It's knowledge. They *had* to know how best to avoid our scouts. Where they came up with the knowledge is something else."

"I still don't think…" Brand began.

"Time's wasting," Rukh interrupted, not wanting to talk about it anymore. He wasn't trying to be gruff or pull rank. He had said his piece. It was enough. The Sil Lor Kum didn't bear thinking about right now…not when there were so many other pressing matters. "We can talk about it later. You heard the lieutenant. We need to gather our gear and get ready to go."

"I'm already packed," Keemo said, gesturing to his bulging saddlebags.

"Same here," Farn said.

"Brand?" Rukh asked.

"I'm ready."

Suwraith's spit. The lieutenant would skin him if he were the last one to have his gear together. He was a corporal for Devesh's sake.

The caravan consisted of Captain Bosna, four lieutenants, each with three sergeants and beneath *them*, two corporals, commanding ten privates apiece; a total of two hundred eighty-one warriors. Virgins were almost always privates, as were many veterans, but in Rukh's case, he'd been bumped up to corporal because of his status as Hume Champion, who, by tradition, was never a private. And it didn't matter if Rukh was only a corporal because of his victory in the Tournament. He was still expected to act like a veteran. And a veteran showed up before his unit.

"Then I guess I'm the only laggard in this group," Rukh said. He nodded to the others and led his horse to his gear. He quickly packed it away and attached it securely to his saddle, taking special care with his bow case, quiver, and round ironwood shield. Wouldn't want to lose his equipment due to carelessness.

He saddled up and heeled his horse into a canter, guiding him toward Lieutenant Pume. With a slight lifting of his heart, he realized many of B Company had yet to arrive. But of the six corporals, he was the last one to make it to muster.

"Nice of you to join us, Shektan," Lieutenant Pume noted as he rode up.

There was no good answer to that. "Yes sir," Rukh replied, hoping the lieutenant would drop the matter.

The lieutenant made a noncommittal sound before turning away.

Rukh breathed a sigh of relief and glanced around to see what else needed to be done. The wagons and their supplies still burned, sending a thick plume of smoke into the air. If the Chims didn't know where they were before, they were bound to know now. Some of the smoke drifted his way, and the horses shifted nervously. The stallion stayed rock steady, and Rukh stroked the horse's neck in appreciation.

He studied the assembling warriors. The men were young; in their early-to-late-twenties – only a fool left the safety of an Oasis past his thirty-fifth birthday – with more than half the guards Kummas and the rest Rahails or Murans. The Kummas were the best fighters, but it would probably be a member of the other two Castes who stood the best chance of surviving the coming battle. Only a Muran or a Rahail could conduct *Jivatma* to form a Blend: a near-perfect camouflage of sight, sound, and smell that veiled the men and wagons of a caravan from the piercing eye of Suwraith and Her servants.

Concealment sounded like a good Talent to have right about now.

Several companies, B Company among them, were ready to go. However, A Company of Lieutenant Ulrit, still had a few stragglers.

"Stop jerking around!" Sergeant Lathe of A Company roared at several lingering guards still leafing through their belongings. "We leave in one minute. Any dumbass who doesn't have his gear and his horse ready is out of luck."

The men, suitably chastened, hustled to get their gear stowed away and their horses saddled.

After they had finished assembling, the captain spoke to all of them. "Ashokans," he said. "This will not turn into a rout. There will be no panicking, especially when we haven't even seen a single Chimera yet. We will go forth in an orderly fashion. Remember who we are. We are men of Ashoka, and we will not shame our ancestors with cowardice! Am I understood?"

"Yes sir!" the men shouted as one.

"Good. Stay frosty and sharp. The northern scouts haven't reported back yet. Hopefully, that means it's clear in that direction. With a little luck, we will get through this and return home. Now move out."

"Devesh save us," Brand said, sounding earnest in his prayer, which wasn't surprising. He was a Rahail, and while they weren't as devout as Murans, they were far more pious than Cherids or Kummas.

"Glory to Devesh," Rukh intoned automatically, feeling a hypocrite. He had no confidence Devesh would heed his prayers, and he was sure many others shared his doubts, but they still offered up their dutiful entreaties to their so-called deity.

Rukh distractedly pushed aside the stallion's muzzle as the animal reached back for his thigh. He had other matters on his mind. His insides churned with a mixture of fear and excitement. He knew his duty, and if death was the result of keeping his oath, then so be it. He had accepted the possibility from the moment he had learned what it meant to be a Kumma. It didn't mean he was eager to die.

Most of his concentration, however, was on Captain Bosna's words. The captain wanted to make sure someone, anyone, would make it back to Ashoka and carry warning to the city. Maybe there was a way to see it happen. In a battle, Kummas were taught to always fight alongside other Kummas, Annexed into Duos or Triads or even Quads. It was thought to be the best way to stay alive, but in this instance, maybe there was a better way. A stealthier way.

He leaned toward Brand. "Stay close," he told the other man.

The Rahail frowned, puzzlement on his face.

"We can protect you better than you can protect yourself against the Chims," Rukh explained, nodding toward Farn and Keemo, "but we can't Blend. We need each other if we're going to make it back."

Brand gave a tight nod of agreement, saying nothing. He looked as scared as Rukh felt.

Well, Rukh wasn't *quite* that scared.

The captain waited a few more seconds for the last of the stragglers to report in before giving a sharp nod to the lieutenants. Bosna wheeled his mount and led the guards north.

Four tightly bunched columns, one for each lieutenant, followed Captain Bosna. The warriors were twitchy and full of bundled energy. They glanced in all directions but maintained a disciplined silence. Sounds carried far in the low hills northwest of the Hunters Flats, and there was none of the banter that had marked the day when they had left Ashoka six weeks earlier – a lifetime ago Rukh mused. The only sounds to be heard, other than the noises of nature, were the creaking of saddles, nervous whinnies of the horses, and their steady, staccato hoof beats.

They rode at a quick pace but it was one their mounts could maintain for hours on end if need be, and the need probably would be. As the day lengthened, they pushed further north of the Hunters Flats and were now amidst the steep foothills of the Privation Mountains. Rukh saw a wispy cloud of dust rising from the northeast. It looked like it was from a small, swift-moving group. Whoever it was had already adjusted their course and would intersect the Ashokans within the hour.

Warriors from the column raced off to intercept them.

"Hope it's not Chims," Brand muttered.

Rukh was pretty certain they weren't. He suspected those kicking up the dust cloud were the northern scouts. They were early. And looked to be riding flat out.

Unfortunately, it seemed like he had been right about Chims to the north.

Damn.

Soon enough, the northern scouts became visible, flanked by the warriors the captain had sent out to meet them. Their horses were lathered and blowing hard. The riders didn't look much better. Their grim faces spoke of the news they carried.

Rukh shared a knowing glance with Keemo.

"You were right," Keemo mouthed.

The columns came to a halt as the northern scouts rode through, making directly to Captain Bosna, who waited on the crest of a low hill.

"There are Chims up north, aren't there?" Brand said more than asked, having nudged his chestnut mare closer.

"Probably," Rukh replied. The scouts wouldn't have ridden so hard for any other reason.

Brand nodded, looking glum. "Suwraith's spit."

The word came down the line for a halt.

The low, rounded mounds north of the Flats had given way to the taller ones of the Privation Mountain foothills. The column wended through a narrow valley, mostly cast in sunlight and surrounded by treed hills with out-thrust spears of gray stone. A narrow, cold stream cut across their course, and the warriors took the brief pause to dismount and give their steeds a quick breather as well as some water.

Rukh led his stallion to the creek, and while the horse was drinking, he took a long pull from his canteen. The stallion wanted more water, but hot as he already was, it wouldn't be good for him to drink too much.

Farn sauntered up, wearing a smile. "Looks like a load of Chimera bilge is coming our way."

"I think it's been heading our way since we left Ashoka," Keemo said in a sour voice as he arrived, over-hearing Farn's words. "We just didn't know it until today."

"So then why is Farn smiling?" Brand asked.

"Because he's got the sense of a turkey in the rain?" Keemo guessed.

Rukh let their conversation wash over. He was watching the officers.

The captain and lieutenants were poring over their maps. They reached a quick decision, and the lieutenants had all their units bunch up, drawing closer to the captain. Bosna wanted to address them again.

"We've got terrible news on top of bad," the captain shouted. "Many of us may not make it home. The scouts from the north report five Fractures coming south like an avalanche. With that and the other Chims ringing us, we face almost a full Shatter. Twelve thousand of Suwraith's beasts, and likely another three Fractures out there whose whereabouts we don't know yet." His face firmed; his jaw clenched. "They think they'll roll us like a pride of lions on a single wildebeest," he said, pausing slightly. "Well let me tell you, we aren't a wildebeest, we're a fragging bull buffalo, and this fragger has horns. I'll be damned if any warrior of mine goes down like a lamb to the slaughter!" The men cheered, but settled down quickly when the Captain raised his hands for quiet. "We've found a place to get out of this trap, but we'll have to ride hard. We'll have to ride the wagon horses or a remount until they drop. Save the best horses for when we need them. Dump everything we don't immediately need. No pots or pans. Speed is going to be more important than supplies. Tomorrow will have to take care of itself."

Upon his words, the column became a beehive of frenzied activity as men did as the captain ordered.

Rukh found himself riding a wide-backed wagon horse. The beast was a gelding; placid and gentle in comparison to the stallion, but even he must have caught a whiff of the danger they were facing. His eyes rolled, and his tail swished with nervousness.

When they were ready, the captain gave the call: "Ride!"

The column thundered along the shoulder of a rocky, boulder-strewn hill and down the other side into a slender ravine.

Rukh found the gait of the placid workhorse almost unbearable. The animal ran in a lumbering trot, tossing Rukh about with every stride, but the horse had a great heart and never quit. Soon enough, the gelding was lathered and blowing hard, and Rukh had to leave the heavy-gaited horse behind. He switched back to the stallion. The gelding had given his best, and after Rukh had cut him loose, he found himself hoping that somehow the wagon horse wouldn't find itself in a Chim cookpot.

The warriors had already been given a rough outline of where the captain intended for them to go – a narrow pass leading into the Privations, a place that could be held by only a handful of warriors, allowing the bulk of the Ashokans to escape – so when the column shifted southwest, the direction nearly opposite of where they needed to go, Rukh was surprised. He glanced back and sighted dust to the north and southeast. He bit back a curse. The Chims must have spotted them and moved to intercept the column, herding the Ashokans away from the relative safety of the Privation Mountains.

The captain led them out from the foothills, and the column found itself once more on the relatively barren round hills north of the Flats. The sun was just past its zenith. The heat, so prevalent in the Flats, baked the earth, drying the red clay of the ground into a hard, dusty shell. The column received temporary relief when they raced along the shadows in a deep vale. They followed a small stream which winded south before likely becoming a part of the Slave River. They crossed the brook, muddying the water, and on the other side, they darted between thickets of gray-leaved thorn bushes. The flanking hills on either side were now brush and pine covered hillocks.

Perspiration trickled down between Rukh's shoulder blades and beaded on his forehead, dripping into his eyes. He blinked, trying to clear his vision from the sting of salty dirt in his eyes. The stallion was covered in a sheen of sweat, but he breathed easy with a steady, willing gait.

"Good boy," Rukh murmured, patting his horse's shoulder.

The stallion's ears flicked back in response.

They exited the thickets and cut north, racing the Fractures, hoping to escape the noose around their collective necks. Rukh urged them all to greater speed. The column ran silent but for the drumbeat thud of horse hooves; all of them keeping an eye on the dust cloud that marked the Chims to the north.

Rukh closely watched the west as well, where they'd swung wide. Surely they must have closed with the Fractures coming from that direction.

A few minutes later, he cursed. He had his answer. Dust clouds to the west. Fast closing. No more than an hour away.

The captain led them due north, straight back toward the foothills. In the narrow valleys and ravines, the larger Chims forces would be hindered. Hopefully, it would slow them down long enough for the Ashokans to slip the trap and make for the mountain pass where they could escape and head back to the city.

The current race would be a close run contest.

Rukh tried to keep his vision focused ahead, but he couldn't help but look to the sides. The Chims to the north and west had shifted to cut them off, but as the hours passed and the late afternoon sun blazed over the hills, it became clear that the Ashokans were pulling away. They passed the northern Fractures near enough to hear the rumble of the enemy's pounding feet. When they crested one hill in particular, they could even see the swarming Chims for a few brief seconds.

Until this moment, Rukh had never seen a living Chimera. All he had to go on were pictures, descriptions in books, and dead examples of each species of Chimera in Ashoka's City Library. Now, he could see them all.

He took a moment to study Humanity's enemies.

He didn't see the Braids, but he saw the other breeds making up the Fan Lor Kum. He saw Ur-Fels, small and dog-like. They fought in well-disciplined nests of eight or ten, and if they had the advantage, they took it, but otherwise they were cowards. Kill a few, and the rest of the nest scattered. The Tigons appeared to be upright saber-tooth cats: strong, powerful, and fast, but thankfully, their preferred tactic was to scream and leap, often with weapons discarded. Once enraged, they were easy to take down. The hooting Balants towered over their brethren, a hideous mix of baboon and elephant. Strike them on their bright-red butts or their long noses, and they went berserk, becoming as much a danger to the other Chims as to the people they were fighting. Rukh smiled without humor. What could Suwraith have been thinking when She made them?

Had Suwraith's armies been composed of only those breeds, Humanity could have easily held off the Chimeras. It was the Baels who shifted the balance. They were midnight black and walked upright on the thick, heavy legs of the bulls they resembled. Upon their heads were curved horns, each arching three feet or more. Their preferred weapon was a trident and a barbed chain whip that glowed red as their eyes and burned with the heat of a furnace. However, what made the Baels most dangerous was a combination of their intelligence and their ability to control the other Chimeras. They brought focus and discipline to the armies of the Fan Lor Kum, the Red Hand of Justice, accounting for as many Human deaths over the centuries as Suwraith Herself. Rukh held a special hatred for them. Fragging demonseeds.

Just then, he smiled.

The column was going to make it through, despite the best efforts of the damn Baels. They had slipped through the trap laid before them, and he dared hope that he might see Ashoka again. The cold finger of fear tingling down Rukh's spine slowly eased off. He shared a triumphant grin with Brand, Farn, and Keemo. Losing Suwraith's beasts in the high, rugged foothills of the Privation Mountains wouldn't be easy, but it was most certainly possible.

The word came down the line. They were going for the mountain pass, and the captain shifted their course northeast. They ran like that for several hours, and slowly, the pine and scrub covered hummocks gave way once more to rock-strewn slopes where dwarf oaks and maples clung to steep-shouldered hills. The footing became more difficult, and their pace slowed. They picked their way along the bases of scree slopes, sometimes slick from a burble of water that had found a seam in the stone, dribbling down and across their path.

Twilight: with the sun lowering and shadows measuring long, they traversed a rock-strewn hill, and the column came to a disjointed halt.

The lonely call of an eagle on the hunt came to them.

Rukh shifted nervously in his saddle and glanced around. The column was riding along the eastern base of a stony hill, deep in shadow. He didn't know why they had stopped. They had an hour or so of daylight to get deeper into the foothills, but for some reason, Captain Bosna had called a halt. Rukh could see the captain studying his maps before rolling them up and putting them away.

He seemed on the verge of speaking, but just then a harrowing cry rose into the air from directly ahead of them. It was one Rukh had never heard before, but he knew what it was. His heart sank. It was the hissing, grating howl of the Braids, the snake-like Chimera scouts. From hills to the east and west came answering cries.

The Ashokans had been discovered. The other three Fractures the captain had warned of must have been lurking in the foothills in case the column escaped the trap to the south. The fragging Chims must have seen through the Ashokan Blends, which couldn't mask the heavy fear and excitement hanging over the warriors like a fog.

The Ashokans were in deep trouble. It didn't take an old veteran to understand that.

Rukh saw the captain pull out his maps once more. On Bosna's face was none of the fear and desperation Rukh was feeling. He was calm and controlled as he quickly but coolly studied the maps, his eyes narrowed in concentration. Another cry came, and Rukh's heart skipped. The captain rolled up his map and heeled his horse forward, drawing his sword.

The word was passed down in whispers: they would attack the Braids. Generally, the Chim scouts hunted in groups of five, known as a trap. If the Ashokans could break past this grouping of Braids, they might still lose the Chims in the high hills bordering the Privations.

They picked up their pace, kicking up stone and grit. Howls continued from the east and south, answered in the farther distance. Braids in those areas would converge on the initial cries of their brethren. It would be those other traps that the Ashokans would have to work to avoid.

Rukh remembered all he could of the Chims scouts. Hairless and scaled in black with a tuft of green hair atop their heads. A serpent's head with a forked tongue tasted the air. Excellent sense of smell and hearing but relatively poor vision. And despite their reptilian appearance, they were warm-blooded. They slithered on the ground or walked upright, depending on the need. Typically, they fought with a sword, but their tails could also be used as a weapon. It took an entire trap to take down a Rahail or Muran and several traps to defeat a Kumma in the open field.

The Ashokans kept to their initial path, and the column bunched for the briefest of intervals. Rukh saw mangled flesh pass under the stallion's hooves, and he realized they must have run down the Braid scouts who had discovered them. They circled the hill, and took a trail east. Howls directly ahead were picked up by more traps further in that direction followed by a chilling roar. It was a sound he had been trained to recognize, one he was hearing for the first time in his life on this grim day. It was the basso roar of a Bael, the leaders of Suwraith's armies.

The Chim commander was close. If he was a Jut, he would lead a Smash, one hundred Chimeras, something the Ashokans could easily handle. But, if he was a Levner, a Fracture commander, that meant a thousand of Suwraith's creatures. The Ashokans could still take them on and win through, but it would be a hard fight; long enough for the other Fractures to arrive and tip the balance in the favor of the Chims.

The trail split, and the column surged west, away from the roar of the Bael. Rukh urged them on, glad to be on the stallion even though the rock-strewn trail made footing unsure and slowed them to no more than a deliberate trot, almost a jog. A few horses whinnied in fear as they slipped on the scree, and a few even went down, screaming in panic. Luckily, none of them were injured, and their riders quickly remounted as their friends disregarded orders and waited on them. They rode for hours, past dusk, into the edge of night. Watch fires lit up the hills along their path, signaling their location.

Rukh cursed. Fragging Chims.

They switched directions, now heading northwest through a wooded valley. The smell of moss and mold lingered in the dry air. Oak, elm, and maple loomed large, their trunks dark and thick in the fading light. The branches high above hid them from the lurking Chims in the hills, and the ground, littered with leaves and fallen branches, made footing nearly as tricky as the rock-strewn slopes but the detritus softened the hoof beats, muffling their sound. They made better time through the woods and exited a half hour later, moving up the slope of a granite hill along a narrow trail. The path widened, and the captain pushed them into a canter.

Another half hour and no further cries came to them. Rukh

started to breathe easier. Maybe they would make it out of here after all.

No sooner had the thought crossed his mind when a yipping howl, like a dog in pain, rose before them.

Ur-Fels. And judging by the number of barks, three or four nests. Suddenly, a number of arrows clattered against the rock around them. They chipped the stone but none of them struck the column. The warriors unlimbered their small, round shields and held them at the ready even as they pushed forward.

More arrows followed and now came the hissing grate of Braids and the basso roar of several Baels.

Rukh swallowed heavily, once more feeling the cold finger of fear. They were surrounded. No way to escape. He glanced at Farn and Keemo. Their faces were tight with worry. Even the veterans looked uneasy.

"We aren't done yet," Lieutenant Pume growled. "That's for the damn Chims." He leaned past the side of his mount and spit before turning to glare at the men of B Company. "We *will* carry out our mission. Remember who we are."

Rukh took a steadying breath. The lieutenant was right. They were Ashokans. Most of them might die in these hills today or tonight, but all they needed was for one of them to escape.

Captain Bosna called a halt as he consulted his maps once more. He glanced around, getting his bearings before leading them off the hill and heading them south east. He spurred his horse almost to a gallop and the rest of them followed close behind. The pace was dangerous in such poor light and footing, but they didn't have any other choice.

Rukh patted the stallion's neck as the horse kept pace, blowing hard but showing no signs of quit. The beast might have been a right unholy terror to handle during most of the Trial, but in this run, he had been worth every moment of his pain-in-the-assedness. He had the power, speed, and endurance to run this race to its end. For that, Rukh was grateful.

The column thundered up a switchback trail, heading for the top of a tall, flat-topped hill. The track narrowed and was open to a harrowing drop on one side and pressed tight against stone and dirt on the other.

The column slowed.

As the trail climbed, it cut deeper into the hillside, and Rukh now found himself flanked on both sides by a rock wall with the quickly darkening sky still open above. Their track was now a small gap, barely wide enough for two or three horses to ride abreast. Just before the crest however, the path opened onto a broad summit, several hundred yards wide and deep, and the column of warriors quickly spread out, making room for those coming behind.

Starb's men, who had been riding point, closed ranks as soon as the last of the warriors exited the narrow gap.

The top of the hill was flat, the rock dusted red with a thin rind of clay. A thick pillar of stone – many yards wide, worn by time and wind to form a laddered terrace – thrust up near the center of the summit, reaching over thirty feet into the air. Parts of it had cracked, falling over into jagged boulders. The granite's serrated edges glistened in places. On the far side of the flat peak, the ground fell away in a sheer cliff, except for a ragged and rocky path even steeper than the hard trail they had just climbed. At the base, a long, forested valley spread out. If they could make it down into the trees, escape was still a possibility, especially with the darkness.

The captain issued orders, breaking Rukh away from his reverie. "We'll make our stand here," he shouted. "That gap..." he pointed to where Starb's men had taken up position, "...will act as a bottleneck, funneling the Chims. Their numbers won't count for as much then. We'll make them choke on their dead! C and D Companies will hold the trail, halfway down the hill. A and B Companies will retreat down to the valley floor. We'll lose the Chims there."

"Sir?" Lieutenant Starb questioned.

For the first time on this hard day, Rukh saw emotion flit across the captain's face: regret and heartache. "Someone has to slow the Chims down," he said. "We have to carry word back to Ashoka."

"C and D are all going to die," Brand said, coming up to stand next to him, his voice sounding hollow.

Rukh nodded, unable to speak beyond the lump in his throat. These were his brother warriors who were about to sacrifice their lives so he and the others might live. "It's a fragging world we live in, isn't it?"

"Suwraith's spit," Keemo cursed, arriving just then. "I wish I was going with them."

"You want to die?" Brand asked, not sounding surprised.

"No. I just don't like the idea of running from a battle while our brothers are fighting and dying. It makes me feel dirty, like some filthy naaja, a tainted bastard."

Rukh nodded. "I imagine we'll be fighting plenty," he said. "The Chims are sure to have scouts on those far hills." He pointed to several nearby peaks, including one looming no more than forty feet away. "They'll be watching for us."

"Unholy hells. We *definitely* should have chosen a different caravan for our first Trial," Farn joked as he dismounted.

"I'm starting to think you might be right," Rukh agreed with a faint smile.

"It was good knowing you the two of you," Keemo said. "And you, too, Brand," he added a beat later. "You're not bad for a Rahail."

Brand smiled back. "And you're not too stupid for a Kumma." he answered.

Keemo chuckled.

Pume rode up. "Form up," he shouted. "We've got point. Ulrit and A Company will follow right behind us. You'll have to lead your horses. No way to ride them down this fragging goat trail. Hustle down as quick as you can. The faster we're down, the more chance someone from C and D Company might be able to make it out of here, too. Shektan, get your men ready. You've got the lead. Go!"

Rukh's men gathered around him, and he led them to the far side of the summit, lined up behind the captain. They dismounted and prepared to head down the sheer path. Rukh glanced down. In the fading light of the early evening, it would be a hard descent, and he took a quick swig of water, his mouth suddenly dry. Suwraith's spit. Men and horses were going to get hurt bad or even killed going down that steep, thread of a trail. What a dumbass way to die.

A roar came from the edge of the wooded valley at the base of the hill.

His jaw clenched as he focused on the sound. The Chims were down there. His heart sank as he saw hundreds of Suwraith's fragging beasts pour out from the gaps between the trees.

The captain sighed. "Damn," he said softly before turning around and calling for the lieutenants.

A moment later. "New orders," Pume said. "We aren't going to live through the night, but none of that matters. We're Ashokan warriors. We don't quit. We fight to the last!" With a roar, the men shouted their assent. "C and D Companies have been recalled. They're to hold the trailhead. A and B will act as a reserve. We're to plug any breaches in the line. But until that time comes, we wait in the heights and empty our quivers. Make every shot count. Now, here's where I want you." He quickly had the men positioned along the rocky prominences of the summit.

Rukh's troop along with Keemo and Farn's were positioned near one another next to the wide column of stone centered upon the summit. The other warriors of A and B Companies were also stationed nearby, some behind boulders or higher up the laddered terrace of the broken pillar. Most faced forward where C and D

43

Companies held the trailhead and where the main force of Chimeras was expected to arrive in minutes. Only a few warriors held the far side of the summit. The Chims who had exited the forested valley and cut off the Ashokans' retreat would take hours to ascend to the top of the cliff. By then, the battle would be over.

"Fight with us, Brand," Rukh urged.

"But if I do, you won't be able to form a Quad," he said, looking confused.

"We'll form a Triad," Rukh said dismissively. "It won't matter if we have a Quad. Besides, we're all brothers in the Trial."

Brand nodded slowly. He straightened, his eyes bright with unshed tears but also filled with a brazen fire. "Unto the last breath, wield the wild sword and scream defiance!" he shouted.

Others heard his words. "Until the sun's demise or Suwraith's death, we war!" Pume's unit roared in answer.

Rukh blinked back tears. Brand would have made a damn fine Kumma.

They made their way to where Pume had indicated, readying their weapons. Their bows were strung, and they sat in silence as warriors from C and D Company rounded up the horses.

No one needed their mounts anymore, but the animals might still have a use. The horses were stampeded down the hill. Many would run off the trail into empty space, screaming until they crashed on the hard, rocky floor hundreds of feet below, but a few might make it to the Chims host, causing some damage, however minimal and fleeting before being put down. Regardless of how they died, they would all end up meat for the Chims horde.

Rukh saw his white stallion – he had never named the animal – look back at him several times before he followed the rest of the herd down the trail. If Rukh didn't know better, he'd have thought the horse had sorrow in his eyes.

"Here's where it ends," Keemo said.

"Or where it begins," Brand countered. "Devesh waits on the other side of life."

Rukh considered Brand's words, wishing they were true. "I envy you your faith," Rukh said in a soft voice.

Brand smiled. "We'll all talk about it one day over a cool beer in Ashoka."

Rukh smiled while Farn chuckled softly.

Keemo licked his lips. "A cold beer sounds great about now," he said.

"Cold beer and a warm woman," Brand agreed. "In that order."

Rukh laughed. "Now isn't that something to live for?" he asked.

They murmured assent before once more falling silent, waiting for what was to come.

Soon enough, sounds came, close and unmistakable. The yipping of Ur-Fels; the trumpeting hoots of the Balants; the gravelly roars of the Tigons; and the hissing cry of the Braids. And over it all, rumbled the deep roar of their commanders, the Baels.

It wouldn't be much longer. Only a few minutes.

The last light of the sun had long since set. A waxing, gibbous moon hung low, and stars twinkled uncaring. A cold wind blew on the heights. At the base of the cliff, seven Fractures, half a Shatter – more Chims gathered in one place since the fall of Hammer almost three centuries before – announced their presence with a cry of triumph.

It was a sound to chill the soul.

"Form the Triad on me," Rukh ordered.

"It's not as effective," Keemo reminded him.

"And it doesn't matter," Rukh said. "We're facing seven thousand Chims. It won't make a difference if we have a Quad."

"Weren't you the one saying we aren't dead yet?" Keemo asked. "Now you're all fatalistic."

Rukh shrugged and smiled. "Consider it wishful thinking," he replied.

"Here they come!" someone from the gap shouted.

"Make those arrows count. Strike at the Balants if you can. Otherwise, hit the Baels," Pume ordered. "And if any of you see an opening, take it. Especially the Rahails or Murans. Blend. Not now, but during the height of the battle. With all the confusion going on, one of you might be able to get clear. Ashoka must know what's coming. That is your mission. All of you."

"Yes sir!" the nearly seventy men of B Company shouted back.

Rukh conducted *Jivatma*, thick and rich, from his Well. As always, it filled him with a heady sense of invincibility. He stretched his inner senses and found Keemo and Farn even as they reached for him. They Annexed. A languid peace stole over Rukh. His thoughts drifted and were distant. They felt like they were covered with a thin film of icy water. His mind soon stilled.

The Triad was born. It held all the knowledge of its hosts – all their memories, likes, dislikes, strengths, and weaknesses – but was itself simply a construct, an ephemeral being. It had been tasked with a simple directive: fight and survive. It would do so by any means necessary.

The Triad looked through the eyes of its hosts. The enemy was vast, but the Triad knew no fear.

B rand looked at the three men in confusion. Nothing had changed as far as he could tell. "Rukh...?" he began, hesitantly, unsure if he was interrupting something important.

All three men pivoted their heads as one. It was eerie. Rukh spoke, but it sounded nothing like the corporal. *"Rukh is not here,"* something answered. *"We are the Triad."*

Brand was startled. He had seen Quads, Triads, and even Duos, but before now, he had never actually spoken to one. The voice was emotionless and strange; not like his friend at all. "What about Rukh and the others? Do they know what's happening?"

"They watch. They are aware. They wait."

Brand gave Rukh…the Triad…whatever it was…a brief, uncertain glance before turning away, unnerved by the way they stared at him in unblinking unison. He looked to the trailhead where the men of C and D Companies had bows drawn or were holding Fireballs.

It was time. The enemy was in range.

Brand set an arrow, ready to draw. He had a moment's startled awareness as Keemo, Farn, and Rukh lifted their bows in perfect unison. Other Kummas along the ridge, also in Quads or Triads or Duos, had similar dulled features, and they too moved with uncanny precision. The Rahails and Murans along the ridge wore looks of grim determination.

At that moment, with death soon to come, the words of his proctors from the Shir'Fen, one of the three Rahail schools in Ashoka, came to him. They taught that futility was a rescindable state of mind, but duty was one's everlasting master. Brand finally understood what his teachers meant. Right now, their actions were essentially pointless, but duty impelled them. Futility was a choice, and if he so chose, he could surrender to its hollow embrace. It was a cold comfort he would not allow for himself.

"Devesh guide my arrows," Brand breathed, before coherent thought was lost. The Chims were in range.

C and D Companies had already engaged the enemy. Fireballs and arrows blew forth, hissing or roaring through the air, ending with the scream of an injured and dying Chim. It was a beautiful sound.

But Suwraith's beasts pressed the warriors. The sheer mass of the Chims made it impossible to hold them back. Soon, close-in fighting with swords raged along the edge of the summit.

Brand fired his arrows as rapidly as he could, aiming for the Chims emerging from the trailhead. The ones who had already gained the top of the hill were mingled in amongst the Ashokans and sending arrows their way would risk the lives of his brothers. C and D would have to fight them on their own while A and B worked to keep the Fractures of Chims off the summit. His heart pounded with adrenaline. Beside him, the Triad aimed and released with metronomic precision, killing with almost every shot. The arrows were spent, and the Kummas unleashed a withering wall of fire, straight into the maw of the onrushing Chims. Suwraith's servants incinerated with screams of anguish, and the smell of burning flesh hung over the ridge.

"Frag them!" Brand yelled. He was stupid enough to stand and pump his fist, but quickly ducked low when a flight of arrows came his way. Nests of Ur-Fels, Suwraith's best archers, had reached the top of the hill and were clustered behind a wall of hooting Balants. Some of the dog-like Chims had laid down a flight of arrows in answer to A and B Companies' withering attack. But most aimed fire directly into the mingled mass of their fellow Chimeras even as they battled bloody combat with the Ashokans. The damn dogs were killing as many of their own as they were the warriors of C and D.

Another flight of arrows came their way, and Brand hastily threw up his shield.

Just then, the ground trembled like an earthquake, and the Chims were thrown from their feet and off the cliff. But it wasn't a temblor. It was something better. Brand smiled. It was the Murans. The farmers had a Talent to move earth.

The captain roared a command, and the booming scream of over one hundred Fireballs followed, incinerating the Balants and the Ur-Fel archers crouching behind them.

For a brief moment— a painfully brief moment – it seemed the Ashokans of C and D Companies might be able to hold the line and push the Chims back. But they never had a chance. The sheer numbers of the Chimera horde carried the day. They surged forward like a misshapen tide, howling, hissing, roaring, and baying for blood as they rolled over the warriors of C and D Companies.

"Swords!" Lieutenant Pume called out. "Fill the breach!"

With the hiss of a thrown, rusty gate, the Ashokans of A and B Companies drew their matte-black spidergrass swords.

The Chims charged forward, led, as usual, by the Tigons. Close on their heels were Braids, their shiny, sinuous, snake-like forms seeming to change color as they raced forward. Ur-Fels, small, fast, and cunning, hid behind and amongst the shambling, massive forms of the hooting Balants. Scattered amongst their brethren strode the commanders: the Baels. Their eyes glowed as red as their chained whips as they spurred the Fractures onward.

The men of C and D Companies battled desperately, but so many of them were already down. Some lay unmoving, frozen in death, while others moaned in agony and anguish before the hordes of Chimeras trampled them into the blood-soaked ground.

The warriors of A and B Company rushed forward and briefly threw the Chims back, giving their brothers in C and D a chance to regroup. It was a small pause in the carnage. For a moment, sound seemed to mute to a dim and dull cacophony before the violence took hold once more. A Bael loomed large, urging his Chimeras forward. A cool breeze carried the smell of blood, burnt flesh, and feces. The moment was gone and sound returned with thunderous roar. The battle was joined once more.

Such fleeting impressions impinged on Brand's mind, but he gave them no thought. He wielded his sword instinctively, letting the repetition of ten thousand lessons form his movements. At his side, the Triad of Rukh, Keemo, and Farn fought in eerie silence.

The Triad leapt forward, into the midst of the enemy. Tertiary threw Fireballs. An injury-crazed Balant allowed Secondary to press forward. Primary, the most skilled, wasted no movement and danced death amongst the Ur-Fels, Braids, and Tigons. Blows glanced against the Shields of the hosts, but none penetrated. A Bael stepped forward. The bull-like beast pounded the friend of Primary into the ground with his glowing, chained whip. It could not be allowed. Primary was unleashed. The Bael died.

Rukh awoke, anesthetizing the link. "Brand, you alright?" he asked.

"Liver shot. Hurts like hell," Brand said, getting shakily to his feet. "Thanks for saving me."

"You're not saved yet," Rukh reminded him.

The bulk of the Bael provided some cover, and Rukh took the momentary reprieve to reassess their situation. The Chims were swarming over the defenders. Scores of Suwraith's servants had died but, little by little, they were whittling away at the Ashokans. Pockets of Kummas fought on, but even as he watched, Rukh saw three warriors rolled over by the sheer weight of the creatures they were facing. Few, if any, Murans and Rahails were left. Rukh hoped some of them had Blended and were simply waiting for the opportunity to slip away. Rukh doubted it was true, but he mumbled a prayer anyway. There were too many Ur-Fels and Braids about. The Chims could scent out fear through a Blend.

Hopeless. It was over. Resigned to death, Rukh prepared to re-form the Triad's link. Kummas didn't die meekly.

His gaze snapped north. Someone was out there. Watching. He was certain of it. From one of the further hills. He looked for the telltale signs of movement, but saw nothing. He frowned. The feeling was gone. His gaze drifted back to the closer hills, and his eyes narrowed. A deep chasm, over forty feet wide, separated their ridge from the nearest hill: a smaller, rocky prominence. He glanced about. The Chims still hadn't noticed them.

"Can you make that leap?" he asked Brand, pointing out the rise in question.

"Only if I rode a catapult," Brand answered.

Rukh took a deep breath. "Then we'll just have to throw you," he said with a grin.

"Absolutely not," Brand protested.

"Absolutely yes," Rukh said. "Blend us and follow. We can do this."

Brand nodded, unsure of Rukh's plan, but he did as directed. He had no chance for questions, though. The Triad was back. It dashed toward the cliff's edge, and Brand followed, running flat out, pushing past his exhaustion. The liver shot from the Bael that Rukh had put down had him gasping in pain. It was like a knife digging into his side. Just then, eight Baels swarmed the Triad.

⸺ ● ⸺

"Looks like we missed it," Jessira Viola Grey observed, as she scanned the battlefield with her spyglass. She was Blended, as were all the members of her squad, the Silversuns, and they lay hidden and unobserved within the shelter of a cave in a nearby peak. There were only four of them: Jessira, her younger brother Lure, cousin Court, and Cedar, her older brother and the commander of the Silversuns.

What had been a routine scouting patrol had turned into something else when they had run across several Chimera Fractures. So many of Suwraith's beasts in one place hadn't been reported in quite some time. Cedar had ordered them to trail the Chims. He, along with the rest of the unit, had wondered what the Sorrow

Bringer's creatures were doing gathered in such numbers.

Later in the day, from the south, they had heard the hissing cries of Braids on peaks all along the foothills of the Privations. And then, carrying on the wind, had come the basso roar of a Bael. The Silversuns had shared looks of confusion and worry. There were even more Chims out in the mountains than the Fractures the Silversuns had been following. Something important was happening.

It turned out the Chims had been hunting a caravan – maybe out of Ashoka – and were in the process of decimating it.

The Silversuns had hunkered down a half mile away and watched. There was not much else they could do. By the time they'd arrived, the battle was all but finished with only a few scattered pockets of fighting still raging. What little they *could* see had been an indistinct and confusing series of images, made more so by distance and dim light. The large pillar rising from the summit of the flat-topped hill hadn't helped matters either.

"It looks like some might be trying to escape," Cedar said, pointing out four fleeing figures.

Lure brought a spyglass to his eye. "One of them might have sensed us," he said. "He looked right at me."

"No way," growled a stocky man, their cousin Court. "Not when we're Blended."

"I'm telling you: they saw us," Lure replied.

Court snorted in disbelief.

Jessira watched a moment longer, before setting her spyglass aside with a sigh. "Well, whether he knew we were here or not, it doesn't matter. They didn't make it," she said. "They just got cut off by eight Baels."

Court looked to Cedar. "Think we've seen enough?"

"I suppose so. Not much to be gained by sitting around watching men die. We need to report back to Stronghold," Cedar said, spitting into the dust.

"What do you suppose this gathering of Chims is about?" Lure asked.

"Other than killing those warriors down there?" Cedar shrugged. "Nothing good."

———◆———

*T*he Triad fought. It did not know desperation, but survival was difficult because Primary insisted on defending the friend. Had the Triad been allowed to leave the friend, it could have survived. The friend was not a part of the Triad, and so his actions could not be controlled or anticipated. It made him very hard to protect. Something had to be done.

The Triad reached through Primary and did the inconceivable. It lunged with Jivatma, grabbing hold of the friend. Well melded with Well. Annex was complete.

The hosts were stunned. Never had a non-Kumma been incorporated into an Annex. To the Quad it did not matter. Primary was the battering ram; standing at the prow while Secondary and Tertiary maintained the flanks. Quaternary defended the rear.

Wells had grown weak. Jivatma thin. No Fireballs or Fire Showers. Survival depended on blades and escape.

Primary blurred into motion. He faced four Baels, cutting down two of them when their whips tangled. He took a hammering axe from a third against his Shield and thrust up, disemboweling his opponent. The fourth Bael had time enough to blink in slack-jawed disbelief before Primary lopped off his head. A somersault leap backward and Primary was behind the Bael pressing Quaternary. The beast never saw his danger. The last three Baels were quickly dispatched.

The way across the chasm was open. Primary's plan. They were unobserved. Time to run. The Quad drew the last dregs of Jivatma from all four hosts. After an adjustment to Quaternary – another impossibility – strength and speed flowed *through all. A further adjustment and the hosts were Blended.*

The Quad sprinted toward the brink of the plateau and leapt. Quaternary slipped, barely making it across the chasm. Secondary reached and pulled Quaternary to safety. The mission was complete, and the Quad was no more.

———————•◆•———————

All four men were spent.

"Keep us Blended," Rukh said to Brand. "The Chims can't know we survived."

Brand nodded and concentrated for a moment. "It's done."

"We need to find a place to shelter for the night," Rukh said. They stood on a small ledge, but about twenty feet up was a cave. The cliff wasn't sheer. They could climb it. "Come on," he said to the others.

"They're feeding!" Farn cried out, disgusted.

"Lower your voice," Rukh commanded in a whisper, but they all turned to witness the depravity of the Chims.

The Tigons fought amongst the corpses, tearing flesh and biting off great mouthfuls. Ur-Fels and Braids lurked nearby, lunging for their own pieces of meat. The Chims fed on the bodies of men the four had called 'friend' just a short time ago.

Rukh watched silently, his face a mask of disgust and loathing. He'd seen enough. "Let's go," he ordered. He turned his back on the Chims and sheathed his sword.

Again, he shot a glance to the north. There again was that eerie sense of a nearby presence.

"What is it?" Brand asked.

"I'm not sure," Rukh replied. He concentrated on the hill directly north of them. "It's just…" The feeling was gone again. "It's nothing. For a moment, I thought there was someone out there."

"Survivors?"

"Let's hope so."

"There's a cave up there," Keemo said, staring upward.

Rukh nodded. "I saw it. Stay quiet and alert. I don't know if anyone else made it, but if they did, they might be up there already."

"Isn't that good?" Farn asked.

"Not if they survived because of promises made to the Chims."

"Sil Lor Kum," Keemo hissed, hatred in his voice.

They climbed, taking care to move quietly. Even Blended, sounds might betray them. Rukh silently cursed the crunch of rock and gravel under his boots, certain that it sounded as loud as thunder. They reached a small ledge directly in front of the cave. It extended further on either side.

Rukh gestured. Farn and Keemo flanked one side while he and Brand flanked the other. Rukh peered into the gloom. Nothing. He felt Keemo and Farn's Shields flicker to life. He startled when Brand lit a Shield as well. Impossible. That was a Kumma Talent.

He shook his head in disturbed wonder. Deal with it later.

Rukh unsheathed his sword and Shielded. He darted into the cave, pressed close against a wall as he searched the interior for signs of life. The others crowded in as well.

There was no one else there. The cave was empty.

Chapter Three
A Varied Test

Ashoka, awash in the brightness of the sea
and the sweet aromas of fields of flowers...
be cautious of her thorns.

~From the Journal of Writh Far, caravan master out of Fearless AF 1638

"Watch your step, missy," the Duriah drover shouted as Mira Terrell almost stepped in front of his wagon.

The drover's words snapped Mira's attention back to the present, and she leapt out of the wagon's way with a start. She nodded thanks to the Duriah and mentally chided herself for her carelessness.

The only reason the Duriah hadn't said anything more coarse to her was because of her appearance. She was a Kumma, and most people showed members of her Caste a great deal of deference. Especially the women, whom Mira had heard described as being as prickly as a porcupine and irritable as a badger with a sore tooth. She didn't think it was an entirely fair assessment, but she understood where the sentiment came from: Kummas were warriors and *very* proud of the fact. It was not wise to test them.

Which wouldn't have helped her one bit if she'd been trampled to death by a wagon. And it would have been her own fool fault. She had been lost in thought, unheeding of her surroundings. It was a flaw Nanna – her father, Janos Terrell – jokingly attributed to Nannamma's influence – her father's mother. *'Your nannamma gets so lost in the canyons of her mind, it's a wonder she even remembers to breathe,'* Nanna would jokingly tease. Of course, Nanna never dared say so if Nannamma was in earshot. Nannamma *was* as prickly as a porcupine and irritable as a badger with a sore tooth. Even Amma, Mira's mother – one of the strongest women Mira knew – stepped carefully around Nannamma.

Right now jokes and thoughts of her family would have to be set aside. She was on business, headed to a warehouse in the Moon Quarter, the wharves and industrial heart of Ashoka. Mira was in the last week of her yearlong internship with House Suzay, and Tol'El Suzay, the ruling 'El of his House, had tasked her with a problem. It also happened to be one affecting House Shektan, Mira's own House. A Sentya had reported an infestation of some sort with the saffron stores shipped from Kush. It was Mira's job to figure out what to do about it. Saffron was expensive, and if the entire shipment were ruined, it would put both Houses at a loss for the caravan from Kush. It was a potential disaster, and Mira was proud of the trust Tol'El showed her. If they were lucky, they might be able to salvage some profit from the situation by simply hiring a Muran to exterminate the pests in question.

With a wry grin, Mira wondered if such work could also include the workers who had allowed the contamination to happen in the first place.

After the Duriah and his wagon passed her by, Mira took stock of her surroundings.

She walked along Bellary Road, one of Ashoka's main thoroughfares. A very busy street, Bellary began in the southwest, directly off the Inner Wall gate of the same name, cutting diagonally to the northeast and passing all the way down to the Moon Quarter on the opposite side of the city. Along the way, the street transformed many times. At its beginning, just past Bellary Gate, it thrust through Trell Rue, a fashionable neighborhood of artisan shops and new restaurants, where young, ambitious artists came to hone their craft and make their mark before relocating to more well-heeled, desirable areas. There, Bellary was constricted and shadowed amongst tall buildings looming large, but further on, the road entered into the shade of Mount Cyan and passed by Glory Stadium before intersecting with Martyr Hall and Triumph Street at the Plaza of the Martyrs. At that point, Bellary widened and the buildings lining it became old, well-kept row houses and apartments, tightly fitted against one another with a thin median of palm trees providing some greenery in the center of the street. Bellary also provided the northeastern border of Semaphore Walk, Ashoka's theater district and home to elegant, stately mansions. Further on, however, in the area where Mira walked, the road was wide but thick with traffic as Bellary pushed on toward the Moon Quarter, Ashoka's beating industrial heart. The thin median of palm trees had disappeared as drovers hauling wagons laden with goods and materials made their way to various parts of the city. Square, blunt warehouses and workshops lined the road, and a light haze of dirt floated on the air, coating everything with a patina of dust. The bellow of machines as well as the ringing shouts and curses of various workers carried along the street. The smell of smoked spices, hot oil, and burning wood drifted on the mild, spring breeze, mixing with the stink of nearby tanneries and Ashoka's paper factory. It made for an unpleasant odor. The Moon Quarter was most definitely not Mira's favorite place to visit, and she pitied those who were so poor as to be forced to live within its malodorous confines.

Mira smiled wryly when she had to pull up sharply as a group of children ran by. They played a game of Slay the Chimera, darting in out of the traffic and crying in delight as only children without a care in the world can. Of course, there were some who were blessed to be happy no matter what their circumstances.

"Mira, hold up," a familiar voice shouted above the din.

Mira paused and searched for whoever had called out to her. She smiled in greeting when she saw Bree Shektan approaching.

The only daughter of Dar'El Shektan, the ruling 'El, and his wife, Satha Shektan, was a tall woman who had inherited much of her parents' vaunted talents. From her nanna, she had been gifted with a formidable intelligence. She had achieved the highest scores of any graduate in the past ten years from the Fan and Reed, one of Ashoka's all-female Kumma academies. Of course, Devesh must not have been satisfied to grant her a keen intellect. From her mother, He had also graced Bree with a languid beauty. A slow smile from Bree was guaranteed to get a man's pulse racing, be he young or old. Mira grinned as the young woman caused men's heads to swivel on their necks simply by crossing the street. In the world of Arisa, there was a strict precept against inter-Caste intimacy of any kind. It was what allowed the Castes to remain pure, each able to do their duty as Devesh had decreed. But an even older law was that men were men. Put a beautiful woman in front of them, and they would notice...although those not of Caste Kumma had to be careful. It wouldn't do for them to overly ogle one not of their own Caste. Such men could be easily identified by the manner in which they kept their heads preternaturally still and their gazes locked forward. But Mira knew they were aware of Bree.

While she waited on her, Mira was also reminded of Bree's older brother, Rukh. She didn't know him well. Rukh was older by a year and almost always away at the House of Fire and Mirrors, busily training for his time in the Trials. In fact, training seemed to be all he ever did. Bree's brother had been relentless in his pursuit of perfection, and it had paid off. Rukh had become the ideal of a Kumma warrior: strong, fast, and graceful – he made the simple act of rising from a chair appear to be a dance – and his proficiency with a sword...in a few more years, he would be unbeatable. Which made his abilities all the more unusual given his lineage. None of his ancestors had been counted as great warriors. They had been fine and brave, but for the most part, they had been, at best, competent, including Dar'El Shektan. Rukh, though, even from early on, had been a prodigy. He was a sublime talent, going so far as to capture the Tournament of Hume in his first attempt and becoming the first Virgin Champion in history. Pity he lacked the wit to match his fierce warrior's heart. Though he was handsome, Mira did not find Rukh inspiring. In fact, he seemed rather dull, a bore. Swords, it seemed, were his only passion. On the other hand, his odd, yet somehow intriguing younger brother Jaresh, the only Sentya, or for that matter, the only non-Kumma of any kind ever adopted into a House, was the brighter of the two men. He was also more approachable and funny, but not in a clownish way. In their few interactions, he had always struck Mira as being clever and witty. Of course, it was said Jaresh was also training as a warrior. She had even heard he might leave Ashoka for the Trials.

She grimaced. The Devesh damned Trials. At best, they were a necessary evil, always taking the best of Castes Kumma, Muran, and Rahail and bringing them home broken in body and often in spirit. Like most Kumma women, Mira hated the Trials. She didn't necessarily like Rukh, but still she paused and said a quick prayer for his safety, even as she knew Devesh probably paid little heed to the concerns of Humanity.

"I think we should give those responsible for this disaster a boot in the ass," Bree declared when she caught up with Mira. Bree's forcefully voiced opinion didn't surprise Mira. Despite being two years younger and only eighteen, Bree typically had strongly held views. She got her forceful personality from her nanna as well.

And Dar'El Shektan was a *very* forceful man. He was only the fifth 'El of their young House, but he had already turned it into a prosperous one. Such a rapid ascent in fortune was bound to raise the jealous enmity of some of the older Kumma Houses. Some of them went so far as to hate House Shektan, especially after Rukh's success in the Tournament of Hume. Mira believed it was a price worth paying. Through Dar'El's skillful maneuvering and financial acumen, her own family, once all but destitute, had risen to become a respected and honored member of the rising power that was House Shektan.

"Maybe we should get the facts first before putting a boot up someone's back passage," Mira suggested with a smile.

Bree smiled back. "Never stopped me before," she replied.

Mira rolled her eyes. "Which is probably why you kept getting switched when you were a child," she said. "Speaking without thinking is not an attractive feature."

"You may have something there," Bree said with a laugh. "I'll follow your lead and try to learn wisdom." She bowed mockingly.

Mira rolled her eyes again. "I wouldn't expect to learn too much if I were you."

"You shouldn't be so hard on yourself," Bree advised. "I think you're quite clever."

"Thank you. But that's not what I meant," Mira said. "I'm sure I could try teaching you something. Whether you can understand it…" Mira arched a questioning eyebrow before turning and walking off, smiling when she heard Bree's squawk of outrage.

Bree quickly caught up and gave Mira a playful shove. "Nicely done," she said. The two of them shared a smile.

One of the qualities Mira liked about Bree was the younger

woman's ability to accept some harmless ribbing.

They walked on, and the weather grew warmer. It was a fine spring day, and the sun blazed bright heat on the world below. Fluffy, white clouds occasionally eclipsed the sun, casting the world in temporary shadow, while heavier clouds, gray and pregnant with rain could be seen passing ponderously far to the southwest of the city.

The two women topped a hill, and Bellary Road ran straight to the water's edge, offering a view of the harbor and the bay. Mira paused. She liked looking out at the water. It reminded her of the larger world beyond the borders of Ashoka's Oasis. Many boats were out; some already near the horizon. The fishermen must have cast off early in the morning. Mira watched as several vessels slipped from view as they broached the terminator.

"We need to go," Bree reminded her.

Mira nodded, and they walked in silence until they passed a pub named *The First World*.

"You think those old stories are true?" Bree asked, pointing to the faded sign over the tavern entrance.

Mira smirked, and spoke in a portentous, high-pitched tone, a dead-on impersonation of Mistress Volk, historian and headmistress of the Fan and Reed. "It was a legendary time of peace and prosperity when the First Mother and the First Father walked among the people, protecting them and bringing life to a once desolate and dead land. In those days, great works were raised; creations which we now believe to be the stuff of dreams. A grand civilization of enlightenment and culture arose and understanding of *Jivatma* reached its peak. Grace and elegance were the hallmarks of the era."

Bree laughed. "Yes, that. Do you believe any of it?"

"I don't have a firm opinion one way or the other," Mira replied. She shrugged. "Besides, it doesn't really make any difference to how we live our lives now, does it?"

"No, it doesn't," Bree agreed.

Though Mira's words were spoken dismissively, they in no way reflected how she truly felt. In reality, she was a romantic, and she spoke as she did to shield her romantic heart from disappointment – whether from her own fears or the mockery of others, she wasn't sure. It didn't matter. Mira had always had a deep longing for the glory found in the First World: a world of peace, tranquility, and beauty, where the highest goal of one's art was to reflect the glory of Devesh. She had loved reading the stories of the First World. The tales from that time were a mix of legend, myth, and history spun into a wondrous fable. Mira wistfully wished it was all true. Her own era seemed so much emptier and gray in comparison.

And how the First World had ended, two thousand years earlier was still a mystery. Supposedly, it had died in a single night of blood and death, starting with the murder of the First Mother and First Father. It had been the Night of Sorrows when a demon desolated the world. A demon named Suwraith – the Bringer of Sorrows, the Queen of Madness. Those who survived Her appearance spoke of how She had raged across the land, unstoppable as a flood and powerful as a hurricane, sacking all the cities She came upon. Lightning and thunder had pounded a bruised earth with the fury of a cataclysm, leaving behind only rubble. The few people who had endured Her coming had huddled in their cities, sheltered in the unexpected embrace of an Oasis, a powerful manifestation of *Jivatma* unseen prior to Suwraith's arrival. No one knew how the Oases had come to be, but some historians claimed they must have been the final, desperate act of the First Mother and First Father, a means by which to protect Their children before They perished. It might even be true, but if so, why then had They not protected all the cities in such a fashion? It was one of the great mysteries of time, but whatever the reason for their sudden appearance, the Oases proved impervious to Suwraith's power, and the cities sheltered within them were able to ride out Her fury.

The legends spoke of how Suwraith had hurled Herself against the Oases, again and again, howling with greater anger each time She was rebuffed. They described a sky groaning under Her unceasing madness as thunder rolled in an endless peal, its roar an echo of Her rage. The deafening noise seemed to herald the world's demise, but the Oases had stood, and with them the cities.

In the end, the Queen finally understood defeat, and after a century of merciless attacks – the Days of Desolation – a new civilization of sorts arose. The cities, widely scattered now, devised a means to maintain contact with one another through large caravans of wagons or ships: the first Trials. Initially, only goods and materials were sent from city-to-city, but it was the open exchange of knowledge and learning that proved to be the true impetus for the Trials. Hoarding information in a world made savage was a recipe for disaster. Advancements in every field, such as farming and medicine or philosophy and law were freely given. Even newly minted poetry, music, and plays were included. It was the only way to ensure Humanity's survival.

Over time, the Trials had achieved the status of sacred but, given the imminent danger involved with leaving the Oases, a financial remuneration was needed. As such, those who volunteered and were chosen to guard the caravans were compensated with a percentage of the profit as payment for their protection. Such men and their Houses and Castes became extremely wealthy, especially the Kummas since they were the ones who provided most of the warriors. But for Mira, prosperity wasn't measured merely by the number of coins in one's pocket. In the ways that mattered most, Kummas, and to a lesser extent, the Murans and Rahails, were all impoverished. Too often their men died young to fulfill this so-called holy mission, and those left behind had to bear the burden of grief.

Bree glanced at her and must have noticed her expression. "What's with the sour face?" the younger woman asked.

Mira shook her head. "Just thinking about the Trials," she answered.

Bree sighed in sad acknowledgment. "Rukh won't be back for at least two years," she said. "And Jaresh wants to set out this time next year. Idiot."

So the rumors were true. Mira was mildly disappointed. She had expected better of Jaresh. She thought he had more sense.

"He thinks going on Trial will make him more of a man in the eyes of my parents," Bree finished.

"Will it?" Mira asked, hoping Dar'El wasn't so shallow. As far as Mira was concerned, a boy did not become a man by simply surviving the Trials. A true man needed so much more than fighting prowess alone. Dying was often easier than the weight of living.

"Of course not," Bree said, sounding offended. "Jaresh is loved for who he is. He always has been. It was *his* choice to continue his training as a warrior, not my parents'."

Mira was relieved. She greatly admired Dar'El and Satha Shektan, not least because of their adoption of a child not of their own Caste. They demonstrated an open-mindedness far too lacking, not just amongst Kummas, but most Ashokans. She would have thought less of them had they forced Jaresh along the path of the warrior.

Their conversation dwindled, and they walked on, soon arriving at their destination. They carefully crossed the busy street before entering the squat, square warehouse in question. It stood on the western corner of Bellary and North Moon Street, a few blocks from the harbor where the smell of the salty Sickle Sea and drying fish from the day's catch mingled with the rest of the Moon's stench. The warehouse was a grimy gray color, faced in what might have once been white brick – a foolish choice given the nature of the Moon – with high, narrow windows along the top of the first floor and the lower part of the storage lofts above.

Mira glanced around after they entered through the raised front gate. The interior was a brightly lit open space with materials stacked in the corners while the center was left clear for wagons to be loaded before they exited on the far side of the warehouse through the rear gate. All of the workers within were Duriahs or Sentyas. The Duriahs – typically engineers and builders – were easily distinguished by their bull-like build, olive skin, and midnight black hair and almond eyes. The Sentyas, in contrast, were slighter of frame and darker of complexion with aquiline noses and curly blond-brown hair. They sported their Caste's customary even white teeth when they smiled. Great physical strength was not their forte, which was understandable since most Sentyas were employed in bureaucratic positions. Those here were unfortunate fellows, unable for whatever reason to gain a position more suited to their Talents and forced to do menial labor instead.

Upon seeing them, a Sentya, balding and thin, rushed over. He wore a yellow shirt stained orange and smelling of saffron. "Deal Welt," he said, introducing himself without preamble. Mira had been told to expect him, and she eyed him askance. He was supposedly in charge, which meant he was the possible reason for the misfortune of Houses Suzay and Shektan. "Good news. We were able to isolate the infestation. It only affected twenty percent of the shipment. Some damn pest from Kush," he grumbled. "We should charge them the cost of our expenses with the next caravan."

Mira blinked, pausing a moment to take in his words. She smiled. Her work had just become *much* easier. "That is good news," she said, wanting to shake the Sentya's hand. She couldn't, of course. Men and women of different Castes took pains to avoid touching one another.

Bree was frowning. "How do we know the pest in question was Kushian in origin," she demanded. "It could have been you or your men who were lax."

Mira winced. She preferred a light touch, especially since Deal

Welt had just managed to recover a tidy profit for both their Houses.

Welt gave Bree a measuring assessment. "Your nanna tried that tone once," he said. "I wasn't scared then, and I'm sure not going to be frightened by some stripling filling out her bra for the first time."

Bree squawked in outrage.

Deal Welt waved aside her indignation. "Don't get your undergarments in a bind," he said, only adding fuel to Bree's fire. "The reason I know it was Kushian, *Miss* Shektan, is because I asked the Muran entomologist I hired. He believes he can salvage the infested saffron, and the insect in question is subtropical and native to Kush. Our winters get too cold for it to survive here."

"Well done," Mira said with a smile. She looked over at Bree, hoping the younger woman would follow her lead and give Deal Welt his just due.

Bree still glowered, and Mira had to hide her irritation and desire to slap the girl. Bree was reputedly brilliant, but right now, her actions and reactions were beyond foolish. The Sentya had taken the initiative and efficiently handled the problem. He had staved off what could have been a disaster. Bree was smart but apparently she still had a lot to learn about handling people. Either that or she would have to start liberally spicing her feet if she insisted on shoving them in her mouth.

It took them a little longer to settle the situation than Mira would have liked, especially since the main problem had already been dealt with, but Bree insisted on personally inspecting the saffron to verify no other portion of the spice was infested. She even stopped the Muran exterminator before he could depart, questioning him at length to learn what could be done to prevent such a problem in the future. All the while, she threw challenging glares in Deal Welt's direction. The Sentya never showed any sign of intimidation, but the other workers in the warehouse caught the scent of an angry Kumma female on the prowl. They made themselves scarce.

Mira gritted her teeth. The girl was a hammer when a helping hand was needed.

After they finished, Bree turned to Deal Welt. "My father will send for you," she said in a haughty tone. "He'll want a full report on this issue in person. If satisfied, he may even offer you direct employment by House Shektan." She said the words as though offering a grand position before turning to Mira. "That is, if House Suzay has no objections?"

Mira shook her head. "I'm sure Tol'El will voice no concerns on the matter." After Bree's treatment of Welt, there was no chance the Sentya would hire on with House Shektan, but fine, he could say 'no' in person. Besides, setting aside his fine decision-making with the saffron, Deal Welt couldn't be any great prize. He was still a free agent after all, and at his age, he should not have been. Any Sentya worth his salt would have found a posting in a ministry office or hired on with a high House by their late twenties at worst. Welt had not been able to do so, which meant despite his good work in the warehouse today, something else was wrong with the man. His competence had to be lacking.

"I await his word," Mr. Welt said with a fractional nod. A brief smile flitted across his face.

Bree smiled back, all her previous hostility gone as she tilted her head in brief acknowledgement before turning aside and making her way out of the warehouse.

What was that about? Mira wondered as she followed Bree outside into the bright sunshine. She suddenly felt as if she had just overlooked something important.

Before Mira could ask anything, Bree spoke first. "He'll do well," she said, sounding smug.

Mira frowned in confusion. "What do you mean? What just happened back there?"

Bree glanced at her sidelong. "Nanna wanted me to test him, so I threw a tantrum to see how he'd react. He did fine. No cowering in fear. Mr. Welt has a spine, just as Nanna said he would." She nodded. "We need smart, tough, efficient people, not gibbering morons in House Shektan. The only reason Mr. Welt's still working the docks is because he lacks the family connections for a higher post."

Mira's mouth dropped open. She should have realized. The nepotism of Caste Sentya was legendary. She shook her head. Deal Welt wasn't where he was because of incompetence. He was where he was because he had no one who could speak for him and place his name in the ears of those who might further his career. But despite the setback with which he had been born, he had done his job well enough for Dar'El Shektan to learn of the man's abilities. And Dar'El hadn't held Mr. Welt's lack of lineage or connections against him as some might have. He'd looked past it and likely just hired someone who would help his House – her House again soon enough – become even wealthier.

Mira whistled in appreciation. First Mother, the Shektans were subtle.

And upon the completion of her internship in just a few days, she would be expected to live up to that level of proficiency.

She gulped in trepidation.

At least Tol'El should be happy about the saffron.

———— • ————

She and Bree went their separate ways once they entered Jubilee Hills, the exclusive and wealthy area where most Kummas made their homes. Unlike Bellary and Ashoka's other main thoroughfares, which were made of crushed rock bound with Cohesion and stone dust, the quiet streets of the Hills were paved with long red bricks laid out in a herringbone pattern. The raised sidewalks on either side were lined with live oaks draped in wispy strands of gray moss. Street lamps atop tall, black posts, evenly spaced every hundred feet or so, added to the loveliness of the area. A number of cherry trees had been planted along the median, and right now, they were in bloom, fragrant with pink blossoms. Mira inhaled deeply, taking in their perfumed aroma. It was a distinct pleasure after the stink of the Moon Quarter.

The houses in this part of Jubilee Hills, hidden as they were behind large compound walls, were similarly beautiful. They sat on long, narrow lots and were built of cement blocks faced with stucco and painted vibrant shades of blue, red, yellow, or green. Most were two or three stories with tall, peaked roofs tiled in slate or terra cotta. All had a multitude of covered porches, balconies, and wide windows to take advantage of the views out to sea and over the rest of the city, including Mount Bright looming in the near distance.

Mira eventually reached the cul-de-sac upon which the seat of House Suzay was found. Unlike the other homes of Jubilee, the House Seats rested upon acres of land, usually at the summit of a hill. Within the confines of their compound walls could be found room for barns and training rings for horses as well as well-trod areas for the instruction of the House warriors. Some Seats even had what amounted to a small farm tucked inside the borders of the estate. And, of course, the houses were also correspondingly larger, looming over any other nearby homes. House Suzay's Seat was typical, with two wings – each three stories – stretching back from the large, main entrance, which alone was as big as most family homes in Jubilee Hills.

Mira passed through the open, black gates and stepped onto the wide, brick-paved drive, taking the smaller right hand path toward the barn. Her next task would take her past the Inner Wall, and travel would be easier – quicker as well – if she were mounted. Inside, the barn was dim and filled with the warm, familiar scent of hay and horse. She glanced around, hoping to catch sight of a groom, but other than a few horses milling in their stalls, the barn was empty. She frowned in annoyance. The custom of the Suzays did not allow a woman of the House to saddle and prepare her own horse if she wished to ride. It was a task that was supposed to be left to the grooms, but it was also one Mira was more than capable of handling by herself. And right now, she was feeling rebellious. She didn't feel like waiting around like a helpless fool until a groom arrived. Instead, she glanced over the available horses and chose a placid, roan mare she had ridden before. She saddled the mare and rode out, smiling at her insignificant defiance.

She took Shalom Street to Sickle Road before going south on Bright Rose Road. Along the way, she came across a patrol of the City Watch – Kummas all. The Watch, along with the Ashokan Guard and the High Army, made up the three branches of Ashoka's military. While the Guard and High Army had the duty of defending Ashoka in case of attack from Suwraith's hordes of Chimeras, the Watch – far smaller at only three hundred men – was tasked with keeping the peace for the entire city and her surrounding Oasis.

Luckily, their responsibility was made easier by several simple facts. First, if someone committed an offense, they either paid for it with coin or with the acceptance of severe corporal punishment – or both. Second, beyond Ashoka's borders was the Wildness, a perilous place full of danger and death. If someone couldn't get along with his neighbors, his choice was simple: correct his behavior or leave the city.

As a result, crime was *very* rare in Ashoka.

To Mira's way to thinking, it was also *exactly* what the degenerate lawbreakers deserved. The city lacked the resources to coddle the criminal.

She nodded to the patrol and set her horse to a trot. Soon enough, she came upon the massive Inner Wall that protected

Ashoka proper. The crenelated battlements soared fifty feet, and the evenly spaced towers reached up another twenty. The wall was thick enough to allow troops to march five abreast. Even now, warriors of the Ashokan Guard paced the wall, keeping watch over the fields and looking toward the distant outer wall. The protection of Ashoka was a duty shared by the High Army and the Guard. While the Guard was a reserve unit, it was also highly professional, which wasn't a surprise since most of the ranks were filled by every able-bodied Kumma male who had completed the Trials. The rest of their approximately 23,000 warriors were veterans from Castes Muran and Rahail with a smattering of Duriahs thrown in as well. And though they only trained four days a month, there was little difference in quality between the Ashokan Guard and the High Army.

Mira passed into the cool shadow of the Kubar Gate, one of the three gates of the Inner Wall. Each gate was forty feet thick and wide enough for two large wagons to pass one another with room to spare on either side. The gatehouse loomed above as a menacing presence with murder holes all along its length, and the heavy portcullis, made of thick ironwood, was always kept ready to crash down at a moment's notice.

The traffic was light with only a few wagons and pedestrians traveling through the gate. Mira would have been quickly through the Kubar, but everyone had to pause and step aside for a returning Ashokan Guard patrol. From their camouflage clothing, tired demeanor, and grimy faces, Mira guessed they must have been out in the field, scouting beyond Ashoka's borders. Regular reconnaissance for up to a three days journey into the Wildness was standard procedure for the Guard and the Army. Mira studied the returning warriors and recognized a few of them from Houses Suzay and Shektan. It was Fifth Platoon – 23 men – of Third Company, Second Brigade, Third Legion. Their commander, Lieutenant Rector Bryce, saw her and saluted.

Mira waved back, more out of courtesy rather than any real feeling of affection. The lieutenant was someone Nanna had mentioned as a potential husband. She wasn't sure what she thought of the man given how little she knew him, even though, like herself, he was of House Shektan. He'd only recently returned from his fourth and final Trial – a respectable number – choosing to settle down while he still had his health. From what she remembered of him when she had been a young girl and before he had left Ashoka, Rector had seemed warm, generous, and lively. Not so much now. The lieutenant was ruggedly handsome, but his time in the Wildness had returned him weather-worn and grim.

Her Nanna wasn't like that. While he might have been similarly worn down by his time outside Ashoka, Nanna was still bright and cheerful. Even with over twenty years of marriage behind them, Nanna could still make Amma smile with just a word and a glance; implying a hidden meaning only the two of them understood. Mira wanted the kind of closeness her parents shared, and she doubted she would have it with someone like Rector Bryce.

After the Guard patrol passed by, Mira was able to quickly make her way through the Kubar, exiting back into the warm sunlight. In the hazy distance, she saw the thin line representing the Outer Wall: the even more massive fortification bordering the very edge of Ashoka's Oasis. The Kubar Road continued on past the Inner Wall, still wide and true, and Mira continued on it for another few miles. By then, most of the other travelers had already dispersed, and when she took a turnoff onto a narrow track, a path paved in gravel and barely wide enough for a single wagon, she traveled alone.

She was out amongst Ashoka's farms. They took up all the space between the city's two walls and were already verdant under the influence of the warm, spring weather. The air was filled with the pungent smell of turned earth, manure, and hay. Gentle, rolling hills were etched in straight rows of green: wheat and soybeans, the first crops of the season, though it would still be a few months before they were ready for harvest. The temperate climate of Ashoka allowed for three growing seasons. One of the most important crops, though, wouldn't be planted until well into the heat of the summer: the city's famed spidergrass.

Since metals of any kind were scarce in all the Oases, and any ore mines were inaccessible thanks to the Queen, people had to rely on other materials with which to make products requiring strength and hardness. For the most part, they had turned to ironwood and spidergrass, a thin, reedy type of grass with a green blade so dark as to be almost black in color. Despite its slender appearance it was tough and grew to over six feet in height, capped by a brilliant orange, feathery tassel. Over time, the Muran farmers had developed several different strains of spidergrass, each one useful in a different way. The *mericene* cultivar was used for tools such as wagon axles, nails, and hammers whereas the *japchin* was shaped into spears and arrows – shaft and tip – as well as armor.

A very special and rare variety, the *sathana*, was used for swords.

Mira had once seen the making of such a blade.

It had been the work of a Duriah smith, which was only to be expected given their Talent. Just as no other Caste could compare to Kummas when it came to battle, Duriahs were experts in their own fields: they were unmatchable artisans. Through their ability to Cohese, Duriahs could work with various objects and substances, transforming them into something more useful. They had developed an innate understanding of materials and manufacturing and had become experts in the creation of everything from wagons to fine furniture to retaining walls. Even the alchemy needed in the careful mixing of various ingredients within a glass vase until it glowed like a firefly – the eponymously named firefly lamp and the most common means of lighting throughout the world – was a skill only the Duriahs possessed.

In the case of the *sathana* sword, the Duriah smith had Cohesed hundreds of strands of spidergrass into a thick block, a spibar. Afterward, he had hammered the spibar flat and folded it onto itself before gently heating it, using *Jivatma* to make sure it didn't burn. Then came more hammering and heating. More hammering and heating. The Duriah had kept at it for hours, forcing out all air, water, and other impurities from within the spibar. When he was done and had forged the spidergrass block into the shape of a blade, he had then carefully glazed it with a thin, translucent layer of black ink made from the sap of the cerumen tree, which grew best in Arjun. Next came the kiln, and when the blade came out of the oven seven days later, it had a matte black finish and in Mira's imagination, oozed menace.

The resultant *sathana* sword, according to the Duriahs, had properties similar to those of the finest steel: hard and flexible, yet able to accept an edge sharp enough to slice a feather in mid-air. Of course, how a spidergrass blade would really compare to a steel weapon was a question never likely to be answered. After all, very little of that famed metal still existed, and the few remaining pieces were all priceless family heirlooms, not to be broken and wasted on foolish stress tests.

Mira pulled the mare to halt in sudden realization. She'd never actually seen steel. She shook her head in bemusement.

She gently heeled the mare back into motion, glancing about at the surrounding fields and their low-lying crops. Every so often she crossed a wooden bridge spanning a stone-lined and arrow-straight stream. The brooks were irrigation canals sourced from the Gaunt River. They spread like veins or arteries throughout the wide area between Ashoka's Walls and brought needed water to the farms. The Gaunt River coursed into Ashoka's Oasis as a powerful flood, carving a deep canyon through the heart of Mount Creolite north of the city proper before emptying into the Sickle Sea. But with the need for water from both the surrounding fields and the city itself, the river was but a rivulet by the time it reached its delta.

Mira crossed another bridge, entering a familiar village. The buildings were of tan stucco and wood with roofs of yellow tile or thatch. Most were two or three stories tall, both wide and deep with short alleys paved in brick passing between a few of the structures. The road Mira travelled grew finer and wider, paved in crushed stone and mortar and Cohesed by a Duriah. It became the main thoroughfare for the small but lively village.

This was a place peopled entirely by Murans, who were tall, well-built with golden-brown skin and dark hair. Their clothing was generally severe, dark and full length. In addition, the men wore wide-brimmed hats and if married, grew full, thick beards. They would have appeared grim or imposing if not for their generous smiles and their bright, lively emerald green eyes, a hallmark of their Caste.

Most Murans lived in ten such villages, each between two and five thousand, scattered throughout the land between the Inner and Outer Walls. Where they chose to live wasn't surprising since their Talent was the ability to bring life to most any kind of ground. As such, most Murans were farmers, with the men and women sharing equally in the work. Those who didn't live a life in the fields went on Trial, joined the High Army, or became private gardeners. But the glory of Caste Muran was borne by those who could sing. The finest singers were always Muran, and a Clan was highly honored if one of their own was chosen for the Larina, Ashoka's School of Song.

Mira nodded greeting but didn't slow or stop, and she soon left the village behind her. Once more, the road became gravel, her horse's hooves crunching loudly. She passed a field where a small herd of cows munched contentedly. Further in the distance, she saw men and women walking the fields, examining the crops for pests or blight.

The road rose into a series of low, rolling hills, which let her know she was nearing her destination: a *sathana* spidergrass plantation, co-owned by House Suzay and Clan Weathervine of Caste Muran. Several Suzays had recently graduated from the Fort and Sword, the Martial school favored by their House and all of them required an *Insufi* blade – the sword given during the *Upanayana* ceremony. It was the religious rite which represented the transformation of a boy into a man and consecrated a young Kumma to his duties. It was a holy ritual, sacred to Devesh, and even though most members of her Caste weren't religious – unlike the Murans who, along with the Shiyens, were the most devout of all of them – the *Upanayana* was a ceremony no Kumma would think to disregard.

She pulled her attention back to the road when she saw the turnoff, kneeing the mare onto a gravel drive. The small lane was lined with thick, lush azaleas in bloom; pink, red, and white, and Mira breathed in their seductive fragrance. The drive continued toward a large barn in the distance, but a brick footpath also curled to the left, ending in front of a large, two-story house with yellow clapboard siding and a large, wraparound porch. The roof was shingled with cedar shakes, and a set of chimes gently jingled in the mild breeze. It was a typical Muran dwelling, in which several generations of a Clan shared the same home.

Mira dismounted and tied her mare to a nearby rail before passing through a small gate into the fenced yard. Within, chickens roamed, clucking as they ran alongside her. Mira walked up the stairs, onto the large, neat and tidy front porch. Near the door, several green rocking chairs were arranged around a small, round ironwood table upon which a glass of tea gathered condensation. From inside, a sweet contralto voice sang a song of glory to the sun and rain.

Mira knocked on the door.

A woman in her mid-sixties answered. Like all Muran, she had emerald green-eyes and golden-brown skin. Her once dark hair was mostly gray now and her face was lined with wrinkles, a reflection of a life spent outdoors. She still stood straight and tall, almost able to look Mira in the eyes.

"Mistress Shull," Mira said with a nod. "It is good to see you again."

"And you," Mistress Shull Weathervine said, throwing open the door and letting the pleasant aroma of some sort of stew waft out. "Please come in. It's been too long." She glanced upward. "I hope you don't mind, but Trellis is practicing. We pray she might be accepted into the Larina next year."

Mira smiled. "Not at all," she said. "A glorious voice raised in song is never to be condemned." In fact, hearing Shull's granddaughter sing so beautifully raised a lump in Mira's throat. She wished she had a Talent so lovely, but she was Kumma. Though women of her Caste were taught to fight, there was little beauty in killing.

She stifled a wistful sigh. *To each their own.*

Mistress Shull led Mira through the foyer, a small wood-paneled space with a large firefly lantern hanging from the ceiling, and on into the kitchen in the rear of the house from whence the delicious aroma arose. Several shelves hung from the knotty pine walls, holding well-used pots and pans as well as ceramic dishware. A small window gave a view out over the fields and the barn, while the back door was thrown open, allowing a fitful breeze to help cool the room. Mistress Terras, Shull's mother, stood next to the sink, methodically chopping vegetables – onions and potatoes likely from last year's harvest – and tossed them into a simmering pot. Mistress Lace, one of Shull's daughters and but a few years older than Mira, glanced up from her work at a large, butcher-block table where she was de-boning a chicken. A slop bucket rested on the floor between the two women, and they were preparing a hearty dinner for later in the day. And this wasn't the entirety of their Clan. The rest of the Weathervines were likely out in the fields.

Mistress Terras glanced up and her heavily wrinkled face broke into a smile. She set aside her knife and wiped her hands on her apron before straightening as much as she could, a dowager's hump bending a once proud woman. "It's been a long time since you last visited us," she said. "What brings you out to the plantations after all this time?"

"The fortunes of House Suzay," Mira said. "We need spidergrass for several *Insufi* blades," Mira answered.

Mistress Lace's face broke into a smile. "Congratulations," she said. "Your apprenticed House is blessed to have more than one candidate ready to take his place as a man."

Mira smiled acknowledgement. "Thank you. Do you think we'll have enough *sathana* for them?" she asked.

"Absolutely," Mistress Shull answered. "We had an excellent harvest three years ago, and the spidergrass from that season was quite healthy. It should do."

"Then we only need to negotiate a price," Mira said.

Mistress Terras stared Mira in the eyes. "You've grown child, but know this: we bargain hard."

Mira felt the corners of her lips turn up in a faint smile. "Then let's get started," she suggested. Kumma women couldn't engage in battle – they were too valuable to waste in such a manner – but it didn't mean they didn't enjoy a good fight.

It took some haggling, but eventually they settled on a price, one Mira believed Tol'El would be pleased with.

"Will you stay for tea and some food?" Mistress Lace asked.

Mira was tempted, but there was one final task to complete. If she finished quickly enough, the evening would be hers, and she had plans. A new production of an old play she had loved as a child was opening tonight. Bree had promised that Jaresh could get them tickets.

"Thank you, but I can't. I have one last task still to complete,"

Mira said, adding a regretful note.

"Tol'El wants to make sure he gets the most out of you before you return to House Shektan, eh?" Mistress Terras asked with a twinkle in her eye.

"He has been pushing hard lately," Mira said before making ready to leave as she said her goodbyes.

"You did well," Mistress Shull said with a smile as she walked Mira to the door.

"Thank you," Mira replied, relieved to hear the older woman's good opinion. "Can you have it ready for delivery in a month?"

"We have it ready now," Mistress Shull said. "Why wait so long?"

"The caravan from Arjun is late," Mira said with a grimace.

The sap of the cerumen tree, which grew best in Arjun, was the key ingredient in the final glazing of a *sathana* blade before it was placed in a kiln. A Duriah could make do with something else, but for an *Insufi* sword, nothing else was acceptable.

Mistress Shull frowned. "A pity," she said. "Arjun is rumored to have a Sentya who they claim is the second coming of Kubar. I looked forward to hearing his compositions."

"As did I," Mira said. "Hopefully, the caravan will arrive shortly, and we can both hear the truth of Arjun's boasts." With that, Mira said her goodbyes and headed back to Ashoka proper.

CHAPTER FOUR
A NIGHT OUT

Can a man offer compassion to one for whom
he holds nothing but contempt? It seems unlikely..

~Sooths and Small Sayings by Tramed Billow AF1387

Saresh Shektan waded his way through the heavy traffic of Martyr Hall, the southernmost road marking the border of Semaphore Walk, Ashoka's theater and performing arts district. He cursed under his breath as he bumped into a clumsy, heavy-set Rahail and offered a half-hearted apology. The thick crowds weren't a surprise. The Semaphore was a popular destination on most evenings for couples and families, or a group of friends wanting to go out for a night of entertainment by seeing a play or listening to some new music.

He glanced at his sister with bemused envy. Bree wasn't having any trouble. There she was, walking alongside him without a care in the world. He rolled his eyes. Of course not. She didn't have to worry herself with such mundane concerns as moving to avoid others or mumbling apologies as one tried to slip through the crowd. Her beauty and Kumma heritage allowed her to live without the need for such simple courtesies. Men stepped aside at her approach as did women, although rather than favoring her with an admiring glance, the latter were more likely to give her one of judgmental jealousy.

Jaresh sent an angry glare at one particular Cherid, a young man who was staring at Bree with a bit too much appreciation. He was happy to see the man's wife or escort slap him for the almost rapacious expression he had worn. The man was a Cherid. Bree was a Kumma. An admiring glance was relatively benign, but the open look of lust on the man's face was disgusting. The Cherid needed to be taught the limits of what was considered proper behavior.

He felt sympathy for Bree. She hadn't missed the interaction. Her giveaway was the mildly derisive smile she wore and the tension Jaresh could see in the carriage of her shoulders. Bree sometimes complained that her beauty was as much a burden as a boon, which was true to a certain extent, especially at moments like this, but it was also utter bat guano when fully considered in all possible contexts. True, her appearance often granted her unwanted attention, but it had also never stopped her from using her attractiveness to its full advantage. She exploited every gift available to her just as their nanna had once pithily advised: *don't be too proud to use what you've got to get the job done.* Bree didn't always like the unsolicited interest, but Jaresh knew she wouldn't have it any other way. Better to be beautiful than ugly.

Jaresh, on the other hand, was as plain as yogurt. Not even vanilla since that was an actual flavor. He was unassuming like a good Sentya should be. Nothing special. Move along, people. Nothing to see here. He had the features typical for his Caste: an aquiline nose perched proudly above his well-tailored goatee; sparkling hazel eyes, accented to his unending embarrassment with long, feminine lashes; and dusky skin, though not so dark as a Kumma's. The one aspect of his appearance setting him apart as unusual from the rest of his Caste was his build. Like most Sentyas, Jaresh was of average height, but unlike the other members of his Caste, who tended to be slender, he had a thick and well-muscled physique.

He could thank his upbringing for the latter, which was as unique as anyone could ever recall. Jaresh was of the Kumma House Shektan and even carried the surname Shektan but was *not* himself a Kumma. Nobody could recall a similar situation ever occurring in the past: a Sentya raised in a Kumma House, and by the ruling 'El, no less.

It was all because his Nanna – Dar'El; not his birth father – fell out of a boat.

When Darjuth Sulle – Nanna's name before his elevation to ruling 'El of House Shektan – had returned home after his last Trial, he had taken to spending many an afternoon out on the sea. He had whiled away the hours; resting, healing, or just trying to forget. His final two Trials had been difficult. Painful. He had ended up in Mockery, a city on the far eastern edge of Continent Catalyst near the Mourning Ocean. It was about as far from Ashoka as any place in the world. Darjuth had eventually joined a Trial heading from Mockery to Defiance. The caravan had been large, with a complement of over five hundred warriors, and they had initially made good time. But somewhere north of the Highmark Hills, several Fractures of Chimeras had attacked them. While Suwraith's beasts had been crushed, the creatures had still managed to cause heavy damage, setting fire to the caravan's food stores and rupturing their water casks. By the time the caravan had reached Defiance, fully half of the warriors had died, most from dehydration in the unforgiving desert of the Prayer.

After a long respite, Darjuth had then joined another Trial, the short sea voyage from Defiance to Ashoka. It was regarded as the safest and easiest Trial any warrior could make, but it too, had proved ruinous. An unexpected storm had blown down from the Privation Mountains, sweeping the ships of the caravan north where many of the vessels had smashed against the Needle Points, a graveyard of spiky rocks and outcroppings with impassable water and heavy waves. Only one man in four survived by the time the remaining ships had limped their way home to Ashoka. The two journeys, occurring consecutively as they had, were disasters unlike any recorded in decades.

The Trials were harsh, but the sudden death of *so many* close friends…it took time to come to terms with such loss. The sea was a place where Darjuth could occasionally forget his pain and search out his way in the world once more; where he could reconcile himself to his guilt-ridden survival in the face of the senseless death of so many good friends, men he had loved and who would never again return home. The sea was a place where he had hoped to find some semblance of peace.

On one particularly fine day, Darjuth had gone out by himself on a small, wide-beamed catboat. It should have been easy to handle with its one sail, but during a moment of distraction, the boom had unexpectedly swung around and smashed into his head. He'd been knocked unconscious and thrown from the boat.

Meanwhile, Jaresh's birth father, Bresh Konias, already in middle years by then, had seen the entire accident. He later described it as a terrible event he could almost presciently guess would happen but had been powerless to prevent. But he had prepared himself for what he knew was about to occur. Before Darjuth had even hit the water or been struck by the swinging boom, Bresh had already aimed his sloop toward where he had guessed the Kumma would fall. An unpredictable riptide and choppy swells had made the ocean dangerous, but Bresh had disregarded the peril. At great personal risk, he had leapt into the sea and managed to save Darjuth. In gratitude, Nanna had offered any boon he could legally promise.

Bresh had been the unwanted third son of a poor Moon Quarter dock worker. He had no claims on those with wealth, and his kinfolk

– the Konias' – couldn't help him either, being, at best, of only middling-to-minimal wealth. They had been unable to help Bresh with anything beyond the bare necessities for living and the rudimentary schooling in Sentya learning. However, without advanced training, he had nothing to commend him to a potential employer. He had no specific skills or knowledge, which might have allowed him to rise to a higher station in life. His fate had essentially been sealed in childhood: in poverty.

And after his childhood, in poverty he had remained. At an age when many of his contemporaries were readying homes for grandchildren, Bresh had remained single and childless. After all, who would offer their daughter to someone in such dire straits? His livelihood – a for-rent fisherman leasing his sloop at usury rates – had been the only job available to him. Even the Moon Quarter where his father and two brothers worked had been a posting unaffordable to him. His life as a fisherman allowed his survival but little more. Day-to-day drudgery was his existence.

Saving the life of a Kumma, though, everything could change from that, and Bresh had known it. Being unschooled didn't make him stupid, and he had understood his good fortune and recognized how best to turn it to his advantage. So instead of one boon, Bresh had begged Darjuth for two. The first was simple: money to buy his own fishing boat. After eyeing Bresh's tattered clothing and old, poorly maintained sloop, it was a request Darjuth had expected, and one he could easily afford. It was Bresh's second wish that had caught Nanna by surprise.

With halting words, Bresh had begged for a simple provision: any children the Sentya might someday father would be personally sponsored by Darjuth. It was a bold supplication, and Nanna had been curious as to the reason for it. Bresh's explanation had been rational and straightforward: with his own boat, he would no longer be poor and with the promise of a Kumma sponsorship for his children, overnight, he would become a sought-after prospect for marriage. More importantly, his children would have a chance for a future Bresh couldn't even dream of experiencing.

Upon hearing his reasoning, Darjuth had agreed to all of it. He had been thoroughly impressed with Bresh's judgment. A lesser man would have asked for more selfish and fleeting needs. Bresh's choices reflected a more shrewd intellect. Even then, Nanna had prized competence and intelligence above all else, reasoning from a purely practical level that any children from a man like Bresh should be nurtured so their acumen could flower. They could be of great benefit to House Shektan.

And Nanna couldn't help but feel empathy for Bresh's pain. So much longing and desire trapped in a life of drudgery. It was a tragedy.

Soon after, Bresh had married, and several years later, he and his young wife, Shari had their first child: Jaresh. Witness to his birth had been Darjuth himself, holding to his promise to sponsor Bresh's children. Life must have been an unexpected, endless wonder of possibilities for Jaresh's birth father. It all ended several years later when a drunk in a downstairs apartment had failed to close the grate to his stove and a stray spark had sent the whole building up in a wall of flames. Jaresh had been three when the apartment fire had claimed the lives of his birth parents. Darjuth and his wife, Satha Sulle, had come for him. He didn't remember much from back then – except for the fear. He had been certain he would have to go live with his Aunt Veldik, who hated him.

Instead, for reasons he doubted even his father truly understood, something in Jaresh's soot and tear-stained face must have touched Nanna's heart. Perhaps it was the voice of Devesh. Perhaps it was a moment of weakness. Or, maybe it had been simple pity. Whatever the reason, Darjuth had followed his feelings, and on the spot, without even consulting his wife, he had decided to adopt Jaresh.

Even now, most Kummas hadn't quite come to grips with the

ridiculous peculiarity of such a decision. What could be the purpose of a Kumma adopting a Sentya? It made no sense.

Jaresh wondered if his nanna sometimes questioned his decision as well.

Adoption into House Shektan had provided Jaresh with a loving home, but it had not solved all of his problems. Far from it. It wasn't easy being the Sentya son of a Kumma. For his own birth Caste, Jaresh was an oddity. He was one of their own, but he acted and dressed like a warrior. As far as he knew, it was something never before known in Ashoka or any other city. As a result, other Sentyas weren't sure whether his status counted as a point of pride or as a matter of revulsion. They simply didn't know how to relate to him. As for Kummas, Jaresh often served as an affront to their ego. He was someone who could never measure up to their lofty warrior standards and yet carried one of their surnames. It was a disgrace for one so incapable to be counted as a member of a Kumma family. It only grew worse upon Nanna's election as the ruling 'El of House Shektan and his children's assumption of the House name. Despite all this, Jaresh was grateful for his place in the world. Dar'El and Satha were the only parents he knew. They loved him.

On most days it was enough.

Jaresh was broken out of his reverie when he bumped into Bree. She had come to an unexpected halt as, wonder of wonders, the crowd had *not* parted before her. She turned with a frown.

"Be careful," she admonished. "You almost stepped on my dress."

"Sorry," he said. "Just thinking about other things."

Her eyebrows arched in an unspoken question.

"Did you know that tomorrow is my seventeenth year as your brother?" Jaresh said.

Bree smiled. "Of course I know. Amma plans on throwing you a surprise party," she said.

"Oh. Had no idea."

"That's why it's called a 'surprise party'," Bree explained in an overly patient tone. She tapped her chin in consideration. "We don't want Amma to be disappointed. So act surprised," she advised, giving him a condescending pat on the cheek before turning away.

Jaresh smiled at his sister's patronizing tone. She must be slipping if she thought she could irritate him with such a transparent ploy. For whatever reason, the two of them had always been competitive, even when it came to schemes meant to annoy one another. It was childish, and Jaresh sometimes wondered if they should grow up about it, but the look on Bree's face when he punctured her inflated sense of importance was absolutely priceless. He imagined she felt the same way, else she wouldn't also continue with their game.

He hid a grin as an idea came to him. "I'll make sure to remember," he said. "And you have to promise not to tell Amma I told you her dinner two nights from now is only a ploy to get you together with your potential future husband."

"What!" Bree said in shocked disbelief. Onlookers turned at her shout. She grabbed Jaresh's arm in a painful squeeze. "What do you know?" she demanded in a menacing whisper.

Jaresh carefully pried his arm free. Bree feared marriage like most people feared falling from a great height; it might be survivable but the pain was sure to be awful. Up to a point, Jaresh sympathized with her. Kumma women could only marry a man who had completed at minimum three Trials, which meant their spouses were at least ten years older than them. Bree claimed it must be a horrible fate – like being shackled to an old man.

"Just kidding, little sis," Jaresh said grinning broadly.

"Not funny," she said, glowering.

"Was to me," Jaresh said with a carefree smile. "Now, if you're done with your tantrum, the crowd's opening up. We should get going."

"I wasn't throwing…"

Jaresh grabbed her hand and yanked her forward, cutting off whatever she was about to say. "Come on before it closes up again," he said.

They took a large thoroughfare branching off of Martyr Hall and headed deeper into Semaphore Walk. Another turn had them on a small street, close to their destination: the Blue Room. It was an older playhouse, one more willing to take on a challenging project eschewed by most of the larger theaters.

Even here, the streets remained crowded. Well-dressed men and women, perfumed and coiffed, mixed with rougher looking folk; most of whom were Murans coming in from the fields. Restaurants and cafes opened out on the street, and the smell of sizzling meat and spices filled the air. A mild spring breeze filtered through the crowd but did little to cool the warmth raised by the press of so many people.

Jaresh was soon sweating. He looked forward to the cool of the theater.

Tonight they meant to see *The Magistrate Divan*, an old comedic satire written two hundred years ago. It chronicled a week in the life of a Cherid Magistrate of a fictional city and the foibles of the supposed ruling Caste. Of course, no Caste had been spared by the author, Deside, and his humorous and cutting pen. He had added everyone into the scope of his satire; from the arrogance of Kummas to the lickspittle nature of Sentyas to the earthy know-it-allism of Murans. All were mocked, some more than others. It was supposed to be hilarious, but Jaresh wouldn't know. He'd never seen it before since the last time *The Magistrate* had been produced was over a decade earlier. Tonight was opening night of a fresh interpretation of a classic.

At the playhouse they were to meet Mira Terrell, Bree's friend. The two women had always been close. Both of them were Shektans and had gone to the same schools throughout their lives. Couple this with the fact that she was the only daughter of Sophy Terrell, one of Nanna's closest advisors in the House Council, and Mira had ended up spending a lot of time around the House Seat. However, despite her frequent presence, Jaresh felt like he hardly knew her. The two of them had never spent much time with one another. On the few instances they had, Jaresh had found himself charmed by her wry, self-effacing humor. He found her…interestingly unique.

He couldn't say the same for Rukh. His brother thought Mira a bit eccentric.

Rukh. Jaresh sighed. Where was he and how was he doing? He'd left six weeks earlier, but it felt like a lifetime. Jaresh did some rough calculation. Rukh was probably somewhere northwest of the Flats by now. Jaresh sent a silent plea heavenward, praying for his older brother's safe return.

Jaresh still remembered the first time he saw the young boy who would become his older brother. Rukh. It had been in the parlor of their original home, a large three-story house on a hill north of Scythe Cut with a view over Dryad Park. Jaresh had entered his new home with trepidation, still teary-eyed and covered in soot from the apartment fire wherein his birth parents had died. Rukh had greeted him at the door with open arms and a ready smile that promised a mischievous sense of humor. The two had been close from the very first, driving Amma to distraction with their over-abundance of boyish energy. There had been an episode when they had chased a nonexistent housefly all around the kitchen, pretending to smash it flat. Jaresh could still recall Amma's cry of horror when Rukh had pretended to promptly gulp down the imaginary insect. And then there was the time he and Rukh had donned matching Tigon masks and walked in on Bree while she'd been brushing her teeth. She had shrieked in fear and tried to flee; tripping on her own feet and promptly fell into the toilet. Her howl of anger when she realized what had happened had been priceless. The switching the two of them had received was worth it. All these years later, Jaresh still laughed over the memory.

He missed Rukh.

"It's right over there," Bree said, breaking him out of his reverie.

Jaresh looked to where she pointed. There, across the street and a few buildings down, stood the Blue Room. The area around the theater was congested as people milled about, waiting for their friends and family. The three sets of double wooden doors leading into the playhouse were thrown open. Attendants, young men and women, stood beside them, collecting tickets, ensuring no one tried to skip in for free. A few hardy souls stood at the box office, hoping to find a seat even at this late date. There might still be a few available, but they would be likely high up in the balcony.

"There she is," Bree said, pointing out Mira. Now it was her turn to pull Jaresh along.

"I've got the tickets," Mira said to the two of them. "You pay for dinner, and we'll call it even."

"But that wouldn't be fair to you," Jaresh protested. "You bought two tickets, and we'll only be buying you one dinner."

"You haven't seen her eat," Bree warned.

Mira wrinkled her nose at Bree before breaking out in laughter. "Nanna says I must have a tapeworm. He even had me tested."

Jaresh smiled, charmed again by Mira's self-deprecating humor. "You're joking, right?" he asked.

"I wish she was," Bree answered.

"Let's go find our seats," Mira suggested with a gentle laugh.

Jaresh led them across the street. He paused on the other side, grimacing when he saw someone he despised heading their way. "Like flies at a banquet, so is Suge Wrestiva's presence," Jaresh said. "Don't look now, but the bilge breather is heading our way."

"Great," Bree replied sourly. "Let's get inside before he sees us.

He's always drunk and looking for trouble."

As the only remaining child of Hal 'El Wrestiva, the powerful ruling 'El of his House, Suge had always been spoiled and overly indulged. The leniency shown toward Suge had allowed him to skirt the very edge of what Kumma society considered proper decorum. He had grown up into a coddled man-child, always protected from facing the consequences of his cruel actions – behavior certain to have earned severe censure for any other Kumma.

Jaresh cursed. One of Suge's sycophants, the idiot identical twins, Han or Wan Reold – Jaresh could never tell the two apart – had spotted them and was pointing them out to Suge. An ugly sneer appeared on the Wrestiva's face as he moved toward them. Suge hated Jaresh with a loathing bordering on the pathological. In times past, it had only been Rukh's swift sword that had stood between Jaresh and a beating from Suge.

"Let me handle this," Mira commanded.

Jaresh's jaw hardened. He wasn't a Kumma by breeding, but a horse would stand on its legs and sing before he hid behind a woman. "No."

Bree looked at him, surprise and worry in her eyes. "Be careful," she warned. "He's a wastrel, but he's still a Kumma."

"I'm not looking for a fight, but I won't run from one either," Jaresh said, infusing his words with more confidence than he felt. "Let's head on inside. We only stop if we have to."

They had taken but three steps when Suge's challenging words reached them. His voice was like the rest of him: thuggish and guttural. "What's this? A dog escorting two women." He brayed as his hangers-on joined in the laughter.

Jaresh froze in place before slowly turning around. There was no way to ignore such an insult. It had to be answered. His jaw clenched with resentment. Why couldn't the dung eater have let them be? Jaresh had only wanted to enjoy a play. There was no rational reason for this confrontation, but reason wasn't a factor when it came to Suge Wrestiva. The man was a bully. He enjoyed throwing his weight around, spoiled and protected as he was by his wealth and position. The man represented the worst of what it meant to be a Kumma. He was a stain on the entire Caste. Jaresh's anger got the best of him, and he spoke without thinking. "Speaking of animals," he said to Bree, "look who's here. A talking jackass."

Bree's hiss of dismay was distant in Jaresh's hearing. There was only the now. He wouldn't let this prick – this pig of a man – ever bully him again.

Suge's face reddened as he scowled in ugly anger. "Careful what you say, Sentya. Your brother isn't around this time."

"He was never needed," Jaresh said, stepping forward and getting straight in Suge's mug. "You need your friends to handle me coward?" he asked, glancing pointedly at the twins who were glowering in warning.

"Step away from him, Jaresh," Bree urged, tugging on his arm.

Suge smiled, humorless and full of malice. "You should listen to her, little bitch. Hide behind her skirts. That's all you Sentyas are good for anyway. Not a real man in the whole Caste." He snorted in derision. "You Shektans are weak."

"Maybe so," Jaresh said. "But I was called for Trial. I leave in six months. First one in my Caste ever to do so. *That is* what it means to be a Shektan. We breed champions and heroes."

"You? A champion?" Suge laughed in contempt. "You're no more a champion than my dog's ass."

Jaresh smiled thinly. "No, I'm not a champion, but soon enough, I won't be a Virgin. When I return from Trial, where will you be?" Jaresh asked. "Still here with these two cretins? Doing nothing, achieving nothing, and being nothing as you hide behind your nanna's name."

Suge lunged forward, swinging and missing.

Jaresh easily dodged the blow, surprised by how slow Suge moved. Rukh was a blur in comparison. Even Keemo and Farn were far faster.

By now a crowd had gathered. Included was Rector Bryce. What was he doing here? Jaresh grimaced in annoyance when Bryce blocked Suge's next blow. He didn't want or require anyone's protection. Not anymore. He had to stand on his own two feet.

"What's going on here?" the lieutenant demanded as he glanced at the two men. Bryce was a member of both the Ashokan Guard and the City Watch, and the look on his face said he expected a swift answer.

Suge wrenched free his arm. "None of your business, warrior," he growled.

Jaresh was disappointed by Bryce's interference. He knew it was foolish, but for a moment there, he thought he could have taken the thug. "Suge was just demonstrating his many deficiencies," Jaresh said.

Suge smirked. "Deficiencies you say? Maybe so, but I'll always be a Kumma, and you'll always be a Sentya. Never forget it. You'll always know I'm a man and you aren't."

"You would count yourself as a man?" Bree challenged, coming to stand next to Jaresh. "You, who have never dared the Trials?" She froze Suge with a look of scorn and loathing. "You are no man Suge Wrestiva. You are a weakling and a coward."

Suge stiffened, outraged. "Frag you, whore. You think you're so prim, proper, and perfect. We've all heard how you sell out your pretty pony, giving it up for any Kumma with a coin or smile."

Jaresh was incoherent with rage, fists balled. No one spoke to Bree like that – or any woman for that matter. "Apologize now, you fragging bastard," he demanded from between clenched teeth.

Suge drew himself up proudly, chest thrust out. His stance was ruined by his sneer. "Or what, Sentya bitch? I've nothing to apologize for. I'm just telling the truth. Hell, I even heard how she gives you a free ride now and then, spreading her legs for your tiny prick." He thrust his pelvis rhythmically.

Shocked intakes of breath met Suge's words. Everyone had heard them. The world stopped as all conversation ceased.

Jaresh wanted to kill. What Suge had said…it was an unforgivable insult, one demanding violent retribution. Nothing less would do. Rector Bryce must have felt the same way. His face was a blank mask of hatred as he stepped forward, looking ready to attack.

Jaresh grabbed the lieutenant's arm, pulling him back. "A brother has first right to satisfaction."

Bryce paused, unwilling to pull back before finally nodding in grim acceptance and stepping aside.

Even the twins, Han and Wan Reold, despite the haze of their stupidity, must have recognized the severity of the moment. They nervously edged away from Suge, as if wanting to separate themselves from the stink and contamination of his crude insults. This wasn't something Hal'El Wrestiva could paper over with coin or coercion. House Shektan would demand blood. Suge's blood. Not necessarily his death, but certainly a painful beating with his abject apology and humiliation. Whatever the Shektans deemed just. And House Wrestiva would have no standing to deny them.

Bree broke the tableau. She stepped forward and slapped Suge, raking his face. Trails of blood slowly oozed from the cuts left by her fingernails.

"Satisfaction. Now," Jaresh demanded. "No weapons."

"As you wish," Suge replied boldly. His brave words were betrayed when he nervously licked his lips. The thug must have finally understood the enormity of his mistake. Suge worked to mask it, but Jaresh could see the dread lurking behind his eyes, but it wasn't Jaresh he feared. Stupid as he was, by now even Suge realized that retribution was certain to come from House Shektan and would land on his fool head like a load of bricks. It was a promise made manifest by the imposing figure of Lieutenant Rector Bryce standing at Jaresh's shoulder.

The crowd moved back, leaving a twenty foot opening around them.

"After him, me," Bryce promised.

"Get in line," Suge said. "I'll smear you across the pavement, old man."

Jaresh doubted anyone watching was fooled by Suge's false bravado. Bryce certainly wasn't. He answered Suge, mocking the Wrestiva's lack of experience in any kind of real fight. Their words washed over Jaresh. He had stopped listening. He was about to be on the receiving end of a painful whipping. Possibly even the fatal kind. He tried to control his fear. His hands shook, and he wanted nothing more than to throw-up. He could just step aside, let Bryce fight in his place, but Jaresh knew the task was his and his alone. He had to be the first one to face Suge.

Damn it! Why couldn't Rukh be here? As the eldest, it would have been *his* responsibility to stomp Suge's mudhole dry.

Jaresh took a deep, calming breath. Complaining about it wouldn't help him any. His duty was clear. Alright then. Time for some pain. "Let's do it," Jaresh said to Suge, glad his voice didn't crack as he spoke brave words he didn't feel. Without warning, Jaresh kicked. His hips twisted, and he whipped his foot around. It smacked with a dull thud against the meat of Suge's thigh.

Suge winced and stepped back, taking up a fighter's pose. "Only shot you'll get on me, bitch."

Jaresh didn't bother answering. He drew on his Well, and his thoughts grew sharp and clear. His focus was like a crystal lens, drawing in the weltered and rainbow coruscated confusion of his thoughts until only a single, fierce white light remained. This was the Talent of the Sentya: to understand the truth in a way that burned away all illusions. A multitude of evaluations was completed in less time than a heartbeat. The kick shouldn't have gotten through, and yet it had. Even distracted as he was, any Kumma should have been able to block and counter before Jaresh had even regained his balance. Something was wrong with Suge. The advantages were still with the thug but perhaps they weren't insurmountable. Will to win counted for much.

Jaresh's thoughts were tested a moment later as Suge landed a stiff jab followed by a straight right. The last rocked Jaresh, causing his knees to buckle. He stumbled back on jelly legs, needing distance and time to regain his bearings.

Suge feinted a jab and shot forward as Jaresh ducked the punch, still clearing the cobwebs. Suge was on him, attempting to take him to the ground and pound his head into the bricks. Jaresh managed to get his arms under Suge's. His legs stiffened as he worked to keep to his feet. He couldn't afford to have Suge on top. Jaresh barely managed to hold off the bilge-breathing jackhole, and with a frustrated growl, Suge disengaged.

Jaresh saw an opening. The Wrestiva didn't do a good job covering up. Jaresh jumped forward, knee leading. He felt satisfaction as he connected with Suge's forehead. Suge took a halting step back as he shook his head and glared. Jaresh wanted to smile as another opening appeared. He needed to thank his sister. No doubt, she'd done it on purpose. Hers had always been a cold anger, allowing her full control of her actions no matter how furious she might be. Her rake of Suge's face had ripped a line of cuts, two of which were slowly dripping blood into Suge's right eye, blinding him.

And Jaresh was a lefty. The thick-headed thug would never see the punches coming from that side. Jaresh swung a left hook, connecting solidly with Suge's cheek. A kick – same side – smashed into Suge's forehead. The coward stumbled back, legs buckling.

With a rush of exhilaration, Jaresh rushed forward. He couldn't believe it. He was about to whip a Kumma's ass! A flying leap and a straight punch, connected with Suge's nose, crunching it in a spray of blood. The Wrestiva crumpled, falling to the ground.

He was down but not out. Jaresh stepped forward. A vindictive thought led to action. One final kick to Suge's chest. Cracked ribs. Asshole wouldn't breathe easy for weeks. Suge groaned and passed out.

The world returned. Jaresh found himself hugged by Bree. Mira smiled widely and congratulated him.

Rector slapped his shoulder. "Incredible! I never suspected you had such skill." He saluted. "The honor of our House is avenged."

Bree laughed. "I would love to see Hal'El's face when word of this humiliation reaches him." She hugged Jaresh again.

The twins knelt next to a supine and unconscious Suge. One of them put a head to the Wrestiva's chest and fingers to his nose. "He's dead," he said, speaking into a sudden quiet. He glared at Jaresh. "You killed him."

All the glory left Jaresh in a rush. Emptiness and horror replaced it. How could Suge be dead? Impossible.

He pushed Han or Wan, whoever it was, out of the way, hoping and praying the man was wrong. Suge wasn't breathing. No pulse.

An elderly Shiyen stepped out of the crowd. He shoved Bryce aside. "Move, you lump. I'm a physician." He moved to the side opposite Jaresh and knelt, feeling for Suge's pulse. He shook his head and ripped open Suge's shirt. "You know resuscitation?" he asked Jaresh.

"I…I took a class a few years back," Jaresh mumbled. He wasn't thinking clearly. He wasn't thinking at all. He reached for his Well and clarity came. "I remember what needs to be done."

"Good. Stay close," the Shiyen ordered. "I might need you soon." The Shiyen's eyes went blank, and a glow quickly built up around his hands. "Heart quivering. All four chambers. Fibrillation.

Suwraith's spit." He placed his hands on Suge's chest, one directly under the right clavicle and the other one below and to the side of the left nipple. "Stay back," he said loudly. The glow bled out of his hands and flowed like streaming lightning straight into Suge's chest.

Suge's torso jerked. He still wasn't breathing, and still no pulse. The Shiyen's eyes remained blank. Once more, the glow built in his hands. "Stay back." Again came the streaming lightning but Suge remained unmoving. The Shiyen shook his head and shifted position. He began chest compressions. At thirty, he tilted Suge's head back, pushing the chin up, and gave the Kumma two breaths. As he restarted chest compressions, he glanced at Jaresh. "I'll need you to take over soon," he said.

Jaresh nodded, still too shocked to sort out what had happened. How could Suge have died? Jaresh hadn't hurt him *that* badly. And what did this mean for the relations between House Wrestiva and House Shektan. The two families, one of ancient lineage and the other relatively new, were already fierce rivals, with ruling 'Els who despised one another. And now, the heir of House Wrestiva was dead by the hands of not just any member of House Shektan, but the Sentya son of its 'El. The repercussions from what had happened here could go on for years, possibly even leading to a blood feud.

The Shiyen gestured and Jaresh knelt opposite him. He picked up where the physician had left off, applying chest compressions and calling out the numbers. Time distorted, twisting and changing. They could have been at it for hours or only seconds, trying to resuscitate Suge.

In truth, it was a few short minutes.

The Shiyen leaned back and waved Jaresh to stop. "It's over," he said, his voice tired. "His spirit is with Devesh." He rose to his feet with a series of creaks from various joints. "Young fool. Too much fire in his loins and stupidity in his damn fool eyes," he muttered.

Jaresh sat back on his haunches, stunned by the sudden finality of it. He studied Suge's slack features, still and unmoving as they were. Death had granted the Wrestiva's brutish features a tranquility and grace they had never possessed in life. Suge's empty gaze stared heavenward, and Jaresh dimly noted a faint blue tinge to the whites of the man's otherwise wide-open eyes.

By then members of the City Watch had arrived. Fortunately, none of them were of House Wrestiva. Their Captain took one look at Suge and removed his cloak, draping it over the fallen Kumma. He sent a runner to House Wrestiva, and the rest of his unit took statements from the crowd, most of whom still lingered and spoke in hushed tones. A sense of unreality settled over those who had seen the fight. How could a Sentya have defeated, much less killed a Kumma? It was the question on everyone's mind.

The Captain turned to face him. "Dorn Esap," he said by way of introduction. "You're Dar'El's boy, right?" At Jaresh's nod, the Captain looked over the rest of them. "Someone want to tell me why Hal'El Wrestiva is about to bring Suwraith's own sorrow down on all of you?"

Jaresh answered. "He insulted my sister," he began. He explained the argument and escalating series of insults that had eventually led to the words Suge had spoken about Bree. "I demanded his apology." He shrugged. "He chose to fight." Jaresh paused, uncertain now. How *had* he defeated a Kumma? It should never have happened. In the heat of battle and the aftermath, the unlikeliness of such an outcome hadn't had time to sink in. Now it did. "Somehow, I won..." A pause. "And he died."

The Captain scratched his head, confused. He turned to Rector. "Lieutenant, we've known each other awhile. You saying this scrap of a Sentya took down a Kumma?"

Han or Wan, whoever, leapt to the fore. "There must have been some trickery. The Sentya coward must have poisoned Suge. How else could one of the craven Caste defeat one of our own?"

The Captain looked to the twins. "The whys and what-fors are for others to figure out. Not my job. Did the argument take place the way the Sentya described? Did your kinsman speak the words to the Shektan girl?"

Han and Wan shared a mulish look before turning back to the Captain, nodding reluctantly.

"Good. That's settled. The fight was legal. Now, Lieutenant Bryce, what did you see?"

Rector shrugged. "Don't ask me how, but what Jaresh described...it's exactly how the fight occurred. For whatever reason, Suge never drew from his Well. He moved no faster than any non-Kumma. He fought very stupidly. I've seen children do better. But even without the advantage of speed, he should still have had the skill to win."

Jaresh glowered. Suge hadn't been *that* bad.

Bree caught his scowl and shook her head. "Not now," she mouthed.

Jaresh nodded acknowledgment, nevertheless, annoyed by Rector's assessment.

The Captain stepped away and met with the other members of the Watch. After a few seconds of conversation, he gestured and set them to dispersing the crowd. He turned back to Jaresh and his group. "The rest of the crowd pretty much confirms what you lot told me. You four..." his gaze included Rector "...should get going before the Wrestivas show up. The last thing I want is for a bunch of hotheads to have a battle in the middle of the city. Go home. I have your names, and if anyone needs arresting, I can do it in the morning."

Jaresh nodded. Bad trouble would come about from this.

"I really wanted to see that play," Mira said softly.

"A man is dead," Bree responded tartly. "Our House may have a blood feud on its hands. How can you think of a silly play at such a time?" she asked.

Mira was instantly contrite. "I didn't mean it the way it came out," she said. "I just wanted..." She shrugged. "Nevermind."

"I understood what you meant," Bryce said, sounding gallant. "This could have been a very pleasant evening. You only wish it could have remained so, rather than have it end the way it did."

His words were kind, but to Jaresh they sounded overly obsequious, almost toadying. Wasn't there some rumor about Bryce and Mira possibly marrying? Whatever. It wasn't his concern.

"There's a lot better ways this night could have gone," Jaresh agreed with a sigh. "Nanna's going to be livid."

Bree smiled tightly. "I may have to find a nice little hole to hide in while you explain what happened."

"Thanks for the support," Jaresh muttered.

CHAPTER FIVE
A GAUNTLET THROWN

*Who then must explain to a man of power how it is he has a
dearth of a currency? Does one so cursed not have courage?*

~A Sentya aphorism (attribution unknown)

"That is…unfortunate news," Dar'El Shektan murmured in
his inimitable and classically understated fashion after
Jaresh and Bree related the events of the evening. His
coarse features – few would have labeled him handsome – creased
into a frown of concentration as he idly rubbed his ruby earring,
punched through the scar where his left ear had been neatly bisected
during one of his four Trials. He stood and paced, crossing his study
in three long and efficient strides. While time had robbed him of
much of his strength, speed, and grace – even some of his height –
Dar'El, like all Kumma men, remained in fit and fighting trim,
practicing daily with the sword since one never knew when the City
might again need his blade. Right now, warring with Chimeras was
likely the last thing on his mind. A battle of a different sort occupied
his thoughts, a concern reflected in his brooding eyes.

"It's a Devesh-damned disaster," Amma said, glaring angrily.

Though Satha Shektan, their mother, stared at the chessboard, she didn't seem to be paying any attention to it. Amma and Nanna had been playing when Bree and Jaresh had come home, although Bree didn't know why they bothered any more. Bree could count on one hand the number of times their father had won against their mother. Certainly Satha Shektan's elegant loveliness had softened over the twenty-five years of her marriage, but her mind was still as keen and scalpel-sharp as ever. In fact, Amma was as much the reason for House Shektan's current fortunes as Nanna. Together, the two of them were formidable, taking a small and lowly House and turning it into a rising power, one only a few rungs below the acknowledged leaders of Caste Kumma. Amma had recently stepped back from the day-to-day management of the House, but she still made sure to keep abreast of the important details. And Jaresh killing the only living son of Hal'El Wrestiva certainly counted as important.

"It should not have happened," Nanna said, flicking a glance at Jaresh. "You should not have been able to overcome the Wrestiva."

Jaresh grimaced sourly. "So I've been told," he replied.

"I still can't believe Suge is dead," Bree added.

The four of them were alone, meeting in Nanna's study. It was a large, square room, huddled in the back corner of the House seat. Floor-to-ceiling bookshelves took up two adjacent walls, and they groaned beneath the weight of Nanna's collection of scrolls, manuscripts, and oddities from his Trials. A large leather sofa and a number of sturdy, yet comfortable upholstered chairs, surrounded a low, marble-topped table placed before the fireplace. Hanging above the mantle was a map of Arisa. A trellis chandelier with a number of firefly pendants was centered upon the high, coffered ceiling and provided a bright, warm light. Several tables of various sizes were scattered throughout the rest of the room, and the largest one — upon which rested the chess set — took up much of the library's center. Tall firefly floor lamps, one in each corner, provided more lighting, and a globe of the world rested on a pedestal near one of the bookshelves. Nanna stood next to his heavy, mahogany desk, which faced the door, and behind him was a wide, bay window. During the day, it offered a view of the gardens and Mount Bright, but right now, with night upon them, it reflected the contents of the room.

"And yet he is dead," Amma said. "Jaresh may have the blood of a Sentya, but his heart is Kumma." She sounded both proud and sad at the same time.

Nanna nodded. "And it is because he is of House Shektan, an almost-Kumma and not simply a Sentya, that Hal'El will require blood as payment for the death of his son."

Jaresh frowned. "Blood payment? Won't he have to prove I acted in a malicious fashion?" he asked. "He can't do that, can he? Not after what Suge said about Bree."

Nanna steepled his fingers beneath his chin with eyes closed while Amma stared out the large windows of the study, both lost in thought.

"We will see," Amma said, breaking the silence, neither agreeing nor disagreeing.

Bree had already considered the matter from every angle she could imagine. She was not as sanguine as Amma.

Her nanna noticed. "You have something to say?" he asked.

Bree paused to compose her thoughts. Long ago, she had been schooled by both Amma and Nanna to think first before speaking. It was a habit meant to help her organize her thoughts, and one her parents had insisted she practice. By now, it was second nature, and it had been years since she had been treated to her mother's languid opprobrium of 'interesting', a single word used to convey both dismissiveness and contempt in response to rambling or disjointed explanations.

"Hal'El is sure to understand his dilemma just as well as we do," she began. "He knows the preponderance of proof will demonstrate that Suge's actions demanded a physical confrontation. If he wishes to challenge us, he must first determine if it is in the interest of his House to do so."

"There won't be much honor in challenging a Sentya," Jaresh said with a derisive smile. "But in challenging the only Sentya son of an upstart rival…"

"We must assume he will come for you," Amma said.

"The most important question still remains. How?" Jaresh replied.

Bree found the other three looking at her; Jaresh with curiosity while her parents wore bland and polite expressions of interest, as if they assumed she would have an answer to Jaresh's question and would be disappointed if she didn't. She held in a sigh. Sometimes their expectations could be tiring, but now wasn't the time to complain about it. "House Wrestiva is powerful and old. They wield far greater influence in the Chamber of Lords than we do. Hal'El might have to call in a few chits, but the Wrestivas are wealthy enough to absorb the cost. Younger Houses will not want to cross him, and the older Houses will be all too happy to link arms and help throw down an upstart. He'll find a way."

Jaresh nodded in understanding. "He'll bribe those who owe him nothing, call in the favors owed by those who rely on his House, and the older families will look to his leadership to prevent us from threatening their power."

"It all depends on if he can convince a majority of 'Els to bring the matter before the Chamber of Lords," Bree said. "If he manages to do so…" she shrugged, "…then it becomes a toss of the coin as to how the 'Els will decide."

"Hal'El has never required much reason to hate our House. This will simply lend greater impetus for his desire to seek our destruction," Dar'El said.

"He'll force you to acquiesce to his desires or see me die," Jaresh said, looking sick. "It will set the House back for years."

Nanna nodded. "You see the problem. If I bend to Wrestiva's will to the detriment of our own House, how can I reasonably name myself ruling 'El?"

"We won't bend," Amma vowed.

"And if Hal'El manages to put the matter regarding Suge's death to the Chamber of Lords? What then?" Jaresh asked.

"Then we'll deal with the matter if and when it happens," Nanna said, clapping his hands and calling the meeting to an end. "Let's not stir up a hornet's nest of panic until we learn what he intends. Go get some rest, both of you. If you can. I imagine tomorrow will be an eventful day."

Jaresh looked heartsick as they left Nanna's study, and Bree felt a surge of sympathy for him, her brother with a Kumma's heart who tried so very hard to be a warrior even though he was born to be an accountant. "We'll find a way out of this," she said, infusing her voice with as much certainty as she could.

Jaresh looked her way for a moment before facing forward as they marched through the rear foyer and past the intersection with the long hallway running along the back of the house. The hallway was dimly lit with the small table lamps turned down for the night. A floating, elliptical staircase took up the back of the foyer.

"You think Nanna's right?" Jaresh asked. "About maybe nothing seriously bad coming from all this?"

Bree could have told him 'yes', but it wasn't in her nature to tell a comforting lie. "I think we need to be ready for whatever Hal'El Wrestiva tries. I think he'll do his best to bring the matter to the Chamber of Lords."

"It won't be easy to beat him in the Chamber."

"Life is a summer rain," Bree reminded him. "Sometimes it replenishes.

"And sometimes it storms," Jaresh finished.

"But we'll pull through," Bree said.

They reached the top of the staircase, which ended at a broad landing. Branching off in both directions was a smaller hallway, which also ran along the back of the house and was also dimly lit with turned down table lamps. It was on the second floor that Bree's bedroom and those of her brothers were to be found. Their parents slept downstairs in their own wing of the house.

Jaresh paused at the landing. "I feel like we're missing something," he said. "I don't know what it is, but it seems like it should be important."

Bree nodded in understanding. Something about the fight – or the scene after – it bothered her too, but she couldn't put her finger on it. "I keep going over what happened tonight," she said, voicing her concerns. "Everything leading up to it and how it ended." She paused and glanced at Jaresh, not wanting to hurt him but also knowing he needed to openly acknowledge what was true.

"It's alright, Bree," Jaresh said with a sardonic smile. "You were going to say I had no business beating Suge. It should never have happened. Even I knew that when we were fighting." He shrugged. "I just wish sometimes it wouldn't have been so unexpected a victory."

Bree understood what he was trying to say. "Because then instead of being Sentya, you would have been a Kumma?"

Jaresh nodded tightly. "Yes. Because then I would have been a Kumma."

Bree's eyes teared up. How lonely Jaresh must be sometimes. She hugged him, an unexpected expression of support and love since growing up, the two of them hadn't always been close. Of course, she also felt the same way about Rukh. For whatever reason, she had usually been the odd person out amongst her siblings. Thankfully that distance had closed as they all grew older, and while Rukh and Jaresh were still closer, right now Bree was all Jaresh had. Right now, he needed something to smile about.

"By the way, say hello to your counselor for me," Bree said, deadpan.

"My what?" Jaresh asked, confused.

"Your counselor. Nanna is going to make you see one since you've just killed a man."

Jaresh chuckled. "With everything that's happened and will happen, I hadn't considered it all that much," he said. He sobered a moment later. "I know I should feel bad about killing someone, and I suppose it'll hit me eventually, but right now, I've got other things to worry about."

Bree was surprised. "You don't feel any remorse at all?"

Jaresh shrugged. "I don't feel much of anything. I'm just numb, but I also don't think I did anything wrong. However it ended, it was an accident. I didn't mean to kill Suge, but I sure don't regret defending your honor."

Bree hugged Jaresh again, touched by his concern for her. "It is really a shame Suge died," she said. "I mean beyond the obvious. Just think of the humiliation he would have had to live with: the first and only Kumma in history to lose a fight to a Sentya."

Jaresh laughed, the worry dropping away from his face, even if only for a moment.

Bree smiled. Better.

***

Jaresh awoke the next morning, bleary-eyed and tired. He hadn't slept well, which wasn't a surprise given the events of the night prior. His mouth was dry as sawdust, and he was certain his eyes were red with fatigue. They certainly felt full of grit anyway.

He hauled himself out of bed and made his way downstairs to the kitchen. Cook Heltin was already up, swiftly chopping vegetables on the butcher-block table. Behind her, the tandoor oven had already been heated, and from it came the delicious aroma of baking bread. Jaresh's stomach rumbled. Cook glanced up from her work, took one look at him and magically produced a glass of fresh-squeezed orange juice. She somehow always knew a person's needs. One of her gifts. Plus, as a fellow Sentya, she had a soft spot for Jaresh. "The bread should be ready soon," she said, "and there's some cinnamon butter in the ice box. I'll put some aside for you."

Jaresh smiled his thanks and quickly drained the juice. It was enough to revive him. Afterward, he went back upstairs to the washroom he once shared with Rukh – all his now – and quickly bathed, shaved his day-old stubble, and brushed his teeth with soda. Bree met him as he walked out of his bedroom.

"Good. You're awake," she said. "The House Council is meeting in the study. Nanna wants you there."

Jaresh nodded. "Be right down."

He glanced at Bree as they walked down the flight of steps. There was something he wanted to tell her, but he wasn't sure how she would take it. She could be so prickly sometimes.

She noticed his silent observation and gave him a look of annoyance. "Just say what's on your mind. We don't have all day."

That was more like the Bree he'd grown up with. The woman from last night who had been so supportive and kind must have been an illusion. Even as a child, Bree had been self-assured and commanding, almost to the point of arrogance. She wasn't cruel, but she sure wasn't sweet and compassionate. Where *had* the woman from last night come from?

"I wanted to thank you," Jaresh said. At Bree's look of incomprehension, he continued. "For last night. I wouldn't have wanted to face Amma and Nanna without you around." He hesitated.

"And I know what you were trying to do. Making me laugh. It helped."

Bree gave him an amused smile. "You're welcome," she said. "That's what sisters are for. She playfully jabbed him in the ribs. "Don't get used to it."

Jaresh laughed. "I wouldn't dream of it."

They arrived at the study. The door leading into it was closed.

"Ready?" Bree asked.

"Not really, but I might as well get it over with."

"I'll take that as a 'yes'."

Without waiting any further, Bree knocked once, waited for Nanna's deeply voiced "Come" and pushed open the door.

"We've received a response from the Wrestivas," Amma said without preamble upon their entrance into the study.

"They're very prompt, aren't they?" Bree remarked.

"It is to be expected," said Garnet Bosde. He was one of Nanna's oldest friends. In his middle years, Garnet had taken a deep and abiding interest in Nanna when the latter was a young man and new to House Shektan. Nanna hadn't been an acclaimed warrior, but he had a sharp and ambitious mind, something Garnet recognized early on, and over the ensuing years he had helped nurture and shape that unassuming young man into a ruling 'El of great standing. Garnet was old now, in his late seventies and stooped with age. His clothes hung like a billowing tent from his rail-thin frame, and he walked with a slow, shuffling gait, leaning heavily on his cane. Though he looked like a dodderer, he was no such thing. It was an assumption those opposed to House Shektan often made to their detriment. Even now, with nearly four score years to him, Garnet's mind remained firm and diamond-hard, and no one was better at gauging the will of the Chamber of Lords.

"Sit down, Jaresh," Sophy Terrell advised. Mira's mother was a tall, sturdily built woman with gray shot hair piled into her usual bun.

Given her squared off, blunt features, she would never be confused with beautiful. Rather the kindest and most generous description of her would have been handsome. Other Shektans affectionately named her 'the Hound' because of her dogged determination to complete any task set before her. Members of other, less friendly Houses similarly named her after a canine, but in a less complimentary fashion.

Jaresh and Bree found seats around a long, rectangular, curly-wood maple table. Last night, the chess set had rested upon it.

"The Wrestivas response is enclosed within," Garnet said, passing over an envelope bearing the crest of the Chamber of Lords. "Read it."

Jaresh perused the document, reading it twice to make sure he hadn't misread it. He grimaced in anger. "The Slash of Iniquity. They don't have the justification for something so serious. It's only given out to traitors, rapists, and murderers."

"Hal'El has always been one to quench his thirst in a raging river when a simple glass of water would do," said Durmer Volk, the last of Nanna's councilors. Durmer was a gruff, blunt man, never given to soft-pedaling his words. He was several inches shorter than Jaresh's father, but he carried himself with a very upright posture. It gave him the appearance of looking down his nose at everyone. He was in his late sixties, and his thinning hair was colored black, which gave it the unfortunate hue of shoe polish. His thick mustache curved down past the corners of his lips to his jaw, and his blocky features were held in a perpetual scowl. His main task – the training of young Shektans in the way of the sword – was one he took very earnestly. However, only rarely did the efforts of his students please him. Secretly, he was called 'the Great Duriah' by his charges, a reference to the folk of Caste Duriah who were famous for being *extremely* serious about their duties.

"Jaresh's actions don't come close to meriting such a

punishment," Bree said, also sounding offended. "It's preposterous."

"Hal'El and his House claim differently," Sophy said calmly. "They say Suge was too inebriated to have full control of his actions or his words. They also offer a very unique challenge. One I've never come across. We'll have to have someone research the medical and law journals to find out if it has any true basis in fact."

Amma glanced at Sophy, a disapproving frown on her face. "Will you tell him, or must he guess?"

Sophy smiled slightly and nodded acknowledgment of the mild rebuke. "House Wrestiva claims that you are able to conduct *Jivatma* from your Well, and with it, increase your speed and power. They say you used these…questionable means to defeat Suge, even after knowing he was too intoxicated to offer fair combat. Therefore, it was a purposeful and malicious killing. Thus, the Slash of Iniquity."

Jaresh sat back, not knowing whether to laugh or be offended. House Wrestiva's claim regarding his supposed abilities was utterly idiotic. It bordered on the sacrilegious. A barking laugh escaped him. "They must be as mad as Suwraith if they think anyone will believe such a ridiculous fable. Like Bree said: it's preposterous. Only Kummas can use *Jivatma* like that."

"Not necessarily," Amma said. "According to our preliminary research there may be a few anecdotal cases from other Castes, specifically Murans and Rahails doing exactly what the Wrestivas claim. The Talent only manifested in the heat of battle when death was a near certainty. There is even one supposed case of Kumma casting a Blend."

"Myths more like it," Durmer muttered.

Amma shrugged. "No matter how unlikely the Wrestiva claim, we have to treat it as a defensible argument."

Bree's eyes widened in sudden insight. "They want to claim Jaresh is Tainted. They'll say Jaresh has either learned our Talent having been raised as a Kumma, or it manifested as these others did:

in the heat of battle with his life on the line. Either way, if they get enough 'Els to agree with them, they could decide Suge's death wasn't malicious, but Jaresh's supposed Kumma Talents warrant his expulsion from Ashoka. Either way, Jaresh would be dead."

Nanna nodded. "I agree. That is their ultimate goal: Jaresh expelled from Ashoka, by whatever means necessary."

Jaresh snorted. "It still sounds like a thin line upon which to hang their case."

"So it is," Durmer said. "But that's not the issue."

Jaresh nodded. "I know. We spoke of it last night. They'll use their political influence to achieve the judgment they desire rather than appeal to rationality or facts."

Garnet grunted. "Spoken like a true Sentya," he said, in his hoarse, croak of a voice.

"It is who I ultimately am," Jaresh replied.

Nanna shook his head. "No. You are Sentya by birth and breeding, but your heart is ours. You are Kumma. Never forget it."

"I hardly think..." Jaresh began.

"It is who you are," Amma interrupted. "We never expected you to take to the Trials, but you did and you've been chosen. Your sword is equal to that of the finest Murans and Rahails." She stared Jaresh in the eyes. "In your heart, you are Kumma."

"It is true," Durmer said. His words were unexpectedly kind, more complimentary than any Jaresh had ever heard from the old man. The Great Duriah had actually sounded affectionate.

Jaresh blinked back sudden tears. He'd never expected to hear such words.

Nanna smiled. "And now that Durmer has suitably embarrassed you, we need to move on and discuss our defense. I've spoken to the other House elders, and while some still don't consider you a true Shektan, all of them recognize their personal feelings are immaterial. The rest of Ashoka sees you as being of our House. For this reason alone, your honor – and by extension, *our* honor – must be defended at all costs."

Garnet harrumphed. Jaresh didn't need to guess where the old man's feelings lay. He had never made secret his dislike of a Sentya being adopted into the House. As such, Garnet's next words surprised Jaresh. "The Wrestivas are an ancient House and influential, but they are caught in the past. Much of this complaint is but a mere regurgitation of a triumphal attitude and idea of Kumma supremacy we should have left in the shadows of history. These beliefs have no place in a modern society, and they know it. I would wager that the focus of their arguments will be aimed toward the reactionary elements of our Caste."

"I believe you're right," Durmer replied. "But, we must still make our case unassailable to even the most regressive 'Els, especially in light of how those Houses view our own."

"What do you propose?" Nanna asked.

Durmer gestured toward Jaresh. "I had the training of him for much of his life. He is good for one not a Kumma, but he's never demonstrated our Talents. I would have known. His most recent tutors from the House of Fire and Mirrors would tell you the same."

"In which case, House Wrestiva will have to prove that not only is Durmer Volk a liar but so are many of the Martial Masters of the House of Fire and Mirrors," Bree concluded.

Garnet chuckled dryly. "It won't be an easy task."

"Then they'll say I recently acquired this Talent," Jaresh said. "While I was fighting Suge."

"Again, it is easier said than done," Garnet said. "The Wrestivas must prove what is at best a fanciful notion. Since they can't, they'll rely on their political influence. It may even work, but only if the Chamber feels it has enough substantiation to afford the risk of alienating the other Castes. If the 'Els find in favor of the Wrestivas, it would set a bad precedent: defending one's honor against a Kumma could result in one's expulsion."

"There is one other thing which might be a problem," Jaresh began hesitantly. "I was with Bree and Mira. We shouldn't be surprised if many of the 'Els will be offended to learn that a Sentya was escorting two Kummas to a play."

"I'm you sister," Bree countered. "Accompanying me to a play is part of your brotherly duties. It's irrelevant to the matter at hand."

"I'm curious as to why you would believe so," Garnet asked. "Many of the conservative 'Els might side with Hal'El on this one issue alone."

"Because it happened. We can't do anything about it. When I say it's irrelevant, I mean there is nothing we can say to refute such an obvious fact: Jaresh accompanied me and Mira to a play. It is a fact well known to all by now. We simply acknowledge it as true and move on as though it is of no relevance."

"You think we should brazen our way past it?" Garnet asked.

Bree shrugged. "I don't see what other option we have."

"Besides which, while the Wrestivas will claim Suge was simply trying to uphold Kumma honor, it's nonsense," Nanna said. "Suge never sought the truth of the situation – and what could be more innocent than a brother taking his younger sister to a play. Instead, he interjected himself into a situation where he wasn't wanted or needed. We need to make sure the other 'Els see it the same way."

"A true warrior looks before leaping," Durmer agreed.

"Suge was no warrior," Garnet said with a scornful snort. "The man was a known coward who Jaresh rightfully mocked for his craven behavior."

Amma rapped her knuckles sharply on the table. "It is not enough," she said, forcefully. "This challenge must be crushed." She glanced around, staring each of them in the eyes. "With this perverse assertion, House Wrestiva has directly challenged our honor. We must answer in kind."

Nanna glanced at the others before turning to her. He nodded. "I feel the same way," he said. "If they wish to wallow in the mud, so be it. We'll do the same. If Hal'El Wrestiva sees this as an opportunity to bring dishonor to our House, then we can do the same to his. We will use this trumped up, rabid charge as our own stalking horse and do all we can to destroy his son's reputation, and by extension that of his House."

Jaresh smiled. They were going to take the fight directly to House Wrestiva. Good. He hated playing defense anyway.

Durmer looked similarly pleased. "Yes. Their arrogant House has too long hindered our own." He cracked his knuckles. "How do we proceed?"

Nanna steepled his fingers and closed his eyes, his way of focusing his thoughts. He sat in silent repose for several moments, seeming to almost fall asleep. He opened his eyes and smiled coldly. "We will raise every despicable rumor, no matter how puerile, about his son. We will bring utter ruination upon the already sad and despicable character of Suge Wrestiva. When we are done, Hal'El will wish that the mangy carrion eater he fathered had never been birthed. The standing of House Wrestiva will be brought low."

Amma smiled just as coldly upon hearing Nanna's words. "It begins then. I want a report on Suge Wrestiva from each of you, everything about his birth, his habits, his friends, his training, his girlfriends...everything. I want a detailed dossier so complete that we know Suge better than his own father."

"I'd like to be present at Suge's autopsy," Bree said, speaking up suddenly. "There's something about his death that's bothering me." She blushed. "Other than his dying, I mean. I don't know what it is, but I think it might turn out to be important."

Nanna considered her words. "I had planned on being at the autopsy myself. I see no reason why you can't accompany me."

"I still want your report," Amma warned.

"I'll have it ready," Bree replied.

"One last thing," Jaresh said. "If Suge had lived, how much would have been demanded of him in payment for the insult paid to Bree?"

"He got off easy," Durmer growled. "He should have been beaten senseless even after he offered a public and groveling apology. Until then, he wouldn't have been safe anywhere in Ashoka."

"We should play that up then," Jaresh said.

"Wasn't there some rumor about Suge and a Rahail courtesan?" Bree asked.

"Let's not dredge up old hearsay unless we can prove it," Amma said. "I want absolute verification first, with as much documentation as possible before we assassinate his character."

"Let's get to work," Nanna said.

———— • ————

"They must be mad," Bree said upon hearing Nanna's words. "They admit Suge acted dishonorably enough to be found Unworthy?" she asked. "Why would they do such a thing?"

"Because the story we released yesterday is true," Jaresh said, smiling smugly. "The past week has not been a good one for House Wrestiva, the death of Suge and the destruction of the thug's already poor reputation."

"It was clever finding the Shiyen physician," Garnet said, chuckling dryly.

Once more, House Shektan's advisors were meeting in Nanna's study. Since Suge's death, each of House Shektan's councilors had ferreted out every possible nugget of information about Suge Wrestiva. What they had learned, when put together as a portrait of the man, had made for ugly reading. The son of the ruling 'El of

House Wrestiva was a braggart, a bully, a drunk, and a coward. All of this was well known, but the depths to which he had sunk were absolutely appalling. Even worse, he had fathered a ghrina, an abomination: a child conceived with a woman not of his own Caste.

Jaresh had managed to confirm the rumors about Suge and his Rahail courtesan. The woman had disappeared two years earlier, but the Shiyen physician who had helped care for the woman during her pregnancy had remembered her well. During one of her appointments, the courtesan had tearfully confessed her sin: the father of her child was Kumma, and no less than the son of the ruling 'El of one of Ashoka's oldest Houses. Afterward, the Shiyen only saw her a few more times, and then she was gone, vanished as if she had never existed. The City Watch had been unable to find any sign of foul play, but coincidentally, at around the time of her disappearance, Suge was known to have exited the city, alone apparently and on a training exercise. A small Ashokan Guard contingent had come across him as he passed Ashoka's Outer Wall, and according to the sergeant in charge, Suge had been driving a small, covered wagon.

It hadn't taken much to get the rumor started about what might have truly happened. Suge had probably murdered the courtesan to hide his disgrace, and his thin excuse for leaving the safety of the city had likely been to get rid of the courtesan's dead body and that of his murdered child.

The city was abuzz with every new lurid piece of gossip about Suge's dissolute life, all of it provided courtesy of House Shektan. Of course, the Wrestivas were furious, but they could do nothing to counter the claims made about the deceased son of their ruling 'El. The Shektans had been meticulous, carefully cultivating multiple sources and testimonies for the stories they produced, seemingly one every day, each one more shocking than the one before, with the most recent tale acting as a capstone.

"I still don't understand why Hal'El would say such a thing about his own son," Bree said, glancing at the other advisers.

"Because Hal'El knows what we claim is true, and it doesn't do him any good to try and argue the point," Sophy replied.

"Also, accusations are most potent when made for the first time," Nanna added. "By admitting Suge's corrupted nature now, Hal'El hopes to minimize the outrage such an allegation will raise when we bring it up again in the Chamber." He shrugged. "Perhaps we should have held back this final detail."

Durmer cleared his throat. "I find myself troubled by something else," he began. "I spoke to the masters at the Fort and the Sword, the military school favored by the Wrestivas. They all make mention of how significant Suge's improvement has been over the past few months, in all aspects of combat, both armed and unarmed. It makes what happened with Jaresh even more difficult to understand."

"Any idea on how to explain such a discrepancy?" Dar'El asked.

"No," Durmer said. "Suge's autopsy…you mentioned he had been drinking but not enough to be drunk. Was there anything else that could have caused a reduction in his skills?"

"The autopsy turned up nothing," Bree said. "Suge had dilated pupils and possibly cyanotic digits, both of which might indicate a poppy-based drug, but nothing like that was found in his body. As far as the pathologist could tell, Suge was completely healthy."

"Nothing else at all?" Durmer asked in a hopeful tone.

"That was it." Bree shrugged. "I'll do my best to make sure we aren't missing anything, but I wouldn't hold up much hope on that end."

"It may not matter," Garnet said. "From my initial polling of the Chamber, the numbers are swinging our way. It's still close, but if we're effective in presenting our case in the actual tribunal, we should be fine."

"I would prefer if we had something more concrete," Amma

said. "This entire tribunal is a farce. The Wrestivas haven't paid nearly enough for what they claim Jaresh can do."

No one had a respose to Amma's words, and the room fell silent for a moment.

"Perhaps we should play up the differences between Suge and Jaresh," Garnet said, breaking the quiet. "Consider: we have two scions of ruling 'Els, but only one of them was leaving for the Trials, and it wasn't the Wrestiva. It was the Shektan," he finished in satisfaction.

Bree was surprised by the older Kumma's statement. All knew how little Garnet had cared for Jaresh's admittance into House Shektan, but ever since House Wrestiva's challenge, the old councilor had been painstakingly diligent in searching out every angle through which Nanna and Amma could defend their Sentya son. More surprising, though, were the complimentary words he occasionally paid to Jaresh. It was unusual but welcome.

Her brother had always had a difficult time with many of the other Shektans. Perhaps this would be a turning point for him. Perhaps others in their House would start seeing him as the asset she knew him to be and accept him as someone worthy of respect. She hoped so, but it would have to be a dream for another day. First, she had to help him get past this stupid charge.

"That particular piece of information is not well known," Nanna said, " and I think we should hold off on releasing it until the actual tribunal."

"We've done well so far, but we must ensure the Chamber never comes to believe House Wrestiva's lie about Jaresh and his supposed Taint," Amma reminded them. "And we still lack the final nail with which to hammer the Wrestivas to their yoke. For what they've done, Hal'El Wrestiva must face utter humiliation for even bringing up such a possibility."

Bree shared a smile with Jaresh. Amma had always been the

more hard-nosed of their parents, unwilling to give an inch when she believed a point needed to be made. It was an attitude seen in her child-rearing as well. The three of them – Rukh, Jaresh, and Bree – had quickly learned that Amma's word was law, and to cross her was to invite serious consequences. Nanna could be a disciplinarian as well, but he was also more flexible and more willing to compromise. And besides, Bree had him wrapped around her finger.

"I don't know if we can do what you want," Sophy said to Amma. "I understand your anger and your frustration, but you're asking us to prove a negative."

Nanna sighed. "Sophy may be right," he said. "But we need to keep looking for any other oddities surrounding Suge; something which might explain what happened that night."

The room quieted as they digested Sophy and Nanna's words.

"Or, during the tribunal, maybe we don't attack their claims about me, but just brush them off as though they're unworthy of rebuttal," Jaresh said, breaking the silence. "Instead, maybe we should work to expose the feelings Hal'El has toward the other Castes. If we can get him to admit to them, it will cost him and his House quite a lot in public opinion."

Durmer cackled. "It will ruin them."

"Him," Sophy corrected. "Not them. Their House still contains men and women of great cunning and wisdom. They may limit the damage by doing away with Hal'El and choosing another to head House Wrestiva."

"And the Chamber would have no choice but to look past *all* of House Wrestiva's charges, including this supposed Taint simply to get the matter behind all of us," Bree noted.

"And having House Shektan known as the defender of the interests and voices of the other Castes won't hurt our standing with the general populace," Jaresh said.

"A secondary benefit," Nanna noted.

"Cunning," Sophy said after a moment's thought. "Let them see the fist and hide the knife." She laughed. "I like it."

"I'm impressed," Bree said to Jaresh. Her brother was smart and studious, but in the ways of a Sentya: all accounting and math. Politics was not his forte. "You came up with this by yourself?"

"Nanna helped." Jaresh grinned. "But I'm allowed to have a good idea every now and then."

"I would rather we had something more…forceful," Amma said, still looking dissatisfied. A moment later, she sighed her acceptance. "But if this is all we have, then we will have to make it work."

⸻ ● ⸻

After the meeting ended, the council members left to go about their other tasks. Jaresh left as well. He felt pretty good about his chances, but a twinge of doubt and worry still preyed on his thoughts. Besides which, Amma was right: the House needed to do more than win through lack of evidence or fears about public opinion. They needed – he needed – to erase the Wrestiva claim, utterly and completely. Both he and the House needed to come through this tribunal with a spotless reputation. Otherwise, other jackals would test them, seeing their weakness and inability to defend themselves against what was an otherwise stupid and ugly accusation.

Despite his desire for action, Jaresh ending up spending the next two days cooped up at the House Seat. It was on Nanna's orders. He wasn't to be seen in public where he could come across the Wrestivas. Nothing good would come about from such a confrontation. Being confined to the House Seat was deadly dull and did nothing to settle his nerves.

He did receive several visitors to help pass the time, including Mira Terrell. She had finished her internship with House Suzay, and

123

Nanna was including her in some issues related to their own House. As a result, she had to visit the House Seat more regularly, and occasionally the two of them would cross paths. Along with Bree, she had kept him apprised of the mood of the city. Not surprisingly, the upcoming tribunal was the talk of Ashoka. Suge's death had been scandalous enough – no one had been intentionally killed at the hands of another within the city in over fifteen years – but most people couldn't believe that House Wrestiva was pursuing its case when all agreed it had been Suge who had instigated the fight. The stature and standing of House Wrestiva was taking a beating, but Jaresh knew Hal'El's primary audience wasn't the general public: it was his fellow 'Els, especially the reactionary ones.

Nevertheless, Hal'El had members of his House prowling the streets, telling everyone with an ear House Wrestiva's version of the truth. And the Shektans continued the war of words, ensuring the dissolute nature of Suge's character remained prominent in everyone's mind. The situation was tense whenever a group of Shektans came into contact with a group of Wrestivas as the two camps sniped at one another like angry dogs. Luckily, no blows were exchanged, thanks to heavy patrols of the Ashokan Guard, which had been called in to help the City Watch maintain the peace.

Jaresh spent the last night prior to the tribunal sitting on a bench in the back gardens, looking out to sea. It was one of his favorite spots in all of Ashoka. So peaceful. The gardens took up much of the grounds behind the Shektan seat, curving around to cup the main house. A copse of trees bordered the gardens to the north and a large, red barn did the same for the west. Beyond them, a tall retaining wall, meant for privacy and security, could be seen edging the entire property. The drop-off to the east, where the hill fell down a steep cliff toward the rest of the city, was left unobstructed, giving a glorious view of the Sickle Sea.

"Maybe you need to take a walk," Amma said, coming up from behind and taking a seat next to him.

"I've done nothing but walk the past two days," Jaresh replied. "Walk the grounds, walk the house, walk the drive."

"More like paced," his mother corrected. "You've stalked everywhere like a very large, angry cat. I'm sure I saw your tail swish now and then."

Jaresh smiled. "I don't think I've been quite that bad."

Amma sniffed. "So you say. But the mice are terrified."

Jaresh smiled briefly, but he was a bundle of jangling, nervous nerves. Humor didn't sit well with him right now. "What do you think will happen?" he asked.

Amma didn't pause to consider his question. "You'll be fine," she assured him, stroking a stray lock of his long hair from his forehead. "Garnet believes the votes should go with us, but as long as you're safe with us, I'll be happy."

Jaresh sighed. "That's all I care about, too," he said. "It's just…" He searched for the words to express what he was feeling. "I don't like not being in control, you know? Everyone is doing things for me, and I know Nanna is making sure nothing slips through the cracks, but it isn't the same thing as being in charge myself."

Amma laughed. "So you think Nanna is in complete control of his life?"

Jaresh was puzzled. "Of course he is. He's a ruling 'El, and he's always taught us how our lives are what we make of them. We decide what we become. You've always said the same thing."

Amma shook her head in negation. "Jaresh you misunderstood us. We told you to steer the course of your life as best you can, but we never expected you to master the sea and the wind." Jaresh's confusion must have been evident on his face, so she continued on. "Jaresh, we love you, but we can't make others acknowledge the wonderful young man you've become; not even those of our own House. It breaks our hearts, but we can't do anything about it." She took his hand. "The point I'm trying to make is that community and family, however you choose to define them, will always be a big part of your life, and how they view you may not always be under your control."

Jaresh considered her words. "I think I understand," he said.

Amma drew him into a hug. "We've done good work these past two weeks," she whispered into his hair. "Your nanna will keep you safe."

Jaresh hugged her back, squeezing her briefly before pulling away. While he believed her on an intellectual level, doubt still clung to his heart. But he didn't want Amma to see it. She had enough to worry about with Rukh gone on Trial. "You're right," he said, infusing his voice with false assurance. "But you know me...I always seem to see the worst of a situation."

Amma laughed. "Well, it's hard for me to see the good side of this one."

"I guess all of this would be worth it if the Wrestivas end up humbled, right?"

Amma smiled sadly and pushed back another stray lock of his hair, gently stroking his face. "It would be a small side benefit," she said, her smile fading. "And I know it probably seemed like breaking House Wrestiva was the focus of my attention, but when it comes to my children – you, Rukh, or Bree – I'll settle for safe. I'll do anything to ensure that." She stared Jaresh in the eyes, willing him to comprehend what she was saying.

He nodded. Even though they sometimes complained about Amma's dictatorial manner, they also knew she would battle Suwraith Herself to protect them. They were her heart.

"Amma, sometimes you scare me," Jaresh said with a mock shudder.

"Imagine how the enemies of the House must feel," Amma replied.

Jaresh laughed. "The mind quails."

CHAPTER SIX
THE TRIBUNAL

Their accountant hearts must pump mud thick blood, cold as a reptile.
So it is said…but it is wrong. They can be fierce.

~From the journal of Kol'El Wrestiva, AF 1257

Jaresh woke early the next morning after a night of restless sleep. He was too nervous to stomach much more than a cup of coffee.

Nevertheless, Cook Heltin encouraged him to eat some food. She offered him a bowl of oatmeal sweetened with a dollop of butter and honey. "You'll need to keep up your strength," she said.

Jaresh nodded reluctantly, and accepted the oatmeal. Just as he was finishing his breakfast, Nanna arrived in the kitchen. Jaresh found himself pacing back and forth, waiting impatiently for his father to finish his breakfast. Thankfully, Nanna didn't linger over his food. He ate quickly, and afterward, the two of them left the House Seat for the Chamber of Lords.

At this point, Jaresh just wanted to get the day over. The waiting and anticipation preyed on him like a phantom of menace.

As they passed the front gates, Jaresh glanced back at the seat of

House Shektan. The house stood tall behind them. His home, and Jaresh drank in the sight of it. It really was a beautiful place with the main, two-story house standing on a small rise, facing west. Its pale, pearly-white granite blocks glistened in the dawn sunlight, and the terracotta roof tiles gleamed with dew. A gravel driveway, framed by a lush grass lawn led the short distance from the heavy, black gates to the columned front porch before sweeping on toward the barn.

If he were found guilty of the charges Hal'El had leveled, execution of the verdict – expulsion from Ashoka – would be carried out immediately. This might be the last time he saw his home.

He shivered, and the oatmeal sat like a stone in his stomach.

"We'll do fine," Nanna assured him. "The truth and the right are with us."

Jaresh nodded and tried to force confidence into his stride as the two of them marched the short distance from the Shektan House Seat to the Chamber of Lords, situated like most things Kumma, in Jubilee Hills.

As early as it was, the brick-paved streets they walked were all-but empty of pedestrians. In this section of Jubilee Hills, stately town homes pressed close to one another on small lots with black, gray, or golden fences to mark the property boundaries and enclose elegant ornamental gardens out front. Dew glistened on the flowers and grass, sparkling in the morning sunshine. A few shopkeepers were up and about, and the smell of baking bread and burning wood carried on the air as restaurants prepared their ovens for the day's work. Muted voices and occasional shouts from the open doorways of several shops could be heard, but overall, the streets were relatively quiet. Nevertheless a tingling excitement carried through the streets, a trembling in the air like the presage of a coming storm. He knew it was just his imagination, but the hairs on his arms stood up anyway.

A sudden worry struck him, and he glanced at his clothes, wanting to make sure everything was in order. It was a silly fear since he'd checked his attire twice already, but today was too important to take any chances. He absolutely could not appear before the 'Els looking slovenly. He breathed out a sigh of relief. His gray shirt, dark trousers, and blue coat emblazoned with the House crest – a griffin clawing the air – were perfectly creased and fit him well.

Rukh had always complained that the griffin looked like a stylized housecat. Jaresh smiled at the memory, suddenly wishing his brother was here with him. "I hope Rukh's safe," he said in melancholy.

"Rukh can take care of himself. Right now, you need to focus on this moment and yourself," Nanna suggested.

Jaresh nodded, somewhat abashed. His father hadn't raised his voice, but the mild rebuke was clear. They walked the rest of the way in silence.

The Chamber of Lords was a large rectangular building standing on the flattened plateau of a tall hill and surrounded by a thin ribbon of a green lawn. Much of the exterior was made of red brick, with dark ivy covering it in large swathes. Tall, narrow windows, mullioned with ironwood, sat at regular intervals along the entire first floor. Most of the rooms were dark, although a few were lit, spilling out a wash of light. Gray marble stairs led to a deep portico roofed in copper and made of the same stone where small groups of people lingered. They cast speculative glances at Jaresh and his father. The façade above the entrance was carved with a likeness of Devesh. He held a sword in one hand and on another rested a dove, seemingly ready to take flight. His other two hands were empty, although one was the open palm of friendship and the other was clenched in a fist.

Jaresh prayed the tribunal would see him as the dove, granting him freedom's flight and friendship.

He and Nanna nodded greeting to the two warriors standing guard at the entrance. They were dressed in ceremonial gold-colored armor with spiked helms, but their swords – held unsheathed with the points facing downward – were anything but ceremonial. The heavy ebony doors leading inside were enameled with a coat of clear lacquer and buffed to a bright sheen. They were engraved with scenes of Kumma life, most of them having to do with the Trials and battles with Chimeras.

Inside was a broad foyer, tall enough for a central planting of coconut trees. The ceiling, high above, was paned in clear glass with bright, cheerful sunlight shining down. The walls were frescoed with scenes from *The Word and the Deed*, the sacred writings of the First Mother and the First Father. The book was a moral guide for individuals and society as a whole but also served as an historical record of the time before the First World when the world was rough and Humanity few. An ancient, well-preserved edition of the book was encased in glass at the far end of the foyer.

Jaresh followed Nanna to one of the twin sets of platform staircases on opposite sides of the foyer. They swiftly ascended to the third floor where they were let out into the midst of a wide hallway filled with milling people. The walls along both sides of the hall were lined with paintings of famous Kummas, all of them 'Els. On the right hand side of the hallway, a number of double doors were thrown open.

Each entryway led to the Assembly, the amphitheater where the 'Els actually met. It was a room large enough to hold over a thousand people. Wide planks of a dark wood lined the floor and from the ceiling hung a number of chandeliers. One entire wall, the eastern one, was a bank of windows. Given their position on the heights of Jubilee Hills, Jaresh could see all the way to the Plaza of the Martyrs and even to Mount Cyan in the distance.

Today the Assembly was packed. The 'Els and other high-ranking Kummas took up most of the lower gallery, while the upper level was for lower ranking Kummas and anyone else who wanted to witness the proceedings. Often, several non-Kummas could be found in attendance, and today was no exception. The tribunal had been the talk of the city for the past several weeks, and any non-Kumma with the wealth to afford a seat had purchased one. It was a hearing unlike anything ever reported before with enough salacious details to spur even the most jaded to attend. It was 'El versus 'El; a charge of murder; the killing of a Kumma warrior by a Sentya; and even the rumor that a son of an 'El had fathered a ghrina.

Jaresh took in the buzz of the crowd as he and Nanna descended to the raised stage centered in front of the tiered galleries.

They bowed before the Arbiter, Lin'El Kumma, a spare, older man in his seventies. His beard and full head of hair were white, and he wore black robes, highlighting his role as judge. The Arbiter was typically an elder Kumma chosen by the 'Els for his wisdom and knowledge. Upon his election, he gave up his House name and took on the surname of 'Kumma'. While his was indeed but a ceremonial position – his vote was only offered in the eveent of a tie – it was the Arbiter who administered the Chamber, interpreting the various rules and points of etiquette.

Two lecterns faced the Assembly, each backed by a large, rectangular table and flanking the Arbiter's dais. Nanna gestured, and Jaresh followed. They took the right-hand table. Hal'El Wrestiva sat alone behind the left-hand one, and he stared at Jaresh, following his every move with the flat, deadly expression of a viper. Jaresh tried to ignore him as he took his seat and waited with what he hoped was a polite look of interest rather than fear, while Nanna spoke to the Arbiter. He shot a quick sidelong glance in Hal'El's direction before quickly looking away. Malice seemed to ooze off of Hal'El Wrestiva like a promise of retribution.

Needing a distraction, Jaresh looked out over the crowd as it murmured with excitement. Like most of the families and Houses, the Shektans sat by one another, and all were located on his side of the Assembly. He smiled as they gave him signs of encouragement.

He noticed the Wrestivas, and his smile faded, a frown of confusion taking its place. What was going on with them? Some of the Wrestivas had appeared ashamed, especially when they had noticed his attention.

Jaresh was broken from his reverie when Lin'El gaveled the tribunal into session.

The Arbiter hammered a smooth oval of black granite against a base of white stone, the signal for silence. "The Assembly shall come to order," Lin'El said. Despite his age, his voice was still powerful and carried to the far corners of the room. All the doors leading to the Assembly were closed, and they thudded shut with an echoing sound, cutting off all further conversation. "Honored 'Els, ladies and gentlemen, and distinguished colleagues," Lin'El began. "Before us stands Jaresh Shektan, accused of maliciously killing Suge Wrestiva without cause or need. The punishment being sought is the Slash of Iniquity. Before we begin, I will ask the aggrieved party one last time, will you withdraw your claim?" He turned to Hal'El.

The leader of House Wrestiva stood. "I will not withdraw. My son lies dead by wicked, Sentya hands. Punishment for this crime must be meted out," he replied in a clear and firm voice.

Lin'El nodded. "So be it. The tribunal has begun. The accused is represented by his father, Dar'El Shektan. The aggrieved is Hal'El Wrestiva, ruling 'El of his House and represents himself." He looked to each of the named men. "I will allow each of you to call on attestants and make your claims. You will also be allowed to question your opponent's attestants. The tribunal will be decided by a simple majority of the 'Els who are present. As you know, in case the Chamber is evenly divided, I shall cast the deciding vote." He paused and cleared his throat. "The tribunal begins. To the aggrieved, I say the lectern is yours."

Hal'El stood and made his way forward. He was a proud man, with hooded eyes and a wide, flat nose broken on several occasions.

His gray hair was trimmed in a simple, martial cut, and a slight limp marred his confident warrior's gait. His one adornment was a nose ring, but with his thick frame, it gave him the unfortunate appearance of a bull wearing a nose hoop. However, unlike Suge, who had been similarly built, Hal'El was not slow, and he was not a coward. In his time, he had been a famous warrior, holding the distinction of more completed Trials – eight, all told – than anyone in living memory. The fame garnered from his accomplishments had made him the obvious choice when it came time to choose a new ruling 'El of House Wrestiva. Initially, after rising to his position of leadership, Hal'El had developed a well-deserved reputation for ruthlessness in the furthering of his House's ambition. But five years ago, shortly after the death of his older son during a Trial, something within Hal'El had changed, some vital spark or fire had dimmed. As a result, his energy and focus were not as they had once been, and the fortunes of his House had suffered. Rumor had it that relations among the families of House Wrestiva had grown strained.

"My fellow 'Els, I had but one child left in this world. His name was Suge Wrestiva," Hal'El began, his voice powerful and commanding. "My child admittedly disappointed me on many occasions. I do not seek to defend his actions on the fateful night in question. It shames me to the depths of my soul to know my own flesh and blood could have behaved in such a despicable fashion." He took a deep, shuddering breath, as if burdened by a weight of emotion. "I cannot understand how he came to speak as he did, but he was, and always will be, my son. I loved him, and now he lays dead – and I say, needlessly so.

"As I stated, I don't seek to defend him – he was not a saint – but I must demand each of you answer this one question: was execution the proper sentence for the words he spoke? I say no, and I am certain you all feel as I do. Certainly, he should have been brought to task and given a fitting punishment. But it would have been we, the ruling 'Els of the Caste Kumma, who would have rendered justice upon him, not this puffed up boy, this Sentya, full of pride and anger over some perceived insult from his betters! And we would not have killed Suge. He would have offered a proper and sincere apology. House Wrestiva would have made appropriate recompense, and it would have been the end of the matter. The Sentya had no right to take his life!" He thrust an accusing finger at Jaresh and took a menacing step forward.

Nanna's hands clamped on one of Jaresh's from under the table, keeping him from flinching.

"I know my son, Devesh comfort him, was a poor warrior," Hal'El continued. "I admit it. He was almost found Unworthy, but he was a Kumma. His breeding alone should have sufficed against a Muran or a Rahail, much less a Sentya. And I know you must be asking the same question, which has plagued me since that terrible night: how did a Sentya best a Kumma warrior in his prime? It is madness, but it happened, and there can be only one possible explanation, despite how unlikely it seems: this Sentya, raised as a son by the famed ruling 'El of House Shektan, learned to conduct his *Jivatma* as we do, powering his speed and strength. No other explanation makes sense! I say Jaresh Shektan is Tainted. He is naaja, corrupted. He is no different than a ghrina, a cursed child of two Castes." Hal'El shouted to the Assembly, full of righteous fury and indignation.

The Assembly broke into shouts of feigned astonishment since all knew of the Wrestiva claim from two weeks prior. The tumult went on and on, and it took several minutes of shouting and gaveling from Lin'El to silence the crowd and bring the proceedings back to order.

Jaresh looked to his nanna. "Do you think anyone believes this bilge water?"

His father shook his head. "I doubt it," Nanna answered. "But right now, the politics of the matter take precedence."

"I know. I was only wondering what would happen if this was a fair tribunal."

"Fairness and politics rarely go hand-in-hand."

Jaresh was about to answer, but Nanna motioned him to silence. Hal'El was speaking again.

"As it is said in *The Word and the Deed*, the Castes remain under Devesh's grace only when we are satisfied with the obligations to which we have been tasked. For Kummas, we were given the holy duty to act as guardian warriors for all Arisa. It is who we are and what we do. It is the reason Devesh granted us our Talents and no one else." Hal'El paused and wiped at the beaded sweat on his forehead. "And *that* is why I have brought forth this tribunal," he continued. "This foul and filthy man…" He shot a murderous look at Jaresh. "This offal who should have never been conceived, lured Suge into a fight, thinking to make his fame and his name by defeating a Kumma. He chose my son, a man who was not a skilled warrior as we would measure matters; a man he assumed to be too inebriated to effectively defend himself." Hal'El sneered in disgust. "And with his grotesque and disgraceful mastery of *our* Talents, this so-called man saw his opening and he took it, knowing my son to be easy meat. And with a cold and cruel calculation did he then murder my son."

Hal'El shot another stabbing finger at Jaresh, who couldn't help it this time: he flinched. The ruling 'El of House Wrestiva was a forceful man, and his overwhelming sense of anger and hatred was frightening. Jaresh could tell even Nanna was unsettled by it.

"And so, for *all* of his cowardly actions, the murder of my son; the foul use to which he has put his *Jivatma*, I demand that Jaresh Shektan of House Shektan be branded with the Slash of Iniquity, to be known for time immemorial as a child of Suwraith!"

Jaresh stiffened and slammed to his feet. "How dare you!"

"You go too far!" Nanna said a beat later, also shooting to his feet.

"And yet it is the truth!" Hal'El shot back.

Jaresh was furious. He understood Hal'El's pain, but those words…it was unforgivable. To be called a son of Suwraith was to be labeled a member of Her Sil Lor Kum, Her Hidden Hand of Justice. It was the worst kind of insult.

Nanna still quivered with anger, and he took several deep and calming breaths before speaking. "I will forgive you for your obscene words given your recent loss, but the truth is your craven and dissolute son brought his doom upon himself."

"He did no such…"

Nanna spoke over him. "We've already heard your words once, Wrestiva. Once is enough. Your foolish accusations sound like nothing more than the ravings of a loon."

Hal'El scowled. "How dare you accuse me of madness."

"I do no such thing. I merely accuse you of being a fool and blinded by the loss of your pathetic son."

Hal'El and Nanna stared daggers at one another, neither one flinching or looking away.

"Enough," Lin'El said, speaking into the silence. "If Hal'El is finished with his statement, he will be seated. The floor belongs now to Dar'El Shektan."

With a muttered curse and a last look of anger and disgust, Hal'El took his seat.

As Nanna prepared his words, Jaresh took the time to study the Chamber one more time. The 'Els were silent as they absorbed Hal'El's words. What Hal'El claimed was still ludicrous as far as Jaresh was concerned, but glancing around, Jaresh noted that many of the 'Els wore troubled expressions or had even nodded in agreement during Hal'El's speech. Hal'El Wrestiva possessed a rare combination of charisma and speaking ability. He was the kind of man who could lead others to do great deeds or rouse them to riot.

Jaresh grimaced.

The verdict would be close.

He cut off his thoughts as Nanna began speaking. "Ladies and gentlemen. My fellow 'Els...You all know who I am and why I am here. I am not as eloquent as Hal'El. I can't twist words and events until they bear no relationship to reality. All I can do is tell the truth. And the truth is that my son is a wonderful young man. He has done nothing wrong. He acted as a brother should and accompanied his sister and a family friend, a member of our House, to a play. Nothing more. In the Trials we are repeatedly admonished to understand the truth of a situation before seeking conflict. The caravan is always safest if a means can be found to avoid battle. It is an instruction we impart to our young from the time they can first hold a sword. Had Suge Wrestiva done as he had been taught, the tragedy of his death would not have come to pass. And had Suge Wrestiva not spoken the words he did, words so outrageous and despicable that common decency forbids me from repeating them amongst civilized company, satisfaction would not have been sought or required. My son, a Sentya by birth and Kumma by training, did as a brother must: he defended the sacred honor of his sister. It is what we would have all demanded from our sons."

Jaresh noticed several of the 'Els, especially those from the conservative families, shift uncomfortably in their seats. It didn't take a Shiyen counselor to determine their sentiments. Even now, years later, few accepted the adoption of one not born a Kumma into House Shektan. And even fewer cared to understand the reasons why. For most, it was at best a puzzle and at worst, anathema. The underlying Casteism of Ashokan society was yet another obstacle standing between Jaresh and a fair hearing based on the evidence alone.

Nanna continued. "My son never sought any of this. It is true; he did kill the Wrestiva, but it wasn't because of preconceived ill intent and malice. However, I must say, given the vile insults Suge offered to my daughter, many here would have insisted upon exactly that final retribution. But such an outcome was not what Jaresh intended. He fought to win. That's all. He fought to defend honor, and he should be rightly applauded for his actions. Yes, I say applauded, though it ended with the death of a Kumma. After all, this wasn't a mere Kumma. This was Suge Wrestiva, a young and angry man, full of himself. He was the worst of us: boastful, proud, and a lack-wit warrior. Even his own father admits that he was almost found Unworthy. And he should have been. Hal'El Wrestiva dares claim my son is all but a ghrina! Well, I say Suge Wrestiva *was* a ghrina. Or have none of you heard the scandalous rumors – rumors I know to be true – of an illicit liaison between Suge Wrestiva and a Rahail courtesan? A relationship resulting in conception, and the probable murder of the woman in question. Suge Wrestiva was killed several weeks ago, but he should have died two years ago when he fathered a ghrina. My son did us all a favor."

"Lies! May Suwraith smite you for your calumny!" Hal'El stormed to his feet. "My son is not the accused here. It is your ill-bred son."

Jaresh schooled his expression to stillness. Now wasn't the time for any display of anger on his part. The 'Els would be watching his reaction closely. They would not want to see any emotion, which could be read as disrespect toward Hal'El Wrestiva, given the death of the man's son at his hands. Still, it was hard to have sympathy for the leader of House Wrestiva, given Hal'El's recent words.

He looked to the gallery and sought out his mother. She sat amidst the other Shektans, and she nodded encouragement to him, smiling faintly. Jaresh smiled tightly in response. He searched further, but Bree still hadn't arrived, and he wondered what was keeping her.

Lin'El pounded his gavel. "You will be silent, Hal'El Wrestiva," he growled. "You will have your chance to speak again, but it will be within the dictates and traditions of this Chamber. I will not have this tribunal descend into anarchy. Now sit!"

Hal'El glared a moment longer before returning to his seat.

"Hal'El is right. It is my son, my Sentya son, the boy I chose to adopt, who faces this tribunal, and he should not have to. My son did as he was trained: defend those who need defending. He stood up to a man, a thug infamous for his bullying ways and vicious behavior; a man Jaresh knew he had no expectation of overcoming. Jaresh expected a beating, but he didn't let his fear unman him. My son displayed a courage we should all be so fortunate to possess."

Jaresh noticed the frowns, crossed arms, and uncomfortable shifting amongst the 'Els. His father's words weren't going over very well. By insinuating that Jaresh had a valor equal to that of a Kumma's, Nanna risked alienating the Chamber. While those of the warrior Caste knew others were courageous, such as the Murans and the Rahails, they were unwilling to believe that a mere Sentya might be their equal. After all, the greatest duel that one of the accounting Caste might face would be balancing the books every month.

Nanna smiled. "Did I mention Jaresh was chosen for his first Trial? He will be the first from his Caste to do so."

Astonished murmurs rose around the gallery as the people took in his nanna's words. Jaresh also breathed more easily. Several of the 'Els, including a few from the older, more conservative Houses, who had been frowning in disapproval moments earlier, now smiled or chuckled softly in appreciation.

Nanna smiled. "As I said, I raised him, and while his blood is Sentya, his battle isn't with accounts receivable." Further laughter greeted this statement. "He is of us. Kumma. He has the heart of a warrior, and he did nothing wrong the night Suge Wrestiva died. He used his skills to fight an aggressor who had for too long been protected and coddled by family connections from facing the consequences of his wicked acts, especially his fathering of a ghrina. And so, Suge Wrestiva picked a fight with someone he thought to be an easy mark, speaking words only a naaja would say. Suge Wrestiva was a disgrace, not only to Hal'El Wrestiva, who fathered the coward, but also to his House and our entire Caste. He died at the hands of my son, and I sorrow for Hal'El's loss, but still – and I know you feel the same way – we are the better for it. His own father admits he should have been found Unworthy, but what is the proper punishment for Suge Wrestiva's actions?" Nanna paused a moment, staring out over the audience before he answered his own question. "It is the Slash of Iniquity. He would have been killed for his numerous sins, and his body left to rot on the Isle of the Crows. His death wasn't tragic. In my estimation, it was justice long delayed."

Hal'El glared angry death at Nanna as astonished murmurs rose in the Assembly at the harsh words spoken. Normally, one did not speak ill of the dead in the presence of their family. But just as he had done many times in the past, Nanna had once more broken with tradition, and as he sat, Jaresh gave him a reassuring squeeze on the arm. He knew what Nanna intended. Suge's reputation had already been ruined, and now, in front of the Chamber, they would promulgate the idea that Suge's death was an unfortunate accident, but it was also a long overdue punishment. Whether it would really matter given the underlying politics of the situation was another matter.

The Arbiter gaveled once more. "The aggrieved will now make his case," he said.

Once more, Hal'El took the lectern and called on his attestants. The first to be named was one of Suge's lackeys, Han Reold. He was led through the events of the night in question, lingering on how he and the other two Wrestivas felt upon seeing two Kumma women accompanied by a Sentya.

"So, you were rightly incensed by this puffed up boy daring to spend time alone with a beautiful daughter of our own Caste?"

Jaresh snorted in disgust and reddened in anger. His mood

wasn't improved as he noticed several of the 'Els and Kummas nod in understanding as Hal'El encouraged a testimony meant to make Suge seem like a noble warrior seeking to protect a virtuous maiden from the grotesque advances of a thick-skulled, slavering Sentya. He recognized Hal'El's ploy, but it wasn't the same as accepting it, much less liking it. Jaresh was the son of Dar'El Shektan and Bree was his sister. Why shouldn't he go to a play with her?

Fortunately, his mood improved when Nanna got a hold of the sycophantic rat. His father went straight for the jugular and forced Han to repeat what Suge had said to Bree.

The gallery gasped in shock and horror when Suge's words were made public. Jaresh was pleased to see even the conservative 'Els squirm in discomfort and disgust.

"He said what about my daughter? I'm sure I must have misheard," Nanna said in flat voice, taking a menacing step forward. Upon hearing the words repeated, Nanna turned to face the gallery, fury etched on his face. "Consider those words, and consider what your actions would have been had some sodden thug dared speak such vile curses at your own daughter. Or your sister. Or your wife. Who among you would have held back?"

"I thought his words were disgraceful," Han blurted out. "He shouldn't have said what he said. They were indefensible."

Nanna slowly turned back to face him. "Indefensible? As in words so ugly you would not have protected him from House Shektan's justified retribution?"

Han nodded, looking miserable and unable to face Nanna's scrutiny.

Nanna nodded. "Perhaps you are not entirely without character."

Hal'El stiffened in anger at the words spoken by his kinsman. He shot a look of loathing at Han Reold. It wasn't what he had expected the bootlicker to admit. By agreeing with Nanna's assertion, Han had basically undercut Hal'El's already thin argument that Suge's actions had been justified on the night in question.

A small smile – one quickly hidden – momentarily lit Jaresh's face. Nanna had no further questions and took his seat.

"The attestant is dismissed," Lin'El said.

"A moment," Hal'El said, standing swiftly. "Might I indulge the tribunal with a final question?"

Lin'El allowed it, and Hal'El approached the attestation stand where his kinsmen shrank beneath his 'El's baleful gaze. "On the night my son was murdered, did you have to engage your Well in order to witness the fight?"

"Sir?"

"Are you deaf as well as stupid?" Hal'El snapped. "Did you have to use your Talents in order to witness the fight? Were both combatants moving so swiftly they couldn't be seen with the unaided eye?"

Han swallowed heavily. "I...I don't know. I always conduct *Jivatma* during a fight," he said. "The Sentya was fast but not as fast as one of us. Not even close."

"But faster than a Rahail or a Muran?"

Han looked confused. "I suppose so."

"Yes or no," Hal'El growled.

"Yes."

Hal'El smiled in satisfaction and nodded to Lin'El. "I'm done with him."

Next, Wan was called to the stand, and delivered much the same testimony as his twin. Other attestants were brought forward, and with each of them, Hal'El lingered on the question of Jaresh's speed in relation to that of Suge.

Even Teletheil Foal, the Shiyen physician who had tried to resuscitate Suge was called as an attestant.

"Did you witness the fight between my son and his murderer?"

"Yes."

"And what was your impression?"

"The Sentya was the better fighter."

Jaresh's lips quirked as Hal'El worked to hold back a scowl of annoyance. "Anything else?"

"Both men moved much faster than my poor eyes could follow."

"I see. Thank you," Hal'El said, resuming his seat behind his table.

Nanna stood and approached the Shiyen. "My son's behavior in the face of the Wrestiva coward's dishonorable actions…how would characterize them?"

"Noble. He sought to save the life of the man who spoke so poorly about his sister," the physician said. "All men of decency would have done as your son did."

Nanna turned to Hal'El. "Almost all of us," he replied, earning a sharp intake from the gallery at his unvarnished insult.

Hal'El didn't react. His eyes remained flat and unblinking.

After the Shiyen was released, Hal'El called his next attestant. His choice was surprising. He called on Conn Mercur, the dean of Verchow School of Medicine, one of the two medical colleges in Ashoka.

Like all Shiyens, including Teletheil Foal, Dean Mercur was somewhat short and stocky. His skin was dark as old walnut and his coarse, black hair was cut short. Dark eyes sat above high, prominent cheeks and a ready smile.

Hal'El approached the attestant stand with a warm and welcoming smile. "You are considered one of the finest minds and physicians of your generation, is that not so?"

Dean Mercur smiled slightly in return. "I simply used the gifts with which Devesh saw fit to bless me. If others accord me any honors, it is because I reflect Devesh's glorious light, not furnish my own."

Shiyens had a pious devotion to Devesh, which would have been beautiful if it weren't in honor of a deity who had abandoned and betrayed Humanity over two thousand years ago. Or so Jaresh thought.

"The humility of a Shiyen," Hal'El said, sounding warm and sincere. "So different than the boastfulness of a Kumma." He played to the audience as he chuckled dryly.

Dean Mercur smiled wryly. "Or perhaps we have more reasons to be humble," he replied, earning further laughter from the gallery.

Hal'El laughed in appreciation as well, and after the audience had settled down, he turned to face Dean Mercur once more. "We've heard some harsh words spoken about my son," he began. "I'm sure it's upsetting to all in attendance but especially to an honored physician such as yourself."

The dean paused as though carefully considering his words. "Your son's words were unseemly. Vulgar. I would have expected better from one of your lineage."

Hal'El stepped away from the attestant's stand. "Yes. We all have regrets," he said softly before turning back to the dean. "What do you know of someone conducting a Talent not of his own Caste?"

Dean Mercur frowned. "It has been known to occur," he said. "Very rarely, however. I would estimate less than once a century according to our records."

"Is there a common feature to these occurrences?" Hal'El asked, although Jaresh could tell he knew the answer before he even spoke the question.

The dean nodded. "In times of great need. When one is dying or someone close to you is in dire need, a Talent not of one's own Caste can manifest."

"Like a Sentya battling a Kumma. He would rightly fear such a conflict might lead to his death?" Hal'El asked, staring Jaresh in the eyes.

"It's possible."

Jaresh scowled.

"It will be fine" Nanna murmured. "He won't have the votes for it. I can read the Chamber well enough to know."

"And when it occurred, how was it viewed?" Hal'El inquired.

"Confusion and disgust," the dean answered. "Why would someone not of Caste Shiyen be able to Heal? It goes against the dictates of the First Mother and First Father. From *The Word and the Deed: To each Caste, a Talent and seek not that which is not yours*. It is what They taught us before Suwraith overthrew Their world."

"And the punishment for such individuals?" Hal'El asked.

Dean Mercur appeared perplexed. "It was different for every individual. Some were allowed to remain in their home cities; others were exiled. It depended on the circumstances and decision of their Caste."

"And if their ill-gotten Talent led to the murder of another?" Hal'El asked slyly.

Dean Mercur frowned. "I believe this tribunal has been convened to make just such a determination. Is it not so? To decide if your son was killed in self-defense or if he was murdered?"

"Exactly," Hal'El replied, turning to face his fellow 'Els. "If a Sentya murders one of our own through the use of our own Talent, what is the punishment for such a heinous act?"

He took his seat, Nanna stood. "And like his son, Hal'El leaps without looking. We haven't determined that Suge was murdered. By all accounts, he sought the fight, and he lost the fight. Those are the simple facts. All the rest is idiotic confabulation." He turned to face Hal'El. "Have we really been brought together here at this tribunal, wasting valuable time and effort, on this inane hypothesis of yours? All because you are unwilling to accept your son's flaws?"

"I will show…"

"You've shown nothing," Nanna said, cutting off Hal'El. "And the lectern is not yours."

"How dare you!"

"Silence!" Lin'El thundered. "The lectern belongs to Dar'El."

Dar'El waited while Hal'El settled down with a muttered curse before turning to Dean Mercur. "Given the testimony of all those brought forth today, does it seem likely that my son can conduct his Well as a Kumma might?"

"I don't know," the dean answered. "There are no records to indicate how fast or strong a non-Kumma would be in such a circumstance."

"So then this is all just speculation?"

"I suppose so," the dean agreed.

"In other words, Hal'El has resorted to fables to understand his son's demise," Nanna said. "I have no further questions."

Hal'El stood. "Redirect?"

Lin'El allowed it, Hal'El approached the attestant's stand. "The autopsy report indicates my son was drunk at the time of the fight. On the Gristole scale, he was a two. That would make him slightly impaired, correct?"

Dean Mercur nodded. "So I have been told."

"And can you conceive of any situation or circumstance in which a Sentya could defeat a Kumma with such a modest reduction in his fighting ability?"

"No. It should not be possible."

"No circumstance at all?" Hal'El persisted. "Luck? Greater skill?"

Jaresh held his breath, knowing where this was leading.

Dean Mercur shook his head. "Certainly there is always luck, but the odds would be so great, by all accounts it wasn't what happened. No one said your son slipped or stumbled. He was simply bested, which should also be impossible."

"So how did it happen then?" Hal'El asked. "How did a Sentya defeat a Kumma?"

"I don't know."

"But if we've ruled out luck and skill, what else is there?" Hal'El asked. "What other circumstance could allow for such a bizarre occurrence?"

Dean Mercur hesitated. "The only manner I can think of is if the Sentya was moving much faster than normal. If he was stronger as well."

"Like a Kumma conducting *Jivatma*."

The dean hesitated again. "I…suppose so."

The speculative murmuring of the gallery grated on Jaresh's nerves. They were actually considering Hal'El's ridiculous idea.

Dean Mercur proved to be the last of Hal'El's attestants. After him, it was Nanna's turn. He called all of Jaresh's friends, they simply re-iterated what had already been said: Jaresh had not sought this fight Suge was completely to blame for instigating it in the first place. And with every attestant, Nanna let it be known that House Shektan believed in equality amongst the Castes. He also slipped in the implication that House Wrestiva apparently believed Caste Kumma was superior to all the others. How else to explain this tribunal where a Sentya was on trial for his life simply because he had the audacity to defend himself? It was a deadly precedent House Wrestiva sought. The non-Kummas in attendance muttered in angry agreement at Nanna's words, but too many of the 'Els seemed to be watching in stony silence, although the members of House Wrestiva looked less than pleased at Hal'El's inability to deflect Nanna's insinuations.

Late in the proceedings, as Nanna was finishing up with an attestant, Jaresh noticed Bree finally enter the Assembly.

She quickly made her way down the stairs and across the stage, seating herself next to Jaresh. Whispered murmurs rose at her passing, but she didn't seem to notice. "Let me interview the pathologist, the one who performed the autopsy?" she whispered to Nanna. She seemed pleased and excited at the same time.

"What have you learned?" Jaresh asked.

"Something that should end this entire farce and have it blow up in Hal'El's face." She grinned. "You shouldn't even have to sit at the attestant's stand," she said to Jaresh.

"You're sure?" Nanna asked. "We are already likely to be victorious."

"I'm certain. This will be the final log on the Wrestiva pyre. They'll burn," Bree replied. "But I need to be the one to do the questioning. It's complicated, and I can't explain all the details right now."

"You'll have your chance," Nanna said, "but calm yourself. You need to be clear-headed when you question an attestant."

Jaresh nodded. "I'll help." He reached for his Well and conducted *Jivatma*. One of Caste Sentyas greatest Talents was the ability to instill utter serenity in themselves and thereby organize their thoughts and ideas with near perfect clarity. And it was also a Talent they could share with others.

He encompassed Bree in the glow of his Lucency, and her grin faded. A look of firm resolve took its place. "Thank you," she said, her voice sounding flatter than usual.

"You're more than welcome," Jaresh said, "especially if you can do what you say you can."

A fleeting smile graced Bree's face before quickly fading. "Call the attestant."

Step Lindsar, the Shiyen who had performed Suge's autopsy was recalled to the attestant's stand. The physician was in his late forties and sloop-shouldered. His hair was pleated in long braids but his lean, angular face was clean-shaven.

"I cede the lectern to my daughter, Bree Shektan. She will be the one to question Physician Lindsar," Dar'El said.

Bree stepped forward to the lectern, pausing to clear her throat. "You mention in your report a blue tinge to Suge's fingers and toes as well as dilated pupils. Do you have any explanation for such a finding?" Bree asked. "Any herbs or something along those lines?"

"Nothing other than poppy-based drugs," the physician answered. "But none were found in Suge's body."

"Nothing?" Bree asked. "You're sure? No drug that can do all that and also turn the whites of a person's eyes a barely detectable shade of blue?" Bree seemed to be holding her breath, as though she already knew the answer and was willing the Shiyen to come up with it as well.

The physician thought for a few moments before shifting in his seat, looking uneasy. "There is one," he said, hesitantly.

"And it is...?" Bree asked after a moment's silence.

Lindsar grimaced. "Snowblood."

The gallery exploded into bedlam as the Arbiter hammered his stone gavel for order but to little effect.

"Outrageous! This is a travesty! It was my son who was murdered!" Hal'El shouted as he roared to his feet. "These despicable Shektans shamelessly seek to strip Suge of every last shred of his dignity."

Jaresh was held frozen in shock. Snowblood? It was a powerful hallucinogenic stimulant meant to induce euphoria and a substantial increase in the speed and strength of the user. But, when coming off the high, the drug was known to cause paranoia and rage, as well as a loss of co-ordination and reaction time. Those stupid enough to try it were often addicted within several weeks of regular ingestion. They eventually wasted away as the drug burned them up, leaving them without an appetite for anything but their next use of the drug. Most ended up as skeletal husks, frequently dying within a year of first trying snowblood. As a result, the drug had been banned long ago, and use of it carried a terrible stigma. Jaresh's lips curled in disgust. Suge using snowblood? What a degenerate.

It still fell to Bree to prove her accusation, but if she could, there was no way Jaresh would be found guilty.

Jaresh shared a tight-lipped smile of triumph with Nanna, and glanced to where the Shektans sat. They were openly smiling, shaking one another's hands and doing little to hide their joy. His mother's eyes were shiny, and she wiped aside a tear or two. Even old Durmer Volk and Garnet Bosde were laughing and gave Jaresh a fist pump of encouragement.

It took some time, but the crowd quieted once more with whispers of conversation still rippling here and there.

"I demand that no more questions about snowblood and my son be allowed. He is not facing the tribunal here. The Sentya is!" Hal'El shouted, hot and angry.

"Sit down, Hal'El," the Arbiter said in irritation. "I know how you must feel, but *we* must know the truth. Continue," he said to Step Lindsar.

Physician Lindsar explained the history of the drug and its effects, including the reason it had been banned.

"Your account tells us all we need to know about the drug, but not why Suge might have been using it," Bree said. "Is there anything else you can offer?"

"Well, along with the emotional changes and metabolic changes – by this I mean the temporary increase in speed and strength followed by a terrific fall off – it also causes characteristic physical findings, and among these are dilated pupils, peripheral cyanosis – blue fingers and toes – and a blue tint to the sclera – the whites of the eyes."

"We've heard it said how Suge greatly improved his skills as a warrior over the past few months. Is that a known side effect of the drug?"

"Yes," the Shiyen replied. "But it just seems so unlikely. The drug's been banned for decades. And the son of an 'El..."

"I can understand your skepticism," Bree said. "Who among us would believe such a thing? However, I asked your assistant to test Suge's body for snowblood. Would the findings be accurate given how long he has been dead? Two weeks?"

"They should be. We Preserved him, and the drug has a very long half-life, so if it was there, we would know."

"I see," Bree said. "She handed the physician a rectangular piece of parchment, an official looking document. "Would you please verify this report as being from the City of Ashoka Medical Investigation Division?" Bree asked.

The physician looked over the paper, glancing at its contents. "It is from my office," he replied.

"And it relates to?"

Physician Lindsar looked up from the parchment. "You know who it relates to. It's about Suge Wrestiva."

Jaresh glanced at Hal'El, wondering how he was taking this. The head of House Wrestiva looked like he was going to be sick.

"And can you please read the contents, specifically the results of the drug screen on snowblood in Suge Wrestiva."

"Must I? His soul is in Devesh's hands. What good will any of this do?"

"I know you don't wish to impugn a dead man's reputation, but my brother's life hangs in the balance," Bree said softly. "You must read it."

Physician Lindsar studied the parchment. He cleared his throat, clearly stalling for time. "You must understand, the tissue analysis for snowblood can have a false positive in some circumstances..."

"Please read the report," the Arbiter interrupted.

Physician Lindsar frowned and stared at the parchment once again. "Tissue was taken from four separate sites on Suge's body, and the analysis was done three times on each sample," he begain. "According to the report, all the sites had..."

"There will be no need to proceed any further, Arbiter," Hal'El

Wrestiva said, rising to his feet and interrupting a relieved appearing Physician Lindsar. "I withdraw my claim." He turned to the members of his House sitting in attendance. "I am willing to state, here before this tribunal and my fellow 'Els, my unbiased belief that my son, Suge Wrestiva, was killed with justification by Jaresh Shektan, and further, neither I, nor my family nor my House will ever seek retribution upon him or his."

Hal'El's final words were nearly drowned out by the shouts of joy from the members of House Shektan.

CHAPTER SEVEN
A TRIAL OF A DIFFERENT SORT

Amongst the Humans, they say a mother's love knows no bounds.
She will do all in her power to see her children safe.
Can such a dream be true? Our Mother's love is barren.

~From the journal of SarpanKum Li-Charn, AF 1752

Li-Dirge stood on a stony plateau south of the Privation Mountains, where the land sloped along a series of jagged hills before flattening out into the Hunters Flats. The air was warm and heavy in the late evening, even here in the heights, but it was a mere hint of the summer to come. The sun set quickly in the foothills, streaking the sky with bands of violet, red, and orange. Bats darted in the air, turning sharply in ways no bird ever could. If not for the smell of roasting meat and the raucous shouts of the Chimeras camped at the base of the hill, it would have been peaceful.

Li-Dirge was a Bael, one of the feared commanders of the Fan Lor Kum, the Red Hand of Justice. However, he was no ordinary Bael. Li-Dirge was the SarpanKum, the general of the Eastern armies of the Queen, Mother Lienna, She who the Humans named Suwraith, the Bringer of Sorrows.

153

He considered the events from the day prior, when his Chimeras were engaged in battle with an Ashokan caravan. He switched his tail in annoyance as he listened in on the casualty report. So many brothers dead. The battle with the Ashokan caravan had ultimately been successful, but it had been costly. The Humans, all three hundred of them, had been utterly annihilated, but they had not gone down easily. The price for their deaths had been steep; almost five thousand Chimeras lost from what had originally been a full Shatter of fifteen thousand.

He glanced down at the fires below where the Fan Lor Kum were encamped, celebrating as they feasted on horseflesh, the meat of the Human warriors, and even the bodies of their own brethren. The additional food was most welcome. In general, the diet of a Chimera consisted of Chauk, a thick stew made from whatever grass was available and the boiled meat of a Phed, the beast Mother Lienna had created specifically to feed her Fan Lor Kum. She must not have worried over much about the taste since Phed in any form resembled dirt and bitter roots. Mother had also proscribed the hunting of any other game, but She had relented when it came to eating those who had fallen in battle. As a result, meat of any other kind was a delicacy.

Thus did the Fan Lor Kum gorge themselves on the plunder of yesterday's kills. But then again, in their minds, they had earned their feast. Many of their crèche brothers had died, and today had been difficult as well. Li-Dirge had pushed his warriors hard, wanting distance from the site of yesterday's battle. They had covered over forty miles and were exhausted.

Let them eat their fill.

Tomorrow would be no easier than today. Li-Dirge wanted to regroup with the rest of his forces. All told, he had sixteen Shatters under his command, over two hundred thousand Chimeras – the Eastern Plague of Continent Ember. While most of his forces were widely dispersed, there were three full Shatters gathered far to the southeast, in the Hunters Flats. He needed to reconnect with those warriors. He felt vulnerable out here in the hills, no more than a few weeks journey from Ashoka. There was little chance any force from the city might come for his Chimeras, but there might be another caravan nearby, a larger one and one led more competently. And besides, why take any chances? Humans were unpredictable.

For example, consider what had happened during the battle. It had not gone at all as Li-Dirge would have wished. He frowned in remembrance of the day's events. The Ashokans had fought hard and fought well, but unfortunately, their commander had been a lackwit. The man had trapped his warriors on a high mountain ridge with no way off. If not for the Human commander's decision, some of his men would have surely escaped the noose the Fan Lor Kum had thrown about the Ashokans – in fact, Dirge had been counting on it. If the Queen had not been observing – for the past month, She had been strangely lucid – Dirge might have even managed a means by which most of the column might have survived. Sadly, such was not the case.

He recalled the battle and wondered about the four he'd seen fighting so fiercely, especially the one who tore through the Fan Lor Kum like an engine of destruction. Those four *had* escaped. Li-Dirge had seen to it himself. It had been a great risk, but one he had been all too happy to take. The SarpanKum only wished more of the Ashokans could have fought free of the Chimera trap and fled into the night.

He sighed. The battle had been a success, but still, the Bael wished things could have gone differently. Better.

Most Chimeras had been created by Mother Lienna millennia ago from the twisted wrecks of many species. She had shaped fertile breeders for each of Her various types of warriors, but those made for Her armies were all mule males. From snakes and ferrets, She had made the Braids; from Shylows and monkeys, She had formed the

Tigons; Ur-Fels were a mix of dog and rat; while the Balants were a disgusting blend of elephant and baboon. No one knew the inspiration for the Pheds or the Bovars. Of all the Chimeras, they were the only two breeds without the gift of speech. They were dull creatures, empty of thought, although none of the Chimeras could really be said to be intelligent. All of them were irredeemably stupid as far as Li-Dirge was concerned.

Except for the Baels. The Baels were unique. Born like all other Chimeras in groups of five – a crèche – they had been the unexpected offspring of the bovine Bovars. But unlike their brethren, the Baels were not merely powerful, they were also intelligent. They were everything Mother had sought since the creation of the Chimeras. Prior to their birth, the Fan Lor Kum had been disastrously led by the Tigons. It was with the rise of the Baels that Her armies became far more lethal, and the Human caravans became far easier to kill, their cities easier to sack.

And centuries ago, the Baels had rebelled. Their very intelligence, so prized by their Queen was the reason for their betrayal. They eventually came to understand Mother Lienna's pogrom against Humanity for the evil that it was. Their awakening had changed the Baels, every last one of them. As a race, they had chosen to stymie the Queen's will at every pass, never hinting at their hatred for Her. They no longer hunted the Humans to extermination. Instead, at great personal risk, they ensured casualties amongst the caravans were as limited as possible; generally no greater than one quarter of the Human warriors. They would have managed even lower losses, but Mother Lienna insisted on a tribute of Human heads every six months, a pile as tall as a Balant.

If only his fellow Chimeras were capable of understanding the truth. It was a pity, but they remained slavishly devoted to the Queen.

Thus, the Baels were alone in their rebellion. And no one could learn of it, most certainly not Mother Lienna. If She ever became aware of the true feelings of Her Baels, She would extinguish them. Beyond simply killing them out of hand, without Mother Lienna's blessing, all Chimera breeders were infertile. Only the Pheds and Bovars could procreate without Mother Lienna's direct intervention, but She could simply kill the bovine Chimera beasts of burden out of hand. The extinction of the Baels would occur through simple lack of reproduction.

Li-Dirge put aside his thoughts. He sensed the approach of his Queen, Mother Lienna.

Li-Reg, his SarpanKi, his aide and brother – they had been born from the same crèche – hissed warning. *She* was nearly upon them.

Li-Dirge schooled his unruly thoughts to silence, focusing instead on the prayer all Chimeras spoke at night, re-affirming their love for Mother Lienna: the Prayer of Gratitude:

> *By Her grace are we born*
> *By Her love are we made*
> *By Her will are we shorn*
> *By Her fire are we unmade*
> *And are reborn once more*

A storm – a sound of thunder and coruscating lightning – was the harbinger of Her arrival. Her voice was a howling scream carried on the wind. A calm and warm Mother she was not, although She believed otherwise.

He and Li-Reg fell to their knees, followed instantly by thirty others of their brother Baels. Here were gathered all the surviving Vorsan and Sarpan, the leaders of the Fan Lor Kum. All their foreheads were pressed to the dirt, and they silently incanted the same night prayer Li-Dirge had used a moment earlier to cleanse his thoughts of treason. The rest of the Chimeras, including the junior Baels remained encamped on the northern outskirts of the Hunters

Flats, awaiting the return of their commanders. And not for the first time did Li-Dirge wish he were amongst them, safe from Mother's scrutiny.

Her attention was always dangerous.

"My SarpanKum: to Ashoka you will send Our most trusted child," Mother said. Her voice was the sound of nails on glass. It tore into Li-Dirge's mind. *"One there, a servant of Mine will venture forth, past the accursed city walls and greet him. To this servant I instruct you to give him this trinket."*

A knife, small and plain with a dark, wooden hilt fell from the sky and into Li-Dirge's hand. He had a moment to study it. What he had initially taken to be dark wood was actually maple stained with blood. Further inspection would have to wait for Mother's departure.

"And how shall I know him?" Li-Dirge asked in a firm tone, with no hint of a quaver and no sign of fear. Mother genuinely believed Herself to be gentle and loving. Should one of Her children display even the merest wisp of trepidation toward Her, Mother considered it a cardinal sin. She dealt with such heresy accordingly.

She spoke once more. *"He will be the SuDin to their Sil Lor Kum. He will use the trinket to unlock the gates of Ashoka so that I may lay it low. I will smash her tall towers into the ground such that no brick will be left standing atop another. And then will I turn my gaze to proud Hammer and finally bring an ending to that cursed city as well."*

Li-Dirge held still, no longer surprised by Mother's inconsistencies. Hammer had fallen centuries ago, and yet the Queen persisted in believing it a threat. Early on as a young Bael officer, Dirge's seniors had explained the situation to him, but he had not fully grasped the magnitude of Mother's tenuous grip on reality until he rose through the ranks and had direct contact with Her. Often were the times when She mistook living cities as being dead and dead cities as being alive; not to mention Her irrational demands and paranoid fears, most of which had no basis in fact. Dirge knew the truth, as did all the Bael: Mother Lienna was insane. Not that it mattered because She was still their Goddess, and they had no choice but to obey Her dictates, despite how contradictory and difficult they were. However, they often dreamed, in the deepest depths of their hearts and souls, for matters to be otherwise. They dreamed of freedom and a world without their Queen.

"Now. Go forth and rend My will!"

With that She was gone, taking the whirlwind and the raging storm with Her.

"That was most unpleasant," muttered Li-Urge, one of the Sarpans, the commander of one of the two Dreads of the Eastern Plague.

"Is it ever anything else?" asked Li-Brood, the other Sarpan. "Something not unpleasant, I mean."

"Never," Dirge sighed.

"What did she give you, brother?" Li-Reg asked, glancing at the unsheathed knife in Dirge's hand.

"I don't know, but I don't like the feel of it," Dirge answered. "It tingles against the skin as if it is unhealthy."

Brood snorted. "Nothing from Her hand is clean."

"Even us?" Urge asked. "We should simply lay down our lives then if we believed so."

Dirge silenced them with a hiss and an angry lash of his tail. "Mother had our birthing, but not our forging. We were an accident She was tempted to abort." He shook his great black head, his bright feathers jangled as his ebony horns caught the last of the sun's rays. "It was Hume who had our forging. We are his creation more so than Hers, cleansed by his charity through the love of Devesh."

"Yet he charged us to find a way to pass on his heritage," Urge said. "Generations of our brothers have failed him. *We* have failed."

"Since Hammer fell," Brood said.

"But we will find a way. His heir will be found," Dirge promised.

"His heir will be found," the other Baels intoned.

Far above the world, Lienna, Mother of the Fan Lor Kum, the Mad Queen and Bringer of Sorrows, floated amongst the racing winds of the high heights. She wondered about Her life thus far, measured in long years and millennia. Though She was ancient now, She was but a child compared to Her parents. She shied away from that memory. Mother and Father were best forgotten. It was wise never to think of them at all, else they might speak to Her as they too often did.

Instead, She recalled Her recent conversation with the SarpanKum of her Fan Lor Kum. She smiled. The Bael was a fool. So trusting and noble. So humble and devoted to Her. The Baels had always been Her greatest creation, but they were also Her greatest failure. They were too much like the detestable Humans, and so in the end, She would have to end them as well. For now, however...they had their uses.

"You were once Human," Her Mother murmured in Her ears, a voice only She could hear.

"Silence, shade!" Lienna shouted to the sky. Lightning arced all around Her as thunder pealed in counterpoint.

"Daughter, you are a fool to trust the Baels," Father told her. *"They seek to destroy You."*

"You think I know it not?" Lienna laughed. *"Though their appearance is vastly different from that of a Human, still their heart is quite the same."*

"The only good thing You have ever made," Mother murmured.

"The only good thing You will ever make," Father said.

"Begone! Both of you," Lienna shouted. *"You are dead."*

"As You would know better than anyone," Mother murmured, Her voice fading.

Lienna seethed at the reminder, lightning forking across the sky with thunder and wind following. She eventually forced stillness to Her heart, but even then echoing rumbles of Her anger still made their way across the cloudless sky. Her Mother and Father were dead, but who then were these Others who spoke with Their voices? It must be Mother and Father's revenge.

Or something else.

A sick dread made a cold and damp path through Her mind. What if Mother and Father were alive?

Impossible.

"Hammer mocks Us," said a voice, gentle as a spring shower, biting as a blizzard.

Lienna winced. Had She a face, it would have been frozen in a mask of fear. Arisa, the unknowable Spirit of the very earth, Lienna's Goddess and Mistress to all Creation, terrified Her. *"I have done the best I can,"* Lienna said, hating the sulky note in Her voice.

"The best You can?" Mistress laughed derisively. *"With all the gifts I have granted, this is the best You can do? You are a fool. I curse the day I ever listened to your entreaties. I should have chosen another, one more worthy, you stupid girl."*

"No. I can do better," Lienna whimpered. *"I can accomplish what…"*

"You have accomplished nothing!" Mistress' voice was a whiplash. *"Succeed with Ashoka, and then destroy Hammer. She is the key to ending the blight of Humanity."*

"And then My Baels will usher in a new golden age?"

"As I promised." A cold dagger slid into Lienna's mind. *"Try to achieve more than mere incompetence."*

"What would You have me do?"

"Gather the Fan Lor Kum upon the fertile fields of the Hunters Flats. The Shylows must be taught respect or hunted to extermination."

"I thought We were to destroy Ashoka?" Lienna whined.

"You think? A wonder for the ages." Mistress laughed again, that same derisive taunt. *"Do as I command. The Flats first."*

"Then Ashoka."

Mistress sighed, seemingly reaching the bounds of Her patience. *"No. Then Hammer."*

Lienna recalled something just then. *"Is Hammer not destroyed?"*

She winced as She sensed a building rage from Her Mistress.

"If it was destroyed already, why would I want it destroyed again?" Mistress thundered.

Lienna was too scared to answer. Mistress Arisa was fearful and disturbing at the best of times. And this was not the best of times.

"Fine. I see where Your mind wishes to go. Ashoka then, coward."

"And the Baels?"

"The Baels are Our greatest ally."

"A new age will issue forth from Our loyal servants." Lienna said, speaking fervently.

"Yes. But only if You gain the merest grain of wisdom, dull and stupid girl."

Her orders given, the Mistress was gone just as suddenly as She had arrived. Lienna shivered in relief.

"The Baels will betray you," Father said.

"I'll kill them all when they are no longer useful to Me."

"You were once loved by all," Mother murmured. *"Your name means 'gentle soul'. Now, all fear and hate you, even the Baels."*

"Our greatest ally," Mistress Arisa said.

Once again, Lienna wondered which voice She should believe.

CHAPTER EIGHT
A RECKONING

The crucible of tragedy teaches us the truth of our dharma:
we sacrifice all so others need not. It is a weighty burden.

~*The Sorrows of Hume, AF 1789*

Rukh knew when Brand Blended. Worse, he knew *how* Brand Blended. This was a Talent given over only to the Murans and Rahails. Never to the Kummas. But then again, no one other than a Kumma could Annex their *Jivatmas*, and yet, Brand, a Rahail, had been joined with Rukh, Farn, and Keemo only a few minutes earlier.

What did this all mean? And should he mention his possible abilities to the others? He didn't want to. It went against everything he had ever been taught. It was wrong. *He* was wrong. And if he spoke up, loathing was the best he could expect from his friends. It was how he would have reacted if one of them admitted to something so repulsive. In that case, wouldn't it be better to just keep it quiet and not say anything? It would certainly be easier. After all, why did anyone need to know this one little secret? He could just keep it to himself. No one would really be hurt if he remained quiet.

But then again, the Martial Masters of the House of Fire and Mirrors taught how a true warrior strove to cleanse himself of all weaknesses, no matter how shameful. He was expected to fight against his sins as hard as he would any Chimera, and it was the duty of his brothers to aid him in the attempt. And those who chose to fight their demons alone were fools, especially if their hidden flaws somehow led to the death of their brothers. There was no salvation for such a coward. Was this the situation Rukh was in? Could his secret lead to the death of one of the others? He worried it might, and he wavered in his decision, torn between hard duty and the easy lie of omission. His heart wanted to follow the path of least pain, but his mind knew he couldn't. He had to tell them. They had to know the truth.

"I think I might be able to Blend," Rukh admitted in a whisper. "Or learn to."

Keemo and Brand looked confused, but Farn immediately seemed to know what Rukh meant. His head snapped around, and he wore an expression of disgust as he locked gazes with Rukh, looking at him as if he were a deadly serpent.

"What do you mean?" Farn hissed. "That's impossible. Don't ever speak of something so grotesque ever again. It's…"

"I can *feel* the presence of a Blend," Rukh insisted, his voice more forceful this time. For some reason, he was unwilling or unable to remain silent. It was like a wave had crashed over him, sending him tumbling and rolling down a path not of his own choosing. He was sick over what he had become, but he couldn't hide from it, and he couldn't hide it from his friends either.

The others wore uneasy expressions.

"I think I can too," Keemo said into the echoing quiet. "I felt it when Brand Blended us."

Farn gasped. "Devesh save you," he whispered in horror. "What have you two become? You're naajas. Tainted. Both of you."

Rukh couldn't face him, and he turned away, feeling wretched. His gaze fell on Brand. He was the only Rahail amongst them. "How did you end up in our Annex?" Rukh asked, his voice unintentionally coming out as a gruff challenge.

Brand's mouth gaped open in surprise before he finally spoke. "Why are you asking me?" he protested. "I didn't *try* to join your Triad. I was just fighting to stay alive when suddenly I'm Annexed with the three of you in a Quad."

"I know you didn't intend to, and I'm not saying it's your fault," Rukh said, forcing calm and patience into his tone. "But you *were* Annexed, and suddenly you could do things only we can. You shouldn't have been able to make that leap." He gestured to the narrow canyon outside. "Do you have our Talents as well?"

Brand stared back in flat-eyed, angry silence. He swallowed heavily and broke with a shuddering sigh. "I think so," he replied, looking miserable.

"You did this to us!" Farn cried out instantly.

"Shut up!" Rukh hissed. "We don't want the Chims hearing us. And what's this about 'us'? Can you sense a Blend, too?"

Farn shifted uncomfortably. "I don't know what I can do," he muttered. He turned to Brand. "But if I can sense them – if any of us can – it has to be his fault. Until he joined the Annex, we were fine. He changed us somehow."

"Go frag a goat," Brand shot back. "I don't care what you believe. If anything, it's you lot who've done something to me. I didn't ask to be in your Annex. You pulled me into it against my will."

Farn looked angry enough to draw blood, which was ironic given how much blood and gore they were all covered with. He, Keemo, and Brand argued in harsh whispers, trying to assign blame for what had become of them, their voices growing steadily louder.

Rukh vaguely listened in, but none of what they said mattered anymore. All of them were naajas. All of them were Tainted. They might as well be ghrinas for all anyone else would care.

"You stupid jackass. How can you take his side?" Farn growled at Keemo.

Rukh's jaw firmed. He'd heard enough. Right now, there were more important issues to address. "Shut up! All of you," Rukh ordered. "In case you've forgotten, our fragging caravan was annihilated only a few minutes ago. Our friends have been slaughtered, and the damn Chimeras...look at their bonfires." He gestured across the canyon to the flat-topped knoll where so many of their brothers had recently died; to where the Chims were joyously celebrating their victory, laughing loudly. The smell of meat carried on the air, the scent of Human flesh roasting. "What do you think they're eating, you fragging idiots?" He glared at all of them, challenging them to look him in the eyes. "They're feasting on the corpses of our brothers while you're standing here barking like scalded dogs. Whatever happened on that plateau saved our lives. We should be grateful for it. So shut up. It's done. Settle down and try to get some sleep. No fires. I'll take first watch."

"Who in the unholy hells put you in charge?" Farn challenged.

"He has rank, jackhole," Keemo said.

"Or do you want to determine this with swords?" Rukh asked, glancing at Farn's hands, both of which were clenched around the hilt of his blade.

With a shudder, Farn relaxed his grip. "Sorry, Rukh. I didn't mean to..." He shuddered again. "It's just been..."

"It's alright," Rukh said, laying a hand on his cousin's shoulder. "None of us are at our salty best right now. Get some rest." He sighed. "Tomorrow is going to be almost as bad as today."

"I doubt it," Brand muttered.

"It will be." Rukh promised with quiet assurance. "Tomorrow we have to go back across that chasm and see what kind of supplies we can salvage. It's going to be a long hike back to Ashoka." His previous righteous fire was suddenly doused, and his head drooped with doleful weariness. He stared at the ground, not really seeing it. His voice was a pained whisper. "And we have to set fire to whatever's left of our friends."

Early the next morning, after a restless night of little sleep, the Ashokans woke and studied the distant ridge upon which the caravan had died. Even though they had seen the cook fires doused as the celebratory armies of Suwraith made their way back down the steep mountain pass in the middle of the night, Rukh ordered them to maintain their position. No moving out yet.

"Why are we still here?" Keemo asked. "The Chims are long gone."

"*Some* of them are long gone," Rukh replied. "There might still be a trap of Braids or a nest of Ur-Fels hiding in ambush over there. They might be hidden, just waiting for survivors like us to show up. We can't afford carelessness right now. Too much depends on our survival."

Rukh left unsaid why the four of them were suddenly so important. They were the only ones left who could carry word of the caravan's destruction back to Ashoka. The city had to be made aware of what had happened: the Chims were massing and planned on attacking the city sometime later in the summer. If Rukh and the others died, the city might remain ignorant and unprepared for what was to come.

So Rukh had them stay in the cave, searching and studying until they were as sure as possible that no Chims were on the other side of the ravine. They ended up waiting for hours, gazing at the flat-topped hill, looking for Braids or Ur-Fels or any other Chimeras.

Nothing.

Rukh motioned, and they moved out. Slowly, carefully, they descended the steep expanse down from the cave in which they had sheltered to the base of the rocky ravine. In the shade of the canyon floor they briefly paused to catch their breath before pushing on to climb the high-walled cliff where the caravan had fought its last battle. It was a difficult ascent and they were all soon panting. They clambered up the last few feet, struggling to reach the top of the ridge, where they hunched over in exhaustion with hands on their knees as they worked to get their breath back.

Rukh was the first to straighten up, but he still needed deep lungfuls of air as he waited for his heart to slow down. He walked about, taking short, stiff steps and shaking out his arms. He didn't want to start cramping.

As he recovered, he tried not to look around. Three hundred good men had died here yesterday, and while very little was left of their remains, there was enough. Mixed in amongst the slowly congealing pools of blood were a few torn up, unidentifiable corpses along with meat-picked bones and burnt pieces of flesh. Some broken swords and spears lay scattered about as well as a few blood-stained clothes, rent and tattered as they fluttered on a cool breeze.

Rukh battled to hold down his gorge. He doubted he was the only one.

Once the others were able, they set about their first task and gathered together the few wretched remains of their brothers in order to lay them to rest. They worked in a strange silence with only the sound of the wind to break the hallowed quiet. The vultures and crows and other carrion eaters hadn't arrived yet, and if the Ashokans had their way, they would never have need to.

Rukh was sick at heart – they all were – as they gathered the remains scattered about like refuse. This might be all that was left of Lieutenant Pume or Captain Stryed or so many other men who had been close friends and even family. He had shared drink, food, and laughter with all of these men, and now there was nothing of them except these torn up chunks of flesh and bone.

What a waste. These warriors – his brothers – had died on Trial, and maybe doing so *was* holy, but it still seemed so senseless. The Murans would sing of the gallantry of these men, and a statue for their bravery might even be raised somewhere in Ashoka, but what difference would it make to those who had given their final, full measure on this lonely hill? They'd still be dead, hacked apart and eaten, their lives cut brutally short in some faraway and savage place. He swore in anger and disgust. He hoped the men had died quickly. It would be a mercy. Some of the veterans said the Chimeras, especially the Tigons, didn't always wait until their victims had stopping moving before they began to feast.

Rukh studied the small pile of body parts the four of them had collected. He shook his head again. So damn pointless. His throat clenched as tears stung his eyes. He had to step away and take slow, deep breaths as he tried to settle his sorrow and anguish.

"We can't light a fire," Brand remarked. "The smoke would give us away."

"Yes we can," Rukh said, his voice shaky with suppressed emotions. He motioned to Keemo and Farn. "We'll flash-burn them with Fireballs." His voice steadied as he focused on the work at hand. "You'll have to Blend it all and hide any smoke, but after we're done, we should get them covered in a cairn."

"Or we could Blend them ourselves. We all seemed to have picked up that Talent," Farn muttered, shaking his head in disbelief. "What kind of naaja bastards have we become?"

Keemo stiffened. "What's your problem?" he demanded.

"We're fragging naajas, dumbass. That's my problem," Farn snapped back. "We're unnatural. How are we supposed to live with this? What will our families think? We might as well slit our throats right here and right now."

"I don't feel any different," Keemo said. "Shouldn't we expect to feel wrong if we're as bad as you say we are?"

Farn laughed. "Do the Chimeras think they're evil?" he asked. "Or do they suppose that serving the Mad Bitch is the height of holiness?" His voice held an edge of panic.

"Fragging hell, keep it together," Rukh said, grabbing Farn by the collar of his shirt and frog-marching him to the small mound of bones and body parts. "Look around you. Our friends are dead. All of them were butchered and eaten. And you're bitching about some Devesh damned Talent we've picked up?" he asked in disbelief.

"I was just saying…"

"I don't care what you were saying," Rukh said, cutting him off.

Farn's attitude pissed him off. It was selfish. They were alive when so many others had given everything. Their lives. Their loves. Their futures. Who cared if the four of them were ghrinas or naajas or some other kind of freaks of nature? They could still do what they were trained for. They could protect Ashoka. Nothing else mattered. It was their Devesh damned duty, and he would be fragged and fried in the unholy hells before he quit on his city.

But if Rukh didn't stomp out Farn's whining, and damn quick, his cousin would destroy them all by wiping out their unit cohesion. Right now, the four of them were it. They had no one else to rely on. They had to be strong and tight with each other. There was no room for whining or complaining about how life was unfair. When had Devesh ever made life fair? They were alive. It was enough. It had to be.

Rukh pulled Farn closer, getting straight into his face and looking the taller man in the eyes, forcing him to meet his gaze. "Unless you have something useful to say, shut up. Because the truth is, I'm damn grateful to be alive. We're naajas. We're ghrinas or something even worse. Who the frag cares? We're the only naajas who can bring warning to Ashoka. We may be our people's only hope, and if the price to pay is being some kind of unnatural horror, so be it. We're Kummas. We pay any price."

170

Farn looked chastened, and he averted his eyes, unable to meet Rukh's scrutiny.

Good.

Rukh released him.

"I'm ready," Brand said, interrupting their argument.

Rukh sighed and stepped away from Farn. "Then let's lay our friends to rest. We can talk about the rest of this bilge water on the way back."

"Let's do it," Keemo said.

Farn also nodded his readiness and he shuddered as some of the fear leached out of his eyes. "I'm ready."

"As soon as we get started, get the Blend up," Rukh directed to Brand. He looked to his cousins. "On three."

As soon as the bodies were aflame, Rukh nodded to Brand who instantly threw a Blend over the corpses.

Rukh wished he didn't have a sudden sense and awareness of the Blend. He could even tell how Brand had formed it. It was delicate work, conducting *Jivatma* like that, but with practice, Rukh knew he might be able to cast one himself.

Just lovely.

Despite his earlier words to Farn, Rukh wasn't comfortable with what had happened to them. He was no less disgusted by the entire situation than his cousin. It was horrible, like being violated. He'd been forced to accept a Talent he had never sought or desired. As a result, he no longer knew who he was or even what he was. He wasn't a Kumma. At least not as most would define the warrior Caste. Not anymore. This new person was Tainted, a naaja, and Rukh hated him. All night long, Rukh had tried to convince himself that whatever had happened, it would just turn out to be a trick played on his tired mind, like an illusion or something. It had been a slim reed of hope, and now it was burned away and gone.

But Rukh couldn't dwell on his loss, not now when he knew the hard work that they had to do. "Let's go," he said a few minutes later.

"Ashoka?" Keemo asked.

"Yes."

"There's a Blend under that pile of rocks," Brand said, pointing to a large mound of small boulders and stones. "I wasn't able to sense it with all the death here until just now."

"He's right," Farn agreed, immediately realizing what he had said and grimacing in disgust.

"We've got to get them out," Rukh said, suddenly filled with hope. He prayed more earnestly than he'd ever prayed before. *Just a small blessing today. Devesh, please...give us a chance.*

"Could it be the Sil Lor Kum?" Keemo asked as they worked.

Farn rolled his eyes. "And why in the unholy hells would they come back here and bury themselves under a pile or rocks? Pretty stupid thing to do if they wanted to survive yesterday's massacre."

Keemo reddened with embarrassment. "I was just saying...we don't know who those people are."

"They're our brothers," Rukh said. "Let's get them out."

They worked quickly and soon had a Kumma, a Rahail, and a Muran free of their encasement under stone. The three men had fought together, and when the caravan had been over-run, the Kumma, Jorn Streedout of House Priyatel, had blasted apart a section of the rock face with a Fireball, effectively burying the three of them. As the rocks had fallen, he had hastily thrown up a protective Shield, while Blok Dam, the Rahail, and Simil Triosole, the Muran, had hidden them with a Blend. They hadn't slept a wink the entire night. If Jorn had let slip his Shield, the rubble would have crushed them, and if the Blend had dissolved, the Chimeras would have promptly known of their presence.

It took the rest of the morning as well as most of their water and scavenged food for the three men to recover.

"Any others?" Blok asked, his head drooping wearily.

Brand shook his head. "You're the only ones we've found so far."

"Suwraith's spit," Simil said, looking weary and sick.

"He was heading back to his home city. Nestle," Jorn said. "He and his brother."

"On Trial, all men are brothers," Rukh said automatically. A moment later, he swore softly under his breath. In most instances, the phrase was trite to the point of losing all meaning, but now, it tasted like ash on his tongue. For the first time, Rukh truly understood what the words meant. But it was an understanding he wished he'd never gained. Too much death had been the tuition for his education.

"Damn Chims," Brand muttered.

"Devesh damn them all," Keemo agreed.

"What do you intend to do?" Jorn asked.

"We're heading back to Ashoka to warn the city," Keemo said.

As the others talked amongst themselves, Rukh remained quiet. A nugget of a plan – still in its formative stage – had settled in his mind, and he needed time to think it through. Eventually it came to him. "We're not all going back to Ashoka," Rukh said, interrupting their conversation.

"What do you mean? You aren't coming with us?" Blok asked.

"Not yet," Rukh said. "You three will go back and warn the city. The four of us…" he indicated Brand, Keemo, and Farn, "…are going to track the Chimeras. We'll follow them to their home."

"Are you sure about this?" Brand asked. "Wouldn't it be safer to go back to Ashoka?"

Rukh turned to him. "Those Chims are the key," he said. "If we can locate their staging area, we can take the fight to them." His jaw firmed and a look of implacable hatred stole across his face. "And when we find them, I mean to help lead the Army of Ashoka straight to their houses and burn them all to ashes."

"Now that's a plan," Keemo said in agreement.

They followed hard on the Chimeras' path, journeying as fast as they could. Their quarry was nearly a full Shatter of filthy Chimeras, and the Ashokans should have been able to close the distance much more quickly than they did. Their biggest obstacle was the need to hunt for food every night. It slowed them down, and it didn't help that Suwraith's creatures were also moving swiftly. The Chims had cut straight out of the foothills of the Privation Mountains and onto the Hunters Flats, picking up speed on the savannah.

During the hunt for the Chimeras, Rukh and the others didn't speak much of the caravan. It was too soon, and the hurt was too close. Better to focus on the task at hand and not dwell on the past or what was lost.

So the days went, but even as they chased the Chimeras, Rukh insisted all of them practice their new Talents. He made the other Kummas learn to Blend. It was an exercise that felt wrong on a bone-deep level, and it left Keemo and Farn – and Rukh – feeling disgusted with themselves. All three of them hated it, but Rukh wouldn't let up. As far as he was concerned, Blending might be the difference between life and death. Dying was easy, but duty demanded they live. All of them took lessons from Brand an hour every morning before they broke camp and an hour before they settled in for the night. They weren't skilled and probably never would be, at least compared to Rahails and Murans, but they learned enough. They could hide themselves if the need ever arose and had even managed a shaky Link of their Blends so that at a distance, they could still see one another.

And, of course, Brand took instruction from the Kummas on *his* new Talents. A Fireball was the first skill he learned.

Several weeks into the hunt, they caught sight of cook fires. It was the Chimeras who'd annihilated the caravan. Rukh shared a smile of anticipation with others, one of their few moments of pleasure since the caravan's destruction.

Rukh signaled the others, and they pulled aside to make camp several miles away in a small thicket of trees.

Brand went off to scout – being the best at Blending, his role was obvious – while the others ate a cold meal of wild carrots and roasted meat. They knew better than to bother with a fire this close to the Chimera encampment.

"Let's hope we don't run into any Shylows," Keemo whispered.

"They'd go for the Chims first," Rukh whispered back. "From what I've heard, they hate them nearly as much as we do."

"Not nearly," Farn corrected in a growl.

Just then Brand suddenly emerged back into view. "The caravan punched the Chims pretty hard," Brand said. "They're down to a little over ten Fractures."

Farn smiled in grim satisfaction. "Then we killed over four thousand of them," he said. "A good start."

"There's something else," Brand added. "Something strange. All the senior Baels – the ones with the most feathers hanging from their horns – they're all gathered in a shallow vale about four or five miles from the rest of the Chims."

"Any idea why?" Keemo asked.

"Of course. We've all of us known what the horned bastards get up to at night," Farn said with a derisive snort. "We just didn't feel like telling you."

"Do you actually know then?" Keemo challenged. "Or are you just blowing bilge out your backhole as usual?"

Farn shook his head.

"Then piss off."

Ever since the caravan's destruction, Farn had become

increasingly sarcastic and impatient with Keemo's admittedly asinine questions. Usually, their jeering banter grated on Rukh's nerves, and sometimes he even had to hold himself back from knocking some sense into their fool heads. Tonight their arguing didn't bother him. He barely even heard them. Something more important occupied his attention. But first, he had to stifle the uncertain excitement building inside. He needed to carefully think this through.

The senior Baels had separated from their main force. Could they do it? If there weren't too many, then maybe...

"I need numbers and location," Rukh said.

"There's about fifty Baels and the same number of Tigons and Braids hanging around nearby acting as guards," Brand said. "Last I saw, they were about two miles northeast of us. It's just about a straight shot given how flat the land is around here. Why?"

All at once, the budding anticipation drained away and left Rukh feeling hollow. A hundred of them. Too many. Damn.

"What were you hoping to do?" Keemo asked.

"Kill them," Rukh said.

"Kill who? The Baels?" Farn asked. "There's no way. Even if there were only twenty of them. In case you hadn't noticed, there's no cover around here except for a few scrub trees and bushes. They'd see us coming from a half-mile away."

"And you think I'm stupid," Keemo replied with a contemptuous shake of his head. "We can Blend now, dumbass, remember? They wouldn't see nothing, not until we were right on them, like ugly on your face..."

Rukh wanted to mentally slap himself. Keemo was right. They could Blend. Rukh was seized with sudden excitement. They *could* do this.

"If these Baels are their senior staff, and they're having some kind of meet up, we could decapitate their army in one fell swoop," Brand said, catching the fever of Rukh's enthusiasm.

Rukh smiled, a predatory gleam in his eyes. "We're still faster than they are," he said. "Even Brand since he's been practicing our Talents just like we have his. We can evade the Tigons and Braids and get close enough to Fireball half the Baels before the others even figure out who's sending them to the unholy hells. And when they try to fight us…" he smiled again. "We slip away like ghosts."

An answering gleam lit Farn's eyes. "And then we hit them again when they try to return to their main army."

"Yes," Rukh answered. "We can't take all of them, but we can whittle their numbers down, especially if we get the feather wearers."

Keemo grinned. "Let's do it."

"Time to get some vengeance," Farn said. "For all our fallen."

Brand shook his head. "My Amma always warned me to stay away from you crazy Kummas. Always racing off from one desperate battle to another."

Farn laughed. "Didn't anyone tell you? Kumma crazy is contagious. By now, you've got it just as bad as the rest of us."

"As long as I'm not Kumma stupid," Brand replied.

"The Tigons and Braids are excited," Li-Dirge noted, standing with his back to the large bonfire at the center of the vale.

"We shouldn't have brought them," Reg said. "In the best of times, they are no more than idiots. When Mother arrives, they'll discard whatever small wits Devesh was kind enough to grant them and lose themselves in their religious fervor over a false deity."

"We need their blades in case the Shylows decide to visit," Dirge said. "If nothing else, we can throw our fellow Chimeras at the damn cats until we can make good our escape."

Li-Brood laughed. "It's all they're good for anyway: fodder."

Dirge glanced to the darkened skies. The stars gleamed, twinkling and warm, while a half-moon shone down on them, making visible the heavy clouds lumbering slowly to the northeast. It wasn't the lovely sheen of heaven's vault that caught his attention though.

There was a power in the skies.

He searched and found a distant place where the clouds swirled madly, lit by lightning. The sound of thunder carried to him on the night breeze. Soon it would become a whirlwind.

He trembled. "She comes." He glanced around, gathering the attention of the other Baels. "Prepare yourselves."

As one, the Baels fell to their knees, foreheads pressed to the grass of the vale. And as one, they chanted the prayer taught to them as young worms in the crèche pouches of their Bovar mothers, the improperly named Prayer of Gratitude:

By Her grace are we born
By Her love are we made
By Her will are we shorn
By Her fire are we unmade
And are reborn once more

Mother Lienna arrived in a torrent of lashing wind and sound. *"My SarpanKum, you have ensured delivery of the trinket?"* the Queen demanded in a voice of pealing thunder and cracking bones.

"It is done," Li-Dirge replied in a voice far steadier than he felt.

"Good. It is as it should be," She replied. *"Now listen well for this is My will. Carry it forth."*

Li-Dirge sweated as the Queen spoke insanity. In his mind echoed the Prayer of Gratitude, the only means to hide his fear and contempt from Mother.

178

CHAPTER NINE
INDISTINCT FOES

Before waging battle, the ferocious warrior is certain of his friends.
But the wise warrior is even more certain of his enemies.

~*The Warrior and the Servant (author unknown), AF 203*

Rukh crouched next to Brand, Keemo, and Farn behind a pile of boulders, the crumbled remnants of a small monolith that had once jutted up from the wide savannah of the Hunters Flats. The grass was long and itchy, and the smell of the nearby eucalyptus trees – a lemony kind of scent – blew their way during a restless breeze. The day had been hot, and the evening humid and muggy. It was perfect weather for mosquitoes and other pests. They buzzed around the Ashokans but never settled, their senses thrown off by the Blend each man had conducted. Sweat beaded on Rukh's forehead and trickled down his back, but he didn't bother wiping it away. He kept still – it was the stillness of a predator waiting to strike.

Before him, meeting in a shallow bowl of land about a hundred feet in diameter, were a number of Baels clustered in small groups as they spoke to one another. Based on the number of feathers they wore, all of them looked to be senior Chimera commanders. So far, the Ashokans had managed to avoid the Tigon and Braid guards with ease. The Blends – even the ones conducted by the Kummas – worked perfectly…or at least well enough. Thirty or so feet from the boulders behind which they crouched stood the Bael commander. Rukh assumed it likely since this was the only black-horned beast with red feather tassels hanging like confetti from his ebony horns.

The Baels were armed with their traditional trident and chained whip, and some even wore sheathed swords at their hips. The last were likely of Ashokan make, probably weapons the Chimeras had picked off the corpses of those they'd killed in the caravan. For the Baels, they would merely serve as long knives.

Bastards.

They wouldn't be able to take down all the Baels, but the Ashokans could do some heavy damage. Rukh prepared to give the order to attack. It would only be a small vengeance for all those killed in the caravan, but it would have to serve. Just as he was about to give the final command, he paused. A small voice in his mind whispered for him to wait. He frowned and rapped the side of his head, not sure where the thought had come from. He decided it wasn't important. Once more, he was about to signal for the Ashokans to attack, but again came the whispered voice, urging him to wait. Rukh paused, suddenly unsure. Something was going on here. Something a part of him felt was important. He stayed his order, choosing instead to remain silent. He ignored the questioning look in Farn's eyes. He wanted to know what the Baels were discussing.

The beasts were in conference, and surprisingly, they spoke Human. Who would have guessed the creatures would share the same language as their enemies? The Baels spoke in an old-fashioned manner, but otherwise, they were easy to understand. And what they discussed shouldn't have surprised him. The Baels apparently had little love for their fellow Chims, but the ease with which they discussed disposing of the Tigons and the others in their command was repulsive. Rukh's lip curled in disgust. The primary duty of any commander was to use his warriors wisely and never waste their lives. Or so Rukh had always been taught. The Baels believed otherwise, and tonight only served to emphasize how utterly brutal and treacherous all Chimeras were. It wasn't much of a surprise given the nature of their Mother.

A flicker of lightning caught his eye, and he looked to the south where a storm was building and heading their way. His eyes widened. The storm was moving against the prevailing wind. He stared harder at the oncoming inky dark clouds moving toward them. It raced forward, covering the distance more swiftly than any wind could possibly account for. Rukh's heart pounded. He knew what was coming, or rather *who* was coming. The swirling clouds, moving in warped and incomprehensible patterns...no one had seen Her in a hundred years, but there were enough descriptions for him to know who it was.

"Holy Devesh. Please tell me I'm not seeing what I think I am?" Farn said, his voice quaking in terror.

"Quiet," Rukh replied, the sweat on his brow suddenly turned clammy. "Focus on your Blends. If She sees us, we're dead."

This was a moment rarely reported in Human history: a close encounter with Suwraith, the Sorrow Bringer in all Her horrific glory. The clouds raced and swirled before a hurricane wind and lightning coruscated, shooting from sky to earth and back again, while thunder rumbled continuously. Despite the din, Her voice could be heard, a howling sound like crushed stone and the anguished scream of the tortured. Rukh had never heard anything so awful or terrifying. Her voice was like a nightmare made flesh, and he had to stifle an urge to plug his ears and flee for his life. He had never in his life expected to be so close to the hated being responsible for carnage and murder on such a vast scale that words couldn't describe the true horror of what

She had done. This was Suwraith. She was evil made real.

He reached out to Brand, who had risen from his crouch, a look of utter panic in his face. His fellow Ashokans weren't doing much better, but after a moment, the four of them got their fear under control. They settled down behind the boulders, waiting and listening to find out what would happen next.

Never before had a meeting between Suwraith and her commanders been recorded. Until this moment, no one even knew how the Sorrow Bringer communicated with her armies. After all, the only other times Suwraith had been seen was when She was in the midst of annihilating a city. Very few people survived such an attack.

She rushed toward the Baels, flattening the grass for hundreds of paces around with a wind that threatened to lift the Ashokans off their feet and hurl them skyward into the teeth of the storm. Dust and grit billowed in the air until the only safety was for the Ashokans to mimic the position of the Baels: knees on the ground with bodies curled up and foreheads pressed to the earth.

Suwraith spoke, and Rukh forced himself to listen, despite the awful and hideous sound of Her voice. Ashoka's existence might depend on what he learned in the next few minutes.

What was this about a trinket? And why did the red-feathered Bael, the general, look so fearful?

"And now take yourself to the gathering of My army. There you will empty this plain and feed the breeders of the Eastern Caverns so I may have three Plagues with which to attack Ashoka as soon as possible."

Rukh risked a glance and caught the startled expression on the general's face. "Three? I can take the city with just two. Your Sarpans and I are certain of it."

"And your bravery and great leadership has been noted," Suwraith said. *"But I will have three, for after Ashoka, cancerous Hammer, which mocks Us even now, will be destroyed utterly and completely."*

Hammer?

Rukh's brow creased with uncertainty. Hammer was dead.

"Yes. I shall rend Hammer and crush the very marrow from her bones. Rumors reach Me of a supposed hero from that foul nest of vipers, a Kumma by the name of Hume Telrest. One who dares challenge Us, treading the green fields of Arisa without fear or regard. He despoils Her with his very touch. Him I will end so grievously that Humanity will quail in fear at the memory of his death for a thousand years and more."

Hume? He was centuries dead. What were they talking about? It made no sense.

"If Humanity exists for another thousand years, then am I to assume our great task has changed?" the Bael asked, sounding confused. "Are we no longer to extinguish the Human vermin?"

"Absolutely not," Suwraith snapped. *"Nothing has changed. It is as I have stated from the very beginning when I first birthed the Fan Lor Kum: Humanity is a pestilence upon Arisa, a plague which must be eradicated."*

"Yes, Mother," the Bael said.

Rukh risked another glance, doing his best to peer through the grit and dirt swirling about. He sheltered his eyes.

The Bael appeared lost in thought, but a moment later, he spoke again. "Perhaps rather than Ashoka, we should level the fabled city of Craven?"

"Craven?" It didn't seem possible, but the Queen sounded just as confused as Rukh. Her voice firmed. *"Yes. I may consider your plan,"* She said. *"Speak on, for Craven should be ended as well."*

What in the fragging hells was Craven? Were they talking about some other city? The Bael and the Queen both spoke Human, but neither of them were making any sense. It was all gibberish garbage. They spoke as if dead cities and heroes were still alive and imaginary cities were real.

He shared a baffled glance with the other Ashokans.

"What the unholy hells?" Brand mouthed.

Keemo and Farn shrugged.

"Exactly. As we know, Craven is the hated sister city to Ashoka," the Bael commander said, sounding disgusted. "They support one another as grass holds the shape of a hill and prevents the fertile earth from being swept away by the raging spring flood. When we break Craven, Ashoka will fall like a ripe plum."

"An interesting idea, my SarpanKum," Suwraith said. *"Explain further."*

"Give me five months, and I will have the Fan Lor Kum trained for winter combat. They will need it as Craven sits in the northern fastness of the Privation Mountains, a place of perpetual snow."

"How will you breech Craven's walls?"

"With your help and guidance, Mother. Craven is a mountain fortress with fierce warriors but weak walls."

"So you say," Suwraith replied. *"And what of my extra Plagues?"*

"Allow the Fan Lor Kum to feast on Craven's corpse, and within three years, in a place of safety, I can deliver the extra Plagues you need for Hammer. Were I to attempt to do all such work here, the Shylows would perpetually work to undo all we attempt. Or worse, the Ashokans, or some others, might learn of our presence and somehow sabotage our efforts."

Suwraith did not speak, seemingly lost in thought as the wind roared and danced about the shallow bowl of land where the Baels huddled. *"Yes. It is a good plan,"* She said. *"See to it. With your fine leadership, Craven shall easily be felled. And then with several seasons to rebuild the Fan Lor Kum..."* Thunder rumbled and Suwraith seemed to smile. It was something in Her voice and the racing clouds. *"The trinket will ease our passage, and the Fan Lor Kum will herald My dread arrival as Ashoka is ceased."*

The Bael might have smiled as well. "Two cities to kill rather than just one."

Her words spoken, Suwraith left, taking her shrieking and tearing gale with her as She soared into the heights. With Her absence, a thunderous silence settled over the bowl of land as the grit and dirt slowly fell back to the ground in wispy streams of dust. The Baels remained bent over until the last of Her lightning was no longer visible.

Several eucalyptus trees had been felled, their limbs denuded, and the sharp tangy smell of lemon pervaded the area.

Keemo nudged Rukh, nodding toward the Baels, a question in his eyes. "Now," he mouthed, asking if the Ashokans should attack.

Rukh shook his head. They were missing something. He didn't know what it was, but he needed the Baels to talk amongst one another. Perhaps then this nonsensical conversation he'd just heard might make sense. He urged the others to stillness. The Baels were stirring.

"It was a great risk you took," one of the Baels said to the general, a larger one and obviously important judging by his feathered horns. "If She were but slightly more sane, She would have seen through your ruse, and we would have all been fodder for the cookpot."

Rukh shared another confused glance with the others. What in the *unholy hells* was going on? The Bael general had lied to the Queen? Why? The Baels couldn't mean to betray their Mother, could they? It made no sense. Why would they? There was something potentially world changing going on here. He knew it. He could almost taste it. He urged the others to silence.

One of the other Baels, also important judging by his feathers, laughed. "I had to struggle to contain my laughter when She actually believed your Balant excrement about the 'fabled city' of Craven," he said with a chuckle. "My SarpanKum, you have giant, brass ones. And where did you even come up with that name?"

"But how could She not know there is no such city as Craven?" one of the younger Baels asked.

"Has She always been this…" another younger Bael spoke, searching for a word.

"Crazy," the chuckling Bael supplied.

"No. Evil."

The large Bael, the one who had initially cautioned the general, was the one who answered. "She is both insane and wicked and so much more," he said. "The question before us, however, is this: what do we do now?" He turned to the general.

"We do as I told Mother: we train for a winter campaign."

"Against a non-existent city?"

The general smiled. "Yes. And once we're in the mountains, marching on this non-existent city, we destroy the Plague," he said it as matter-of-factly as Rukh would have mentioned taking a walk through Jubilee Hills, as if the decision had already been made. "I understand avalanches are prevalent in the high mountain reaches."

"But, we would die as well," a younger Bael said hesitantly.

"Yes we would. Many of our brothers will perish," the large Bael said. "But it is a price worth paying. I, for one, will not have the death of Ashoka on my conscience. Not while I can act to prevent it."

The general nodded. "All of us will die at some point. It is a fact. We are not like Mother Lienna: unnatural and immortal. We are warriors in an army of evil, and our Queen thinks us slaves to do Her bidding. But we are not. Hume taught us what it means to be free. While She can end our lives, we do not have to live those lives in bondage to Her fears and insanity. We can choose who and what we will be. It was bad enough we had to destroy the caravan, but what She demands now...it is too much. Every SarpanKum since Hume Telrest first came to us and taught us of honor and our shared brotherhood has found a means to confound Mother's will." He searched around him, forcing all of the other Baels to meet his eyes. "I will *not* be the weak link who fails our unbroken chain of honor. We will yet redeem the Bael. I say it would be better to slit our wrists right here and now rather than raise tridents and chains against Ashoka."

"And the Humans...you are certain they are worth this?" one of the younger Baels asked, sounding doubtful.

"Yes. They are our brothers though they know it not," the high-ranking Bael who had been laughing said with a nod. "It is as Hume taught us: all who can reason must be counted as our brothers."

Many things Rukh might have expected to hear coming from the mouths of the Baels, but this was most definitely not one of them. He sat back in shock. The other Ashokans looked as stunned as he felt. It had to be some kind of trick. A lie. The Baels actively disobeyed Suwraith and hated Her? Impossible. And this talk of Hume...had he really gone to the Baels and taught them of honor, of devotion and brotherhood? He didn't believe it. Hume was the greatest of Kummas. He could *never* have felt kinship with the Baels. The very idea was sickening.

But then why had the Baels said all that they had? What was the point? The Ashokans were hidden, and no one knew they were here, listening in on the private conversations of the Chimera commanders. So, what did the Baels have to gain by speaking like this? At no time in Ashoka's long history of war with the Fan Lor Kum had the possibility of peace with the Chimeras ever been considered. Two thousand years of history didn't allow for it. The Baels were Humanity's enemy. They had no soul for compassion. They had amply demonstrated this simple fact over and over again.

Rukh growled in frustration. What to believe: a lifetime of learning, or this one strange and absurd conversation? And there the Baels still stood. Even now they continued to plan the most effective means of destroying Suwraith's Plague, the very one intended to help annihilate Ashoka.

Rukh shook his head, uncertain what to think.

"It has to be a trick," Farn whispered fiercely. "They can't mean what they're saying."

Brand clamped a hand over Farn's mouth, flicking his eyes at

Farn's shadow, briefly visible for a moment in the bright moonlight.

Rukh held his breath and tensed. The general had looked their way. Was the Bael aware of their presence? Things might get very interesting in a bad way if the horned beast knew of the Ashokans. A moment later, Rukh let out a relieved breath. The Bael commander was issuing orders and didn't spare another glance in their direction.

"Take the Tigons and Braids back to the army," the general said.

"And what of you?" the large Bael asked.

"I need a moment for prayer. Some silence away from the encampment."

"Do not stay too long out here by yourself, brother," the large Bael said, placing his hand on the general's shoulder. "The Hunters Flats is not a safe place for our kind."

"Is there anywhere in this world that is?" the general asked with a smile. At the larger Bael's frown, he relented. "I will be back shortly," he promised. "You'll see me within the hour."

The large Bael nodded, clapping the general on the shoulder. "I will hold you to keep your promise," he said.

Rukh held himself still as a statue as the Baels moved past the four of them. He poured concentration into his Blend, willing himself to fade into the grass beneath him, the rocks and stones around him, and the night sky above him. He sensed the others also focusing their Blends, holding preternaturally still. Thankfully, all of them were supplemented by Brand's greater skill.

Now would be the time to strike. The general was alone. They could kill the head of the Fan Lor Kum with a single Fireball. But would it be the right thing to do? Rukh couldn't believe he even had to ask. A half hour ago the question would not have even occurred to him. But now he was plagued by a haunting possibility: were the Baels really his enemy? The rest of the Fan Lor Kum, certainly, but the horned commanders...maybe not.

Farn signaled him, pointing to where the other Baels were swiftly departing. They were almost out of view. He gestured urgently toward the general, who knelt in the grass with his eyes closed and face raised to the sky.

"We'll never get a better chance," Farn whispered into Rukh's ear.

Rukh nodded. Farn was right. He raised his hand, readying a Fireball.

———————•◦•———————

"How in all the unholy hells do they know about us?" Jessira Grey asked, shocked by what the Baels and Suwraith had just discussed. She shook her head; still having trouble believing the Queen Bitch Herself had been here.

She and her brothers, Lure and Cedar, hunched down behind a large hummock of grass and dirt. It was not the best cover, but it had to do. There were some boulders on the far side of the bowl which would have served better, but there was no way to reach them without the risk of being spotted. And then the Queen had come, and all thoughts of edging closer to the Baels had been thrust aside. At that point, all she and her brothers cared about was simple survival.

While Suwraith spoke to Her Chimera pets, the three of them had spent the time huddled behind their hummock. It seemed quite small during Her fell presence, but either their prayers to Devesh must have worked, or their Blends had been good enough. Whatever the reason, Suwraith had not seen them for which they were grateful. With her departure, the dirt She had thrown into the air had slowly settled, covering the three of them in a film of gritty dust. The Sorrow Bringer had torn apart a nearby acacia tree, and a floral, orange smell permeated the air.

"Maybe it's a trick," Lure whispered.

"Some trick," Cedar replied with a scoff. "Somehow, they've learned of Stronghold, even if they have the name wrong, and think we're allied to Ashoka."

"Our people have to learn of this," Jessira said, her voice grim. "We've tracked the Chims long enough already. It's time to head home and report."

Lure nodded. "Jessira is right."

"I agree," Cedar said. "We'll head out, link up with cousin Court and hustle home."

Jessira shook her head. "I'd still like to know how they learned of us. After the attack on that Ashokan caravan, I thought for sure they'd head straight for Ashoka?"

"It doesn't matter," Lure said, his lips curled in a snarl. "How or what...they know. And they're coming."

"A full Plague," Jessira said, fear making a hollow pit in her stomach. "I doubt if even the Purebloods could handle that many."

"They could," Cedar replied. He sounded certain, although Jessira had her doubts. "They have a proper Oasis, remember?"

"What are they going on about now?" Jessira asked. The Baels were having a discussion, and since the general was no longer shouting, she couldn't hear what they were saying. She would have loved to listen in on their conversation. Maybe it had to do with training schedules and troop deployments or something along those lines. Even the smallest scrap of information could be of use. Jessira hissed in annoyance. "I need to get closer."

"There's no cover," Cedar warned. "You'd be found out in a heartbeat."

Jessira grinned. "I'm pretty damned good at Blending, lieutenant. Better than you two, anyhow," she said with false bravado, hoping her fear didn't show. "I can sit at the Bael's feet and play the pipes if I wanted."

Cedar poked his head over the hummock of grass and studied the Baels clustered no more than fifty feet from their huddled position. He looked at her with pursed lips before studying the Baels one more time. He turned to her. "Do it," he ordered.

"Linked Blends are more effective then a single Blend," Lure warned. "You sure you're up for doing this? We won't be able to see you or know what you're doing if you end up needing help."

Jessira nodded in understanding. By forming a Link, the three of them could combine their Blends and make them stronger. It was a skill she heard the Murans and Rahails didn't always bother with given their reputed ability to Blend so effectively on their own. She snorted. Right. Everything a Pureblood could do was always supposed to be better than what her own people could accomplish. She didn't believe it. The Purebloods weren't better than her people.

At any rate, without the Link, she would be on her own. She would be vulnerable. She knew it, and so did her brothers, but the risk was worth it. Stronghold needed the information.

She unstrapped her bow and quiver, seting them aside. She kept her sword and brace of knives before easing her way from behind the hummock of grass. She belly crawled across the ground. The heaped up pile of stones and boulders on the far side of the shallow vale was her target. If she could get to the rocks, she should be able to listen in to what the Baels were talking about. Fear had her tight and tense. The muscles in her shoulders and back began to cramp. She briefly paused to work out the stiffness, breathing out as much of her trepidation as she could. She moved forward again, slowly and carefully, holding to whatever minimal shade she could find and staying as downwind as possible of the Baels. Her Blend was good, but all it would take would be the slightest loss in concentration and the red-eyed bastards would have her. She silently mouthed a prayer to Devesh as she edged closer.

Soon enough, she was able to hear bits and pieces of their conversation. Just snippets here and there, but nothing she could really understand. The words grew clearer as she slithered closer. What she heard nearly caused her to gasp in disbelief.

The Baels knew nothing of her city. Their general had fabricated the entire story, spinning a load of lies to his Mother; which explained his use of the name Craven. And Suwraith had been none the wiser. Jessira frowned. How could the Queen not know when she was being lied to by Her own creations?

Jessira's brow furrowed in further bewilderment. What was this about Hume? Everyone honored the man; even her own people who wanted as little to do with anything Pureblood as possible. Hume was the one exception. Beyond his status as the greatest warrior in Arisan history, Hume Telrest had also been openhearted enough to love and accept Jessira's kind, which was much more important as far as Jessira was concerned. Had his charity been great enough to extend to the Baels? Jessira grimaced. It's what the Baels were saying, but she thought it more likely to be some devious Chimera trick. It was simply too good to be true, which meant she would believe a horse could stand and talk before she trusted a word from the black-horned bastards. The Baels had hunted Humanity across all corners of Arisa for over six hundred years. To have them suddenly voice honor to Hume and profess brotherhood with their foes was a leap well past believability. It was insane.

Jessira crept closer to the boulders. She couldn't be hearing right. The Bael general was saying something about decimating his army within the icy spires of the Privations. Now *that* was definitely too good to be true. She inched further. She was only about twenty feet from the boulders when the Baels began moving out, their meeting apparently ended.

Jessira's heart hit her throat, and her eyes widened in sudden panic. Suwraith's spit! They were coming her way. She sidled as quickly as she dared to the edge of their path and prayed for safety.

She prayed to Devesh and to his greatest servants, the First Mother and First Father. She knew one day They would come again and walk the hills of Arisa, and when They did, They would end Suwraith's tyranny and the evil of Casteism. Right now, none of that mattered. All she prayed for was Their protection.

Focused and fearful, she eyed the line of Baels as more than two score of the red-eyed beasts walked by, some close enough for her to reach out and touch. She held her breath as they strode away, only letting it out, slowly, silently, after they had passed from view. The general had remained behind. Maybe he had something more to do? And maybe she and her brothers could take him out. She glanced to the rocks. Almost there. She crouched on the balls of her feet and made her way toward them.

She smiled in relief as she approached. Only a few feet more, and she could unBlend and signal her brothers. She realized her mistake an instant too late.

Her eyes widened in shock as a Blend, deeper and richer than any she had ever encountered suddenly Linked with her own.

At the same time, a hand clamped across her mouth, muffling any noise. A voice whispered in her ear. "Be silent," it ordered. She was held in a grip of iron.

She twisted and saw him. He was Kumma, and he had three companions. Two other Kummas and a Rahail. All of them were holding Blends. Impossible.

First Father! What had she fallen into?

CHAPTER TEN
A BANEFUL COMPLEXITY

Strike with merciless swiftness and ensure your survival.
Hold your blow and you may learn wisdom. Or you may earn a fool's death.

~Kumma aphorism

Rukh's grip loosened as he stared in puzzlement at the girl he was holding. Who was she, and what was she doing alone out here? She was equipped like a warrior, wearing camouflaged clothing and even had a short sword and a brace of knives strapped to her waist. He looked closer, and his confusion deepened. She had the emerald eyes of a Muran, the honey-brown hair of a Rahail, and the delicate features and red-golden skin of a Cherid. She was like no woman he had ever seen before.

"What in the unholy hells," Keemo whispered. "Where did she come from?"

"And what is she?" Brand whispered. "She looks like…"

"Let me go," the girl whispered furiously after working Rukh's hand off her mouth. "I've done nothing to you."

A shock, like lightning, raced through Rukh, and his blood ran cold. On a night of surprises, this one was just about as startling as all the others. He knew what she was. Words from childhood lessons came to him as he struggled to hold back his sudden disgust and anger. She was a ghrina, a child of two Castes. She was an unholy abomination, warned against by the First Mother and First Father in *The Word and the Deed.*

But her presence here should have been impossible. A ghrina and its parents were immediately evicted from a city as soon as they were discovered, even those as young as a newborn. It was a death sentence. No one could survive the Wildness. Between the Queen, her Chimeras, and the brutality of the wilderness itself, anyone caught out alone beyond the safety of an Oasis would quickly die. Or so everyone had always assumed.

Obviously, their assumptions had been wrong. Some ghrinas must have managed to survive and live on in the Wildness. The proof of this disturbing truth sat before him: an adult ghrina, living, breathing, and healthy.

Rukh didn't know what to do. Should he simply kill her out of hand? It was what might have been done back in Ashoka. Death was supposed to be a ghrina's proper punishment, but it seemed so barbaric. He growled low in frustration. This was the last thing he needed to worry about right now.

He shook his head in frustration.

And to think several months ago, he thought he had the world figured out: there were the Castes and the cities and there was Suwraith and her hordes. Life was simple, and he liked it that way. Now...he sighed as he came to a decision. He couldn't kill the girl, not yet anyway, and he wasn't sure if doing so would even be moral, no matter what *The Word and the Deed* commanded. If nothing else, he had to learn more about her and where she came from.

"I'm afraid we can't let you go miss," Rukh said. He gestured to the motionless Bael general who was praying or something. "He'd kill you, eat you up, and pick his teeth with your bones. And if you're lucky, in that order."

The girl snorted in derision. "My name isn't *miss*, and the Chim out there would have to catch me first. I don't think he can."

"I caught you," Rukh reminded her.

She stared at him, taken aback by either fear or surprise. A moment later, she struggled anew against his grip. "Let me go. You have no right to hold me," she said.

Rukh shook his head at the girl's misplaced confidence. Women weren't weak. That went without saying. His mother was about as indomitable an individual as he could think to name. But women were also to be sheltered and protected. They were the hope of Humanity, the only ones able to bear the next generation. To put them unnecessarily at risk in the Wildness was folly beyond measure.

The ghrinas – Rukh doubted she was the only one of her kind – didn't seem to care as much about their women. Rukh wondered what it might mean for what they were as a people to put their women in danger like this. Who were they, and where did they live? None of it mattered – not now anyway – but he was curious. Or maybe he was reading this all wrong. Maybe this girl was a criminal and running from her own kind. But then why was she dressed as a warrior, and why had she been spying on the Baels? She looked and acted like a scout, not a criminal. He glanced at her again, taking in more details. Well, she wasn't a girl. In fact, she looked to be about his age, and she was most definitely a woman. A strange looking ghrina woman but somehow compelling. She might even be considered beautiful if not for her oddly mismatched features.

He grimaced in abhorrence at the idea, but something in his face or posture must have given away his thoughts. She noticed, and her eyes were suddenly hot and full of anger. "That's right. I'm a ghrina, an abomination. Take a good look."

Rukh didn't bother answering. He was still angry with himself. He had thought the ghrina was beautiful? Disgusting.

"We should…" Farn began, a look of hatred on his face as he stared at the woman.

"No," Rukh ordered.

Farn wanted to kill the woman. He had no qualms about the matter. Rukh could see the urgent desire in his eyes. His cousin had always been more of a reactionary, and with all the sudden changes pushed onto him; he could see Farn reaching his breaking point. But right now he needed his cousin to hold on a little longer. They could always kill the ghrina later, although Rukh hoped it wouldn't have to come to that.

But..." Farn protested.

"I said no." Rukh cut him off, his voice as hard as the spidergrass of his sword. "Not now. We don't have time for it anyway." He pointed to the Bael, still praying. What in the unholy hells could a Chim pray for anyway? "First, we deal with the Bael. Then her."

Farn simmered down into an unhappy silence.

"Burn the Chim from a distance," Brand urged.

"I want to talk to him first," Rukh said.

"What!" Keemo said, in a strangled voice. "Rukh, no..."

"I have to understand..."

The woman took advantage of his inattention and nearly freed herself. Suwraith's spit! The stupid ghrina would give all of them away. Rukh's Blend was adequate at best, but not good enough to disguise the noises she was making.

"I've got it," Brand said. "I'm Linked with her, remember?"

Rukh exhaled in relief. He'd forgotten. Rukh nodded 'thanks', grateful for Brand's help. The woman still struggled, though, and that had to stop. Rukh put her in a body lock, his legs cinched tight around her waist with one foot tucked behind a knee. His right arm snaked under her chin, and he had her in a chokehold as well. "Don't," he warned. "I'll put you to sleep if I have to."

She slowly and resentfully subsided.

"If you've been here as long as I suspect you have, you probably heard everything the Baels said. I need to understand what they meant, and I think you want to know too." Rukh carefully relaxed his grip. "Now, I'm going to release you to my friend over there." He gestured to Keemo. "Don't try to run, and I'll tell you everything the Bael tells me. And then you can tell it to your ghrina commander over there by that little hummock of grass."

The last had been a guess, but judging by the woman's open-eyed expression of shock, it had been a good one. "How did you…who are you?" she asked in a furious whisper. "You're Kummas, but you can Blend."

"We're men you don't want to mess with. Now, shut up." Thankfully, the woman stayed quiet and still, even if she looked like she wanted to run him through with her sword.

Brand gave Rukh a look of uncertainty. "How did you know she wasn't alone? I can barely sense anything," he said. "After Suwraith, the ground around here…it's like someone shouting in my ear. I can't feel Blends like I normally can. I could barely tell the girl was there until she was right on top of us."

"It was a guess. If she had backup, I figured they would have to be nearby. They're probably all ghrina like her, and the only other place around here a person could hide is behind that little hillock." He glanced at the woman. "So what do you say to my offer?"

She considered his proposal, frowning angry murder the entire time before reluctantly nodding. "Fine. But two things first. Stop calling me ghrina. We're OutCastes. And second, let go of me. I won't be wrapped up like fried fish in paper. I'll wait here quietly without someone's thick hands all over me. And I won't run or signal my unit. On my honor."

Rukh briefly wondered what she meant by fried fish in a paper. It sounded unappetizing. He shrugged. A mystery for another time. At least she sounded sincere about not running away. "Agreed," he said, accepting her terms.

With that, he released her and watched as she scooted away from him and the other Ashokans, but at least she remained behind the rocks.

Rukh looked at Farn, who eyed the ghrina distastefully. "Remember, nothing happens to her," he reminded his cousin.

Farn eventually nodded before moving his angry gaze away from the woman, turning it toward the Bael instead. "Are you sure about this, Rukh? You really want to talk to him?"

"If I can. If he doesn't attack, then I won't have to kill him…"

The woman snorted in derision. "Think much of yourself?"

"You have something to say?" Rukh asked, annoyed by her mocking tone.

"You four are pretty young. I'm guessing this is your first time out in the Wildness, right? *Virgins* is how you Purebloods put it, I think." She smirked as they shifted uncomfortably. "You'll find Baels, or even Tigons for that matter, aren't as easy to kill as you seem to think."

"We could kill him from here if we wanted," Farn growled.

She rolled her eyes. "Right. The vaunted Kumma Fireballs," she said, clearly disbelieving them. "But if you close with him, you lose the advantage of distance, and in close quarters, he'll have you. You'll be easy meat."

"Then there will be one less of us you need to worry about," Rukh snapped.

He stood slowly, keeping his Blend in place as he stalked the Bael on silent feet. He slid to the general's side, leaving Farn a clear shot with a Fireball if need be.

As far as he knew, other than in the heat of battle, no one had ever been this close to one of the creatures. The Bael kneeled on heavy knees and sat back on his hocks. The beast's legs ended in wide, bovine hooves. Standing, he would be eight feet tall and full of heavily muscled fury. His horns, each about three feet long and several inches thick at the base, were curved slightly. They faced forward at the tip and were wreathed with a number of feathers, the most prominent of which were the red ones, proclaiming his position as general. His bristly tail with its terminal tuft of hair occasionally switched at the flies buzzing about him. The Bael was thickly wrinkled in places, especially the joints, and his tough, black skin was covered in a dense coat of short, coarse, black fur. It twitched at times to shake off the same flies. His hands were massive, with thick nail-less fingers wrapped firmly around his trident. His only garments were a crossed-leather harness and breechcloth from which his whip was hung. His red eyes were closed, and he breathed slowly and steadily, as if meditating. A heavy scent, like musk and cut grass, lingered about him. But the beast didn't stink – not like the manure smell of a cow.

Rukh eased his sword from its scabbard, aiming it at the Bael's neck. He let the Blend fall away and cleared his throat.

The general slowly lowered his closed-eyed gaze from the sky and looked at Rukh. He blinked, but otherwise evinced no surprise. His lips pulled back into a smile, revealing teeth disturbingly Human in appearance, especially considering his bull-like face. The Bael let go of his trident, letting it fall to the side as he bowed his head. "My life is yours, brother," he said, his voice carrying and commanding. "Do with it as you wish, but I will not fight you."

Rukh kept his face still, hiding the surprise he felt. He had expected the Chimera commander to roar with rage and charge, trident leveled and chained whip aflame. Not this meek surrender.

In just about any other instance, Rukh might have been moved to pity. Had it been a person, even someone he hated, bowing down and asking for mercy, he would have granted it. But the Baels were different. They had too much blood on their hands. Again and again, history described the evil of the red-eyed bastards and their undying hatred for Humanity, a hatred returned in fullness. Even now, despite his earlier words to his cousins and Brand, the pent up desire to kill the Bael, the commander who had ordered the death of all his friends and brothers on the caravan, ate at Rukh's soul. It overwhelmed his desire for any knowledge the beast might give him. Death would be too good for the creature.

His grip tightened, and he prepared the killing stroke.

"Thirty Tigons approach from the south," the Bael said, softly. "They have seen you already. Stand and fight with me, brother."

Rukh didn't bother answering. Fight alongside a Bael? He'd rather burn in the unholy hells of Suwraith's pit.

Just then, fast approaching from behind him came the sound of claws and hardened feet tearing at the ground along with hoarse cries and roars. Fragging hell. The Bael hadn't been lying. The damn Tigons really *were* coming up fast.

Rukh shifted position, moving to place the general between him and the onrushing Chimeras. He Blended. He felt a Link brush against his mind, and he locked in on it. The world blurred briefly, as he Linked with Brand and the others. He could see them again. They had stalked closer, remaining hidden as they took up positions behind and beside him.

"Stay Blended," Rukh commanded. "Unleash Fireballs as soon as they are in range." He glanced back at the rocks. "Where's the woman?"

"The ghrina hides behind the boulders," Farn said, contempt lacing his voice.

"Well, considering you wanted to kill her on sight, it's probably not a bad decision," Brand muttered.

Rukh glanced at the general, who still kneeled, trident still lying on the ground. "Will you fight alongside me?" he asked, flickering back into view as he let go his Blend.

The general smiled. "If you allow it. It would be my undying honor, something of which I've dreamed since my Nanna taught me in the crèche."

Rukh cursed. More Devesh-damned mysteries. The Baels had nannas? He thought the Baels were born of the dimwitted Bovars, Suwraith's beasts of burden. Was the Bael saying the Bovars could talk? He exhaled in frustration. Leave it be.

The Tigons had arrived. They stumbled to an uncertain halt, their clawed feet digging into the ground. Their ears, tented and peaked, twitched as they shuffled about nervously. Their fur – some long, some short – varied in color and patterns with everything from a gold to a tabby to a pure white and black. All were tall, taller than a Kumma, but stout through the chest and sinewy and lean through their hocked legs. Their hands, similarly clawed like their feet, clenched and unclenched, although most were empty of weapons for now. That would likely change very shortly. Their wide, blunted faces wore identical looks of hunger as their vertically slitted eyes expanded as they took in the sight of Rukh standing next to the SarpanKum.

The general stood, taking up his trident, and Rukh quickly moved beyond the circle of his reach.

The lead Tigon stepped forward. He was spotted in yellow and black rosettes, like a jaguar. Though he must have been braver than his brethren, he was no less confused. "Why not kill Human?" he asked. "Mother kill all them. Vermin."

Rukh could barely understand the creature. His mouth, full of daggered teeth, wasn't meant for speech.

"Mother has a special role for this one. He will be the means to our victory over Ashoka."

Rukh forced himself not to look at the Bael. Once more the creature was lying, this time to his own warriors. But, what was his ultimate ploy? Surely he and the other Baels hadn't been serious with all their talk about Hume and all the rest?

"We go Craven," the Tigon said, sounding even more confused. "Li-Reg said."

"After Craven," the Bael replied smoothly.

The Tigon lifted his snout to the air, seemingly tasting it. His jaguar-like visage lowered as his gaze came to rest upon the general. The Tigon's ears flattened and he snarled. "Another Human nearby?" He turned to face the rocks. "Hiding."

Suwraith's spit. The Chim must have seen through the ghrina's Blend. Well, there went that. Rukh rolled his shoulders, loosening them. Thirty Tigons against three Kummas and a Rahail. Not great odds, but possible, especially if the Bael really did help them out.

"Ready the Quad," he whispered to the others.

The first Tigon again tasted the air. "Li-Dirge, what means this?"

"It means you should remember who commands."

"Mother commands. She hate Humans. Not save them."

The Tigons were working themselves into a killing fury. Rukh could tell it, and apparently the general could as well.

The Bael smiled as he leveled his trident. "There are greater mysteries in this world, oh foolish kitten, than your dim and empty head could ever hope to comprehend." The smile faded and a look of grim purpose stole over him. "Remember who I am. I am the SarpanKum, chosen by Mother Herself! Who are you to gainsay Her will? Stand down!"

The Tigons glanced at one another, their earlier anger fading away as they shuffled about in uncertainty.

"Return to the encampment and forget all you saw here. Tell no one," the Bael barked, his voice a whiplash command. "Go!"

Long years of discipline and habit took hold. The Tigons turned and began to shuffle away. The general appeared to have convinced the cats to disengage, and Rukh relaxed, but his grip upon his sword remained firm.

As the Tigons retreated to the south, a Fireball exploded into their midst, and all became chaos.

Rukh spared a disbelieving glance at Farn, who was no longer

Blended. It had been him. They'd been so close to walking out of this without a fight. Fragging idiot! Now, one or all of them might die here tonight.

"Form the Quad!" Rukh shouted.

The Tigons were on them before they could get off more than another few Fireballs.

———■●■———

J essira peered over the small boulder behind which she hid, watching as the Kumma leader, the one named Rukh, steadily advanced on the Bael. She hated to admit it, but the man was brave. Foolish, but brave.

Kummas were supposed to be the foremost warriors of Arisa, and they might be, although Jessira figured their supposed skill was probably more than a little exaggerated – nobody could be *that* good. Regardless of their reputation, they sure weren't bright. The best way to handle a Bael was with an arrow from a distance, preferably a very long distance. Trying to take one on with a sword was madness, a guaranteed trip to the funeral pyre.

Although the other Purebloods didn't look worried. They must be either too stupid or too ignorant to know any better. It might even be their first battle. She rolled her eyes, feeling contempt for the stupid jackholes. At least they were alert and wary, even if nothing in their faces or stances indicated concern for their leader. Or maybe they just hated him. She glanced at the one who made her blood run cold, the one who looked at her as if she were a maggot in his meal. He looked tense, and his hand was raised. It glowed dimly.

Ah! So the stories about Fireballs were true! In that case, their leader might be able to escape his idiotic decision with nothing worse than a singeing, depending on the aim of his fellow Kummas.

Jessira's eyes narrowed, and she returned her attention to the Bael. Something was happening. The Bael had dropped his trident and had bowed his head to the Kumma leader. She couldn't hear clearly, but it sounded as if the general had called the Kumma his brother and had offered his life to him. That couldn't be right. She didn't believe the Baels' bilge water from earlier about brotherhood with Humanity and taking instruction from Hume. They had been lying for some reason. The only Humans the Chims didn't automatically kill were those who chose servitude under Suwraith.

Her eyes widened with sudden recognition.

What did she know of these men? They were far out in the Wildness, in the Hunters Flats, a place she knew Purebloods only traversed if part of a large group of warriors. The nearest such caravan had been ambushed in the foothills of the Privation Mountains a few weeks back. So then how were these men here alone within the Hunters Flats and meeting with Baels?

What if these men were of the Sil Lor Kum? It made sense. Kummas who could Blend. The Human followers of the Sorrow Bringer were said to have powers, gifts given to them by Suwraith and possessed by no one else.

Jessira looked at the others in sudden revulsion as a knotted bramble of fear curled in her stomach. What had she gotten herself into? Baels who lied to the Queen? Men who might be Sil Lor Kum? And a plan meant to destroy a city named Craven, a place that might or might not be her own home of Stronghold? She had to get free. Her brothers had to know what they faced. She held back a sudden urge to jump and race away. It wouldn't have worked, and she knew it. More likely, she would have been quickly recaptured, either by these men or the Chimeras or both.

Patience was required. She would have to wait for the proper moment. She turned slightly in order to better study the men holding her. Good. None of them were watching her. Despite her earlier vow to the Kumma leader, she didn't feel beholden to it; not if he was Sil Lor Kum. First chance to run, she would take it.

A shocked hiss from the Rahail drew her attention back to the Bael and the Kumma. Rukh had stepped behind the general.

Jessira frowned. Where had all the Tigons come from?

She watched as the other three – the two Kummas and the Rahail – left the shelter of the boulders and slowly advanced, taking up positions next to and behind their leader. She remained Linked to their Blends and watched as all held up hands that glowed.

Jessira sat back on her heels.

So. The Rahail had the gifts of a Kumma.

It was a certainty then. These men *were* Sil Lor Kum. Time to go. She prepared to crawl back to her brothers when a scream rent the air, followed by an explosion.

She froze in place and risked a look over the boulders. Her eyes widened.

The Tigons were attacking their general. And the Purebloods fought with him, which meant they would all be dead soon. The Tigons were too tough. They were best faced by a large group of warriors, hopefully with a sizeable advantage in numbers. The Purebloods must not have been taught that lesson. They had waded straight into the heart of the fight, to where the Tigons were massed most thickly. They were fearless, she had to admit, but courage alone wouldn't save them. They would all be dead inside of…her thoughts broke apart as details of the battle took shape.

"Holy Father," Jessira murmured in awe.

The Rahail was good. Before tonight, she would have said he was as good as anyone she'd ever seen, even her brother Cedar, one of the finest warriors in Stronghold, but the Kummas were something else entirely. They could *fight*. Their movements were liquid. They flowed across the ground, dancing with a graceful, eye-blurring speed and precision. Their technique was perfect, and they utterly devastated the Tigons. Wherever they went, the Chimeras fell.

And they weren't deadly with just their swords. Fireballs screamed through the air, killing and maiming the Tigons, decimating their numbers.

It seemed the Kummas were everything the legends said. Jessira was suddenly glad she and her brothers hadn't somehow stumbled upon these men. She would never have wanted to face them in battle.

In moments, nearly all of the Tigons were either dead or dying. Only a few were left standing. Three Chimeras encircled the leader of the Kummas, Rukh, and his men weren't close enough to offer him support. He never needed it. The Kumma took the fight to the Tigons, and in the space of three breaths, all three of the creatures were down and dead.

It had been a slash across the throat of one Chim before the beast could even get his blade up. A hamstring cut to another followed by the decapitation of the third. The Kumma had returned to the disabled Tigon. A straight thrust through the beast's armor and into its heart and the battle was over. All three blows had been perfectly placed and delivered with a speed and power that Jessira had never believed possible.

"Unholy hells, they're good, aren't they?" Lure asked, suddenly appearing at her side as he crouched down next to her.

Jessira was momentarily startled but quickly regained her composure.

The Purebloods were the deadliest fighters Jessira had ever seen, but now wasn't the time to discuss or admire their skill. They might very well be the enemy of all Humanity. At the least, they were Purebloods, which meant they were certainly the enemy of her kind, the OutCaste. No matter how it was measured, they sure weren't friends, not by a long sight. She and her brothers had to flee if they wanted to get out of this situation alive. Stronghold needed to learn what they had discovered.

Jessira urged Lure into motion, back toward Cedar, who still huddled behind the hummock. "Move. We have to get out of here," she said to her older brother when they reached his side.

"Why?"

"The Purebloods...I think they might be Sil Lor Kum," Jessira said, quickly explaining her reasoning. "If we don't back our butts out of here right now, we might not ever be able to. We can't hide. The Rahail can sense our Blends better than we can. And you just saw what the Kummas are capable of."

Cedar's mouth thinned into a tight-lipped line of worry as he quickly considered her words. "Let's go," he said. "Don't worry about being quiet. Just run. Swift and silent."

They slipped away into the night, moving as quickly and quietly as their Linked Blends would allow.

No more than several hundred yards from the shallow vale where four Purebloods had crushed thirty Tigons, they ran into a nest of Ur-Fels, spread out along their path. The creatures, each one the size of a large hound had a fox-like appearance with triangular ears, narrow noses, and bushed tails. The Chims sniffed the air. They couldn't see the Strongholders, not through a Blend, but they could sense powerful emotions such as fear and excitement, both of which Jessira knew she and her brothers exuded like cologne.

Cedar signaled a different direction, and just as they were about to go, a strange call, deep and carrying, echoed across the night sky.

The Ur-Fels yipped and yammered and bounded away in the direction of the cry.

Jessira exhaled in relief.

They broke into a run, but had taken no more than a few dozen steps when they almost ran full on into a troop of Baels – ten of them – looming out of the darkness like a dark, ugly fog.

Jessira silently swore, hoping against hope that somehow the Chimeras hadn't heard the grass tear as she and her brothers had come to a stumbling standstill. She prayed as fervently as she ever had. *Please let the Blends hold. Please let them pass us by.*

For a moment the world was still except for the creak of the leather harnesses worn by the Baels as well as the jangling of the feathers from their horns. The beasts smelled of hay, cut grass, and musk. They breathed heavily as if they had been running.

The world snapped back into motion.

"Three Humans out for a stroll on this dimly lit night, so near our encampment," one of them said sounding amused. He was a huge brute, one of those from earlier, with Suwraith.

Icy fingers clutched at Jessira's heart. She cursed their bad luck. Why did the Baels have to be right here and right now? Why hadn't they returned to their camp as their general had ordered? She sought an escape, looking for any place to hide or run, but all paths before them and to the sides were blocked. Perhaps they could turn around and race back in the direction from which they had come. Baels were slow, and Humans were fast – especially scouts. The Chimeras knew they were nearby, but they probably didn't know *exactly* where. She and her brothers were still Blended after all. They could...

A whipcrack from one of the barbed, metal whips the Baels favored snapped less than a foot from Jessira's head. There went that plan.

"UnBlend," the huge Bael ordered. "And sheathe your weapons. We won't kill you yet, but try to flee, and we'll snap your necks before you take another step."

Cedar flickered into view, causing a few of the Baels to mutter and gesture, pointing him out. Jessira followed her brother's lead, as did Lure, but she still furtively cast about, searching everywhere for a means to escape. "What do you intend to do with us?" Cedar asked.

"Nothing too horrible. Maybe the cookpot," the large one said with a laugh.

"We aren't moving a step until we know what's..."

"You are in no position to make demands, Human," the Bael

snapped, cutting him off. "Come with us and maybe live. Stay here and you'll die. Either way, I care not. A patrol of Ur-Fels heads this way. They can't see through your Blends, but they can sense when emotions run high and hot, and right now, your fear runs like lava down a mountainside." The big Bael stepped back. "Your choice, but you should understand this: Mother's other children are not as hospitable as we." His lips pulled back into a menacing grin, exposing flat, white teeth.

Jessira kept her breathing easy and steady. It wasn't time to panic yet, but it was close. Stay alive. It was the only thing that mattered.

Cedar reluctantly accepted the big Bael's offer, and Jessira and her brothers were quickly surrounded and marched back in the direction of the shallow bowl of land from where they had come. When they arrived, the general and the Purebloods stood amongst the scattered corpses of the Tigon dead. The ground was slick; red and puddled in places with blood.

She noticed the Rahail had a bad cut on his bicep. It might be through muscle, which was a hard injury to recover from. The crueler Kumma was also hurt, and his sword arm hung limply at his side, obviously broken, and one eye was blackened. Good. She had no pity for those who hated her. The shorter, stockier Kumma had a nasty slice across his hip and a stab through the meat of his thigh. He limped about in obvious pain. As for their leader, Rukh, even he was injured. He looked like he was having trouble breathing and he held his arm protectively against the side of his chest. He probably had a broken rib.

All of them were covered in gore and blood, looking like they had waded through the worst parts of a slaughterhouse. The place smelled like one, too. The prior clean scent of acacia and eucalyptus was overwhelmed by the stench of shit, piss, and blood. It was stomach-turning.

"I found these morsels wandering all alone in the night," the large Bael said as he stepped into the firelight. He gestured, and Jessira and her brothers were shoved forward.

"And I take it, Li-Reg, they came with you because of your legendary powers of persuasion? It had nothing to do with threats?" the Bael general asked, a laughing tone in his voice.

The larger Bael's lips twitched, but he didn't smile. "On my honor, Li-Dirge, I have been nothing but a gracious host. Although..." his lips quirked into a grin, "...I might have implied deadly harm would be inflicted upon them if they didn't accompany me."

The general snorted in amusement. "Well enough, Reg. The Ur-Fels would have found them before they could have made good their escape."

The large Bael looked at the dead Tigons. "What happened here?"

"A couple of foolish claws decided to countermand our orders."

"Brainless cats," Li-Reg muttered. "Wheresoever Mother appears, the Tigons follow, considering it a holy site and one worthy of a pilgrimage."

Jessira wasn't sure if the Bael called Reg was joking or not, but he seemed to be earnest.

"And who are these individuals," the general asked. "Have you learned?"

"Not yet," said the large Bael. "We kept them silent until we could speak in privacy."

The general nodded. "Send someone to tell the Ur-Fels to stand down."

"It is already done."

"Good. Then gather a detail and clean up this mess," the general said, indicating the Tigon corpses. He didn't bother to see how his order was carried out as he turned to Jessira and her brothers. "The Ashokans are known to me now."

Ashokans? Had they been part of the destroyed caravan?

The general glanced at Rukh. "Thankfully, they chose to spare my life until they heard me out. What of you, though? Who are you?"

"We have nothing to say to you," Cedar said. "Or to your Sil Lor Kum pets," he spat toward the Purebloods.

Of course, it had to be Farn who had to take a threatening step toward them.

What a prick.

"Why would you think we're Sil Lor Kum?" Rukh asked. Jessira noticed the sudden tension in his bearing. "And what are all these Baels doing here?" He glanced at the general. "You should answer quickly."

The Pureblood looked ready to explode into action, injury or no, as did the other Ashokans.

Reg looked to his general, who gave him leave to answer. "The Ur-Fel nests nearby must have sensed the death of the Tigons. They were out in force. I've sent word for them to return to their dens. If we hadn't rounded up your friends when we did, they would likely have been caught."

Rukh looked at Jessira. "Is this true?"

She nodded reluctantly. It felt too much like ceding authority to him.

"We don't need your protection," Cedar said. "We need nothing from the Sil Lor Kum."

Rukh turned to him, a deadly earnestness in his face. "Two times now you've called us that. If this was Ashoka, I'd have already handed you your head." He never raised his voice, but Jessira heard the chill warning in his words.

"And what? I'm supposed to be afraid of you? The big, bad Kumma? I'll cross swords with any of you fraggers," Cedar said. "I'm not afraid to die. The greater death is failing to fight and give quarter to evil."

"You'll want to be careful, or you'll find yourself facing death of a more certain kind," Rukh replied, his voice flat.

Cedar didn't back down, meeting him glare for glare and not giving an inch.

Rukh's hand slid to his sword.

"For the sake of sanity! Leave off, Cedar," Jessira said, pulling her brother back. Her brother was good, but broken rib or no; he wasn't anywhere close to the Kumma's level. "We believe you Ashokans are Sil Lor Kum because you cavort with the Chimeras..."

"We do no such thing!" Keemo interrupted. "How dare you!"

Jessira turned to him. "Then explain *his...*" she nodded to Rukh "...brotherly conversation with their general. You call us ghrina, but at least we don't treat with Humanity's enemies."

"You are Humanity's enemies," Farn muttered.

"Leave off," Rukh said in a tired voice to Farn before turning back to Jessira. "It was curiosity," he continued. "I needed information on where the Plague was staging and what was going on between the Baels and their Queen." Rukh glanced at the Chim commander. "After he helped with the Tigons, the general had an interesting story to tell. All I did was hear him out."

"And what of your abilities?" Cedar asked. "You can Blend. Only Murans and Rahails can do that. We know how strict you Purebloods are with your Talents. If anyone from any other Caste could do as a Muran or a Rahail, you'd think them no better than a ghrina."

"We aren't ghrinas," Keemo said. "We're naajas. We're Tainted."

"But we weren't made so at birth or by choice," Farn said, glaring at Cedar. "Bad luck sealed our fate."

Rukh glanced at the taller Kumma and shook his head, looking disappointed. "It happened when our caravan was pinned against a cliff. The three of us..." – he indicated the other Kummas – "...formed a Triad. Somehow, Brand was drawn into it and we became a Quad. I never even knew something like that was possible."

"But it happened," Brand said. "And now we can all do the same things. The Kummas can Blend, and I can throw Fireballs."

It was a nice story – although Jessira had no idea what they meant by Triads and Quads – but it was just too neat and tidy, just like everything else she'd heard tonight.

"A pretty explanation," Cedar said, apparently disbelieving as well. "But in *our* histories, Purebloods do not suffer those whom they label ghrinas or naajas."

Rukh nodded. "And we will likely be expelled once the city fathers learn what we can do."

"We may get marked with the Slash of Iniquity," Keemo said. "But we are Kummas."

"And Kummas serve," Farn said, drawing himself up proudly. "We will protect Ashoka even though our lives there are ended. We know our duty."

"And this Rahail feels no differently," Brand added.

Their words rang true, and Jessira found herself confused and conflicted. She actually *wanted* to believe them, and she hated her nascent compassion. While the Purebloods hadn't killed her out of hand when they had captured her, murder *had* been in their hearts. She had seen it in their eyes. Jessira had been moments from death, and she still wasn't sure why their leader, Rukh, had allowed her to live. It made no sense because there was a simple truth to her world: Purebloods, whether they were Sil Lor Kum or not, hated the OutCastes. According to the dictates of *The Word and the Deed*, a ghrina's just punishment was death.

"Your story explains your abilities, but not why you have sought alliance with the Baels," Cedar said, obviously still holding onto his own suspicions.

"We made no alliance. We seek none either," Rukh replied. "We came to kill the Baels. All of them if possible."

Lure openly laughed in derision. "Unbelievable. You Purebloods and your arrogance. There were fifty of the red-eyed bastards." He glanced about upon hearing the unhappy mutterings of the Baels, meeting their challenging stares with an unyielding one of his own. "I should apologize for what I said? After what your kind have done to Humanity for two millennia?" He snorted in derision. "You're lucky I don't call you worse."

While Jessira wanted to cheer Lure's words, she also wanted to slap her younger brother and tell him to shut it. A smart warrior knew when to keep silent, and a smarter warrior knew to never poke the bear. Lure needed that instruction. "They took thirty Tigons without loss," she reminded her younger brother.

Lure's mouth snapped shut.

"We wouldn't have gotten all of them," Rukh said, "but then we didn't expect to. If we took out maybe twenty…"

"Twenty-five," the general said. "With your presence, I would guess twenty-five of us might have been felled."

Rukh shrugged. "Fine. More importantly, out of those twenty-five, the first to die would have been those with the most feathers: the senior commanders. After that, we'd have melted into the night and waited for a chance to hit them again."

"And what stayed your hand?" Cedar asked.

Rukh's lips quirked into a grin – a surprisingly winsome and boyish smile, Jessira was annoyed to note. "Well…The Queen showed up. You might have noticed. We listened to their conversation, but none of it made any sense, and I hate it when things don't make sense." He shrugged again. "Then the general's…"

"Li-Dirge," the Bael commander corrected. "I am known as Li-Dirge or simply as Dirge."

"Then Dirge helped us kill the Tigons, and told us a story to make everything else we've learned tonight sound sane."

Jessira turned to face the Bael general, wondering what he could have said to convince an Ashokan not to split him on the spot?

Unless, of course, the Ashokan was Sil Lor Kum. She asked as much, turning to face Rukh.

"We are not Sil Lor Kum!" Rukh growled. "Hear Dirge out for yourself. And the fact the three of you still live when the Baels had you dead to rights tells me maybe there is something to his story after all."

She and her brothers fell silent as they considered the Kumma's words.

Finally, Cedar grunted. "Tell us what you told him," he said to Li-Dirge.

The Bael general sighed. "Certainly. But perhaps we can sit? I've been standing since lunch."

"I think we can all use some time off our feet," Rukh said.

"Can you Heal their injuries?" Cedar suddenly asked of Lure, nodding toward the Ashokans.

Jessira turned to her older brother in surprise. What was he up to?

"Only Shiyens can Heal," Farn said, jaw set firm.

Jessira's eyes rounded in shocked disbelief. What an idiot. He might even be stupid enough to refuse their help. "You mean like only a Rahail and Muran can Blend?" Jessira asked, doing her best to hide the disdain in her voice.

Farn stiffened but said, and did, nothing more.

"If you can Heal, we'll take it. Help Brand first," Rukh said, pointing to the Rahail. "He's the worst off. After him, Farn." He pointed to the tall, bigoted Kumma. "Then Keemo. And if you still have the strength, I would appreciate being able to breathe without feeling like I'm being stabbed in the chest."

"What are you doing?" Jessira whispered to Cedar.

"I'm not sure," her brother answered. "I suddenly have a weird feeling is all."

Jessira studied her brother. His intuitions were rare and never predictable, but when they occurred, it was best to listen to them.

"I can't Heal all of you," Lure said. "But Jessira might be able to help." He turned to their brother. "What do you think Lieutenant?"

Cedar considered the request before eventually nodding agreement. "Go ahead."

While Lure Healed the Ashokans, the general spoke.

"We were never wanted by Mother," he began. "Our birth was unexpected and unplanned. We were a mistake She never desired. The Bovars were, and are, beasts of burden, bereft of all but the most simple of wit. They are as dumb and dull as the cows and bulls they resemble. With our birth, however, Mother had a moment of clarity, a path through Her madness, and She allowed us to live." The general paused. "Humanity would have been better served had She not."

"Are we supposed to pity you for your existence?" Jessira said.

"It was not my intent," the general said with a sad shake of his horned head. "We are glad for our existence, but the simple truth is that if not for us, Humanity would not have suffered as grievously as it has. After the Night of Sorrows, no other Human city died until the first Baels walked Arisa. For the first fourteen hundred years after Mother's murder of the First Mother and First Father..."

"The Queen murdered the First Mother and First Father?" Lure interrupted, pausing, as he was about to set Farn's broken arm. "How do you know this?"

"Mother told us; from Her lips to our ears," the general replied. "When the guilt from Her evil becomes too great; when Her madness no longer suffices to hide the truth...She rages across the heavens, full of sorrow and regret during Her moments of ephemeral self-revelation. She eventually calms and speaks to the Baels, telling us of Her childhood with the First Mother and the First Father, Her parents."

"Her parents?" the Kumma leader asked. "Most believers might find your claims blasphemous," he added in a bored voice. He could have been discussing the weather for how much the information disturbed him.

Jessira felt quite differently. The Bael's words weren't just possibly blasphemous; they *were* blasphemous. The Queen could never have been the child of the First Parents. It had to be another lie. Another trick. How could something so evil be birthed by the personification of good? She cast a look of disbelief toward her brothers who appeared as disturbed as she.

"*Our* histories indicate no such relationship," Cedar said, tersely.

"She was Their Daughter," Li-Dirge repeated. "On this matter, She is completely clear."

Cedar waved aside his explanation. "I don't want to argue about it. Move on. Tell me what you meant to say about the birth of the Baels."

"In the first fourteen centuries after the Night of Sorrows, the Fan Lor Kum, the Red Hand of Justice was under the command of the Tigons. I am sure their instability has not escaped your notice," the general said, with a quick smile, while the other Baels chuckled. "They are perhaps more deadly to the Fan Lor Kum than they are to Humanity."

Cedar stilled and Lure ceased his works on Keemo's sliced hip. Jessira trembled with anger.

Cedar spoke for all of them. "I'm not laughing," he said, sounding furious. "You Chimeras have been nothing but a pestilence of death for all of us – Purebloods or OutCastes alike. You'll pardon me, but I don't think the Tigons are all that comical."

"I should not have made light of their actions," the general agreed. "But you must understand, we use the aggressive nature of Tigons to aid our brethren whenever we may."

"By 'brethren', he means Humanity," Rukh explained. "I felt the same way you look, but listen to the rest of what he has to say."

Jessira shot the Kumma a surprised look of speculation. The Ashokan believed the general. She heard it in his voice and in his stance, but most importantly by the fact that Li-Dirge still lived. Judging by the sour looks on the faces of his companions, though, it was a belief his fellow Ashokans didn't share.

"With our birth, the Baels became the leaders of Suwraith's armies. And it was through our competence that Goshen became the first city to die since the Night of Sorrows, followed shortly by Anvil and then Ajax and then Karma. Eventually, the greatest prize, mighty Hammer, was crushed three hundred years ago."

"Confessing your crimes is a poor way to earn our trust," Cedar said, a look of impatience on his face. "We know all of this. What else is there?"

"Perhaps you do," the general said, unperturbed by Cedar's annoyance. "But what is unknown to your kind until now is what happened after the fall of fabled Hammer. In your histories, I understand you believe Hume Telrest, the last son of Hammer and the greatest warrior to ever walk Arisa's fertile fields, died when his city was sacked, but it isn't true. Hume fell during the battle, yes, but not because of heartbreak or by the sword of a Fan Lor Kum. The great warrior was felled by more cowardly means."

Li-Dirge paused a moment, presumably to build up the drama and the tension, and Jessira had to grudgingly acknowledge the Bael's story-telling ability. She hated the interest the tale inspired, and based on their expressions, Cedar and Lure felt the same way. Of course, while the general was good at spinning out a tale, his skill wasn't the real reason she and her brothers listened patiently to him. The real reason was the ten large Baels standing around, and the four Ashokans, who might or might not be in league with them.

"Hume Telrest was poisoned," the general said into the silence he had built. "Prior to the decisive battle, an unwise Sil Lor Kum thought to make a present for Suwraith in the form of Hume's corpse. Somehow, Mother knew of the great Kumma and hated him as She's never hated anyone before or since. I suppose the fool Sil Lor Kum reckoned such a prize would allow him to live on after his city's demise, but sadly for the idiot, Hume was hardier than the traitor realized. He swiftly threw off the poison and as soon as he had his wits about him, he ended the unlamented life of the unknown Sil Lor Kum. Afterward, with his city a burnt-out husk, he left his home, taking refuge in the gullies and valleys of the foothills rising toward the Horned Mountains. It was there, near the confluence of a silver spring and a mirrored lake, that he came upon our ancient forebear, the SarpanKum of the time. His name was Li-Charn, and with him were his ten senior-most commanders. These were the very Baels who had led the sacking of Hume's home, lovely Hammer. Mother spoke to them there, demanding some impossible task or another, and after Her departure, their words about Her were less than complimentary." Li-Dirge paused again. "For reasons unknown, Hume chose not to strike down the Baels, although he could have. He had the skill. Instead, he sought to converse with my forebears, and changed the course of our history and yours."

"What a load of bull…" Lure began.

"How so?" Cedar asked, cutting their brother off.

Jessira glanced at Cedar in worry. She couldn't believe her brother was taking this bilge water seriously.

"History was changed because for the first time, the Baels heard a voice other than their own or that of Mother. Hume explained concepts such as honor and compassion and forgiveness," Dirge said. "He explained how the greatest leaders are the ones who see themselves as servants rather than oppressors. Hume expanded our horizons. He taught us to read and appreciate the beauty of the written word. From the Master, we learned of Lauri, Chulet, Maral, and so many others."

"I prefer Shuson," Li-Reg said. "I have a copy of *Teller of the Sun and Bride* with me at all times." From somewhere beneath his leather harness, he pulled out a slim, battered volume. It was small in his large hands, and he stared at it reverently.

Jessira frowned. Maybe what Li-Dirge claimed really was nothing but bilge water, but if so, he was the best liar she had ever met. Why would he have planned out all this if it was just subterfuge? Would the general have gone so far as to have one of his underlings produce a volume of romantic poetry on command? She couldn't see the reason for it, and that more than anything else had her feeling frustrated. She wished this night had never happened. Life had been so much simpler a few hours ago. And even though she still wasn't ready to buy what the general was selling, she also was no longer entirely sure he wasn't telling the truth. She was still alive, after all, when the damn Baels had her dead to rights.

Damn Chims. Why couldn't they just behave the way they were supposed to?

"May I see that?" Jessira asked Li-Reg, pointing to the volume of poetry he gently held. Stronghold wasn't a place for arts, but poetry was the one exception. Shuson was one of her favorites, and the copy in the Bael's hands was a rare edition, one not found in her home. She shook her head in disbelief. Who would have believed she would find herself sitting in the Hunters Flats, talking with a Bael as if the Chim was a civilized individual? And discussing poetry no less.

Li-Reg reluctantly passed her the book, and she thumbed through it, wishing she could have a longer perusal. She glanced at Li-Reg, the large, menacing Bael. His eyes were focused on the book, following its every movement like a cat watching a floating feather. If he was anything other than what he was, the plaintive look of worry on his face might have appeared comical. Nevertheless, it was mildly amusing, and she held in a chuckle at the Bael's obvious relief when she passed the volume back to him.

"For romance, I've always favored Kyrian," the general said.

Remembrance of love and
My tears fall in silence.

Your laugh,
My tongue grown mute.

A smile for me alone,
My heart was yours from the first.

All ends but our life endures.
Why so sad, beloved?

As we have forever been,
Love is always.

"Shuson says it better with *Sing the Long Lament*," Li-Reg said.

"Why would a Bael care about romantic love?" Farn asked, for once sounding curious instead of hostile. "Are there even any females of your kind?"

"There are no female Baels," Dirge answered, sounding defensive. "We are all of us male, but even a Bael can dream of falling in love."

Jessira had trouble getting her head around such an incomprehensible concept: the Baels as romantics. A bubble of laughter worked its way up her throat. The notion was just so ridiculous.

Cedar had the flat, pained look of someone unable to feel further surprise. "Just finish your story."

The general cleared his throat. "There's not much more to tell. The Baels studied and learned all Hume could teach us. He even directed our forebears to Hammer's library, which thankfully still stood, and with Master Hume as our inspiration, this knowledge was shared with all our brethren. Over time, we all came to believe as SarpanKum Li-Charn."

"And what do the Baels believe?" Lure asked.

"We believe all those who can reason are our brothers, and we believe it is wrong to kill our brothers."

"It doesn't seem like that particular lesson took hold very well," Jessira said.

"I know it seems like it hasn't but it actually did," Dirge replied, turning to face her. "Since Hammer's fall, no other cities have been razed. Very few caravans even. Even the ghrinas..."

"OutCastes," Jessira corrected, interrupting the general. She hated that word: ghrina.

Dirge tilted his head slightly. "Even those OutCastes who were thrust from their homes were spared as much as we could, and now, here you are, representatives of a place hidden and protected from us and Mother. We allowed the survival of your forebears. The Baels. For the three centuries since Hammer's fall, we've done all we can, often at the cost of our own lives, to deceive, delay, and subvert all of Mother's plans." He turned to the Ashokans. "Or have your war colleges not studied our stupendous incompetence? In battle, you kill ten or more of us at the cost of only one of your own. We are not so stupid as you might believe. We decimate the ranks of the Fan Lor Kum by design."

"Why?" Cedar asked. His eyes bored into those of the general. "Why did you believe Hume and these books your people claim to have read and not your own Mother? Your creator."

Li-Dirge hesitated, and it was Li-Reg who answered. "Mother is insane. She has always been, and our forefathers knew it as well as we. Master Hume's words were simply water in a thirsty desert. We yearned for something other than blood and murder."

"Our appearance seems designed for battle, but appearances can be deceiving," the general said. "War is not for us. Our size and strength allow us to fight well, but our will to battle has always been weak. We are more naturally historians or philosophers."

"I'm done for," Lure said just then. "The last one is yours." He'd just finished with Keemo, and, Jessira's younger brother looked tuckered out. He had the ashen look of someone completely exhausted. He swayed on his feet and would have fallen if a Bael hadn't reached out and gently helped Lure find a seat on the ground.

Jessira didn't want to Heal any Purebloods, but Cedar had asked her to do so. She moved to stand next to the only Pureblood still injured: the Kumma Rukh. "I can help with your rib," she said.

"Thank you," Rukh said, sounding genuinely grateful. "Breathing easily makes life so much more pleasant."

Jessira didn't smile at his quip. "Yes it does." She had to step closer to examine his chest. Her nose wrinkled. The Kumma stank. He smelled of smoke, sweat, and blood, but she probably smelled just as bad.

"You don't believe the general, do you?" Rukh asked.

"No," Jessira replied curtly, hoping the Kumma would leave her be. Cedar had ordered her to Heal the Purebloods, but right now, she didn't want to talk to anyone. She needed time to think over the night's revelations.

Rukh lowered his voice. "The general mentioned something to us, something he didn't tell you," he said, softly. "Have you ever heard of *The Book of First Movement?*"

Jessira didn't bother replying and just shook her head 'no'. And she didn't care to learn about this *Book of First Movement*. Couldn't the Kumma take a hint and shut up?

Apparently not, because he kept talking. "Legend says it was written by the First Father. It was supposed to be the last work of his hands and lost during the Night of Sorrows. The stories also say the pages of the Book are blank to all but the purest of heart, but the general said Hume was once able to read a single line of the book. It said: *Believe my song and serve greatness.*"

Jessira didn't bother hiding her eye roll. "Amazing," she said in a flat, disinterested tone.

Rukh grimaced. "I can tell you're not impressed," he said, "but you need to hear this. You know, when I first met you, I thought my duty was to kill you out of hand just for being alive. Many Ashokans would have."

By the barest of margins, Jessira overcame her sudden fury and disgust for Rukh. Though she would have loved to tell him to take his words and shove it up his back passage, duty wouldn't allow it. Whatever was going on here, Stronghold needed more information. And what better source than this Ashokan, a possible leader of the Sil Lor Kum? Her people's survival might depend on what Jessira learned, which meant she had to follow the same advice she'd wanted to give Lure: never poke the bear.

"Then why didn't you?" she asked, masking her anger with a flat, lifeless tone to her voice.

"I have a brother who is a Sentya. His name is Jaresh."

She paused, studying his face, searching for the lie. A Kumma with a Sentya brother?

"It's the truth. Our nanna is the ruling 'El of our House, and he adopted him when Jaresh was only three."

"Why do you suppose I might care?" Jessira asked, interested in his answer despite her anger.

"Because I *didn't* kill you. I could have, and I didn't because of my brother. Jaresh was an orphan, and Nanna saw it as his duty to raise him because of a promise he made to Jaresh's birth father. There's never been someone adopted into one of our Houses who wasn't also a Kumma. It cost Nanna quite a bit at first when he did what he did. We lost a lot of contracts with other Houses, and they wanted nothing to do with us, but my parents never regretted their decision, and I'm grateful Jaresh is a part of our family. I love my brother."

"Why are you telling me this?" Jessira asked, some of her anger cooling.

"I don't know," Rukh said. "Maybe I don't want you hating us and thinking we're all the same."

"Hate isn't what I feel toward you Purebloods," Jessira replied. "It's pity."

Rukh rolled his eyes. "Fair enough. I guess we deserve that from your way of thinking." He sighed. "Look, I said what I said to let you know Ashoka is changing. Maybe there will come a time when ghrinas – I mean the OutCastes – will have a place among us."

"How very generous," Jessira said with a smirk. She knew he was trying to make a connection with her, but she couldn't help but mock his eagerness. He sounded so sincere, like he was offering her some great prize by accepting the OutCastes. His sentiments didn't impress her. If Ashoka evolved as Rukh said it might, it would be a cause for celebration but also for sorrow. It shouldn't have taken them so long to act in a moral fashion.

"Fine. Hate us. Pity us, feel contempt …I don't care," Rukh said, a surge of annoyance in his voice. "All you need to do is listen. What I know can't be lost. You need to hear this."

Jessira forced down her own anger, burgeoning once more in response to the Kumma's. She didn't want anything more to do with Rukh Shektan, but Stronghold needed her to keep him talking. "What is it?" she asked as patiently as she could.

"Before I left Ashoka, I found a reference to *The Book of First Movement*. There was only one, in all of the volumes, scrolls, and books in all of Ashoka's libraries; just one, and this in someone's journal. And what the author of the journal said matched exactly what the general claimed. He was from the last caravan from Hammer to Ashoka, and he claimed it had been Hume who had read that first line."

"So. The general knew this line…it doesn't prove anything."

"No. Not when taken alone, but we have records of how all the other cities fell…Ajax, Rock, Goshen, Karma…the Chimeras were led much more effectively in those campaigns; better than they have ever since Hammer's fall. Since then, they've always attacked in ways guaranteed to maximize their own losses and minimize ours. Our war colleges have noted this, and we've wondered about it. We thought it was because the Baels weren't too bright, but it turns out they are. You've met the general and his aides. They should be better at tactics and strategy than what we've seen."

Jessira glanced about. The Ashokans were clustered a few feet away, while Cedar stood guard near Lure. Her brother lay on his back with eyes closed on one of the few areas of the nearby ground free of blood and gore. The Baels had finished stacking the Tigon corpses and spoke quietly in small clusters, their voices deep rumbles. A few of the beasts stood beside the large fire still burning in the center of the bowl. Someone ignorant of the lethal history between the three groups might have believed this to be a peaceful scene.

Jessira wasn't fooled. Cedar was tense, as were the Ashokans. None of them looked happy.

"Even our own caravan…we killed four thousand of them," Rukh continued, interrupting her reverie. "Did you know that? With a little over three hundred warriors. The Baels could have chosen from a whole host of options to launch their assault and limit their losses, but instead, they attacked uphill and against what was essentially a fortified position. They paid dearly for their stupidity, but I'm thinking it wasn't stupidity."

"Your caravan paid a dearer price, and our histories tell nothing of the Baels' supposed compassion," Jessira replied, put off by Rukh's expertise in battle. She was a scout. Nothing more. The Kumma, like all his kind, had probably studied the art of war from childhood.

"We paid a heavy price for the captain's mistake," Rukh said. "He shouldn't have kept our forces unified. He should have split us up. If he had, more of us might have slipped the Chimeras' trap."

Jessira shrugged her shoulders, annoyed. "I'm still not sure what you're trying to say."

"When you put it all together: the Baels' incompetence since Hammer's fall; what happened here and the conversations we've overheard; and the line for *The Book of First Movement*, which they could have only known if Hume told them...I think they're telling the truth. Your people need to know that."

"I think you're being naïve. It'll take more than a nice story to make me believe that what Dirge told us is the truth," Jessira replied. "Now, can we please stop talking and let me just fix those ribs?" she asked, changing the topic to something she knew more about.

Rukh smirked. "As angry as I've made you, I'm surprised you didn't tell me to Heal myself."

Jessira grimaced. How had he guessed her thoughts? "Just be quiet."

"As you wish."

"This might hurt," Jessira warned as she pressed her hands gently against Rukh's ribs, seeking the locus of his pain.

A sharp hiss was her only warning before his hand, viper fast, clamped against her wrist.

"You found it," Rukh said. "No need to push any harder."

"It feels like you have two broken ribs," Jessira said with a frown. "You're lucky you didn't puncture a lung."

"Tell me about it."

"You Kummas are tough. I'll give you that," Jessira said. "Are you ready? I'll have to press again."

Rukh nodded. "Do it."

"Take off your shirt," Jessira ordered.

Rukh did as she asked. He was lean and well-muscled, but not heavily so. And against the right side of his chest was a bruise the size of a melon.

Jessira put her hands over his broken ribs and pressed gently. She conducted *Jivatma* through her arms and into her hands, changing it so it bled through her fingers and into him. He hissed when her mental touch poked at his cracked ribs.

She took a breath, exhaling sharply. Now came the challenging part. She stretched out her *Jivatma*, teasing it until it was needle-thin and precise – not a raging torrent. It was so difficult. *Jivatma* had a natural tendency to flow like a flood. It was hard to keep it tight and focused. Sweat beaded on her face by the time she was finished.

Jessira studied his chest, feeling over her work. The ribs were healed, and the bruise was faded, as though the injury was weeks old.

Rukh took a deep breath, sighing with relief. "Thank you," he said, trapping both her hands in his.

She quickly withdrew from his grasp. "You're welcome," she said, confused by what she thought she saw in his dark, brown eyes. For a moment, it seemed like they had held admiration and respect, which was impossible. Purebloods despised OutCastes.

"Get some rest," she said in a gruff tone meant to hide her puzzlement. "Healing takes a lot out of a person."

CHAPTER ELEVEN
THE SIL LOR KUM

Are those who choose the path of the Sil Lor Kum evil or merely pragmatic?
The question has been a thorn in my side for years, and what I've decided is that
we are both. We are pragmatically evil. It is the life of a coward.

~SuDin of Ashoka in year AF 2054 (name redacted)

In a nondescript, windowless room in the back of a nondescript restaurant somewhere in Ashoka, the Sil Lor Kum, Suwraith's Human agents, met for an emergency session called by the SuDin, the Voice Who Commands. The restaurant was to the south of East Vineyard Steep – the traditional home of the Sentyas – along a road running from Style Rod Privet to Palm Court. It was a middle class street with nondescript homes, all of them unremarkable in their modesty and well-kept exteriors. It was always so with the Sil Lor Kum. Although they were wealthy, they never flaunted their affluence. It was better to hide in the shadows, in places no one would think to look. In a place such as this one: a room with unfashionable knotty-pine paneling and a too small fireplace; an ugly, bronze-colored chandelier with a single firefly lamp hanging from each of the arms to provide barely sufficient light; and a rug worn and frayed in the corners, its better days years past but still serviceable. Everything in the room was perfectly plain and unassuming.

As it should be, the SuDin mused as he glanced around. He sat in a high-backed chair with sturdy arms at the head of a large, oval, golden oak table. Around it were the MalDin, The Servants of the Voice. Despite their submissive title, these men and women were the true captains of the Sil Lor Kum, standing just below the SuDin in importance. This was the Council of Rule. There were seven all told in this room – six MalDin and the SuDin – one for each Caste and each one a hidden power in Ashoka. As always, the men and women here were masked, wearing stylized visages of their own choosing. It had always been this way since no member of the Sil Lor Kum – much less the Council of Rule – would have wanted their true identities known. It was safer for all if they worked in the shadows, in anonymity, as their name itself indicated: Sil Lor Kum: the Hidden Hand of Justice. Despite their precautions, the SuDin knew the true names of all his fellow Council members. He suspected some of them knew his as well.

Certainly, the Rahail did. Varesea Apter was a lovely woman in her early forties. She had a way about her: of dressing, speaking, and thinking...in all ways she was a lady, a woman of many charms. She and the SuDin had been lovers for ten years now. At first, their coupling had been that of two people angry at the world and their lives in it. Now, however, there was tenderness and even laughter in their lovemaking. It was odd, and the SuDin wasn't sure what it meant. He recognized the affection he felt for Varesea. She was an intoxicating woman, and she made him feel alive as his own departed wife never had. But he also wondered if their relationship was less complex than he sometimes believed. Maybe they were two people who liked to live beyond all constraints. After all, they faced two death sentences: first, their membership in the Sil Lor Kum, and second, their illicit, carnal relationship. The two of them *were* from different Castes.

As for the others, there was Yuthero Gaste, the Shiyen. He was young to have risen so high to his post as MalDin, and he was also young to be a Professor of Surgery at Alminius School of Medicine. Gaste was proud of both accomplishments, rightly believing his intellect and Talent as being the main reasons for his current success. He was overly proud, though, never understanding others might be equally brilliant and equally Talented in their own ways. His arrogance blinded him, leaving him vulnerable to a manipulation he never suspected could occur. Thus, his greatest assets were also his greatest liabilities. Nevertheless, he bore watching, but the SuDin didn't fear him. Not yet anyway.

Moke Urn, a slimy weasel of a man with the unprepossessing build of his fellows, represented caste Sentya. He was skilled with numbers and seeing a way to squeeze the last profit out of a venture. It was for this reason he had been elected to the MalDin. The man had but two great loves in life. The first was the Sil Lor Kum. Urn had been born in poverty, without any hope of making his mark on the world, at least not in the traditional nepotistic Sentya way. The Sil Lor Kum had offered him the chance to prove his worth. Second, the oily man was in love with the voluptuous Mesa Reed of Caste Cherid. Of course, she knew it and led the fool on. The SuDin doubted Mesa had let Urn so much as touch her, but with every throaty laugh at the Sentya's poor jokes; with every flash of thigh; with every slight bend at the waist to allow Urn to see her décolletage, he could see the man squirm with heat and desire. A cruel woman was Mesa Reed. The SuDin was wise not to share her bed, although Mesa had been more than clear on several occasions that she would be happy to share his.

Then there was the personal pain in the SuDin's backside: the Duriah, Pera Obbe. She was a bundle of anger, anxiety, and ambition; a woman who questioned everything and everyone. And yet, she stiffened with outrage when anyone questioned her. The SuDin wished he could just kill her, but there were no competent Duriahs to take her place. He glanced at Obbe and *tsked* in revulsion. Was there an uglier woman in all of Ashoka? From her potato nose to her piggish eyes to her jackass laugh, Pera Obbe was hideous.

And finally, there was Ular Sathin, the Muran. He was the oldest of them, quiet and unassuming, hardly ever voicing his thoughts in the meetings. He was efficient and quick with his work, and others in the Sil Lor Kum thought him mousy. The SuDin knew otherwise. Ular Sathin might be the most dangerous one of all the MalDin. He was smart enough to hide his true intelligence and his abilities, the greatest of which was his consummate capacity to lie. The man could deceive Devesh Himself and bore close scrutiny. Ular Sathin's one saving grace was the fact that had he truly wanted the title of SuDin, he would have reached for it decades ago. His opportunity had long since passed by.

As for the SuDin himself, he represented the Kummas. It hadn't always been so. In fact, the current situation was actually somewhat unusual. More often than not, just like in society as a whole the leader of the Sil Lor Kum, was typically a Cherid. The SuDin had held his position now for almost a full decade. But very few of his Caste would have appreciated his success or their representation by him in the Sil Lor Kum. If they knew the truth, they would have demanded his head on a pike and his corpse discarded upon the Isle of the Crows.

The SuDin noticed Varesea's subtle gesture. He always noticed Varesea. She had bent over slightly, allowing him a brief glimpse of her breasts. They were no longer as firm as they had been when they had first met, but the sight still stirred his loins. He saw the questioning, challenging look in her eyes, and he nodded, briefly, a bare movement of his head. They would meet after the others had left.

The rest of the MalDin spoke amongst themselves, and the SuDin allowed it, letting his mind wander as he ignored their inane mutterings. He reflected on his life in the few minutes before he had to call the meeting to order. How had he come to this? The SuDin had once been pure in both heart and mind. Now look at him. He was a naaja, a Tainted fornicator with one not of his Caste, and a member of the Sil Lor Kum to boot. His younger self would have happily killed his older self for either of the two sins.

But time, loss, and death had provided the SuDin with a perspective his younger self lacked: Humanity was doomed unless a different path was taken, a path beyond the Castes, a path aiming for more than simply surviving Suwraith but actually defeating Her – or at the least thwarting Her. And if he had to commit acts others might deem evil so as to turn back the Sorrow Bringer, then so be it. He was still a Kumma, and he knew of duty. He would wear the stains on his soul with pride if it meant Humanity would be free.

He called the session to order. Today's meeting would be as momentous as any the Sil Lor Kum of Ashoka had ever had. It should be interesting to see how the others reacted. "The Queen came to me in my dreams last night," the SuDin began. No one needed to describe who was meant by 'the Queen'. All knew it meant Suwraith. And dreams were the only means by which She could breach an Oasis. "We have been given orders. She comes for Ashoka."

As expected, the others greeted the news with hisses of dismay. "How will we survive?" Pera Obbe wailed as the others, even Varesea, asked similarly nonsensical questions.

Their fear was understandable. The MalDin controlled all shady commerce within Ashoka, everything from gambling to prostitution to illicit drugs. If it involved debauchery, the Sil Lor Kum had a hand in it, and the small-minded criminals who ran the operations never knew for whom they really worked. The money from such enterprises was the reason for the fabulous wealth of the Sil Lor Kum in general, and the Council of Rule in specific. It was a great attraction and temptation, and the MalDin feared to lose all they had worked so hard to acquire. So, yes, the SuDin understood the source of their fear, but he had little sympathy for it.

They should have known better. Joining the Sil Lor Kum meant more than merely making money or gaining power. It was more than just running a gambling house or funneling drugs to various restaurants and bars. At its most fundamental, joining the Sil Lor Kum meant service to the Queen, and if She demanded their obedience, then obedience would be offered – up to and including – aid in the destruction of their homes. The MalDin had never expected this day would come, blinded as they were by ambition and the easy acquisition of money and power. But now the Queen was calling in Her chits, and the MalDin had to pay. They were afraid.

Frag them. The SuDin listened with contempt as they bleated on about surviving Suwraith. They were all fools. They should have better prepared for this eventuality. The Queen was coming and no one had *ever* survived Her, possibly not even the Sil Lor Kum. A man of vision, though…he could save his Caste or maybe even the entire city. The SuDin smiled. And the Queen had perhaps given him the means to do so. She had given him the Withering Knife, the legendary blade that myths claimed could steal *Jivatma*.

He rapped his knuckles and told the MalDin a mixture of lies and truth. He showed them the Withering Knife, but feigned ignorance as to how it worked. They listened closely as the SuDin explained his plans, a small alteration of the one with which Suwraith had charged him.

"And we're to survive how exactly?" Pera Obbe asked in her grating voice.

The SuDin smiled generously, as if happy to field her question. He answered, assuring Pera and the others of their safety. He told them what they wanted to hear, letting them believe that places had already been prepared for them in cities throughout the world. He continued on, explaining how easily their wealth would be transferred to these new homes abroad. All of them would survive in prosperity and happiness. They stared at him after he finished speaking, wearing the hungry and desperate looks of the condemned who suddenly saw a means to their survival.

He wanted to laugh in their faces.

None of it was true. They would all die, and the SuDin would be glad. He would miss Varesea, though. He glanced and caught her gaze. She knew he was lying. He could see the realization in her eyes. She understood there was much he wasn't telling them. Varesea knew him too well, and he could see he would have to explain his plans more fully to her later tonight. It went without saying: she would not hear the entire truth.

Smooth lies continued to flow from his lips as he gave false hope to the MalDin. Suwraith would kill them all.

***

Steen Trist awoke early in the morning, well before dawn. He read through his anatomy notes one last time, trying to burn the information into his head. *The origin of the long head of the biceps brachii is the supraglenoid tubercle of the scapula, while the short head originates from the coracoid process. The two heads then insert into...!* Where did they insert? Damn it! The radial tuberosity.

Idiot.

Why couldn't he remember something so basic?

Steen glared at his notes in frustration. He was a first-year student at Verchow College of Medicine, and he had his finals in anatomy later that day. He felt woefully unprepared. The test would only cover the upper extremities and the thoracic cavity, but it was still a lot to learn.

His parents were extremely proud of Steen, and he wasn't as afraid of failure as he was of disappointing them. Their family hadn't produced a physician in over three generations, and although the larger Shiyen community did not look down upon them – his parents were skilled craftsmen and quite well-to-do in their own right – they both still felt an underlying sense of doubt about their own worth. They were Shiyens and Shiyens were supposed to Heal. It was the Talent of the Caste.

But, to become a physician, a person had to do very well on the rigorous entrance exams, and only the best were selected to attend either Verchow or Alminius, the two medical colleges in Ashoka. Steen had been overjoyed, just as his entire family had been, when he had been accepted to Verchow.

A year into his studies, though, he wasn't sure if it had been the right choice for him. It wasn't because the material was too hard for him but because the material was so deadly dull. Steen couldn't imagine anything more boring than some of the topics they were expected to master. For instance, why did they have to memorize the blood vessels in the brain? No one ever did surgery on the brain, so why did it matter? Steen couldn't drop out, though. His parents would be crushed if he did.

He shook his head, trying to clear his thoughts. No time to think about that now. Focus. *Alright, let's see. The triceps brachii has three heads. The long head originates below the infraglenoid tubercle, the lateral head from the posterior shaft of the humerus above the deltoid tuberosity, and the medial head comes from the posterior shaft below the deltoid tuberosity, all the way to the lateral epicondyle. The three heads insert into the ulnar olecranon.*

He felt a small measure of triumph. Yes! One simple fact memorized, a thousand more to go. He kept at it for another few hours. By then, the sun had risen, and the delicious smell of pastries filled the air. His nanna was a jewelry maker, but he also loved baking. He took pride in making his own sweets and breads to serve the customers as they tried on the various necklaces, pendants, and jewels in the store.

Steen closed his books. If he didn't have the material memorized by now, another few minutes of studying wouldn't help. He stood and stretched, yawning mightily. He was about to leave his room, but noticed how rumpled his clothes were. His hair was also a mess. He took a moment to straighten up before trotting down the stairs. He darted into the kitchen, meaning to grab some bread and eat it on the way to school.

Nanna glanced up from the counter. He had already cut several slices of bread and even had them buttered. Looking at Nanna sometimes made Steen cringe. His father had the walnut complexion, high, prominent cheekbones, and midnight dark, almond eyes of their Caste, but while most Shiyens were merely stocky, Nanna was fat. It was a cruel thing to say, but it was true. And unfortunately, Steen could easily see himself following in his nanna's footsteps. He glanced down at the large roll bulging around his midsection. Maybe he should cut back and get some exercise.

The smell of the buttered bread made his mouth water

Some other time. He needed the fuel for his mind and today's test. He swiped the bread, thanking Nanna before heading out.

"Good luck, son," Nanna yelled to him as he stepped out the back door and onto the narrow lane that ran behind their house.

Steen took a deep breath. Ah! Warm weather. Summer was almost here, which meant an end to the school year. He smiled in anticipation. No more classes or studying for two solid months. He paused as he was about to pass by the alleyway running between his parents' home and that of the Barnels next door. There was something down there, lying on the ground, deep in the shadows. Something vaguely man-shaped. He frowned as he tried to figure out what he was seeing. His frown cleared as he realized what it was. It was probably just some drunk, passed out after getting lost and wandering into their neighborhood. He hesitated but eventually decided he had to make sure the fool was alright.

Steen stepped into the alley. "Hello?" he queried.

He waited for a moment, but there was no response. The drunk must have drank enough to sink a boat.

Steen stepped further into the alley.

The person on the ground was unmoving.

A sense of foreboding took him. Suddenly, the shadowed alley seemed darker, more menacing. Steen swallowed heavily as a trickle of fear made its way down his back. He tried to set aside his rising anxiety, seeking to replace it with anger, mostly at himself for being afraid. After all, there was no reason for it. He'd been down this lane a thousand times. It had never caused him a moment of worry before. So then why were all these chills racing up and down his spine? He glanced back to the entrance of the alley. The bright sunlight looked so far away.

He approached closer. Dread rose. His instincts told him to run. Something bad had happened here. He could *feel* it.

He inched closer. Details became clearer. He recognized the coat the person was wearing. It belonged to Master Barnel, the next-door neighbor. The man was lying face down, hands tucked under his body. His clothes looked strangely large, billowy about the man's unmoving frame, and Steen wondered if this might be someone else. Maybe a relative? But then again, there was Master Barnel's white hair.

"Master Barnel?" Steen croaked, his voice cracking from his nervousness.

Silence.

Steen turned the man over and screamed.

He stumbled away from the corpse, terror gripping his heart.

What could do that to a man? He stood up, and without a backward glance, ran out of the alley, still screaming. It had indeed been Master Barnel or what was left of him. All that remained now was a brittle husk. A corpse with a gaping bloodstained wound in his chest.

Master Barnel had been murdered.

CHAPTER TWELVE
AN UNUSUAL CRIME

The most holy room in a man's house should be his library.
It is the same when it comes to one's city.

~*Sooths and Small Sayings by Tramed Billow, AF 1387*

Mira followed Dar'El into the City Morgue. It was a dimly lit space in the basement below Ashoka's main hospice. A bone-deep chill penetrated the dark, windowless hallway and rooms, all of which were colored a drab gray. A smell, acrid and harsh, hung in the air, but it couldn't completely mask the smell of blood and death. Mira couldn't imagine a more uninviting and depressing place. The bodies temporarily stored in the morgue were generally of those who had died accidentally or for whom a post-mortem was required. Then there were the bodies of the impoverished, whose families couldn't afford a proper funeral pyre. The City's Treasury took care of those unfortunate cases.

According to rumor a new category of dead was now to be found in the Morgue: a murder victim from yesterday, the first in over fifteen years. The killing had rocked the city and everyone seemed to have an opinion as to what had happened. It was the primary topic of discussion in most of the restaurants, pubs, and theaters throughout the city, capturing the attention of all. It didn't matter if they were rich or poor or to what Caste they belonged – most everybody was busy gossiping about the murder.

Mira had been no less entranced and horrified by the death as anyone else. She and her friends had endlessly theorized as to what might have happened, and their guesses had gyrated wildly between the ludicrous and the hideous. Occasionally, they had laughed or felt guilty over their morbid fascination, but it hadn't ended their speculation. However, during all those conversations, Mira had never suspected she herself might soon be involved in the solving of the murder. But then why else would Dar'El have ordered her to meet with him here at the morgue? It was the only explanation she could think of, and it left her feeling more than a little trepidatious. She had only recently completed her apprenticeship with House Suzay, and her first assignment with House Shektan might be something of potential importance for the entire city. It was a bit daunting, but also very exciting.

As they walked the echoing and empty hallway, her nervousness grew and she finally had to break the silence. "Why are we here?" she asked.

"We're here for him," Dar'El said, opening a door and gesturing to a plain, black granite table centered within the room and held up by a single stone pillar. Upon the slab was laid out a corpse, covered by a black sheet and leaving only the face exposed. The only light in the space came from a set of firefly lanterns hanging from the ceiling, their brightness focused on the stone table.

Mira glanced at Dar'El. "This is the man who was murdered yesterday, isn't he?"

Dar'El nodded. "Dr. Redhes, the chief of pathology, has never seen anything like it," he said. "Pull back the sheets, and you'll see what I mean."

Mira approached the body. At first she thought the victim must have been tremendously old since the face and head had the tight, pinched look sometimes seen in the elderly, but this was different. The man's skin didn't have the thin, almost translucent look sometimes seen in the aged. Instead it was dry and brittle, appearing like it had been baked and pulled so tightly against the bones of his face that the teeth were exposed in a rictus of a grin. Mira swallowed back her revulsion. This had been no ordinary death. She pulled back the sheet and gasped. A gaping maw was all that was left of the man's chest. Inside it, she could see his heart and lungs. They were hard nuggets of flesh.

Mira stepped back in horror. "What could have done something like this?" she whispered in shock.

"I don't know," Dar'El replied. "The means of his death is as much a mystery as the murder itself."

"Who was he?" Mira asked, tearing her gaze away from the corpse.

"His name was Felt Barnel. A Muran glassblower, and according to his wife, he was alive and healthy the evening prior to his discovery. His neighbor's son, a student from Verchow, found him on the morning in question, murdered in the alley between their two homes."

"You're saying he was alive one evening and dead by the next morning?" Mira asked in disbelief. "He looks like he was left out for weeks in the sun or put in a kiln or something like that."

"And yet his corpse shows no evidence of exposure to the elements or charring."

Mira stepped away from the table. What had happened to Felt Barnel was too horrible for words, and she was both embarrassed and guilty for the selfish excitement she had earlier felt. Yes, she might be able to help solve the mystery of his murder – she had no idea how – but Master Barnel would still be dead. Justice would be too late for him.

"And my role in all of this?" Mira asked. "Aren't murders under the purview of the City Watch?"

A thin wisp of a smile ghosted across Dar'El's face. "They are, but murders are so rare. No one is an expert in the solving of such crimes." He turned away from his study of the corpse, moving to face her. "But the investigation of the murder isn't why I called you here."

"Then what is?"

He paused, as if searching for a word. "I have my concerns," he said. "And I have a job for you. One suited to your skills."

Dar'El was certainly being mysterious.

"What am I to do?" she asked.

"Let's go to where Master Barnel was found, and we'll discuss it then."

Dar'El re-covered the corpse and led her out of the Morgue and into the warmth of the bright afternoon sunshine.

As soon as she stepped outside, she turned her face up to the sky and the sun, letting its heat warm her chilled skin and heart. She shivered, trying to set aside the horrifying image of Felt Barnel. How painful his death must have been. No one deserved what had happened to him, and anyone who could do such an evil deed was someone she would happily see hang.

She and Dar'El walked the short distance from the hospice to Sunpalm Orchard. This was where many of Caste Shiyen made their home, the place where most of Ashoka's physicians and their families resided. It was a wealthy neighborhood of stately town homes fronting narrow, tree-lined streets built around a central district of taller buildings, typically housing a business on the first floor and flats and apartments above. Many of the roads had a slender median within which were planted a single row of gardenias. The plants were the height of a man and were heavy with ripe blossoms. Their fragrant aroma filled the air, carried throughout Sunpalm and beyond by a warm, spring breeze.

Mira took in their lovely scent, so alive and heady, especially after the harsh, dead smell of the morgue.

"This way," Dar'El said, turning down a side street. He led her into a narrow alley between several homes where the week's refuse and detritus were placed for the city's garbage collectors to pick up. "This is where he was found." Dar'El bent to the ground.

"Felt Barnel lived nearby?"

Dar'El pointed to the house to their right. "He lived there. He had his workshop on the bottom floor. His family lived on the second."

"Business must have been good for him to have been able to afford a place like this, especially being a Muran in a neighborhood of Shiyens," Mira said, looking at the handsome and well-maintained houses in the area.

"I suppose so," Dar'El said. "He was said to have been quite skilled, but I'm more interested in what he did before becoming a glass blower. He was a warrior with two Trials to his name. It is how he made his fortune. I understand he was still an active member of the City Guard as well."

Mira whistled appreciation. "Sounds like he was a tough man."

"By all accounts, he could handle himself," Dar'El confirmed. "And he was all but helpless before whoever attacked him." He pointed out a few details in the alley. "Look: hardly any signs of a struggle. A knocked over refuse urn. A smashed flower pot. A few droplets of blood. That's it. Whoever took him was skilled." Dar'El met her gaze. "Very skilled."

Only one Caste bred warriors so proficient in killing. Mira knew what Dar'El implied, and she frowned in distaste. "Kumma," she guessed, appalled that one of her own Caste could be the murderer.

"Kumma," Dar'El replied in agreement. "Only one of us could have taken him down so easily."

Mira repressed a shudder. The murderer was a Kumma. She still found it hard to fathom. How could a warrior be so debased? The man shamed all of them. Her jaw firmed with resolve. She *wanted* to help bring this traitor down. "You still haven't told me what you need me to do," she said.

Dar'El smiled faintly, but the humor didn't reach his eyes. "I need you to do research for me. I want you to search the City Library for any information you can find on something called the Withering Knife. It might also be called the Souleater. It is reputed to be a weapon once used by Suwraith Herself on the Night of Sorrows."

Mira blinked in surprise. This wasn't at all what she'd expected. What did this Withering Knife have to do with the murder of Felt Barnel? Was it the murder weapon? Master Barnel *had* looked withered. Could that be the reason for its name? It seemed a bit simple and derivative, like from a bad drama. More importantly, though, what was her 'El keeping to himself? "Is there anything else you can tell me about this Withering Knife, and how it relates to the murder of Felt Barnel?"

Dar'El shook his head. "Not yet. I'm not ready to say. It may be nothing more than a guess at this point. Once I have a better idea as to what's going on, perhaps then…" He trailed off. His eyes suddenly bored into hers. "Tell no one. Consider your investigation to be a House secret. I know the research will be hard, so I've asked Jaresh to join you. The two of you have complementary skills. You should work well together. I will want weekly progress reports."

Mira hid a sigh. If she was expected to comb all of the City Library's stacks and all one million volumes, hard didn't come close to describing her newly assigned task. The search was sure to be long, tedious, and frustrating. She might be at it for months. The only solace was that Jaresh would be helping her. He was the family's strongest researcher. Maybe he could help make the time go by more quickly.

T he building housing the City Library was the largest and oldest in Ashoka. The Library was ancient, known to have existed prior to the Night of Sorrows. It might have been established at the very founding of Ashoka, and over the ensuing centuries, it had expanded outward and upward until it now covered several blocks and rose a colossal five stories into the sky with another two stories below the ground. It was a shame none of the expansions seemed to have been built with a regard for exterior aesthetics. Additions had been plunked down in various ways and places, and the resultant mishmash of styles had led to an epic eyesore. The oldest parts of the building were simple walls of granite, glass, and ironwood. Grafted onto the original Library were the architecturally nonsensical additions, such as the one from several centuries ago with its ornate, fluted columns holding aloft a complicated maze of porticos and friezes. Even worse was the most recent from fifty years past: an overdone mess of towers and gargoyles. Absolutely hideous.

Somehow, the same architects who had devised the atrocious exterior had been much more cognizant of the interior spaces. The entrance to the Library was a wide, high-ceilinged atrium rising to the roof. It was formed of thick, white granite with slender ribs of ironwood and spidergrass. All of it appeared too fragile to hold up the space and keep the entire structure from collapsing. However, the Duriah engineers vowed those same frail-looking vaulted buttresses were actually stronger than the surrounding stone. A massive chandelier was centrally placed within the atrium and held countless firefly lamps. It descended from the ceiling and lighted up the space as brightly as the noonday sun. Other rooms, airy and cheerful, branched off the entrance. These were the various departments of the Library, everything from history-to-science-to-art. All of them had vibrant frescoes and murals with broad windows bringing in even more light. The rooms were just the sort of place a scholar would happily while away an entire day of study.

The reserve section, though, where the more rarely called for and esoteric texts were kept, took up the two lowest levels of the Library – the ones below ground. Those sections were definitely not sunny and warm but instead had the claustrophobic feel of a grotto: dark and dingy, full of dust and mold with tall shelves rising toward the ceiling's gloom. A few overwhelmed and ineffectual lanterns provided dim lighting for the spaces. As a result, most people referred to the reserve section of the Library as the Cellar, an apropos if obvious name.

Right now, Mira and Jaresh found themselves in the part of the Cellar given over to the study of Suwraith. Within it were housed over twenty thousand volumes, and nearby were the histories of the First World, Arisa as it had existed prior to the Night of Sorrows. There were also accounts of the Night itself and the years following, the Days of Desolation. Once, these books had been in the public section, but over time, interest in them had diminished until the decision was made a century earlier to move them all to the Cellar.

It seemed few people cared to study the world as it was prior to Suwraith. Perhaps it was because the First World had been so lovely and peaceful in comparison to the one found now.

Mira sneezed. Again. The dust and mold were getting to her. Her eyes itched, her nose dripped, and her sinuses were swelling shut. She should have taken her allergy medication before coming here.

"This is the place," Mira said. "Ready for a few months of painful slogging?"

"Absolutely," Jaresh said with false levity. "Searching through thousands of mildewy tomes…what a way to spend the spring and summer." He sighed. "Tell me again why Nanna asked you to look for this Withering Knife? Is he punishing you for some reason?"

"Not as far as I can tell," Mira answered with an arch to an eyebrow. "Why? Is he punishing you, maybe?"

"I hope not," Jaresh replied. "And he didn't say anything else about why we're down here?"

Mira shrugged. "Not really. You know how he is."

"Mysterious and all-knowing?"

Mira smiled. "Exactly." She sneezed again.

Jaresh chuckled. "Why don't you wait by the table? I can bring the books and scrolls over," he said, gesturing to the shelves around them. "There's probably going to be another cloud of dust billowing into the air when I pull them down, and I don't think your sinuses could take much more."

Mira threw him a grateful look. "Thank you," she said.

"Leave the lantern," Jaresh added as she was turning to leave. "I can't make anything out in this light." He waved a large sheet of paper. On it was the cribbed handwriting of the librarian in charge of antiquities, and a long list of books and scrolls the old Sentya had suggested they start with.

Mira left the lantern and retreated. She waited for Jaresh in one of the few reading alcoves found in the Cellar. It was a small space, able to house a couple of rectangular tables, each with seating for four. An ineffectual chandelier shed just enough light by which to read but not enough to drive away the gloom. The oppressive feel was made worse by the looming, shadowed shelves pressed in all around the nook.

A few minutes later, Jaresh returned with a large stack of books cradled in his hands and against his chest. They were piled one atop the other up to his chin. He dropped them with a grateful sigh, letting them thud onto the old, oak table.

"Sadly, this is only a very small fraction of what we'll need to go through," Jaresh said.

Mira took a deep breath. "Better get to work then," she replied.

Hours later, neither she nor Jaresh had managed to find a single reference to the Withering Knife.

"How many manuscripts do you think we've gone through?" Mira asked.

"Five hundred and twenty nine," Jaresh said, not missing a beat.

"Five hundred and twenty nine?" Mira asked in surprise. "You've been keeping track of the exact number?"

"Sure," he agreed, amiably. He grinned a moment later. "Actually, I have no idea," he said. "I just made it up."

Mira laughed. "I should have known."

"Why don't we just say we've gone through a lot and have a lot more to go through. Enough to sink a boat."

"It's going to take us weeks to finish this task," Mira complained, hating the petulant tone in her voice.

"More like months."

Mira groaned.

"It could be worse," Jaresh said.

"How so?"

"You could be doing this by yourself."

"Don't remind me."

Jaresh looked up from the manuscript he had been studying, a twinkle in his eyes. "Do you think we could get Bree to help us?"

"I think she'd be more of a hindrance than a help," Mira said with a chuckle. She gestured around them. "Or do you actually think she would appreciate hours of solitary, mind-numbing research?"

Jaresh laughed. "Not really her forte is it?"

"No, and definitely not your brother's."

"Rukh?" Jaresh asked, sounding surprised.

"He just doesn't seem the type to work on a project like this. I'm sure he'd rather be off practicing with his sword."

"What's wrong with that?" Jaresh asked. "Reading a text isn't going to keep him alive like mastering the blade." He had the obstinate look of someone who was about to be offended, and Mira knew she had to step carefully with him. Jaresh obviously loved and respected his brother quite a lot.

"No it isn't, and I understand why he focused so much on learning to fight," Mira said. "It's just that your father is so well-read and intelligent. I think Rukh could learn a lot from him," she said. "This isn't meant as a criticism of Rukh. He's a tremendous warrior, but maybe Kummas should value intelligence just as highly. Our Caste traditionally chooses our leaders based on their fighting prowess – the other Houses certainly have – but ours didn't, and it's made all the difference. Dar'El wasn't the greatest warrior of his generation, but he is certainly the most cunning. He and your mother see five moves ahead where most other 'Els might see only two or three. It's why our House has become so wealthy and powerful so quickly."

"And you think Rukh lacks those qualities? Their guile?" Jaresh shook his head. "You don't know him as well as you think you do."

Mira frowned. "How so?"

"He isn't as cunning as Amma or even Nanna, but he can see the larger issues at hand in a way they maybe can't. Rukh has always wanted to understand the truth of a matter. He's never accepted received wisdom without challenging it first."

"Such as?"

"Like whether a Sentya should be trained in the sword," Jaresh replied. "We were only six and five, but he was the one who somehow convinced Amma to have Durmer start teaching me. I remember overhearing Amma and Nanna talking about it after they thought I was asleep. Rukh basically told them that if I was a Shektan, then I was all-but a Kumma, which meant if I wanted, I should be taught the sword. I remember Nanna being impressed."

"I didn't know that."

"Few do, and I'm grateful Rukh spoke up when he did. For me, it's made all the difference." He smiled. "And if Nanna had asked him to help you, he would have. He isn't too proud to get his hands dirty."

Mira leaned back in her chair and considered Jaresh's words.

Rukh getting his hands and face dirty in the Cellar? It was hard to credit. In fact, Jaresh's description of his brother was almost completely at odds with how Mira had always thought of Rukh. He had always struck her as somewhat simple and naive. Nothing more pressing than mastery of the sword to ever clutter his mind. It was hard to reconcile the persona she had of him with the complex, intelligent, compassionate man Jaresh described.

Had she really misjudged him so terribly over the years? Jaresh seemed to think so, but she wondered if his view wasn't colored by a younger brother's adulation of his adored and admired older brother. Indeed, while Bree was undeniably brilliant, it was actually Jaresh whom Mira thought of as the brightest and most levelheaded of Dar'El's three children. Given his good looks, kindness, Talents, and wealth, Jaresh would make some Sentya woman incredibly happy one day, but Mira wondered what he might have been able to accomplish had he been born a Kumma, rather than just adopted into a Kumma House.

Jaresh laughed. "I can see you doubt everything I've said so far, but I guess I can let you in on the secret now that he's off on Trial: Rukh read voraciously. All the time. In some ways, he's even more of an intellectual than Nanna. He's certainly more of a dreamer anyway."

Mira frowned as she mulled over his words. "I think of a dreamer as being a visionary, as someone who accomplishes true greatness. He builds the things others say are impossible and raises us all up higher than we can reach. For example, it would have made more sense and been more practical for Dar'El to have remained with his birth House rather than transfer to House Shektan, but by doing so he helped create something extraordinary." She paused a moment, letting her words sink in. "So what does Rukh dream of building?"

Jaresh didn't answer at first, mulling over her words. "I don't know," he finally answered. "But whatever it is, I hope it is something grand, maybe even more than what Nanna has accomplished."

"You really think it's possible?"

"I think Rukh has true greatness in him. Yes."

Mira smiled. Rukh was a fine warrior, and maybe he was even the man Jaresh believed him to be: intelligent and wise, but she doubted he was also a visionary. It was too much. No man should be blessed with so many gifts.

She didn't want to argue the issue, though. What would be the point? Instead, she changed the subject. "And do you dream?" Mira asked. She was surprised to see a look of fleeting sorrow overtake Jaresh's face.

"I have dreams," he said, somewhat softly.

She waited to hear if he would say more, but he remained silent.

CHAPTER THIRTEEN
AN UNWHOLESOME DISCOVERY

*According to The Book of All-Souls, the sins of a man are said to be burned
away upon his death, and if his Jivatma is made pure, he will be elevated to
Heaven through Devesh's grace, to stand at our Lord's feet as a Holy Mahatma.
But, if he is unable to endure the cleansing, his soul re-enters the cycle of Life to be
re-born on Arisa. Where then are the Mahatmas? Perhaps they are absent
because a man's sins are not his alone. Perhaps they carry on in his blood.*

~Our Lives Alone by Asias Athandra, AF 331

Saresh was lost in his thoughts as he walked the southern leg
of Bright Rose Road and took the long way home. It had
been another long, fruitless day of reading and deciphering
the cramped, cryptic handwriting of scholars from ages past. His
eyes were tired, his head hurt, and he was frustrated. So far, there had
not even been the slightest shred of evidence, the smallest scrap of
information to let them know that this so-called Withering Knife
even existed. It had been a month since he and Mira had started their
search, and they had already worked their way through most of the
manuscripts on their initial list. They might soon have to expand the
scope of their investigation. It was an unpalatable thought.

He walked on, paying only minimal attention to his surroundings. He knew he was nearing his destination. All he had to do was stay on Bright Rose Road, the finely paved, large thoroughfare that circumnavigated Ashoka. No obvious ruts or potholes marred the street's surface, but small puddles of water from the late afternoon thundershower had collected in places where the street had settled. The rain had washed away much of the day's early summer humidity, and there was a fall-like nip to the air with a stiff breeze blowing in from the sea. Jaresh shivered. He was dressed for warmer weather, and the chill cut through his light clothing.

A gust of wind rustled the long line of rose bushes planted along the road's median, carrying a hint of the floral scent to come. The roses were the reason for Bright Rose's name. Right now, it was too early for them to bloom, but in a few months, the road would be a riot of colors: pink, yellow, red, and even purple. It was then, during the height of summer's warmth, that the lush, floral aroma would carry for miles and blanket the city with their fragrance, drawing thick bees and butterflies who would flitter amongst the flowers in rapturous delight.

Jaresh was always surprised by the quietness of this area – Widow Cavern, just west of Mount Crone and east of Hart's Stand along Bright Rose Road. Here, the main boulevard along Ashoka's perimeter was packed with rows of houses as well as shops and restaurants, but somehow, this neighborhood never seemed uproariously loud like the rest of the city. Even with the looming bulk of the Inner Wall no more than several hundred yards away to help encapsulate any noises, it remained relatively quiet. Maybe it was because the area here was mostly populated by Rahails, the quiet Caste. They enjoyed their silence. Even those who weren't Rahails quickly learned to maintain a more unobtrusive manner of speaking when living amongst them.

Jaresh pondered this Rahail sentiment for quietness even as a group of buskers played a loud, lively jig down the corner from him.

Maybe their demand for silence didn't apply to music. He was about to cross to the broad median of rose bushes when a harsh cry, cursing and angry, broke through his reverie. He was appalled to find the words were directed at him.

"Watch where you're going, you jackass!"

Jaresh startled out of his thoughts and came to a sudden stop, two steps into the street and off the pedestrian byway, wondering why he was suddenly standing in shadow. He glanced up, looking into the furious glare of a livid Duriah drover. Jaresh had stepped out directly in front of the man's heavily laden wagon. Only a hard jerk on the reins and a pull to the side had saved Jaresh from getting flattened.

The Duriah breathed heavily, anger still blazing in his eyes. "I almost killed you, fool. Do you not have anything to say for yourself?" the Duriah demanded, speaking in the formal and clipped tones of his Caste.

Jaresh quickly sized up the man. Based on his heavy leather apron, scorched in many places by burn marks, the man was a blacksmith and likely strong as an ox, given his bull-like build. And the look in his almond-shaped eyes didn't bode well. Duriahs tended to anger easily.

Nanna had always impressed Jaresh with the importance of humility and courtesy when dealing with strangers of any Caste. And not getting into a brawl with an angry Duriah was even more reason for a kind demeanor.

Jaresh apologized. "I'm sorry sir. I should have been paying more attention to where I was going. Unfortunately, my mind was elsewhere; on a task set to me by my nanna."

Most would have considered the apology excessively deferential, but for a Duriah it was just right. They were a very formal and polite Caste and quite the sticklers for etiquette. And given the near disaster Jaresh had nearly caused, a *very* obsequious confession was required.

It did help that his mistake was due to his preoccupation with his work, an excuse generally considered good as gold to a Duriah. For them, a man's worth was directly related to how seriously he took his labor, especially one given to him by his elders. Hopefully, the Duriah would see it the same way.

Jaresh sensed an easing of tension as the large drover grunted, the anger slowly fading from his eyes. "I suppose the fault for our accidental ill Cohesion was mine as much as yours," he responded, his voice deep and seeming to echo. A smile flicked across his face. "I'm sure balancing the ledgers waits for no man," he said in a teasing tone, mistakenly believing Jaresh was a typical Sentya accountant.

Jaresh saw no reason to correct the man. It wasn't worth the time. He smiled. "No they do not," Jaresh agreed in an amiable tone. He bowed slightly. "Again, my apologies for your troubles, Cohesor."

He had noticed the tattoo on the Duriah's forearm depicting strips of metal twisted into a braid. The tattoo denoted the man's standing as a master in his Caste. He wasn't just a drover; he was a smith.

The Duriah smiled, all the anger gone as suddenly as it had arrived, another trait of his Caste. "Well, best be moving along. Work doesn't do itself." He nodded in farewell. "Take care young man and be more careful next time."

"Be well." Jaresh replied, glad he had taken Nanna's advice: a kind word could often defuse a tense situation.

Jaresh paid more attention to his surroundings and headed for Hart's Stand, an area of fine trade shops, artisans studios, restaurants, and pubs. It was late afternoon, a few hours before supper, and the streets were starting to fill as folk rushed to finish the last of their work before heading home. Many stopped to grab a quick bite to eat from one of the many portable food carts as vendors sold the last of their hot snacks before supper. The spicy aroma of bhaji, samosas, and falafel filled the air.

Jaresh's stomach growled in response to the fine smelling food, but he ignored his hunger and continued on. He had to hurry if he wanted to be in time for his meeting.

The traffic grew more congested, and he passed several heavy wagons loaded with early summer crops as they crawled through the crowded streets. The Muran drovers sat stiffly in their seats, many with pipes held between their lips as they stroked their full, thick beards. Sentya bureaucrats rushed about with harried expressions, offering profuse if absentminded apologies as they went about their business.

Jaresh respectfully stepped aside as a Brace of Rahail swept toward him, marching through the middle of the street. There were about twelve of them, men and women of all ages, formed up in a triangle with all of them focusing their *Jivatma* on their leader, typically the oldest of them. Everyone gave the Brace a deferential berth, not wanting to distract them from their work, and they worked even as they strode past. Caste Rahail were the only ones with the Talent to maintain and repair the city's Oasis, a task paramount above all others.

As he neared Hart's Stand, the quietness of Widow Cavern ended abruptly. The sound of buskers, most of whom were probably from the Ahura Temple – one of the Sentya schools of music – competed with the cries of vendors and the hammering of Duriah blacksmiths. Hart's Stand was a place where several neighborhoods came together. As a result, it had become a place for commerce. There were many merchants and vendors hawking their wares from canvass covered stalls leased to them by the city, as well as a number of tradesmen, such as coopers, shoemakers, and plumbers with more permanent shops.

Jaresh skirted the edge of Hart's Stand and took a smaller road heading southeast. A few turns later he was past most of the noise of the Stand. Blessed quiet once more. With a sense of relief, he finally came upon his destination – the Long Pull, one of his favorite pubs. An old, wooden sign rattled above the entrance: an overflowing tankard. Months ago, before Rukh's departure, the two of them used to come here a lot. It had been one of their favorite watering holes with the best whiskey in the city. He missed hitting the pubs with Rukh. The two of them never got stinking drunk, but they always had a good time of it.

And after a hard, frustrating day, Jaresh needed a drink – a shot of something strong would be a nice start – but he had another reason for coming. While at the Library, he had received a message. Nanna wanted to meet him here tonight. No further explanation had been included. Not that Jaresh had expected one. He did wonder why they were meeting here instead of Nanna's study. He didn't imagine it was because Nanna wanted to go out drinking. Jaresh smiled at the thought. Nanna rarely drank, and he never got drunk.

Jaresh slapped the sign before opening the door – an old habit – pausing inside the entrance to the pub as he waited for his eyes to adjust to the dim lighting. This early, the tavern was all but empty. Ten or twelve tables were scattered around the large room with several lamps hanging unlit along the pub's brick walls. The bar was on the wall facing the front entrance. It ran nearly the entire length of the pub before ending in the far right corner at a door opening out to the courtyard in the rear. To the left of the bar, a swinging door led to the kitchen while a large, empty fireplace dominated the right-hand wall. Sunlight passed through the floor-to-ceiling mullioned windows facing out onto the street and highlighting the wide-planked wooden floor, faded and worn by thousands of feet and stained with spilled beer. A permanent smoky odor permeated the air, but the aroma of cooking food, chicken tikka maybe, floated out of the kitchen making Jaresh's mouth water.

Three men sat at a table near the bar laughing quietly over a joke. Each held a flagon of beer. The barkeep and proprietor, Gris

Holianth, a stocky man of medium height and middle years, stood wiping clean several dented mugs with a rag. His skin, dark as cured walnut, proclaimed him to be of Caste Shiyen, and his shiny pate gleamed in the dull light. Gris gestured out back.

Jaresh stepped through the open door.

The square courtyard was entirely enclosed with the pub, kitchen, and living quarters for Mr. Holianth's family forming three sides while the fourth was comprised of a stout brick wall. Tall, white candles provided a pleasant light as they burned in hurricane vases placed on all three tables set outside. Otherwise, the courtyard was empty except for Nanna and Bree, both of whom sat with a tall flagon of something foamy before them.

What was Bree doing here? He mentally shrugged, knowing Nanna would explain it all shortly.

He poked his head back inside and called for a beer before joining his family outside.

"How goes the search," Nanna asked as Jaresh hitched a chair.

"It doesn't," Jaresh replied, glancing at Bree, wondering if she knew what they were talking about.

"Withering Knife. Souleater. Search Ashoka's Library. Nanna already filled me in," Bree said, responding to his speculative glance. "I already figured out he had you and Mira working on something related to the murder. The timing of it all with the two of you both suddenly doing research in the Cellar so soon after Master Barnel's death…it was just too coincidental."

Jaresh sat back in his chair, surprised by how much Bree had figured out on her own. "I'm impressed," Jaresh said.

Bree chuckled, a throaty laugh. "I'm just glad it wasn't me down in the Cellar getting my nose all filthy."

Jaresh smiled. "No, we wouldn't want to get the Princess' hands dirty," he replied, teasing her with a childhood nickname she hated.

Bree rolled her eyes. "That name hasn't bothered me in years."

"Then why were…"

They were interrupted when Mr. Holianth set a mug of beer on the table. They waited until after he had collected his fifty pence wooden token and headed back inside before continuing their conversation.

Nanna cleared his throat, gathering their attention. "I asked the two of you to meet with me here because of a rather delicate matter. Should this ever come to public awareness, it will undoubtedly ruin our House."

Jaresh shared a wondering glance with Bree and set aside his mug.

Nanna's voice dropped to a low whisper. "What I am about to tell you is known only to me. It has to do with Kuldige Prayvar, born into House Trektim, and known to you as Kul'El Shektan, the founder of our House," Nanna said. "Several years ago, I found a small diary tucked away in a hidden drawer within my desk, the same desk inherited and passed down by the 'Els of our House since its founding. It was written in the hand of Kul'El, and I don't think he meant for it to be read by anyone else. The information contained within his journal is repulsive." Nanna's voice dropped to whisper. "By his own admission, our founder was a member of the Sil Lor Kum."

Nanna's words dropped into a dead silence. Jaresh and Bree shared a look of stunned disbelief. That could not be right. Only twisted degenerates sought membership in the Sil Lor Kum, not someone noble like the founder of House Shektan.

"That is imposs…" Jaresh began loudly, cut off as Nanna dug hard fingernails into his forearm.

His eyes flashed. "Quietly," he hissed. "There may be no other ears about, but we can't take any chances. It's the reason we are here and not the House Seat – too many chances of being overheard."

Jaresh made himself relax and let out a shuddering breath.

Nanna held a moment longer, but at Jaresh's nod, he released his arm.

"Unfortunately, what I just said is all too true," Nanna said, still grimacing in disgust. "But Kul'El was not just a member of the Sil Lor Kum, he was their SuDin, their commander. In our House records, we know Kul'El was, at best, a middling warrior. He completed three Trials, and somehow, through *extremely* fortuitous investments, he became wealthy enough to found House Shektan. Now, we know how those lucky turns of events came to pass. Kul'El possessed information unavailable to others, and he was able to make those spectacularly prudent investments because of his role as SuDin to the Sil Lor Kum."

Jaresh felt sick. Suddenly, he didn't feel like drinking the rest of his beer. He pushed it away.

Bree looked heartbroken. "Our House was founded on a lie, and by the worst kind of criminal imaginable. How do we walk the streets with such shame hanging upon us?" she cried out. "We've lost all honor."

"His sin was his. It is not ours," Nanna answered, fiercely. "Our honor is intact." He stared Bree in the eyes, willing her to accept his words.

"A home is only as strong as its foundation," she replied, reciting an old adage.

"Our foundation does not stem from the House we were born into," Nanna continued. "I know this better than just about anyone else. Nor does it emanate from the actions of our ancestors. In the end, we will all have to face the divining and dividing sword of Devesh. Our only armor during His final judgment will be how we acquitted ourselves on this world. The actions of our forebears can neither stain nor cleanse us."

Bree didn't say anything. She still looked troubled.

Jaresh understood exactly what she was going through since he was struggling with the same issues.

"There is more," Nanna said after a moment.

"I'm not sure I want to know," Jaresh said.

"I know what I've told you is disturbing…" Nanna began.

"Bit of an understatement," Bree muttered.

Nanna shrugged. "Imagine how I felt when I learned the truth," he replied. "While the two of you can confide your thoughts and fears with one another, I had no one. At least not until Rukh forced me to explain why I was so agitated."

"Rukh knows?" Bree asked. "Should have figured he would."

"I don't remember you being sad or downcast," Jaresh said.

For as long as Jaresh could remember, their nanna had always had a smooth and unruffled equilibrium no matter how difficult the situation. Nanna was a rock – nothing bothered him. It was part of the reason he was such an effective 'El. Others might lose themselves in anger or false bravado, but Nanna did not. He always coolly focused on the problem at hand and never let his emotions get the better of him.

Nanna smiled. "It was a few days after I'd come across the journal. One afternoon, Rukh walked into the library and…" he shrugged. "He must have seen something in my face or my posture…whatever it was, he knew something was wrong." He chuckled. "He badgered me until I told him what it was."

"And he's never said a word this entire time," Bree said.

"For two years now, he and I kept our secret shame hidden," Nanna said, "and so will you," he added, obdurate hardness in his voice.

"We will," Jaresh promised. "Now, what was this other thing you wanted to tell us?"

Nanna took a sip of his warm beer. "The Withering Knife. The Souleater. It is mentioned in Kul'El's journal, but he is frustratingly close-lipped about it. He merely restates what we already know: it is an ancient weapon, used by Suwraith at the dawn of our world, on the Night of Sorrows, and perhaps, on occasion, by the Sil Lor Kum. He suspects it gives the wielder the power to steal *Jivatma* from those who are slain with it."

Jaresh tried to keep the horror from his face.

Jivatma was the essence of a person. It was their center, who they were in their heart-of-hearts. Some even said *Jivatma* was the soul itself, the part of a person living on after the death of their mortal form. And for it to be stolen …it would be the final death. All their futures and choices would be vanished, stolen from them. They could never be re-born on Arisa or ascend to Heaven. With the Knife, their death would be the end of them. They would be expunged from existence, as surely as if they had chosen to deny Devesh's grace.

Learning the truth about the founder of their House had been awful, but this was sickening beyond words. This was evil in its purest form. What kind of a sick mind would even think to fashion such a weapon? It was appalling. Worse was the fact that the Withering Knife might be in Ashoka, and if so, it had already been used on poor Felt Barnel. The knowledge leant new urgency to Jaresh's work in the Cellar.

"But you're not certain it's this Knife we're dealing with?" Bree asked, cutting into Jaresh's horrified thoughts. "More likely, it's some naaja degenerate who needs to be put down."

"I am not entirely sure," Nanna answered. "As I said, Kul'El's journal is frustratingly opaque on the topic." He turned to Jaresh. "We have to know the truth of this matter. Quickly and quietly. If it is the Sil Lor Kum with whom we are dealing, they must have no inkling we suspect their presence. They'll only go deeper underground. We have to let them remain comfortable and confident in their anonymity, certain of their safety in the shadows."

"Until we shatter their smug assurance and kill them all," Bree said with a fierce grimace.

"Exactly," Nanna said. "Which is why you will be helping your brother and Mira in their search."

Despite the sickened feeling in the pit of his stomach, Jaresh had to smile, however fleeting. It looked like Bree would be getting her nose dirty after all.

She saw his half-smile and must have guessed what he was thinking. She stuck her tongue out at him, briefly lightening the mood.

Jaresh chuckled.

Just then, a young man, a Shiyen burst into the Long Pull. Based on his build and preternaturally balding head, the owner's son. He fairly bounced with excitement.

"There's another been murdered!" he shouted into the quiet. "Just like the last one!"

CHAPTER FOURTEEN
POSSIBLE ALLIES

Those who choose the twilight existence of the Sil Lor Kum are fools.
But pity their children. What misery to be raised by such jackals!

~*The Sorrows of Hume, AF 1789*

Silence fell in the pub before shouted questions were thrown at the young man, who struggled to answer them. He didn't know much more than what he'd already said.

Nanna turned to Jaresh. "Find Mira. We'll meet you in my study in a few hours," he said. "We need to discuss our plans."

"What about you?" Jaresh asked.

"Bree and I will go to where the body was found," Nanna answered. "And make sure your mother and Sophy are there also," he added a moment later. "It's time we informed them about this."

The three of them quickly left the bar, with Jaresh heading toward the House Seat, while Bree and their nanna went east along Scythe Cut toward Fragrance Wall to where the body had been found. Nanna wanted to personally examine the area, hoping to learn something more of the killer they hunted. Perhaps there was a clue, something others might have overlooked. It was a reasonable expectation, especially since the Watch had apparently not yet recognized that the murderer was likely a Kumma.

Bree followed silently in her nanna's wake, but her mind was in turmoil. It had been a day of upheaval. So many ugly truths had come to light, and so many falsehoods had been revealed. She struggled to make sense of it all. For instance, who was she now? She was a Shektan and a Kumma. That much was still true, but was she still an upright woman? She feared she was not. Despite Nanna's forceful assurance, she remained disturbed by a single question, one she could not answer: could grace and honesty rise from the wretched foundations laid by Kul'El Shektan?

Nanna said people made their own honor, and Bree understood what he meant, at least from a logical perspective, but understanding wasn't the same as believing. Nanna's words were sophistry, a way to wash clean the sins of the past without actually confronting them. For instance, should a ghrina ever reach adulthood and procreate, the original sin of its birth would still be passed on to all of its progeny, no matter how many generations had passed. The ghrina's stain could never be expunged. And if such things were true on an individual level, how could it not be the same for a House? No matter all the good works done later, if a House was born in sin, would it not carry the mark of such dishonor for the entirety of its existence?

The past determined the present, or so the philosophers opined.

All her life, Bree had been so proud to be a Shektan, part of a rising power, a House of morality, led by a man of goodness and decency. And now this…it was a heartache she wasn't sure she could ever come to terms with.

And she had no one with whom to confide. Who could she tell? No one else could be allowed to learn the dark secret at the heart of House Shektan's founding, and the only other person who *did* know was Jaresh. But he followed unthinkingly wherever Nanna led. Their father had decided House Shektan had developed honor, and

Nanna's words were as much the holy truth as *The Word and the Deed*, so far as Jaresh was concerned. Nothing more needed to be said or discussed. It was done.

Rukh might have understood what Bree was going through, but he was far, far away and wouldn't be back for several years.

She held in a sigh of bitter disappointment and grief.

She would have to struggle with this problem on her own. She would have to find her own peace with the past and come to accept the unforgivable. In some ways, she wished Nanna had never taken her into his confidence and told her what was going on. She wished he had left House Shektan's history and all of the foul details of its founding to himself. Blissful ignorance would have been so much easier.

Nanna slowed. They must be nearing the place of the murder, and Bree tried to rein in her troubled thoughts. Her father needed her help. He needed her eyes to help see what the Watch might have missed. She had to be at her best even if she felt at her worst.

She glanced around at their surroundings.

This was Fragrance Wall, the area of Ashoka that was home to most Cherids. The nearby houses were large and extravagant, with tree-lined private drives leading to immaculate manses and estates. Duriah and Rahail guards warded the gates while Murans tended the extensive gardens within. Caste Cherid was exceedingly affluent in material wealth, but their prosperity did not extend to their ability to procreate. They were the smallest of all the Castes in terms of numbers, usually marrying late and often only able to produce one or two children per couple. While everyone else knew a Caste's true wealth was measured in its people, the Cherids must have believed differently or were simply too selfish to have larger families; too caught up in their own lives to share it with someone as needy as a child. How else to explain their vulgar displays of wealth? It was so tasteless. As far as Bree was concerned, it was a minor miracle the

Caste had not somehow bred itself out of existence. And, of course, the precious little princes and princesses never lifted a finger to obtain their riches. For a Cherid, labor was thought to be nearly sinful. Instead the parasites suckled like leeches off the work of others.

"We're close," Nanna said, breaking into her thoughts as he pointed out the Watch.

They had cordoned off the area in front of one of the mansions, using temporary wooden barricades to keep the press of onlookers at a distance. Members of the Watch, almost all of them Kumma, stood grim-faced behind the barriers, facing outward and denying entrance to anyone from the already large crowd gathered beyond the cordons. Bree couldn't see the body, but according to those standing about, it was somewhere close to the gates, apparently having been found behind a tall hedgerow.

Nanna directed her to the barricades.

"Only Watch allowed through," a warrior said as Bree's nanna was about to bypass the barriers. "You'll have to wait…" His words died off as he recognized Dar'El. "Sorry, sir. Didn't realize it was you."

"I understand. I'm sure you have a lot on your mind," Nanna said, stepping past the man.

They headed to a gap through a tall, tapestry hedge where the Watch was clustered.

"Dar'El, what brings you here?" a voice called out. It was Rector Bryce. Apparently, he was the senior officer present.

"Simply a concerned citizen wanting to help in whatever way I can."

"Concerned citizen?" Rector gave them a penetrating look. After a moment he shrugged and gestured for them to follow as he led them through the opening in the hedge.

Beyond was an enclosed garden where hummingbirds darted

amongst floral gems of many hues. The heart was a blue sapphire pond of still water cupped by a carpet of soft, green grass. Lily pads floated on a slow current. A stencil of fine, white gravel marked the perimeter of the garden. It must have been a lovely haven before it became the site of an inhuman murder.

"You know it's a Kumma, don't you?" Rector whispered.

"The victim?" Nanna asked, sounding surprised.

"The killer."

Bree hid her surprise. Despite his membership in House Shektan, Bree didn't know Rector very well. On the few occasions in which they had spoken, he had never struck her as particularly bright. Rather, she had considered him a stiff and cordial bore, which to her was the pose of the amiable dullard.

Perhaps she had misjudged him.

"And you say this, why?" Dar'El asked.

"The first man who was killed – Felt Barnel – he was a friend of mine. I knew him from a Trial we shared. He was as tough a Muran as you're ever going to meet, still in the Guard, in fact. But even with all his training, he was barely able to put up a fight. I'm thinking the only person fast enough, strong enough, and skilled enough to take him down so easily would have to be a Kumma.

"Your friend could have been taken by surprise," Dar'El suggested.

"Not Felt. Surprise or no, he would have given more than he showed. He wouldn't have been put down so easily." Rector shook his head. "I don't like saying it, but it's the truth. It's got to be one of us."

Nanna studied Rector long enough for the Watcher to squirm a bit. "I've considered the same possibility," Dar'El finally admitted.

"And I also think you know even more. It's why you've had Jaresh and Mira going to the Library for the past two months."

"What do you mean?" Nanna asked, feigning ignorance. But it

was too late. Rector had guessed the truth, and Nanna's fleeting look of surprised acknowledgement had confirmed it.

"Others might ignore Jaresh's worth, but I don't. They only see a Sentya, but I see your son, trained to think critically, just like Rukh and Bree. You trust him, and you trust Mira. You wouldn't have them spending so much time in the Library unless it was important, like a Kumma murderer. I can help."

Again, Bree found herself impressed by the man's insight. She had *definitely* misjudged Rector Bryce …and so had Nanna judging by the expression on his face.

Dar'El considered Rector's offer – a moment stretching into uncomfortable silence – before nodding agreement. "No one else is to know of this. Can you do that?"

"So long as it doesn't interfere with my work in the Watch."

"It will complement it," Nanna said. "We're having a meeting at the House Seat in my study in an hour. Will you be there?"

Rector bowed, a brief bob of his head. "Of course, my 'El," he replied.

While Nanna and Bryce had been talking, Bree had ventured deeper into the garden, to a jarring area of bright red blood marring the pristine white gravel. She studied the ground closely. The body had already been removed, but there was something in the blood splatter. A set of footprints from a pair of boots. She frowned in concentration. There was more. She bent closer and after a few minutes of study, she smiled imperceptibly in understanding. She recognized it now.

"You see something?" Nanna asked.

"The killer has a limp," Bree answered. "See how the left boot heel drags."

Rector swore. "I *knew* there was something wrong with those prints," he said. "I just couldn't put my finger on it."

Nanna smiled. "Well done."

They spent a few more minutes looking around the garden but none of them discovered anything else of importance.

"Come to the House Seat in an hour," Dar'El said to Rector.

"I have a few more things to attend to, but I should be there without delay."

"Check her nails," Bree suggested. "She might have fought back and scratched whoever attacked her."

"Her?" Rector asked. "How did you know?"

"The shape of the body etched in the blood," Bree said.

Rector smiled. "Very clever."

• • •

Later in the evening, almost everyone invited had gathered in Nanna's study. Amma and Mira's mother, Sophy, sat in a corner, speaking softly with one another, occasionally flicking glances at Rector Bryce.

Bree watched the object of their attention as well. Rector stood before the bookshelves, scanning them. He seemed aware of the older women's interest, and based on the stiffness of his carriage, she could tell it made him uncomfortable. She took pity on him and walked over. "They seem to have picked up your scent," she murmured.

Rector smiled. "If they were only hunting me, I could run and hope to escape," he said. "But with the plans I think they have in mind, running would merely postpone the inevitable."

Bree laughed. "You make it sound as if they have a horrid fate in store for you. Isn't your family and Sophy's considering a marriage contract between you and Mira?"

Rector shrugged. "So I've heard," he said. "But I don't know how serious these discussions actually are."

"Even if they directly affect you?" Bree asked, perplexed.

"So it seems," Rector said. "Besides, I don't think Mira likes me much."

"Why do you say that?"

"I'm not sure," Rector said. "Perhaps I'm not quite as clever as she would wish her husband to be."

Bree mulled his words, feeling vaguely guilty. After all, until tonight, she had felt the same way about Rector Bryce. "There's more to you than she realizes," she said.

Just then, Mira and Jaresh walked in with Nanna close on their heels. He closed the door and quickly explained to Rector what he suspected might be happening. Amma and Sophy must have already known because they evinced no surprise at Nanna's words.

After Nanna was finished, Rector, who had listened in stoic silence, exhaled hard. "The Sil Lor Kum," he murmured. "Suwraith's' spit. I knew we were facing a degenerate, but I had no idea *how* degenerate."

Thankfully, he missed the meaningful look Bree exchanged with Jaresh.

"What do we know about the victim from today?" Nanna asked.

"Her name was Aqua Oilhue, a Cherid." Rector turned to Bree. "You were right. She fought back and was not taken unawares. A small piece of gold-threaded cloth was found beneath one of her nails – whoever killed her was wealthy." Rector turned back to Nanna. "From what I could piece together of the blood trail, she was attacked on the far side of the entrance to the garden, in the shadows where no one would see or hear. Somehow, she must have broken free and tried to escape. The killer gave chase. He came up from behind her and stabbed her in the back. It was through the heart. She died instantly. And like Felt Barnel, the first victim, her corpse was desiccated by the time it was found."

"I think I'm going to throw up," Mira said, looking appalled and angry rather than sick.

Her mother frowned. "I understand what you're feeling, but we can't afford such weakness right now."

Mira flushed at her amma's rebuke.

Privately, Bree felt Sophy was overly critical of her daughter. Mira was a smart, intelligent, and tough young woman with a bone deep integrity. After all, she had earned Nanna's trust, which should have proven to Sophy that Mira was no longer a child in need of scolding.

"I think you're plenty strong," Bree heard Jaresh whisper.

Mira flashed him a grateful smile.

Amma cleared her throat, gathering everyone's attention. "So, we have a wealthy Kumma who limps." She grimaced. "Which means we have a list of potential suspects measuring into the hundreds."

"True," Sophy said. "Most of the Trial veterans limp to some extent."

"I think we can narrow our search somewhat," Mira said. "I would bet the person we are looking for is someone older and more mature."

"Why so?" Sophy asked, a demanding and doubting tone in her voice. "I don't see it."

But Mira was right. Bree understood immediately once Mira had pointed it out. She was about to answer, but Nanna spoke first.

"Because the Withering Knife is said to be an ancient and powerful relic. Only someone with years as Sil Lor Kum would be trusted with such a weapon."

Bree nodded. It was how she saw it, too, and based on her nod of agreement, so did Amma.

"I agree," Jaresh said. "Those who choose the path of the Sil Lor Kum may be unalterably evil…"

"What do you mean 'may be'?" Rector interrupted. "By their works, we know they actively seek the destruction of Humanity. They hide in the shadows working to kill us all. How can they be anything other than unalterably evil?"

"A poor choice of words," Jaresh replied.

Her brother looked irritated at Rector's reprimand, but Bree agreed with the Watcher. They needed to clearly understand and acknowledge what they faced. Half measures of 'might be' or 'could be' wouldn't do in describing their enemy. It needed to be said, and repeated over and over again if necessary: any who claimed membership in the Sil Lor Kum *were* irredeemably evil.

"The point I wanted to make is this: just like us, seniority in the ranks of the Sil Lor Kum likely depends on length of service. Whoever has been entrusted with this weapon has to be someone who has risen to a position of power, which means he's been with them for years. He's going to be older."

Sophy gave Mira an approving, if a somewhat condescending nod. "It makes sense. We're looking for an older and wealthy Kumma then."

"Before we start investigating possible suspects, I believe a greater priority is confirming the probability that we face the Withering Knife," Nanna said. He turned to Rector. "I'd like you to work with Jaresh in the Cellar while Mira and Bree search the…"

Amma interrupted. "From the reports Mira and Jaresh have given, it would make more sense to keep them together for now. They've developed a system and a rapport. *They* are the ones best equipped to quickly work their way through the Cellar. Breaking them up might set us back by weeks."

"They've already spent quite a lot of time together," Nanna warned. "Tongues might wag."

He looked to Sophy, who didn't look happy. "In our world, a woman's reputation is her only armor," she said.

"And Mira's reputation will remain untarnished. I'll make sure of it," Jaresh said. "We'll take a chaperone if we have to."

"As can Rector and I," Bree says.

"No chaperones. I want this information sealed. The less people involved, the less chance our prey will learn they are stalked." He glanced at Sophy. "Assuming you'll allow Mira to continue working with my son?"

When put like that, Sophy had little choice but to agree, although she remained reluctant. "I'll hold you to your promise," she said to Jaresh. "Mira's reputation must not suffer."

"You have my word," Jaresh said.

"What about Amma and Sophy?" Bree asked. "What will they be doing?"

"They'll be busy as well, looking through the records of House Shektan and House Primase…assuming you will be granted access to your birth House's historical vaults, Sophy."

She nodded. "I have a good relationship with Tor'El," Sophy replied. "I'm sure it won't be a problem."

"Good. Then we'll put the word out. I've already let others know that Jaresh and Mira are researching a topic integral to House Shektan. I'll confirm Bree and Rector's work is in the same vein."

"How much longer until you finish with the works in the Library?" Amma asked.

"Five or six weeks," Mira answered. "If we don't find anything by then, we'll have to expand the search beyond our initial parameters."

"In that case, Bree and Rector will work their way through the larger secondary Libraries, such as the ones at Verchow and Alminius Medical Colleges. I want weekly reports."

"And when will Garnet and Durmer be informed?" Bree asked. The older Kummas would be certain to have advice critical to the search.

Dar'El hesitated. "Not yet. They both fit the profile of the killer."

Jaresh frowned in disagreement. "I have trouble believing either of them would be involved in any of this."

"They are our honored elders," Rector protested.

"If we're correct, this killer is almost certain to be *someone's* honored elder," Dar'El countered. "The killer is hiding in plain sight, a respected member of our community, and until we know whether this truly is Sil Lor Kum, we keep this information quiet. Until I say otherwise, it's restricted to the seven of us in this room."

Bree's shoulders slumped. She felt tired and beat down. How much worse could this day get? Learning of the foundational lie of her House, another gruesome murder, and now this: two of her most honored teachers, Garnet Bosde or Durmer Vulk, might be the very killer they sought.

Having her childhood teachers named as possible suspects brought home the reality and immediacy of the problem they faced.

"Suwraith's spit," Rector murmured.

"My sentiments exactly," Bree replied.

Mira sighed and rubbed her aching back. For the past three hours, she had been hunched over an *extremely* long and overly descriptive manuscript written by a nameless historian shortly after the Days of Desolation. The man had blathered on in exhaustive detail about everything related to Suwraith, everything from the sound of Her thunderous voice – a horrifying thought to actually hear the Queen speak – to the reasons for Her hatred of Humanity. All of it had turned out to be base conjecture. A waste of time. The author went so far as to state that Suwraith's birth arose from Her murder of the First Mother and the First Father, the Queen's supposed parents. It was a patently absurd and blasphemous claim. Like most Kummas, Mira wasn't particularly religious, but she also didn't go out of her way to insult the beliefs of those who were.

She set the book aside and yawned. It had been a long day. Once more she and Jaresh were huddled over their pile of books and various manuscripts deep in the dankness of the Cellar. The light from the chandelier with its dim firefly lamps did little to remove the melancholy nature of the place. But with all the time she and Jaresh had spent down here, she hardly even noticed the gloom any more. It had been three weeks since the last murder, which meant it had been three more weeks with nothing to show for their effort. The search for this mythical Withering Knife was growing increasingly frustrating.

"You would think something so important would merit at least *some* kind of mention," Mira complained. "But in all the books, manuscripts, and scrolls pertaining to the Sil Lor Kum, I've yet to come across even the vaguest of references to the Knife."

"You would think, but then you would be wrong," Jaresh said with a chuckle. "Supposing, of course, anyone else knew about it."

Mira grimaced. "They knew about it. They just kept it to themselves, so our search would be even more difficult than it otherwise would be."

"Yes, I'm sure it was their intention all along: join the Sil Lor Kum. Check. Learn all about the Withering Knife. Check. Hide all the information, so centuries later, Mira and Jaresh will search fruitlessly for it. Check and double check."

Mira punched him lightly in the shoulder, evoking a patently false squawk of pain.

"Heh!" Jaresh protested.

"You deserved it," Mira said.

"You're lucky I'm a gentleman, or I might hit you back," Jaresh said.

"And if you did, I'd hit you back even harder," Mira replied.

"And you'd just break if I did."

"Well then. I suppose I'll just have to mock you from a distance from now on."

Mira laughed. "I'd still find a way to return the favor," she said.

"You know, for such a supposedly gentle flower of Kumma womanhood, you sure have a dogged determination to cause me pain."

"After all the time we've been stuck down here in the Cellar, how is it you haven't realized the truth about me: I am the utter, diametric opposite of a gentle Kumma woman."

"So, you're a violent, non-Kumma man?" Jaresh asked, glancing Mira over. "You hide it well."

She hit him again. This time, much harder, and eliciting another more sincere squawk.

"I can keep this up all day," Mira advised.

"Why don't we get back to work? I don't think my shoulder can take anymore of our conversating."

"Conversating? Interesting made up description of what you think we were doing?" Mira said. "Sounded to me like you were making fun of me."

"Maybe a little bit, but it sure sounded funnier in my mind than when I spoke it out loud and you punched me." He yawned and stretched mightily. "How many more texts are there before we have to expand our search?" he asked.

Mira looked at their master list of topics, subtopics, comparing it to their catalog of books and manuscripts to review. The list had been her idea, but Jaresh had been the one to put it together. His methodical, systematic Sentya mind allowed him to bring order to the chaos of what she had originally proposed. And thank Devesh they hadn't followed her directions. If they had, they would be weeks behind where they were right now.

"Only a few hundred more," Mira said.

"About two weeks of work then," Jaresh said. "Which would bring us in on time for what we promised Nanna."

While no one else had died since the second murder, Mira and Jaresh both felt the press of the passing days. It was only a matter of time before the killer struck again, and if they exhausted their current list, they would have to greatly expand their search. It was something neither of them was looking forward to.

Mira sighed. She still had trouble reconciling herself to the truth of what they hunted: the Sil Lor Kum. How could anyone be so wicked as to join Suwraith's cult? Evil fools. If all the members of the Sil Lor Kum spontaneously caught fire and burned for eternity – or just a very long time – Mira would have considered it their just rewards. She hated the presence of such depravity in her city, or any city for that matter. Hunting the Sil Lor Kum had been a task she would willingly do over and over again, but she still didn't like having to do it.

In fact, the only good thing to come about over the past few months was getting to know Jaresh. She now understood why Dar'El trusted him so much. He was smart, hard-working, and did his job without complaint, but he wasn't stiff and joyless like Rector Bryce. She pitied Bree having to spend so much time with such a bore. Jaresh was clever and amusing in his own Sentya way. Mira smiled. In fact, without his wry sense of humor, their time in the Cellar would have been far less pleasant. Sure, his mocking tone could grate on her nerves, but all in all, she enjoyed spending time with him. He made her laugh.

Jaresh looked up and noticed her scrutiny. "What is it?"

"Nothing," she replied. "I only wanted to tell you how much I've appreciated your company these past few months. Without you around, the Cellar would have been far more taxing and monotonous."

"Thank you," he said with a smile. "It was nice getting to know you as well."

Mira laughed. "Well, it goes without saying," she replied. "I am a Kumma woman after all. You should consider yourself blessed to spend so much time in my presence."

Jaresh bowed his head. "Of course," he said. "All Kumma women are queens." He paused as if in thought. "Then again, it might not be something to trumpet about given the mind of the most famous of queens."

"Comparing me to Suwraith now? Not very chivalrous."

"I'd never say or even imply such a thing…my queen."

Mira laughed. "You're a good man, Jaresh. Don't ever change."

"A good man," Jaresh repeated, seeming to taste the words. "Something to which we should all aspire."

———————◼●◼———————

Bree was broken from her reverie as Rector sighed in disgust. "What is it?" she asked, wincing as her words echoed through the cavernous hall, which made up Verchow Library. She had spoken more loudly than she meant, but luckily this late at night, and in the summer no less, only one other person shared the Library with them, and her nose was plugged in a book. She hadn't even looked up at Bree's words.

Verchow Library was a long, narrow arcade with rows of medical texts and histories of disease and death neatly placed upon the shelving running perpendicular to the length of the room. The center of the hall was given over to a large number of dark, mahogany tables, each with seating for four. Broad chandeliers of firefly lamps hung above and shed light down below. Murals depicting scenes from the life of Gelan Criatus, the father of modern medicine, graced many of the panels of the vaulted ceiling, which soared thirty feet or more above them.

"Are Shiyens even Human?" Rector growled. "Devesh bless them, but they discuss disease in such an unemotional fashion. It makes me wonder if they really care about the people they take care of. Listen to this:

> *The patient, one Privem Thacker, was found to have an intestinal obstruction and rupture upon arrival to the hospice. Unfortunately, despite our best efforts, the patient expired forthwith. His wife was expectedly distraught. However, she was unreasonably put out when she was quite rightly informed that had she brought Master Thacker (a Muran) for our care several hours earlier, he might have lived.*

"Utterly bloodless." Rector threw down the book in disgust. "A man is dead, his wife grieving, and you'd think the Shiyen was talking about a dead cat."

The idea of Shiyens as emotionless and non-caring was a commonly held view and had essentially become a truism. However, Bree had spent a lot of time with those of the Healer Caste. From what she had observed, Shiyens cared deeply about those they cared for, but it wasn't always easily evident. Sometimes, in order to do their work, they had to maintain a reserved restraint, a decorum others occasionally mistook as a callous insensitivity. In fact, had she been born a Shiyen with the proper Talent, Bree would have gladly attended Verchow or Alminius to become a physician.

"What are you reading?" she asked.

"Eh?"

"The passage you just read...what book is it from?"

Rector glanced at the title. "*Bedside Manners Volume 2: Improper Etiquette When Consoling the Grieving.*" Rector rubbed his chin and reddened with embarrassment. "Maybe this wasn't the best example of what I meant."

Bree smiled. "Or maybe you should pay attention to the book title you're reading."

"How can I when my eyes are cramping?" Rector asked, still looking embarrassed.

Bree laughed. "Your eyes can cramp? It's a medical miracle."

"It's true. There's no explanation for my condition," Rector said. "Besides…someone has to keep the Shiyens on their toes. It might as well be me," he added with a shrug.

"Speaking of staying on your toes…catch." Bree tossed him another book. "I doubt you'll find what we're looking for in *Bedside Manners*," she said. "Try this one instead."

Rector caught the book and squinted at the title, written as it was in a tight, crabbed print. He sighed. "My poor eyes."

Despite his put-upon attitude, Bree knew Rector wasn't serious. From what she had seen, he was as hard-working as anyone she knew. Her nanna would have described him as 'all go and no slow'. She doubted Rector even knew how to be lazy.

Rector settled in with the book she had given him, and an hour later, he set aside the slim volume. "Done," he said. "Hand me the big one over there." He grunted when she passed over the heavy tome. "When we find these lickspittle motherhumpers, I'm feeding them my sword," Rector promised. "Look at the size of this book. Do you know what it's about? It's about unsolved murders in Ashoka. I wouldn't be surprised if the majority of them were due to the fragging Sil Lor Kum."

"Language," Bree admonished.

"Sorry," Rector said, not looking apologetic. "It's just these bastards don't deserve any mercy. They don't even deserve the dignity of a tribunal. We should just execute them. Crucify the whole lot of them, I say."

The venom in Rector's voice took Bree aback.

He must have noticed her expression. "I'm sorry, Bree." This time, he did look apologetic. "I get worked up about these kinds of things," Rector said. "The Trials show us the true face of evil. The Fan Lor Kum are responsible for the death of more warriors in the Wildness than anything else in this world, but in the end, they're only a mob of dumb beasts with no more choice in the matter than an ox hitched to a yoke. They're slaves to their Queen. The Sil Lor Kum, though, they're different. They *choose* to serve evil."

"I agree. They don't deserve any mercy. When we find them, I could easily slit all their throats and sleep well at night," Bree said. "The reason I was surprised is because you're a member of the Watch. Aren't you supposed to uphold an individual's rights under the law? Make sure they have a proper tribunal?"

"Perhaps your father believes the way you describe?" Rector guessed.

"I imagine so."

"Our 'El is a gifted leader of men," Rector said, sounding as if he were choosing his words most delicately.

"Nanna is rare," Bree agreed. "He is generous to a fault, but the Sil Lor Kum don't deserve his mercy. They willingly placed themselves beyond our civilized strictures. Why should we grant them anything? Death is their proper reward. I think you're right: we should crucify all of them."

"Indeed," Rector said. "What do you think should be done with their families? Their children?"

"What about them?" Bree replied. She tried to hide the sudden discomfort his question raised.

"They should share in the disgrace," Rector said. "They'd be forever Tainted. I say exile them as well."

Bree didn't answer. Rector's statement raised doubts she wasn't ready to confront. The whole topic made her uneasy. Rector had no such qualms. He had already decided exile was the proper punishment for children whose only crime was birth to one who chose the Sil Lor Kum. What then would he say of their own House? What would Rector think if he knew the truth of Kul'El Shektan? He would likely demand the immediate dissolution of the House.

Bree couldn't say she disagreed with him, either. She was conflicted in her opinion. Some days she shared Rector's feelings on the topic, but on other days, she thought differently. House Shektan had done a lot of good over the years. It had many just and honorable members. None of them had sought out to do evil. In fact, they had actively fought it their entire lives. Why should they be punished for something they couldn't have ever known or guessed about their founder? It was a question she was no nearer to answering now than on the day she had first learned of Kul'El Shektan's infamy.

"I'm glad we're in agreement," Rector said, mistaking the meaning of her silence.

———•◦•———

"Must you leave so soon, my dear?" the SuDin of the Sil Lor Kum asked.

Varesea turned to him with a coquettish smile. "You know I have to," she replied. "My husband grows worried if I'm out late."

"Your husband is a fool. Were you mine, I would keep you close at hand so we might more easily enjoy one another."

She laughed. "That may be one of the most ridiculous things I've ever heard you say," she replied.

"Speak for yourself," the SuDin said. "I could take you again this very moment if you were willing." He drew her to his lap. "I can prove it," he whispered into her ear as he guided her hand to his hardness.

She gasped in surprise. "Put that away," she admonished. She stood, and he let her go, disappointed. He wasn't sure why or how, but for the past few months, his lust was as it had been when he was young. When he wasn't busy with all the worries of the modern world, foremost on his mind was the next time he could be with Varesea. And given the decline to many of the responsibilities in his other life, the one outside of the Sil Lor Kum, he thought about it often.

He reckoned it might have something to do with the Knife. He was stronger and faster than he had been in decades. Even the limp from his injured left knee was better. At the rate he was healing, a few more killings and he would be as fine a warrior as he had been as a young man. And he had been formidable once, easily as good as any who had won the Tournament of Hume.

"*She* spoke to you again last night, didn't she?" Varesea guessed.

"How did you know," he asked, admiring the line of her thighs as she adjusted her robes. Time might have caused her breasts to sag, but her legs were still lean and strong.

"Your eyes…they're haunted whenever She touches you. Is Her presence really so difficult?"

He laughed harshly "You should be thankful you have never had to suffer one of Her visitations. She is like a razor scraping at your mind."

"And yet, She is the ultimate power in this world." A fleeting look of hunger flitted across Varesea's face.

The SuDin wasn't surprised by Varesea's look of desire. From what he had seen, everyone who joined the Sil Lor Kum yearned for power of some sort. It was rather pathetic. They risked their lives and their good names, even the lives of their own families for something so ephemeral. Too many of the Sil Lor Kum were ravenous pigs, vainly seeking to satiate their gluttonous hunger.

Varesea was like all the others – but in one critical way, she was unlike them. She too lusted for power, but her reason was different. She didn't crave control; she desired safety. It made all the difference in the world as far as the SuDin was concerned. Rather than inspiring contempt, her situation – and he knew her lot in life all too well – aroused his compassion. Because if Varesea had been *entirely* as the others, he wouldn't have been able to countenance even a moment in her bed, much less the ten years they'd shared as lovers.

"So most believe," the SuDin replied to her statement.

"So *most* believe. But not you?"

"Not me."

"Why is that?" Varesea mused.

"We have battled Her for two millennia, and…" the SuDin paused, not sure he was ready to trust her with such a momentous truth.

"And what?" she asked. "We have lost every time She has come against us." A moment later, her eyes widened in alarm. "You can't possibly think to defeat Her. It's an unattainable dream."

"And yet, the dream you dismiss is the very reason I joined the Sil Lor Kum," the SuDin said solemnly. "My only desire has and always will be to protect Ashoka."

"My SuDin you cannot defy Her. She crushes all who do. Remember: all the cities She has visited in times past. They are nothing but powder now. You'll destroy yourself if you defy Her will."

The SuDin smiled at Varesea's concern. It was touching. "I'm not ready to challenge Her yet, but with the Knife, I may have an opportunity to learn Her weakness as no one ever has."

"And have you learned anything thus far?"

The SuDin smiled. "I have, and I believe it is quite valuable." He smiled wider, a lupine grin. "Our Queen is utterly insane, just as the prior SuDins claimed. As they also said, She is easily deceived. In fact, She is quite stupid."

Varesea considered his words in silence.

"Why do you bother?" she finally asked. "Your name has become a byword for humiliation amongst your Caste. In your other life, I have heard how members of your own House openly mock you at times. You hold your position by the barest of threads. Are any of them worth what you've given up?"

The SuDin's jaw clenched. He disliked any reminder of his disgrace. In his other life, he treaded thin ice. As far as he was concerned, he had been all but abandoned by both his House and his Caste. Despite this, he would protect them. Though he lived in the shadows now, working with people who were worse than a Chimera; though his soul had become incurably soiled; though all those proud Kummas of his Caste would gladly stake him out on the Isle of the Crows were he ever found out, he had no regrets. His fallen state was of his own choosing, and all he had done had been for Ashoka's sake. He knew no other way to protect his city. But in the end his legacy would be cleansed; his sacrifices made manifest; and his name as revered and hallowed as that of mighty Hume. It had to be. He had given too much and lost even more for it to be otherwise.

"I will be the one – and in time, all will learn of it – who convinces Her to bypass our city."

"You think it's possible?"

The SuDin shrugged. "I don't know, but I have to try. I know others spit upon my name, but I have always been a loyal son of Ashoka."

Varesea smirked. "You murdered two people and stole their *Jivatma*, and for the past decade, you've enthusiastically shared my bed. Most would name you evil for the first and a ghrina for the last."

He grimaced and looked away. "The dead…I didn't enjoy killing them, but it was necessary." He turned back, and his gaze bored into Varesea's. "I'll murder a thousand more just like them, or even ten thousand, if it sees Ashoka safe."

"An unsettling philosophy," Varesea said, sounding not the least bit troubled. "Kill whoever is needed to achieve your ambition."

The SuDin smiled and tucked a stray strand of hair behind her ear. "I would never harm you," he said, pulling her close for a lingering kiss.

Varesea pushed away. "Pardon me if I have my doubts."

The SuDin laughed. "You need never fear me."

"And what of us and our time shared?"

"Perhaps I am every bit as depraved as my enemies claim," he said. "Or maybe I've simply decided society's restrictions are of only passing importance. I will save Ashoka, but in doing so, I will not deny myself life's pleasures."

CHAPTER FIFTEEN
A PURCHASE OF SANITY

An ancient SarpanKum once questioned Mother's orders, going so far
as to label them nonsensical. No one now knows who he was.
His life was ended on the spot, and his name expunged from history.
The lesson did not escape the notice of his lieutenants.

~From the journal of SarpanKum Li-Dirge, AF 2060

"**W**hy did you murder us, daughter?" Mother asked. Her voice was like sandpaper across Suwraith's frayed thoughts. *"Did we not love you enough?"*

Mother was long dead, but She refused to remain silent, always demanding answers to a question, which on most occasions, Lienna refused to acknowledge.

Sometimes, however, it helped to respond.

"I did what was needed. Your deaths were required for the greater good."

"The greater good? Is that why I was slain as well?" Her Father asked.

"Yes," Lienna answered. *"And I regret it not."* It was a simple truth, and one She shunned facing, but tonight, for some reason, Her ancient dread of Her parents was quiescent.

"Be cautious of the Baels," Father warned, moving on to His favorite topic.

Lienna smirked. Father was a fool, always counseling Her to be fearful of everything. What did She have to fear from anyone? She was the Queen of all creation, the most powerful being Arisa had ever known.

"They are devoted to Me. They serve at My command," Lienna snapped.

"We once believed you served Us," Mother reminded Her. *"That you loved Us."*

Lightning flashed, an echo of Lienna's annoyance. *"The Baels are as I wish them to be: they love Me as I never loved you."*

Good. Such an ugly remark usually quieted Mother.

"And do you love Me?" a softly sinister voice whispered.

Lienna worked to quell Her sudden fear. It was Mistress.

"Of course," Lienna replied. *"I am to you as the Baels are to Me."*

Mistress chuckled, an ugly, mocking sound. *"Then you would betray Me at every turn,"* She said.

"I would never…"

"Be silent, stupid girl," Mistress cut Her off, never having to raise Her voice. *"Look to Me, upon the bosom of My fertile land where Your Fan Lor Kum propagate like lice. See how Your precious Baels conspire with Our enemies."*

Lienna did as commanded, looking to the ground where She had last spoken with Her SarpanKum. She focused on the shallow vale wherein She had commanded the Baels earlier in the evening.

Lightning crackled, and She hissed a stormcloud of outrage.

Humans, and some not even properly Casted. The Human infestation sank ever lower into further abomination. There the parasites stood; proudly and fearlessly beside Her Baels. Why didn't Her warriors attack?

"Because they seek to betray You," Father replied.

"A fitting punishment," Mother said. *"You reap what you sow, Daughter."*

"What now, girl?" Mistress Arisa asked in a derisive tone. *"Will you wreak Your vengeance upon Your children?"*

"Yes," Lienna hissed. *"They were always meant for death anyway."*

"Murder will not avail you Your problems," Mother said.

"And the Baels deserve life," Father added.

"You say this now...after what they have done? You've always warned Me against them," Lienna cried.

"The Baels will betray You, and it is just if they do so," Father said, his voice buzzing loud and angry, a stinging of wasps in Her mind. *"They betray You because You deserve no loyalty. They betray You because of what you have done with Your life, and the lives of countless others. They betray You because You are a wicked curse I wish we had never birthed!"*

"NO!" Lienna cried. *"I am your Daughter. You must love Me. All must love Me."*

"I am dead, Daughter," Mother answered. *"And whose hands are stained with My blood?"*

Mistress Arisa laughed. *"You are weak and worthless. I give You the power to level mountains and You reply with mewling cowardice. You are a feckless fool. I should have ended Your misery ages ago."*

Lienna trembled fearfully. *"I can do what is needed,"* She begged. *"Please."*

For the longest time, there was no answer. *"You have never been able to do what was needed,"* Mistress Arisa replied. Her voice sounded as if it came from a far distance. *"In Your birth was born the flaw of Your unmaking. The Humans of no Caste demonstrate Your failure."*

Lienna cried out in anger and sorrow. She had done everything – *everything* – the Mistress had demanded of Her. She had murdered Her parents, overthrown Humanity, and spent the past two thousand years hunting the vermin to extinction with no company but the clouds and the Chimeras and unknowing trees swaying in the winds of Her passage. And for what? This perpetual criticism where anything She did was met with abrasive ridicule.

Enough!

She howled a hurricane of sound as She poured all Her anger

out into the sky and down to the ground, even into the Chimeras far below. Unknowingly, She filled them with Her unending madness. On and on it went. Distantly, She heard the screams rising from the camps of the Fan Lor Kum, but She was otherwise occupied.

Her mind was quiet. There were no other voices.

What was this?

"Mother? Father?" She queried, hesitantly. Where was Mistress Arisa?

For the first time in eons, Lienna was alone in Her mind, and Her mind was clear. She knew reality. Her parents were dead, and Mistress Arisa was simply a figment of Her madness. For the first time in centuries, Lienna remembered all events as they had actually happened. She remembered the murder of Her Parents, Her ascension, the Night of Sorrows, and all the cities She had sacked on that terrible evening of blood and death. She remembered Her madness, a timeless torment obscuring the truth. She had been blind. Cities long dead, She had thought still alive, and others still thriving She had thought desecrated long ago.

So much of it had been wrong.

And all the while the Baels had deceived Her, telling Her what She wished to hear, or even conspiring against Her wishes with their soft lies.

Lienna screamed at their betrayal, pouring even more of Her anger into the Chimeras. This time She noticed their rising howl of desperation as Her madness took them.

Yes. Let Her Chimeras serve as the vessels for Her insanity. Lienna did not care if they could think rationally. She only required their obedience. She smiled as further sanity returned to Her. Now, She could think and plan, and lo' would Her Baels suffer...

Her smile slipped. She saw with sudden alarm how the Chimeras were attacking one another in their crazed fury. Her madness was driving them to mindless violence. And She could feel how with every death, a very small portion of Her own sanity faded.

No!

The Chimeras couldn't be allowed to kill one another. If they all died, so too would Her newfound lucidity.

She hesitated, unsure what to do, but with each death, She felt the insanity overwhelming Her.

Lienna screamed in frustration.

She took the madness from the Chimeras, just enough so they no longer sought to slay one another. They still raged and snarled, but at least they were no longer leaping for one another's throats.

Her own clarity of thought faded, however. She could feel it slipping away like a wriggling eel through Her hands when She'd been corporal. The derangement Lienna had assumed back within Herself was an infection. It left Her confused and frightened.

The voices would come back. She knew it.

She would have to fight hard to remember they weren't real.

She sobbed, unsure if She would be able to do so.

Once more, Her memories became jumbled, further clouding Her judgment, leaving Her uncertain as to what was real and what was false.

But one thing Lienna remembered.

The Baels would die for their betrayal.

And after them, the Humans in their accursed cities, especially those of the no Caste. From where did they hie? The Oases? Or perhaps some hidden citadel, separate from the bulk of their vermin brethren?

It didn't matter. Not right now.

She would find the truth of their making and eradicate the lot of them from the blessed skin of Mistress Arisa.

She roared groundward, unstoppable as a tsunami.

CHAPTER SIXTEEN
PROTECTIVE ENEMIES

A man aware of his own ignorance certainly has claim to a kind of wisdom.
Sadder by far is the fool who believes he knows the truth
when all he knows is a lie.

~Sooths and Small Sayings by Tramed Billow, AF 1387

Li-Dirge glanced at his crèche brother.

Reg smiled back at him. He understood. The Humans hadn't attacked. They had listened, and their leader, the Kumma from Ashoka, had, however reluctantly, even been willing to believe.

It was the beginning of the dream prayed and hoped for by twenty-five generations of Baels, ever since Hume had taught them of honor and decency as well as mercy and love. With luck, perhaps both Humans and Baels could build on tonight's events and find a way to achieve a greater peace with one another.

Of course, there was the question of these Humans who called themselves OutCastes. They were a mystery. Who were they, and where did they come from? Their existence had been a surprise not only to the Baels, but also to the Ashokans, who quite obviously despised their half-breed brothers.

Dirge didn't know what to make of such animosity. Why hate those who were simply different through an accident of birth? It made no sense. Hume had explained all he could about the Castes, and how interbreeding amongst them was never allowed. Those who violated this stricture were immediately expelled from their city with the expectation of a quick death, but obviously, some had survived. While Dirge was well aware of the law, he didn't understand the rationale for it. It seemed cruel and arbitrary.

Li-Choke, a young Levner, handed the one called Lure Grey a flask of water and a strip of dried pangrill. The young Human had Healed most of the Ashokans and looked spent. Healing was apparently quite taxing.

Lure sniffed the pangrill and took a tentative bite. He promptly spat it out. "Bleh! What in the unholy hells," he spluttered, glaring at Li-Choke, who gazed back at him, surprise evident on his face.

"It is pangrill," Choke replied. "A delicacy amongst our kind."

"Well, it tastes like mint-flavored vomit."

Li-Reg chuckled. "And how is it you know the taste of mint-flavored vomit?"

The one known as Rukh broke out in laughter, as did his fellow Ashokans, Keemo and Brand. Even the OutCastes, Jessira and Cedar, smiled. Only the acid-tongued and angry one, Farn, was immune to the humor.

Lure glared at the others before eventually breaking into a sheepish grin.

Dirge smiled. "Pangrill is made from the grasses growing north of Lake Nest – no finer grass exists on Arisa – and ground Chimera meat – the best is Phed – and dried in the sun for three days," he explained. "Perhaps it is an acquired taste."

Lure Grey appeared discomfited. "You eat the other Chims?" he asked. At Dirge's nod, he set the pangrill aside. "I don't think I'll be acquiring it."

Dirge shrugged. The stories spoke of Hume's finicky feeding habits. Evidently, his behavior was one commonly seen amongst Humans. It was a perspective Dirge couldn't understand. Once dead, meat was meat. Ur-Fels, Tigons, Braids, Pheds, even other Baels...Dirge had tasted them all. Once, he had even eaten Human flesh. It had been stringy and tough, but edible.

Perhaps now would not be a good time to bring up such an observation.

Reg chuckled. "The Tigons would..." he broke off and all the Baels shot to their feet, staring upward.

Mother raged.

She was furious, in a way Dirge had never before seen or heard. The sound of Her wrath was like bones ground to powder or flesh ripped to bloody strings. It was terrifying. **The Humans were frantic, demanding answers for the Baels sudden agitation, but Dirge had no mind to answer. His attention was focused on Mother. He felt it when She poured out Her rage, down into the Fan Lor Kum camped some ten miles distant. A fearsome and incoherent howl roared across the Hunters Flats. It was the sound of pure, unreasoning hatred – a noise to raise the hackles on Dirge's neck and cause fear to work its way down his spine. The Fan Lor Kum had gone insane. The feverish scream rose higher in pitch and volume before suddenly cutting off.**

But a new horror had arisen, and he gazed skyward in abject terror.

Mother was awake, and She was aware.

Oh, Devesh.

The Baels. She knew they had betrayed and thwarted Her, time and again since Hammer's fall.

She thundered toward them, crying fiercely in outrage

Li-Dirge turned toward the Ashokans, terror on his face. "Mother comes. She knows..."

"Knows what?" Rukh asked.

"Everything. She knows everything. Somehow, She has pierced the long millennia of Her madness and poured it out into the Fan Lor Kum. She knows we have betrayed Her. She comes now. She'll kill us all."

Rukh rocked back, appearing stunned.

His fellow Ashokan, Farn, snarled in outrage. "It's a trick," the man snapped. "Don't trust them."

"There is little time," Dirge said. "She will be here in minutes. "A few hundred yards distant lies a small thicket of trees. You may be safe there."

Rukh stared at him, seeming to study him as he considered Dirge's words. Lines of worry and doubt appeared on his face before he turned abruptly to his fellow Ashokans. He barked commands, turning even to the OutCastes.

"We don't take orders from Purebloods," the OutCaste lieutenant, Cedar snapped.

"Then stay and let Suwraith find you," Rukh snapped back. "We need to hustle."

"Can you take a few of us," Dirge pleaded. "You can Blend them. The memory of what the Baels are at their heart must not die."

"What about those of your kind back with your troops?" Jessira asked.

"They're dead. All of them," Dirge replied, a catch in his throat. "I felt them torn apart when Mother poured Her insanity into the other Chimeras. They were attacked mercilessly."

"We can take two Baels," Rukh said. "Any more, and we risk being exposed."

Dirge nodded, relieved. "Take Choke and Brine," he said, pointing out his two youngest and most intelligent Levners. Of the younger Baels, they were also among those most dedicated to the way of brotherhood as taught by Hume.

298

"I still don't know how I feel about you," Rukh said to Dirge, "but we'll protect your Baels as best we can."

The SarpanKum – perhaps the last Bael to hold the title, at least for this Plague anyway – nodded. It was a start. Hume had said brotherhood began with small acts of trust. It was more than Dirge could have hoped for or expected.

"One last thing, Ashokan," Li-Dirge called out. "The other Chimeras require dark caverns in which to birth their young. It is where we hide their breeders, and where the Fan Lor Kum are the most vulnerable. You'll find the breeding caverns housed in a rocky canyon where the Slave River races south from the Privation Mountains." He explained more. "The only Chimeras Humanity has ever seen are the ones in the Plagues, male mules, including the Baels. The breeders, though, the ones who can produce more Chimeras …they are empty-headed creatures, caged all their lives long. Their only duty is to create more warriors for the Plagues, but they can only do so under the direct intervention of Suwraith. Without Her power, the breeders are as infertile as us, their mule offspring."

"What about you? The Baels. How do you reproduce?"

"By accident. We are born to the Bovars through no agency of Mother."

"You know what I'll do with this knowledge."

Li-Dirge smiled. "Yes. I'm counting on it. Consider it a gift, brother. Now go!"

He watched as the Ashokans, along with Choke and Brine raced away, soon joined by the OutCaste.

"It is good to have lived so long," Li-Reg said.

"A life well lived," Dirge agreed. "Hume would have been pleased."

Mother was nearly upon them. Her scream seemed to tear the very sky. But She was too late. The Humans had made it to the copse of trees.

"To brotherhood," Li-Dirge cried, staring heavenward, past Mother's evil. *Devesh offer us grace.*

"Brotherhood!" his Baels shouted back.

Mother struck the ground upon which they stood with an obliterating blast, and Li-Dirge knew no more as he rose into a singing light.

———— • ————

"They're gone," Keemo said into the echoing silence after Suwraith left.

The Baels were dead. They had to be. The Queen had struck as hard as a falling mountain. She had led with streaks of lightning, blazing across the tortured earth as Her strikes incinerated everything they touched. Then came a scouring wind to cleanse the ground of anything still living. Nothing remained of where the Baels had stood awaiting Suwraith's arrival except a deep crater and a cloud of dust hanging in the strangely quiet air.

What a waste.

Rukh didn't want to admit it, but he had liked Li-Dirge. If not for the fact that he was a Bael, Rukh would have described the general as having a near-noble quality to him. Dirge had spoken so eloquently about the history of his kind and how the Bael had changed through their contact with Hume. Rukh had almost believed him. It *was* a nice story, and one Rukh wished were true, but now, with the general's death, it might be impossible to ever know for sure. Rukh wished he could have gotten to know Li-Dirge better.

"The Bael saved us," Farn said, sounding amazed.

"We're going to have one hell of a story to tell when we get home," Keemo said.

"Let's pack up and get moving," Rukh replied.

"What of us?" one of the Baels — Brine maybe — asked.

"We need to find the Western Plague and warn our brothers," Choke said.

"Our city needs to know about this, too," the ghrina lieutenant said. "We'll take leave of you people now. This has been a right proper bastard of a night."

Cries, deep and rumbling, rose from several hundred yards away.

"Just our fragging luck," Rukh cursed softly.

"Damn, damn, and double damn." Brand replied.

"What in the unholy hells was that?" Jessira asked.

"Our deaths," Li-Brine said, grimly. He unlimbered his chain and trident.

"It seems the Shylows have taken displeasure at our presence," Choke added.

"Holy Mother, what a nightmare this night has turned out to be," Jessira said.

"Why don't we all Blend?" Lure asked.

"They see right through them," Brand answered.

"Form the Quad. I've got point," Rukh ordered. "Keemo and Farn hold the flanks. Brand cover our backs." He pointed to Choke and Brine. "Can you keep them off of us with your whips?"

"Doubtful," the Bael replied. "They are too swift."

"That fast?"

"Faster than you would believe," Brine said.

The ghrinas had formed up.

"Protect them as best you can," Rukh ordered the Baels. "They'll try to drive you out from the trees. Don't let them. You won't stand a chance out in the open."

Two Shylows, both males, came into view.

Rukh had never seen one of the great cats before, and as they approached, details swiftly emerged. Both Shylows were similar in appearance with golden-tan fur all over their bodies, except on their backs where they wore a mottled black and yellow pattern. Each cat was thick and powerful, standing over seven feet at the shoulder and twenty-five feet from head-to-tail. Despite their great size, they weren't slow. Far from it. The stories told by Trial veterans, describing the stunning speed of the Shylows appeared to be true. The cats ran with breathtaking swiftness, their over-sized tails pointing straight back as they covered yards with every bounding leap forward. They were only seconds away.

Rukh melded into the Quad, and his consciousness dimmed.

The Quad moved Primary to point. Secondary and Tertiary flanked him. Quaternary held the rear.

Quaternary threw a barrage of Fireballs. They streaked toward the Shylows…and thudded with a dull roar as they slammed into the ground, all of them missing.

Impossibly, the cats dodged all of the Quad's ranged attacks. Had it the ability to fear, the Quad would have trembled. Nothing in this world should move so fast.

The Shylows split apart and charged, one going for the group of OutCastes and Baels, the other for the Quad.

Primary stepped forward to meet the attack, but his straight thrust, usually so lethal, caught nothing but air.

The Shylow had leapt over Primary.

Secondary and Tertiary were ready, but the Shylow dodged past them as well.

Quaternary faced the great cat alone. The others were out of position to support him. The Shylow landed, and gutted the one known as Brand.

The Quad became the Triad.

Dimly, the Triad recognized the anguish of its members. They mourned the death of their friend, but the Triad was untouched by their grief. It had been charged with a mission: defeat the Shylow. Nothing else mattered.

Tertiary charged from the right; Secondary from the left.

The cat spun and Tertiary caught a blow to his arm, breaking it and *sending him soaring through the air. He crashed down, losing consciousness as his head smacked hard against the ground.*

The Triad became Duo.

Secondary, already in the midst of attack when Farn had fallen, cut deeply into the cat's shoulder.

The Shylow howled in pain and anger even as he spun about and raked Secondary across the leg, causing it to buckle. Primary raced in low and slashed the Shylow's rear leg, hamstringing the cat before it could deliver a deathblow to Secondary.

Secondary leapt straight up, stabbing through the cat's lower jaw and into its brain.

The animal keened a nerve-jangling scream as it died.

Duo turned to face the other Shylow. It was engaged with the Baels and the ghrinas. One of their members was already dead, his chest ripped open, the one known as Lure. Another of the ghrinas, the woman, Jessira, lay face down, long hair matted with blood. Duo considered its options. Secondary's leg was damaged. He would be slow. Duo couldn't attack as fiercely as it would have liked. Secondary needed protection and support. Duo moved toward the battle, keeping Primary close to Secondary.

A Bael, Li-Brine, jumped in front of a blow meant for the ghrina lieutenant, and the Bael's chest was crushed. He landed with an unmoving thud.

Primary slashed at an unprotected haunch, but somehow the cat's tail, hard as bone and quick as a viper, struck him, knocking him onto his back.

The Shylow stalked the ghrina lieutenant, who quickly gave way, moving toward the still inert Farn.

Suddenly, the cat howled in outrage.

The other Bael, Li-Choke, had wrapped his blazing whip around the creature's neck. Smoke rose as fur singed and flesh burned. The Shylow pulled hard against the whip, yanking the Bael off his feet and toward the cat where the beast swatted him hard onto the ground.

Secondary used the distraction to press forward, but before he could attack, he was seen. Duo tried to dodge, but Secondary's injured leg made him too slow.

The Shylow caught Secondary on his claws, impaling him. With the last of its focus and the last of Secondary's strength, Duo stabbed, pressing Secondary's sword to the hilt in the Shylow's chest.

The animal screamed once, loudly and terribly, before falling over dead.

Duo became Rukh, who crashed to his knees and sobbed in grief.

He had felt Keemo's death. Brand's also. His friends – both of them like brothers – were now dead. They were gone, their lives suddenly ended on a night filled with so much promise, but right now, no promise or hope could assuage Rukh's guilt. It had been his decision to forgo returning straightaway to Ashoka. He had been the one to insist on tracking the Chims, and his choice had cost Brand and Keemo their lives. They would never again walk Ashoka's tall hills and wide boulevards.

What would he tell Keemo's parents? Or Brand's? Their families would be devastated, especially when they discovered how close their sons had been to making it home.

Rukh sat on the ground, but a moan from Li-Choke reminded him of his duty.

Farn. He had to make sure he was alive. Rukh levered himself to his feet, feeling a soreness in his chest. Even as he did so, hissing calls came from not more than a hundred yards away.

Fragging unholy hells! Couldn't they have a moment's peace?

"Braids," Choke growled. "They seek our deaths. I can taste their anger."

Rukh gestured to the ghrina woman. "Pick her up. We have to move," he said wearily.

Choke nodded, throwing the ghrina over his uninjured shoulder like she was a sack of potatoes. "I'm ready,"

"Too late," Rukh whispered.

The Braids were already fanning out around the copse. They'd be discovered in moments.

Rukh Blended, bringing Choke into it as well. He looked for Farn. The ghrina lieutenant, Cedar was leaned over him, and the two of them suddenly disappeared from view. They must have Blended as well. Rukh wished he could Link his Blend with the lieutenant's so they could see one another, but the distance was too great. Brand might have been able to do so.

Regrets and sorrows would have to wait, though. For now, escape was their only motivation. Rukh guided Choke with a gentle pull on the Bael's arm as they picked their way past the nearest group of Braids. They would be instantly discovered if the Bael stepped outside the narrow range of Rukh's Blend. Several of the snakelike Chimera scouts muttered amongst themselves as they inspected the dead Shylow, pointing out how they imagined the battle had gone. A few toed at Keemo and Brand's bodies, satisfied when they proved to be dead.

Rukh clenched his teeth. He hated leaving the remains of his friends amongst the Braids. Their bodies would end up in a Chim cook pot.

Other Braids had their snouts raised to the air, tongues flicking out. It was said the snakelike Chimeras could taste the scent of Human blood from over a mile away. Just then, one swiveled his head and looked straight at them. Rukh froze, but after an uncertain and fearful moment, the Braid turned away and went back to tasting the air.

Again, Rukh eased forward, gesturing for Choke to step quietly. Despite his warning, the Bael's footsteps still thudded against the ground. Hopefully, the Braids would overlook the slight tremor. Another ten feet, and they were past the thickest collection of the Chimera scouts. Another twenty, and they were in open ground.

The Braids fanned out from the copse of trees, calling to one another and probably also for reinforcements.

Time to pick up the pace.

Rukh led Choke at a dead sprint for a large mound of rocks, a monolith thrown up in the middle of the Flats. Rukh was thankful for the hillock's presence. Blends were good, but they weren't perfect, and Choke was hard to keep hidden. It wasn't his scent or sound or sight that Rukh worried about, though. It was his trail. The Baels had likely never been trained to cover their tracks, and others in the Fan Lor Kum were nothing if not excellent trackers.

The rock formation might be a good place to lose the Chim scouts.

Rukh clambered over the boulders, holding back a hiss of pain as the soreness in his chest became sharper. He hadn't broken another rib, had he? Damn bad luck. Choke followed tight on his heels, carrying the still unconscious ghrina woman.

"Try to keep your feet light," Rukh cautioned. "Don't even turn over a pebble if you can."

Once past the rocks, Rukh led them northeast, toward Ashoka. He briefly wondered if he should wait for Cedar and Farn, but he had no idea in which direction the other two might be headed. Rukh had to look to his own safety. Ashoka had to be made aware of all he had learned.

He and the Bael stretched out into a loping run.

Choke looked like he had it as rough as Rukh felt. The Bael's breathing sounded pained. He, too, probably had either bruised or cracked ribs. Either way, it had to hurt like the unholy hells. The Bael remained stoic, though, never revealing any evidence that he was in pain.

Hours passed.

Rukh had no idea what had become of Farn and the ghrina…no *OutCaste*. It's what they called themselves. He had no idea what became of Farn and the OutCaste lieutenant. Hopefully, Cedar had gotten the two of them out of there. Where they would go after Farn awoke was another question. The OutCaste was sure to head for his own city, while Rukh's cousin would want to return to Ashoka. Farn was strong, but with what had looked to be a broken arm and a concussion, he would have to follow wherever Cedar led. Otherwise, with those injuries, Farn wouldn't last more than a few days out here by himself.

The sun rose, blushing the sky.

Every hour or so, Rukh called a halt so he could check on Jessira. She had been clawed across the left shoulder and down her back, and the cuts still oozed. Rukh worried about her, especially since she still hadn't come to.

"The Shylow have a toxin on their claws," Choke said. "It acts as both a soporific and a blood leecher. She will wake soon enough."

"Blood leecher?" Rukh's brows furrowed in concentration. The Shiyens had a word for what the Bael was describing. What was it? His face cleared in remembrance. "An anti-coagulant? Something to make the bleeding last for a long time?" Rukh asked.

Li-Choke nodded.

"When will it stop?"

"I wish I could tell you, but it all depends on how much got into her."

Rukh examined Jessira's cuts. They were deep. She had likely received a large dose. He hoped the bleeding ended soon. He had to shrug aside his worry for her, though. There wasn't anything he could do for her. Besides, worrying for a ghrina seemed sacrilegious.

Rukh and the Bael pressed on, stumbling as fatigue and pain ate at their stamina.

"There," Choke said, pointing. "Those trees. Will they hide us?"

Rukh looked to where Choke gestured. It was a large stand of scrub pines, junipers, and cottonwoods with a few tall maples rising high in the center of the glade, only about one or two miles away. "It depends," Rukh said. "Are your Chims still searching?"

Choke's expression went flat. "They are no longer *my* Chims.

They were never *my* Chims," he replied. "As we ran, did you not see the claw of Tigons carrying the decapitated heads of my brethren before them?" He shook his head in sorrow. "I am no longer welcome among the Fan Lor Kum."

Well too damn bad. Rukh thought vindictively. Keemo and Brand were dead. So was Lure Grey. And Farn and Cedar were missing. In light of all that, what was the grief of a Bael to him? The black-horned bastards had been killing and destroying Humanity for centuries. Why should he worry now if they were suddenly the hunted? Despite Li-Dirge's pronouncements, Rukh's antipathy toward the creatures hadn't ended. Not by a long shot. It would take more than a fine speech from one possibly noble Bael for him to feel otherwise. Let the damn Chims taste their own Queen's anger for once.

"You didn't answer my question," Rukh said gruffly. "Are we still being hunted?"

Li-Choke cocked his head, as if listening to a sound only he could hear. "No," he said at last. "Though I no longer am a part of Her armies, I can still hear Her…desires. The Tigons lead the Fan Lor Kum now, and She has sent out a call for the Plague to gather northwest of here, before the foothills of the Privation Mountains.

"You can still hear what She thinks?"

"No. I can't hear Her thoughts; only her wishes and desires; Her feelings. At least for now."

"Do you think She'll lock you out?"

Choke nodded. "I would not have believed Her capable of such clarity of thought," the Bael mused. "She was always easily deceived before, but something happened last night. You heard the screams?"

Rukh nodded.

"It was the Fan Lor Kum…all of them. Somehow, Mother emptied Her insanity into the Plague. In doing so, She regained Her own sanity…"

"So She isn't insane anymore?" Rukh interrupted. He swore softly, trying to mask his fear. A mad Suwraith was bad enough, but the implication of a sane Queen was too frightening to contemplate. He shivered involuntarily.

"Not exactly," Choke said. "There is more to tell. The mindless rage She poured into the Chimeras caused them to turn on each other like rabid wolves. If it continued, the Chimeras would have murdered one another down to the last warrior within the hour. It would have ended Mother's moment of sanity, and She must have realized it as well. She took back most of Her madness, thereby preserving the Fan Lor Kum."

"I wish She hadn't," Rukh muttered.

"Perhaps, but what should concern you now is this: Mother is once more quite deranged, but She is far more sane than She was before last night, She remembered and realized enough to understand how deeply the Baels have betrayed Her over the years. It is why She killed us. She has already seen to the death of all Baels within the Eastern Plague. She will likely move against my brothers of the Western Plague soon enough. I fear we face extermination."

"Join the club," Rukh said. "Your kind will have to figure out a way to survive just like we did, but I wouldn't panic yet. Remember, Li-Dirge said Her inability to plan has always been Her greatest weakness. For all we know, this whole episode may blow over when She has another episode of insanity."

"I hope you are right, but I fear you are wrong," Choke replied.

Rukh grunted. The Bael's assessment of the situation was probably the correct one, but it did no good to say so. It was cruel actually, and the small sliver of sympathy worming its way into his heart surprised Rukh. Compassion for the Baels? How unexpected. Only moments earlier he had felt a complete lack of concern regarding their impending slaughter. Perhaps Li-Dirge's words had affected him more deeply than he realized.

They walked in silence the rest of the way to the glade of trees.

"We'll stop here," Rukh said as they approached the large copse. "I can't keep the Blend going for much longer anyway."

Choke nodded, and soon after they penetrated into the deeper shadows under the cottonwoods and junipers, he carefully set Jessira down with a grateful sigh. The Bael looked drained.

As for Rukh, he had been conducting *Jivatma* during the whole of their escape and even before, during the fight with the Tigons. He felt as weary as Li-Choke looked. And the pain in his chest was like an aching hot coal.

"Do we have anything to eat?" Choke asked.

Rukh shook his head. "I left everything but my sword back there." He nodded in the direction they had come from. "Besides, we need water more than food right now. I need to clean the ghri...I mean Jessira's wounds."

"There might be a stream somewhere nearby," Choke said, pointing to a deeper part of the stand, where the maples arose. It was an area marked by the fallen trunk of a thorn tree. "It sounds like one anyway."

Rukh went still and listened.

Choke was right. There *was* a stream nearby.

Rukh stood with a weary sigh and clambered over the fallen thorn tree, careful not to let it scratch him. Directly past it, a small rivulet of water meandered across gray pebbles before disappearing into a soggy bog, forming a small marsh.

"Water means animals," Rukh said. "If we're lucky, we might get to drink *and* eat."

Fate must have been smiling upon them because shortly after they had sated their thirst and cleaned Jessira's wounds, a family of jackrabbits came to the watering hole.

Two Fireballs later, they had food. The meat was tough, both gamey and burnt – the Fireballs hadn't just cooked the jackrabbits, they had nearly incinerated them – but it was edible, and for Rukh, it was enough.

Afterward, he took the first watch while Choke fell into an instant slumber. Rukh insisted on it. He didn't trust the Bael. What better time for a betrayal than now, when he was asleep and the woman was unconscious? Maybe after Jessira woke up, Rukh could sleep – even with Choke nearby – but until then, he would have to try and stay awake.

The Bael rumbled in a fitful slumber.

It was then, during a time of quiet reflection that the images from the previous night came to Rukh. Keemo…smiling and laughing and bringing his infectious joy to all who knew him. His lighthearted banter could lighten the mood of even the most dour. He had always been the most generous of them – so open and honest. He was a rare man. And Brand – so strong and brave. He had always stood unflinching in the face of danger. Never quitting. He had even run with Kummas, a feat no other Rahail could have done. Brand was pure will and determination. Rukh had never known anyone tougher.

They were both gone now. Both lay broken and dead in a faraway place.

He might have cried then, but he forced down the tears. Now was not the time. He could mourn when he reached Ashoka, when his city had been warned and her people saved. Until then, the tears would have to wait.

But the grief remained, a hollow knot in Rukh's heart.

Just then Jessira stirred, briefly lifting Rukh's hopes before she settled down again. Sometime during their long run from the shallow bowl where Suwraith had obliterated her Baels, Rukh had come to equate the OutCaste woman's safety and well-being with that of Ashoka's. It was an odd belief to have, but for Rukh, he *had* to ensure Jessira's survival. If nothing else, her living might give meaning to all those who had so senselessly died last night. It would be a chance to spit in the Sorrow Bringer's face; let Her know that while She could kill some, She couldn't kill everyone. Humanity was too strong. They would live on in spite of the Queen's worst intentions.

CHAPTER SEVENTEEN
AN ABSENCE OF TRUST

*Sometimes we must simply throw open the doors of destiny,
hanging as they are upon the hinges of our choices.*

~*Attribution unknown (dating from circa AF 850)*

ventually, fatigue overcame Rukh's ability to stay awake, and
Li-Choke had to take the watch. It didn't mean Rukh slept
easily, though. Every small noise had him instantly alert, and
he had an ear cocked for the slightest sound of betrayal. He didn't
trust the Bael. More importantly, he didn't *want* to trust him, and the
idea of sleeping while Choke stood watch filled him with worry. By
Rukh's way of thinking, this whole situation might still be an
elaborate deception of some sort.

Who knew what occurred in the mind of a Chimera?

Then again, if this *wasn't* an elaborate ruse, while the Baels were
still Chimera, they were no longer Fan Lor Kum. If so, could one of
Humanity's greatest enemies be made into an ally? Rukh doubted
many people would think so. It was the long shot hope of a
simpleton. Too much blood had been spilled, and all those who had
lost family at the hands of the Baels…how could they ever be

expected to forgive what had been done to them and those they loved.

Still, Rukh wondered at his small niggle of hope where he wished it could be so. Even stranger was the fervent yet fearful *desire* for it to be so.

Rukh was a warrior, but he was finding a warrior's heart was not entirely fulfilling. At times, something else drove him or sought to drive him. It was said a true warrior did not seek battle but sought victory through peace. Rukh had long pondered the meaning of those words. What did they really mean? Whose peace? Peace as he understood it meant the annihilation of one's enemies, or in the case of the Kumma Houses, coexisting with various degrees of comfort with one's rivals.

Was there nothing deeper?

Rukh wasn't sure, but he longed for something else, something richer and more profound.

The words of Li-Dirge had a sentimentality to them, and despite the fact that they had been spoken by a Bael, Rukh still found them touching and appealing. He especially liked the notion of brotherhood amongst all who could reason. *That* was deeper, richer, and a more profound sentiment, and one worth fighting for.

Rukh still didn't like the Baels, but while his heart remained hardened against them, the undemanding hatred he had prior to last night was not as easy to summon anymore. A part of him wished it was. Life would be so much simpler then, safer and more comforting. Before his Trial, all he had to do was just follow his years of training and teaching without giving any more thought to the matter. It was how everyone else back home seemed to think. Why couldn't he do the same?

He knew why. Li-Dirge and the damn Baels and their damn words had introduced doubt into his life. The SarpanKum's explanation of history since the fall of Hammer made sense. Dirge had been right: before Hammer, cities had fallen like kindling, but afterward – nothing. What if Hume, the greatest hero in Humanity's history, had gifted all who came after him with something even more precious than victory over a mountain of Chimera corpses? What if three hundred years ago, Hume had found a means to teach the Baels to love? It changed everything because it might very well be true. If the Sorrow Bringer had genuinely wanted to, She could have easily annihilated Humanity. She hadn't done so, but was Her failure due to a lack of desire on Her part, or was it due to the actions of those like Li-Dirge? Given Her extermination of the Baels, it seemed more and more likely that the Sorrow Bringer's commanders and generals had, in fact, been the ones to block Her will.

The questions such a possibility raised raced through Rukh's mind, and he couldn't get them to stop. Right now, all he wanted was for the thoughts to just go away. At least for a little while. He preferred silence. He wanted quiet so he could grieve. He wanted time to remember Keemo's smile and Brand's courage.

He wanted the bliss of ignorance.

Jessira stirred, and Rukh awoke, turning to see how she was doing.

"She's starting to rouse, I think," Choke said.

"How long was I asleep?" Rukh asked.

"A few hours. It's just past mid-day."

Jessira' eyes flickered open. She groaned. "I feel like I've been mule-kicked. What happened?"

"The Shylows happened," Rukh replied, settling next to her. "Do you remember anything from last night?"

She glanced at Choke, a guardedness to her eyes. "I think I'm starting to," she said. "For a moment, I thought it might all have been a dream." She tried to sit up and instead cried out in pain.

Rukh helped ease her back down. "Don't try to get up just yet. The Shylow raked you pretty good."

"I'm thirsty."

Rukh glanced at Choke.

"I'll get her some water," the Bael said.

"Where are we?" Jessira asked, after the Bael left.

"In a small grove of trees, somewhere in the Hunters Flats."

"What about my brothers?"

"I saw Cedar. We got separated. I think he made it out."

"And Lure?" she asked, dread rising in her eyes.

Rukh shook his head. "One of the Shylows got him. I'm sorry."

She lay her head back and mouthed a silent prayer as tears leaked from the corners of her eyes, tracing a clear line through the dust and sweat on her face.

Rukh turned away, giving her privacy for her grief.

"And you have no idea where Cedar is?" Jessira asked after a moment.

"None," Rukh said. "Last I saw, he was with Farn. Your brother had them Blended."

"What about your Ashokans?" she asked.

Rukh swallowed heavily and turned away. Now it was his turn to hide his tears. "Keemo and Brand are both dead. And Farn...he's with Cedar. Hopefully, they're still safe." Rukh quickly explained all that had happened while Jessira had been unconscious.

Choke returned as Rukh was finishing his account.

"And him?" Jessira asked, gesturing to the Bael.

"The Queen killed all the Baels meeting with us, you remember that?" Jessira nodded. "We Blended two of them and hid them from Her. The rest of the Fan Lor Kum killed all the others back in their main camp. His brother, Li-Brine, the other one we saved, died protecting Cedar. Choke might be the last of his kind."

Jessira glanced at the Bael, a pitiless expression on her face. Rukh could imagine how she felt: the Baels were the enemies of the OutCastes, no less than they were enemies to the rest of Humanity. If they suffered, so be it.

"So what happens now?" Jessira asked.

"We go to Ashoka," Rukh replied. "It'll take us about four weeks to get there."

"You're going to Ashoka. I'm going to Stronghold," she said, trying again to lever herself up to a sitting position.

"I think you're better off staying with me," Rukh said.

"Frag that," she said. "I'll be fine," she snapped, as Rukh moved to keep her from swaying.

"You aren't fine," Rukh countered, privately impressed by the woman's determination. She had courage, he'd give her that, but fortitude and bravery wouldn't serve her now. She needed help, whether she accepted it or not. "You can barely sit up."

She fell back with a stifled moan.

"Drink some water," Choke said. "We also found a date tree. You can eat once you've slaked your thirst."

"I don't want food or water!" she shouted. She was sobbing a moment later. "Did Lure suffer?"

"No," Rukh said. "I think he died instantly."

"Good," she nodded, wiping away her tears. "Help me up."

After she drank and ate, she was able to sit straighter and on her own. Her clothes were a mess. Her outer jacket was ripped into long ribbons along her left chest, shoulder, and back. It was crusted in dried blood and so was the camouflage shirt she wore underneath. The cuts she had suffered had been deep, and they still looked to be seeping blood. Her pants and boots were worn and dusty but at least they were whole.

She would have trouble keeping up with him, and Rukh worried for her. He had to put aside his pity, though. "We need to get going soon," he said. "Choke says the Chims were called to someplace northwest of here, near the foothills of the Privations. The Tigons lead them now, but who knows if the word's gotten out to all of them. They might still be hunting us."

"And you're going to Ashoka?"

Rukh nodded. "No one else is left. I have to warn the city."

"What about Farn?"

"The Shylow broke his arm and the way his head bounced off the ground, he probably has a bad concussion to go with it. I doubt he's in any shape to try to make it home on his own. He'd be dead in a day if he tried."

"Like me."

Rukh nodded. "Like you."

"I won't be going with you," Choke said.

Rukh hadn't planned on taking the Bael with them anyway, and he was privately relieved Choke felt the same way. How would he have explained or protected the Bael? It was one thing for Rukh to relate all he had learned so far, but it would have been a disaster if he tried to bring a living Bael into Ashoka. Choke *and* Rukh would have both been lynched within minutes.

"Where are you headed?" Rukh asked.

"The breeding caverns. I don't know if Mother has killed all Baels everywhere, but if She hasn't, I have to warn them of what's happened."

"Welcome to our life. We've had her unholy attention for two thousand years now," Jessira muttered, echoing Rukh's earlier thoughts.

Choke glanced at her, sympathy on his face. "I understand your sentiments," Choke said. "Perhaps some day, you will find a way to forgive us."

"Not likely."

Choke nodded. "I know. Given how we've killed and hunted your kind, mercy might be too much to hope for." He turned to Rukh. "I have to go."

"Good luck to you then," Rukh replied, surprised by how true the words felt. He *did* wish the Bael good fortune.

Li-Choke smiled. "Thank you," he replied. He stood up, his whip coiled at his waist and his trident clutched in one hand. "In another world we would be brothers."

"And in a better world, we shall be." Rukh smiled at the young Bael's astonishment. "It is the correct response, isn't it?"

"Yes, but how did you know? Hume taught us that phrase."

"It's from the second stanza of *All Truths*, an antiphon dating from before the Night of Sorrows."

Choke stroked his chin. "I only know the one verse," he said. "It would be good to read it in its entirety some day."

"Perhaps one day you will."

"Peace to you, brother," Choke said. With his final words, he left the glade.

Rukh turned, finding Jessira glaring at him.

"So now you trust the Baels? Like they're worthy of brotherhood?" she asked.

"No, I don't trust them," Rukh said, annoyed. "He isn't, and they aren't, and none of them will ever be my brother. I was just telling him where the words to his phrase come from. That's all."

"And what about me?" Jessira asked. "Am I also worthy of the great Kumma's notion of brotherhood? I am a ghrina, remember?"

Rukh gritted his teeth and managed to hold onto his patience. He really didn't want to have an argument right now. "There is much in this world I would change if I could," he said. "I'm not your judge, and most everyone back home would think I'm no less Tainted than you. I'm a Kumma who can Blend and has conspired with the Baels." He snorted in derision. "I'm sure my people will find great fault with both those transgressions."

"Then why save me? Won't my presence in Ashoka be just another 'transgression'? Another reason for your people to consider you Tainted?" She sounded honestly concerned for him, or at least curious as to his motivations.

He wished he *could* explain his feelings to her, but he couldn't. Even for him, they remained a jumbled mishmash of confusing motivations.

"I'm not the barbarian you seem to think I am."

"You haven't answered my question," Jessira said.

Rukh grimaced. His patience left him, and he was suddenly incensed by the whole situation. He'd lost three friends last night; two of them had been as close to him as his own brother. And a few weeks before, he'd seen three hundred Ashokans mauled and killed. In their own way, they, too, had been like brothers, and he had been forced to listen as their killers feasted on their corpses. He'd seen enough death, and he wanted to save a life. So what if it happened to be the life of a ghrina? Who was *she* to judge him or think so poorly of him?

"What do you want from me?" Rukh demanded. "Look around you. We're all alone in the Hunters Flats. As far as I know, we may be the only two Humans still alive out here. We're likely surrounded by a Plague of Chimeras, and the Shylows might be hunting us, too. I will protect you because that is what a Kumma does: we fight and we protect those who can't protect themselves, even to our dying breath." He said it all with hot anger in his voice.

Jessira sat back and appeared chastened. She looked away, sipped on some water, and ate a few dates as they sat in an uncomfortable silence.

"Thank you," she finally replied.

"For what?" Rukh scowled, still angry with her.

"Saving me. Not every Pureblood would have."

"You're welcome," Rukh said gruffly. The apology had sounded forced, but perhaps it was a start.

"What kind of welcome will I find in Ashoka?" she asked, breaking the quiet.

"Not a good one," Rukh said, unwilling to insult her intelligence with a lie. "I'll do my best to make it as…pleasant as possible. You'll be Healed. I'll make sure of it. And I'll protect you, like I promised I would."

"Why do you care so much?" Jessira asked. She appeared puzzled or confused by his attitude.

"It seemed like the compassionate thing to do. The OutCastes don't have a monopoly on it, you know?"

———————•———————

Jessira muffled a cry as the Kumma helped clean her wounds, reaching the ones she couldn't get to on her back. The damn cuts from the damn cats had finally stopped bleeding, but they were still angry and red, showing no signs of healing three days on from the Shylows' attack.

"Sorry about that," Rukh said when she flinched.

On the first day after she'd come to, she'd taken one look at Rukh's breathing and known he'd done something to his ribs again. This time it had only been bruising and pulled muscles, but it had still taken much of her strength to Heal him. She hadn't wanted to, but it made sense, much as she wished it was otherwise. Mauled as she was, she couldn't do much to protect herself. She would have to rely on *his* protection, the protection of a Pureblood. It was laughable when she thought about it. The entire situation was either karma or Devesh's idea of a joke.

Later in the day, after she had Healed Rukh, they had come across a nest of Ur-Fels, about ten of them along with a Balant, all of them likely heading toward the gathering Li-Choke had spoken of. When the Chims charged, she had reckoned she and the Kumma would be dead in seconds. A warrior of Stronghold could handle three or four Ur-Fels at one time, but not ten of them.

She had forgotten how swift was the Kumma's sword.

Rukh had lit into the Ur-Fels like a single-minded engine of destruction. The Kumma had slaughtered all of them in a brief battle, with his Fireballs wiping out most of the Chims in mere seconds. The rest had fallen to his sword, including the Balant accompanying the Ur-Fels. The large, baboon-like Chim had hooted in alarm and anger as the other Chims died around it, but it too was swiftly silenced. Rukh had charged the beast, decapitating it before it could finish trumpeting its anger. After the battle, Rukh had merely cleaned his sword. He had said nothing more. His face had been a stiff, unfeeling mask.

From that moment on, Jessira had warily watched Rukh even more closely than before. She knew men like him; men with hearts of stone whose only purpose in life was to fight; men who were only ever alive while in the white-hot heat of battle. They almost always died young, unable to cope with living amongst civilized folk. Such men lived on the knife's edge of losing control and it wasn't safe to be around them. They were like unpredictable dogs, laying about without a moment's notice or hesitation as they bit or clawed anyone within reach. Jessira could see the Kumma following such a path. If she was right, peace for Rukh would prove to be as elusive as a feather floating on the wind, teasingly far above his outstretched hands.

During all this, while her thoughts had been distracted, Rukh had quickly ransacked the Chims supplies – supplies the two of them sorely needed. He had found water, blankets, and more than enough food for both of them. It had turned out to be some kind of jerky, and while it tasted awful, at least it was edible. There had also been some rancid alcoholic beverage. It worked fine as an antiseptic, stinging like a fiery coal when poured over her wounds. She was willing to put up with far worse if it meant getting through this alive. She needed to return to Stronghold and warn her people of the change in the Sorrow Bringer's sanity, just as Rukh sought to warn Ashoka.

"It's the best I can do," Rukh said, re-stoppering the rancid alcohol. "Put your shirt back on. We have to get going."

Jessira kept her back to him and winced as she lifted her torn camisole from where it hung around her waist. She had hated letting the Kumma know she wore such a feminine garment underneath all her warrior's gear. Next came her thick, linen shirt. She slipped her arms through its sleeves, no longer cringing at the touch of the crusted blood dirtying her clothes. Instead, the pain all along her left side had her attention, whenever she moved her arm or tried to button up her jacket.

Had Lure been here, he would have Healed her long ago.

She stared unseeing at the grass, lost in her memories.

If Lure were here, she'd have boxed his ears for breaking her heart. She'd always been closer to him than Cedar or her eldest brother, Kart, who was so much older he might as well have been an uncle. As for Cedar, he had always been mature beyond his years. He never seemed to have the time to spend with his younger siblings. Even her cousins, Court and Sign, who had grown up in their home, hadn't been as close to her as Lure. The two of them had invented games only they understood and hiked the caverns of Stronghold, pretending to discover new cave systems or battle strange monsters awoken from their slumber deep under the mountains. And as they grew older, their adventures had taken them through the hills and valleys bordering their city, usually just the two of them. She had spent more time with Lure than any other person in her life.

And now he was gone, and she would never see him again. She would never have another chance to tease him or hear him laugh. How would she tell her parents, especially her mother? Lure had been their favorite as much as he had been Jessira's.

"Are you alright?" Rukh asked, breaking her out of her reverie.

"I'm fine," she said, wiping away the tears which had fallen unnoticed down her cheeks. "Let's go."

Of course, the Kumma never cried. She'd never seen him show even the slightest evidence of remorse or grief over the deaths of his friends, Brand and Keemo. No doubt his stony warrior's heart kept him from feeling such frail Human emotions as sorrow and loss.

But then again, why had he saved her and brought her along? She only slowed him down. She couldn't defend herself or even help much with the watch at night. She was too weak, and Rukh ended up having to take the longest shifts. He would have been better off alone, but so far he hadn't made any mention of leaving her behind.

Why was that?

He should have. *She* might have.

The first day after the Shylows attack, he had said it was because of compassion, but did he actually have such an emotion? The one time she had asked about his friends, he had snubbed her with a snarled warning to mind her own business. And when he helped with the wounds on her back, his hands were cold and brusque, as if the feel of her skin disgusted him. Rukh Shektan was a puzzle. His attitude proclaimed how much he despised her, but his behavior did not. His behavior went against everything she had been taught about Purebloods. She couldn't tell which part of him was true.

While she was grateful for his help, Jessira looked forward to her arm and shoulder healing enough for her to split off from the Kumma and find her own way home.

Just then, Rukh held up a hand, and she stopped. His hearing was better than hers. All of his senses were. It was childish to resent his superior attributes, but it just seemed wrong that one man was so gifted.

Rukh stooped low into a crouch and hid himself in the tall, prairie grass in which they traveled, gesturing for her to do the same. "There's a trap of Braids up ahead," he whispered into her ear. "They might have our scent. Don't move." He stared off into the distance, an intense expression of concentration on his face. An instant later, he hissed softly in agitation. "They're coming. Blend yourself. Stay low."

As he slowly eased himself out of his crouch, his sword sliding noiselessly into his hands, Jessira wondered again at his ultimate motivations. At his heart, what kind of a man was he? Taking on a trap wasn't likely to be much of a challenge for him after what she'd seen him do with the Ur-Fels, but still, it spoke of a deeper commitment to her than she realized or wanted to admit.

Jessira Blended, and despite Rukh's admonitions, she stood, preparing to help if possible. She had lost all her weapons when the Shylows had attacked, and now all she had was the looted sword of an Ur-Fel. It was short and poorly weighted for her, but it was better than nothing. Even if Rukh didn't need her help.

Although...she frowned. In his fight with the Ur-Fels, he'd simply burned them where they stood with Fireballs. This time, his sword was unsheathed, but his hands remained unlit. There was no glow to them. Jessira chewed her lower lip in worry. What if he no longer had the *Jivatma* to conduct Fireballs? He might only have the skill of his sword. Long odds at five against one.

The Chims must have seen his movement. They howled out their strange, hissing cries.

Jessira had trouble seeing what happened next. The Kumma moved too fast for her to follow. She saw him take on the foremost two Braids. He kicked one in the gut, causing the beast to fall over and gasp for breath. A block and slice disemboweled the other one. A reverse thrust slammed through the open mouth of the gut-kicked Braid. Rukh blurred forward, and she briefly lost track of his movements. Another Braid died. She saw Rukh bend backward at the waist beneath a blow aimed at his head. He snapped upright and struck like a cobra. His sword arrowed into the creature's heart. He slipped another strike like a twirling dancer. At the end of the spin, his blade came down in a deadly arc against the final Braid's neck.

The battle was over. It had taken less than five seconds, and despite Jessira's initial worry, it had turned out to be anticlimactic.

And once more, to her great disgust, she hadn't been able to offer any help whatsoever. Jessira was used to taking care of herself. She was tired of relying on the skills of another to protect and care for her. She wanted – she needed – to be able to fight her own fights. Just then, even though Rukh had once more saved her life, Jessira found herself hating him, or at least the situation in which she found herself. She hated being helpless, especially before a Pureblood.

She viewed him as he stood amongst the carnage of his killing, not injured in the slightest, barely even breathing heavily. He flicked droplets of blood off his blade, displaying no emotion whatsoever. Once more, his face was a blank slate: no anger, no joy, no fear, no pain, and no pity. At that moment Jessira feared him as she had never feared anyone. In battle, this man was as cold and merciless as a knifing winter gale.

A chill filled her heart. *Devesh, what kind of man have You forged?*

No matter all he had done for her, just then, had she been healthy, Jessira would have run in the opposite direction. Instead, she forced herself to walk to where he cleaned his sword. "Are you hurt?" Jessira asked.

"I'm fine," he said, his voice diamond hard and sharp. The tone reminded her of a scything sickle.

"Good. If you die, I wouldn't last an hour out here." She winced as soon as the words left her lips.

Rukh smiled sardonically. "Yes, and I'm glad to know exactly what my worth is to you," he said. His cutting phrase caused her to flinch. "I'll look through their packs, and then we have to go. There may be more on the way."

"I don't think the wounds are getting any worse," Rukh said. He squatted behind her and dabbed alcohol on the cuts on her back.

"But they also aren't getting any better," Jessira said with a hiss when she felt the sting of the alcohol. "If only you Kummas could Heal as well as you can fight."

Rukh smiled. "We all have our roles to play. Devesh wouldn't want us to be too proud."

"Devesh has nothing to do with it. You Purebloods have simply closed your minds to what is possible. If you'd just let me, I could teach you what to do. Who knows? Maybe you'd even be good at it."

Rukh shook his head. "I've learned enough," he said. "No need to disgrace myself any further."

His words stung, and she flinched. If he thought he was disgraced, all because he had stayed alive through the mastery of Blending, what then did he think of her? Sometimes, she forgot who they were, he a Pureblood and she an OutCaste, but then he would say something casually cruel and it would all come back to her. He would remind her of his true feelings: first and foremost, he thought of Jessira as a ghrina, an abomination.

"I'm sorry," Rukh said. "That didn't come out right. I didn't mean to imply anything about you. You're who you are," Rukh said.

Jessira almost turned to face him, surprised he had guessed what she was thinking. The immodesty of having her jacket, shirt, and camisole draped around her waist kept her frozen in place. "And who am I to you?"

"We have a saying in Ashoka: in a Trial, all men are brothers," Rukh answered enigmatically.

His meaning was obtuse, and Jessira didn't know how to reply.

First he insulted her, then he apologized – sounding sincere in the process, and now – was he paying her a compliment? Did he imply she was a sister to him? Jessira couldn't tell.

Without thinking, Jessira turned her head, meaning to ask him. Instead, her entire torso moved. It wasn't much, just enough to expose a portion of her breast before she quickly moved to cover herself.

Rukh flushed.

Jessira wanted to smack her head for not seeing it sooner. Here they were, all alone in the Wildness: a man and a woman.

The flush on his face gave him away.

Jessira smirked.

Now the truth came out. In a Trial, all men are brothers. What a load of Balant shit. He didn't think of her as a sister. Injured, bloody and filthy as she was, ghrina or not, she was merely a woman he'd like to bed. She shook her head in disgust. What a hypocrite.

He stepped away from her, a look of anger on his face. "You think I'm only helping you so I can get you undressed, don't you?"

"A man has his desires," she said, "and I saw your face."

He ground his teeth, looking like he was trying to rein in his impatience. "I'm keeping you alive because I need your help," he said. "The Castes have to change if we want to have any hope of riding out the coming storm. The Baels say Suwraith can rid Herself of Her madness. Maybe they're right and maybe they're wrong, but if they *are* telling the truth, She'll come for Ashoka, and this time She'll know what to do. We'll be sheep before the wolf."

Jessira snorted. Right. His words were pretty and noble. They might even be genuine, but she didn't believe him, at least not entirely. Rukh wanted what all men ultimately wanted.

"And how exactly am I supposed to help you with this miraculous redemption of your Pureblooded hearts?" she asked.

"By just being you. You've got this way about you, of never

backing down, of never apologizing for who and what you are. We need this challenge. We can't keep going on like we have. We have to change. I think we've needed this since the Night of Sorrows."

"As soon as I step foot into Ashoka, your people will lynch me and forget I ever existed."

"I don't think so," Rukh said. "Some might even understand and agree with me."

"Agree with what? Allowing ghrinas to live?" She laughed. "You're dreaming. People don't change that quickly. And besides, none of this matters. You haven't answered my question," she said. "I saw the look on your face. Don't pretend you're saving me because of some notion of noble self-sacrifice."

"Stop being so self-centered," he snapped. "What you saw wasn't lust…it was embarrassment. I'm not as coarse as you think I am. I would never take advantage of a woman in your situation. It's disgusting. And as for my 'noble self-sacrifice', that is exactly what it means to be a Kumma. It is who we are." He stood suddenly, and she could see the anger in his posture as he marched away from her. "Times burning. Let's go," he shouted over his shoulder.

Hours later, with only an unhappy silence to mark the miles of their passage, Jessira knew she had to be the one to make amends.

"I'm sorry," she said, hating how often she seemed to have to apologize to this Kumma.

"For what?" Rukh asked, his voice curt.

She sighed. He wasn't going to make this easy on her.

"For thinking the worst of you."

"You know, I've saved your life over and over again. I've kept you alive, cared for you, and in all this time, I've never complained about it. The only thing I ask in return is a little gratitude and respect." He was still obviously angry.

"You're right," she said, suddenly feeling the weight of her guilt. He had done all those things for her, and she had given him nothing but suspicion and sharp words. "I haven't treated you very well. I'm sorry."

He grunted in response, not sounding mollified in the least.

She paused, trying to find the right words. "It's not easy for me to trust someone like you."

"A Kumma, you mean," Rukh said. He stopped, turning to face her. "You may not believe this, but I understand how you feel. It can't get much worse than having to rely on a Pureblood for your safety."

His insight surprised her. Once more, Rukh had taken the time to think things through from her perspective. He even sympathized with what she was feeling. She might have misjudged him all along. And if she had, could she also be wrong about others like him? Other Purebloods? She didn't think so, but the certainty she had once felt was no longer there.

"I still think your people will toss me out as soon as they see my face. I bet you think the same thing," she said. "So why do you bother? All I'm doing is slowing you down and keeping you from warning your city."

Rukh shrugged. "I'm Kumma. I told you: it's what we do," he said flashing her a grin of self-deprecation.

Jessira smiled back, her first true smile since that awful night in the Flats. "Then you are a credit to your Caste," she said, her voice only slightly mocking.

"Now you're just making fun of me," he said, frowning so severely that Jessira burst out in laughter.

Jessira stumbled, and Rukh reached for her, keeping her from falling.

"Let's take a break," he suggested.

Wordlessly, Jessira lowered herself to the ground, too tired to talk.

Rukh dropped next to her, feeling the weariness of three weeks of marching on low rations and minimal sleep. Every night after they made camp, Rukh took the longest stretch of the watch. Jessira needed the rest. Her injuries weren't healing, and the pinkness along the edges of some of her wounds were starting to turn red. Rukh was worried infection was setting in. It was already starting to affect her balance, and she leaned heavily on Rukh as they made their slow way through the Hunters Flats.

And Jessira was not a small woman. She was as tall as Rukh's sister or any Kumma woman for that matter, but built with the lean, well-muscled frame of a warrior. It wasn't easy holding her up at the end of a long day of marching. At times, Rukh almost wished Li-Choke had stayed with them to help with the burden of carrying her.

The one blessing was that they hadn't run into any more Chims, but Rukh still worried. He could take Braids and Ur-Fels, but in his current state, any force of Tigons – certainly a claw with its five to seven cats – would probably overwhelm him. And coming upon a Shylow along the northern outskirts of the Flats would be a disaster. His *Jivatma* was thin and had been from the beginning of their long march. Along with the gauntness to his face and the weight he had lost, it was yet another reflection of his weariness, and it wouldn't get better any time soon. He couldn't afford to take a break in order to rest and recover. Not now. Jessira had grown too weak to Blend for herself anymore. As a result, it now fell to Rukh to take on that additional task as well.

He placed the back of his hand against her forehead.

"I'm fine," she said.

Rukh didn't think so, but he kept quiet. Jessira's voice was no longer strong and confident like it had been when they had first met, but there was no reason to state the obvious. "Let's clean the wounds," he suggested.

"Want another look at the twins, huh?" she said with a chuckle.

"My lust knows no bounds," he said smiling back.

After he finished, she sighed, and leaned back against him with her eyes closed. "Why won't you talk about your friends?" she asked.

He didn't answer at first. He couldn't. Reminiscing about Keemo and Brand was too painful. "If I talk about them, then I remember them, and if I remember them, I'll miss them, and if I miss them…I'll break down, and I can't afford that right now. *We* can't. I'll mourn their deaths when we get home."

"Your home. Not mine," Jessira reminded him in a soft, wistful tone. But her voice was without the bitterness and anger she had once so commonly expressed.

"Yes. My home," he said, acknowledging her correction.

"You know, those first few days after the attack, I thought you were the coldest man I ever met. You reminded me of people I knew…you know, men whose only goal is the next battle."

Rukh gave her a half-hearted smile of bemusement. He knew the kind of person Jessira was talking about. Had she really thought of him like that? "I hope you don't feel the same way anymore," he said.

She chuckled. "Well, you've grown on me," she said with a shrug. "I think you'll turn out alright. For a Pureblood, you're not half bad."

He laughed with her. "And for an OutCaste, you're only half abominable."

She protested in mock outrage, punching him lightly on the shoulder even as she laughed. "You deserve that," she said.

Rukh laughed with her. The punch hadn't hurt, but once she was fit and healthy again, he imagined she could do some damage.

"Are you ready?" he asked. "There's still about three hours of daylight."

With a groan, Jessira stood. "I'm ready."

A few days later, they finally passed from the northern edges of the Flats and were into the southeastern foothills of the Privation Mountains. The grasslands had given way to forest, making it a much harder slog as they forced their way up and down steep hills and through wooded valleys. For every mile as the eagle flew, they had to cover four on the ground. It made for frustratingly slow progress, and to make matters worse, Jessira wasn't getting any better. An infection *had* settled into her shoulder, further weakening her.

Today, they had to stop early. Jessira had collapsed.

Rukh set up camp on a small field of grass next to a narrow stream. The air was cool from the late day shower, and the smell of moss and wet leaves from the undergrowth filled the air. Lightning bugs flitted through the warm early summer evening while chirping crickets and croaking frogs competed to be heard over the sound of water burbling over rocks.

Once he had a fire started, Rukh made Jessira as comfortable as he could. He tucked her under the few blankets they had managed to scavenge, but sometimes she still shivered uncontrollably. They were a little less than a week short of Ashoka, and beyond where Shylows were known to hunt. This close to the city jaguars and bears might still be a danger, but the smart ones had learned to steer clear of campfires. The stupid ones were dead, but even if one of them showed up, Rukh knew he could handle it.

What he couldn't handle was Jessira's infection. Pus seeped from the wounds, and she burned hot with fever. At other times, her skin was cold and clammy. Her breathing had also changed, coming in short gasps as if she had been running for miles. She even smelled sick, a mixture of stale sweat, dirt, and old blood, but underneath it all was a sharp, bitter almond-like smell.

He slipped her out of her jacket and shirt, leaving her in her camisole. He didn't know what else to do with her alternating fever and coldness. He also hadn't been able to wake her up for dinner, and with a sinking feeling, he realized she might not live through the night.

Rukh had hoped to be in Ashoka by now, where a Shiyen physician could have Healed her. And if the wounds hadn't slowed them down so much, they might have actually made it. As it was, they were still a good four or five days from Ashoka, which was too far for Jessira. Several days ago, he'd even tried his hand at Healing. Jessira had done her best to teach him, but it hadn't worked out. He had even tried to form a Duo with her. After all, Rukh had learned to Blend while Annexed with Brand in a Quad, but once more they had met with failure.

Now, she lay dying next to him, and there was nothing he could do about it. He was helpless even as he watched her every movement, desperate to see some sign she might be able to rally. He didn't want to lose Jessira. Not so soon after Brand and Keemo, and maybe even Farn. They were so close – just a few more days would see her safe.

Karma. Fate. A fickle God. Whatever the reason, it flew in the face of goodness for Jessira Viola Grey to die this way.

Just then, the sound of a large animal moving through the shrubs and trees came to him. It moved without any subtlety toward their camp.

In an instant, Rukh was on his feet, sword ready and his back to the fire as he scanned the woods. He wasn't too weak to fight. His *Jivatma* was woefully thin, but he had more than enough to speed his thoughts and muscles to take down any animal out there on this night. He welcomed such a challenge; not for the killing, but just to release some pent up aggression. He wanted to hit something, so whatever was out there was in for a beating.

His blood ran cold when he saw what stalked into his firelight.

334

A Shylow.

The cat was a young female with a calico pattern and a black patch of fur surrounding her right eye. She slowly padded forward, ears erect.

What was she waiting for? The Shylows on the Flats had charged straight in, claws out and out for blood. This one just paced toward him, and her eyes didn't appear to hold malice or a promise of death. More than anything, they looked to be filled with curiosity.

She stopped five feet from Rukh and carefully sat down, tail tucked neatly before her front paws.

You have an unusual voice. It is melancholy, and yet soothing at the same time.

Rukh glanced around, not sure where the words had come from.

I sit before you.

Rukh's gaze sharpened on the cat. The Shylow? It couldn't be.

And yet it is.

"Can you speak?" Rukh asked aloud.

No response.

Why do your kind make so many loud noises?

"Who are you?"

Again. No response.

My name is Aia.

Rukh frowned. Was the cat speaking to him through his mind?

Yes I am.

Rukh rocked back. Impossible. He had to be hallucinating, or maybe even having some sort of lucid dream.

If you can hear me, pat the ground three times, Rukh said.

The cat patted the ground three times.

Twice.

The Shylow did as Rukh asked.

Rukh smiled hesitantly. It *was* her.

I already told you that. the cat said.

335

Rukh didn't know what to think. There had never been any reports of a person speaking to a Shylow. As far as anyone knew, the great cats were simple beasts, deadly to everyone around them. It was best to avoid them, and trying to talk to one of them had certainly never been a recommended piece of advice. Yet here he was doing exactly that. It was surreal.

I'm going to put away my sword now. Do you promise not to kill or eat me?

I came to talk. If I wanted to kill and eat you, you would already be dead. My father says Humans taste awful, by the way.

I need a promise.

The Shylow seemed to sigh. *I promise not to kill or eat you. My name is Aia.* The cat repeated politely, seemingly waiting for an expected response.

It took Rukh a few seconds to understand what she wanted. *Hello, Aia. My name is Rukh Shektan.*

Hello, Rukh Shektan. Most of my kind believe Humans incapable of speech, yet you possess it. You are the first Human with whom any Kesarin has ever spoken.

Kesarin?

*We are the Kesarins. You name us Shylows. *

Rukh sat down. *I think I need a drink.*

Aia padded further into the camp. *What is wrong with your mate?*

She isn't my mate.

She is female. You are male. You are alone. And yet you are not mates?

Right now wasn't the best time to go over Human relationships. *It's complicated.* Rukh said. She's sick. I'm trying to get her to some help.*

*I saw you defend her from the Nobeasts. *

A vision of the battles with the Braids and Ur-Fels flashed through Rukh's mind.

You saw?

I witnessed.

How long have you been following us?

Another vision, this time of the battle with the first two Shylow on the night when Brand and Keemo had died.

You've been watching for that long? Why?

I was curious. Why did the Demon Wind strike down Her Nobeast Kezin?

I'm thinking by Demon Wind, you mean Suwraith?

Yes.

We also call her the Mad Queen or Bringer of Sorrows.

So many names?

She's earned every single one, Rukh said. *But what is a Kezin?*

Another flash of information.

The Kesarins were organized into glarings of forty-to-fifty, each one led by a dominant male, the Kezin, or what the Ashokans called the Slayer. There were also many Kesarins who chose to live as solitaries, like Aia. Most eventually rejoined their birth pack, but some never did.

The Kezin lead the Nobeasts.

We call them the Fan Lor Kum. Rukh explained the organization of Suwraith's armies and the role of the Baels.

And these Baels betrayed their Mother?

Yes.

Then it is good they were killed. For the Kesarins the greatest sin is to go against our Father and our Mother. Aia blinked. *They were Human.*

What do you mean?

My birth father is Kezin to the Hungrove. My birth mother is a Secudus, a lower ranking female. But Mother and Father, our Creators, were Human.

Was Aia talking about the First Mother and First Father?

I see you know of whom I speak, she said.

The Demon Wind is not First Mother to the Baels. There is only one First Mother and First Father, and Suwraith is Their Daughter. The Baels say the Queen killed Her parents in order to become who She is now.

The Demon Wind slayed the First Mother and First Father? Outrage tinged Aia's thoughts. *Our stories tell us how after their seasons of labor, the First Mother and First Father lay down to rest. They sleep deeply now, but one day, They shall rise up and complete the path of the Kesarins, as They promised. But you say They are dead? How can this be?*

Rukh explained all he knew of Suwraith and the Night of Sorrows, and Her endless war with Humanity.

It is good I did not slay you when you were in reach of my claws Aia said. *The Kesarins give wide berth to the Demon Wind, and we slay the Nobeasts when necessary.*

And why would you have killed me?

Some believe the Humans have hidden the First Mother and the First Father away so they cannot complete the Kesarins. It is why some Kesarins hate your people.

But the First Mother and First Father were Human. Why would we do such a thing?

Some Kesarins are fools and believe what is most convenient.

So are many people.

I will have to tell my father of this matter.

Rukh nodded feeling a sense of unreality. This was beyond doubt the oddest conversation he could have ever imagined having: 'talking' to a Shylow – a Kesarin – while a ghrina, an OutCaste woman, lay next to him beside a campfire somewhere in the depths of the Wildness.

When the other two Kesarins attacked us, you didn't finish us off. You could have.

Aia seemed to smile, or at least it was the impression Rukh sensed from her. *I am...unusual. Of all the Kesarins, only a few are born such as I: ones who can hear the voices of others. It is said: the Kesarin who can hear all, will understand nothing. We are thought to be dreamers and fools.*

Rukh smiled. *It seems like Kesarins and Humanity have much in common.*

Perhaps. Aia gently nosed Jessira. *But in this way we are quite different. When one of us becomes too ill to even stand, they are left to die. We do not care for them as you have cared for this one.* She blinked. *The wounds are sickened.*

Before Rukh could stop her, the Kesarin bent low and licked at Jessira cuts, scraping off the scabbed crust of suppuration and opening up the wounds until the blood ran clean, without a hint of pus.

Jessira moaned.

You're killing her!

Aia looked at him. *I am not. This is how we clean our wounds. It works for some cuts and illnesses, but it won't help her deeper sickness.* She cocked her head as if she were listening to a sound only she could hear. *In her mind, she wishes you had her knowledge. She believes you could Heal her if you did.*

Rukh grimaced. *I can't do what she can. Believe me, I've tried.*

Jivatma? So this is how your kind throws fire. We wondered. We do not have this Jivatma. Aia looked at him. *She can Heal. You cannot. You only lack the knowledge?*

And the skill.

I can give you her knowledge.

How...

Rukh never had a chance to finish his question. A mind-splitting flash had Rukh on his knees. He clutched his head. The pain must have only lasted a few seconds, but it seemed to go on for much longer. Minutes or hours. It finally eased off. Rukh closed his eyes and waited for the world to stop spinning and the pounding of his heart to settle down.

What did you do? he asked, not bothering to mask his anger. He didn't care if the cat took offense. He was furious at what she had done.

I gave you her knowledge. You can Heal her now, if you wish. Good luck.

Wait! Rukh searched his thoughts, and found he *did* know how to Heal. What had Aia done?

I gave you her knowledge. I'm certain I've already explained this to you. Aia wore a quizzical expression with her head tilted to the side.

Rukh didn't know what to say. He was stunned, but also heartened. He might actually be able to save Jessira. He walked over to stand before the Shylow. *Thank you. It hurt like the unholy hells, so please don't do it again.*

You are welcome. And I won't. Aia paused. *My chin always itches.*

Rukh frowned, not sure what she meant by her last statement. Surely she didn't...maybe she did. Hesitantly, he reached forward and scratched under Aia's chin, rubbing harder as her eyes slitted closed and she purred contentment.

After a moment she stepped back and shook her head. *Utterly perfect. Had we known how well your fingers could groom us, we would have attempted to speak with your kind long before. A proper grooming...Father will find this most interesting. He needs to know of this as well.* She rubbed her forehead against Rukh's chest, knocking him back a step. *Good luck to you, Rukh Shektan.*

With that, Aia walked out of his campsite. Rukh stared after her as she left, and he briefly wondered how his people would view him now. He had spoken with a Shylow and had two Talents not of his own Caste. Perhaps one Talent might have been forgivable, but certainly not two. Most folk would see Rukh as a walking disgrace, only a few small steps short of a ghrina.

He mentally shrugged. Tomorrow would have to take care of itself. He had work to do. He turned to Jessira. Time to Heal.

First, he examined her wounds. He frowned in surprise. There was no pus seeping from them. The edges of the cuts actually did appear to be somewhat cleaner, no longer quite as heaped up with inflammation. They still didn't look good, but maybe Aia's cleansing *had* helped a little.

340

He searched his newfound Talent and tried to recall what Jessira had done when she had helped with his injured ribs.

He knelt next to her and had to slip off her camisole – he still couldn't understand why she wore such a feminine undergarment – to get to all the wounds. It was a liberty no Kumma would have ever taken with any woman in a normal situation, but this wasn't a normal situation. Rukh grimaced at the severity of her injuries. This wouldn't be easy. The cuts extended from just above her breast, over her shoulder, and down her back.

He placed his hands over the wounds on her back and focused his *Jivatma* as Jessira had tried to teach him. He conducted it, measuring it out until it was a fine thread, more slender than a knitting needle and as precise as a Duriah's measurement. This was so much harder than anything he had ever done. Always before, he had simply reached for *Jivatma* and accepted its fierce torrent. This required a fine touch, one of complete focus and discipline.

Sweat beaded on his face moments into the Healing.

The enormity of the work staggered him. The infection had spread beyond the surface wounds, extending into the blood and bone. Jessira's wounds might have taxed a Shiyen, and here he was trying to Heal her on his first attempt at the art. He would have found the situation laughable if it wasn't so serious.

Thankfully, he didn't have to completely Heal Jessira. All he had to do was keep the infection under control until they reached Ashoka. A real physician could Heal her then, and maybe even save her arm.

He worked slowly and carefully, focusing on the infection in the bones of her shoulder. There was a locus there, the source of the sickness spreading into her blood. He spent what seemed like hours trying to Heal it. Eventually, he was satisfied he'd done all he could. The bone was still infected, but at least the sickness was being held at bay, unlikely to spread so long as he continued Healing it until they reached Ashoka. Next came the wounds. They would also have to be dealt with. He couldn't leave them open. Ever so gradually, Rukh worked at it, and the claw marks on her shoulder and back slowly knitted shut.

There. Almost finished. He sat back and panted. It felt like he'd run twenty miles with a full rucksack. Fighting Kinsu Makren had been easy compared to this. He waited for his heart and breathing to slow, taking time to regain some strength before tackling the cuts on her chest.

He was heartened to see Jessira's color looking better. He took it as a good sign, and once he was rested, he knew it was time for her remaining wounds. She would probably kill him for seeing her nearly naked, but hopefully, being alive would alleviate some of her anger.

He took a deep breath before placing his hands over the wounds. He tried not to notice the softness of her breast. Again, all too slowly, the cuts knitted closed until they were nothing more than fine pink lines. Soon, Rukh was panting again, and his vision blurred. He'd never been so tired in his life.

But it was worth it.

Jessira would live.

He knew it.

Her eyes flickered open, and her gaze focused on his worried face.

"You look like I feel," she said with a tremulous smile.

Rukh chuckled with relief. They both did, and when they finished, it was Jessira who broke the silence. "Rukh...you can let go of my breast now," she said.

Rukh quickly withdrew his hand, utterly mortified, but for some reason, her words struck a nerve. He found them hilarious.

He rolled over onto his back and laughed as he gazed into the night sky, unable to stop.

CHAPTER EIGHTEEN
A NEED FOR CAUTION

Those with love in their hearts must sing it out for all the world to see and share.
To do otherwise is to deny the greatest gift I have given.

~The Book of All Souls

Bree followed as Rector led her through the narrow streets of West Vineyard Steep. This was a mixed neighborhood, just north of the Moon Quarter and not a very desirable place to live. Most people here came from a variety of Castes, such as Sentya, Duriah, Rahail, and Muran. There were even a few Shiyens. No Cherids or Kummas, though. No one from those two Castes – the wealthiest in Ashoka – would deign to live in such a poor place. It would have been an intolerable embarrassment to live in such apparent poverty. Not that the place really was impoverished. At least not anymore.

West Vineyard Steep had come a long way since the time about seventy years prior when many of the houses here had fallen into such disrepair that they had become nesting places for animals. As a result, almost half the homes in the area had been razed, including a large number toward the center of the neighborhood. Most of those torn down had never been rebuilt, and instead their lots had been turned into communal gardens and parks. Of the houses left in place, the vast majority were small, narrow, single-story brick houses, well maintained, and with lovely flower gardens in front. This had become a quiet neighborhood of families with a few small shops and restaurants. And while it didn't have the beauty of Jubilee, the extravagance of Fragrance Wall, or the vibrancy of Trell Rue, it looked comfortable and the people walking the streets here appeared content.

"The Trim Chef was one of my favorite restaurants before I left for the Trials," Rector said. "The food there is classic Sentya cuisine with plain potatoes, carrots, and fish. It's not overly spiced like so many of those trendy fusion restaurants everyone seems to like so much these days. It's traditional, a reminder of the old ways of doing things."

He gently guided her by the elbow down a side street, not much more than an alley in Jubilee Hills.

"Jaresh would probably like it then," Bree observed, although she herself preferred the fusion cuisine, which Rector apparently didn't. She gently eased her arm free of Rector's grasp. She didn't want or need his assistance.

"I would hope so," Rector said. "For me every time I pass it by, I remember how the owner and chef have been the same for twenty-five years, and it fills me with a little bit of hope."

"What do you mean?"

"Our world keeps changing," Rector answered. "There's so much intermingling going on now. Instead of each Caste having its own way of being, it's like the city has this formless culture where everyone is just like everybody else. Most of the other cities I've visited aren't like that. The Castes there are distinct and separate. People know their place. It's simpler, and if you ask me, it's better."

Rector was a traditionalist, and his words weren't unexpected. He had a kinship with Ashoka as it might have existed several generations ago. On the other hand, Bree wasn't sure what she felt. Not anymore. Not since Nanna had told her about the founder of House Shektan. She still hadn't come to terms with it. And now, with everything going on – the murders, the Withering Knife, and the Sil Lor Kum – she could see how maintaining one's traditions could be comforting. "I see what you mean," she said, neither agreeing nor disagreeing with Rector. "Nanna says Ashoka is much more complex than it was when he was a child. It's both easier and harder for those of different Castes to interrelate, especially with us, Kummas."

Rector nodded. "It's because the stature of our Caste has declined, while those of some of the others has risen without merit. I always thought of our Caste as being first among equals, but I don't think many other people do. I know it sounds arrogant, but it also happens to be true whether anybody else wants to accept it or not. Other Castes just don't know their place, and they take us for granted. In Forge and Arjun and Samsoul we are still properly honored for our work. It's how it should be," Rector said.

To a certain extent, Bree understood what Rector was saying even if he wasn't saying it well. People didn't respect the sacrifices made by Kummas. They took them for granted, thinking her Caste's wealth was payment enough for all they suffered and endured. But it wasn't even close. Coins couldn't bring back the dead or Heal the men broken on their Trials. Who wouldn't trade wealth for the safety and health of their children?

Of course, her parents didn't feel the sting of ingratitude quite as strongly as Bree did. In reality, they wouldn't even see it as ingratitude. They thought other Castes *should* rise up and voice their opinions when it came to how the city was run. It shouldn't all be left to the Cherids and the Kummas. Amma and Nanna would have disagreed with Rector, quite strongly, in fact. But if Bree voiced agreement with Rector Bryce, it would feel too much like a betrayal of her family, so instead, she kept quiet.

They arrived at the restaurant, and Rector held open the door. It was dim inside, and since the night was still young – the sun having set just a few minutes earlier – only a few other couples were present. Candles burned within hurricane vases on each of the dozen or so square tables, but otherwise there was no additional lighting. The firefly lanterns hanging on the walls were unlit. The smell of grilled fish as well as the heavy aroma of boiled potatoes and roasted garlic permeated the restaurant. The owner, a chunky Sentya, had them quickly seated.

Bree was surprised when Rector held out the chair for her. It was an old-fashioned habit few bothered with anymore since nowadays women were expected to do for themselves. Then again, Rector was nothing if not old-fashioned.

In the six weeks they had spent perusing the various libraries in Ashoka, Bree had learned two facts about Rector Bryce. First, he was blunt and plainspoken about his opinions, never hedging or hiding what he felt. Bree wondered if he was even capable of deceit or subtlety. In some ways, his attitude was refreshing.

There had been a time when all Kummas – men and women, both – would have been like Rector: candid, confident, and upfront. Over the years, though, the insufferable Cherids and their snide habit of carefully cutting remarks had somehow seeped into Kumma culture, replacing honesty with a preening repartee. The women were especially affected. Too often conversations at many parties and gatherings devolved into a cruel banter where words were seemingly chosen for maximum insult, and yet couched in such a way as to allow the speaker to disavow a slight had ever been intended. It was cultural pollution, and the Kummas were not the better for it.

The other thing she had learned about Rector was that he was quite conservative. He longed for the simplicity of prior times and earlier mores, at least where it came to the interactions amongst the

Castes. In the case of the cultural homogeneity which had overtaken Ashoka, she could see his point.

Of course, Nanna might describe Ashoka as having a mélange of cultures, but on this one issue, Bree disagreed with him.

She was Kumma. She knew who she was, and it was enough. She disliked when non-Kummas aped her kind, such as the Rahails who had gone so far as to form their own Houses. And she especially didn't like it when the habits of another Caste somehow infected the culture of Caste Kumma. She wanted nothing to do with that. Let Murans be Murans. Let Duriahs be Duriahs. Let Cherids be Cherids. And let Kummas be Kummas. Each to their own.

Certainly, some influence was good. After all, look at Jaresh. Without a doubt, he had added greatly to their House, but then again, he was an exception, wasn't he? He might have been born Sentya, but his heart was Kumma. Moving beyond her brother's presence, Bree just didn't think it would make sense for House Shektan, or any House for that matter, to further open its ranks to those who were not Kummas. Jaresh was unique.

She shied away from further thoughts on the matter. They led to uncomfortable places where – if her logic was taken to its natural conclusion – she would be expected to disavow Jaresh. And she had no ready answer for the fact that while she loved being a Kumma, she was also fascinated by medicine. Hadn't she privately wished she could Heal, and wasn't it a Talent given only to the Shiyens?

"We've finished exploring the smaller libraries in the city," she said, changing the conversation. "Nanna will expect us to help Jaresh now." She pretended to shudder. "And given my brother's work ethic, he'll never let us have a nice relaxing meal after a hard day of fruitless searching. He'll push us from dawn-til-dusk."

Rector grimaced.

Bree laughed. "I was joking. It won't be so bad," she said, trying to ease his mind.

"I'm not worried about working hard," Rector said.

"Then what is it?"

"It's nothing," Rector said, trying to sound flippant.

"It must be something or you wouldn't have made that face."

Rector didn't answer at first. "It's Jaresh and Mira," he finally began. "Don't you find all the time they spend together...unseemly?"

Bree frowned in irritation. Agreeing with Rector about the melding of cultures was one thing but this was something else. It came dangerously close to making some very ugly claims about her brother, and Suwraith would claim her before she would let someone suggest something so vulgar. "I think you should be very careful what you say next," Bree replied in a soft whisper of warning. "Jaresh is my brother and our nanna's son, which is a byword for honor as far as I'm concerned. And Mira is my close friend, and I can't imagine her being any less honorable."

"I'm sorry," Rector said, sounding instantly contrite. "I didn't mean to speak badly of either of them. I just think its wrong for a Sentya man to spend so much time with a Kumma woman. Others would think so as well."

"Which is why the House Council has made sure everyone knows the two of them are working on a project under Nanna's specific orders," Bree snapped back. "Which also happens to be true. Again, Jaresh and Mira have my full trust, and I don't appreciate your implications."

"You're right," Rector said, shifting uncomfortably in his chair. "I withdraw the question."

Bree wasn't mollified. This was the other side of the coin when dealing with someone who was always blunt in their honesty: in some circumstances, they could sound cruel and thoughtless. Earlier, Bree had found Rector's unvarnished truth-telling to be admirable, but in this instance she didn't like it.

"I'm only worried about the needless ruin of their reputations,"

Rector continued. "I know they are honorable and would do nothing to bring shame to the House."

"If concern for Jaresh and Mira's reputation was why you said what you did, then fine," Bree said. "I happen to feel the same way, but the way you went about it; the question you asked...it was disgusting."

Rector grimaced. "As you say. I shouldn't have spoken. It was not my place."

Bree was still angry and wasn't ready to let the matter drop. "You need to understand, I might agree with you on how some aspects of our city have changed for the worse, or even the standing of our Caste, but when it comes to my family, I won't sit by and let such repulsive insinuations pass without challenge."

"As I said, you're right. I shouldn't have said what I did. I apologize. Perhaps we can move on to a different topic?" Rector suggested, looking annoyed.

"Then don't bring this particular one up again," Bree said. She didn't want to further antagonize Rector, but she also wanted him to understand just how she felt about the matter.

"Believe me, I won't," Rector said, appearing abashed.

Bree figured she'd made her point. She worked to set aside her irritation. "What else would you like to talk about then?" she asked.

"Anything else, as long as it isn't about Jaresh and definitely not about Mira. "

"Oh? You still think she doesn't like you, is that it?"

"I'm certain she doesn't like me," Rector replied.

Bree was glad to see the annoyance leave his face. "She thinks I'm too old-fashioned."

Bree burst out in laughter, which she quickly smothered when other patrons turned and looked over at them. Rector's words were so close to what she had *just* been thinking.

"What is so amusing?" Rector asked, not cracking a smile.

"Because you don't see it," Bree said, surprised by his blindness. "You *are* old-fashioned. Sometimes you act like you're older than Nanna."

"Well, if it's old-fashioned to believe we should use the past as a guide to direct our present and build our future, then count me as old-fashioned. Too many people discount the teachings of our elders. If you ask me, it is the height of arrogance."

"Nanna would say blindly clinging to the past is no way to win the future," Bree responded.

"And he would be right," Rector said. "I don't believe in a future no different than the past, but I see our culture as existing in a balance. We're not always sure when we're tipping too far on the side of change versus stultification. For instance, I don't like having non-Kummas rise into positions of power in our House. And I'm not speaking of Jaresh here. Your brother proved his worth when he fought that pig, Suge Wrestiva."

"And yet, by allowing those not of our Caste the chance to act as arbiters of our commerce, Shektans have prospered," Bree replied. "In other Houses, Kummas hold those posts, and too often don't do a very good job of it. We weren't trained to be clerks or moneylenders."

"True. We were born to be warriors," he said, a pensive look on his face. They fell into a thoughtful silence. "It seems that change catches me off guard more than I would like," he added, breaking the silence. "Your nanna is wise and canny, but he is far more modern than a simple man like me. It seems his daughter is cut from the same cloth." He grinned.

"What? Wise and canny? Or modern?" Bree asked with a glint in her eyes.

"Both."

"Now it is *you* who are wise and canny."

Rector laughed. "Never."

———————•———————

"**Y**ou forgot your allergy medicine again didn't you?" Jaresh asked as Mira sneezed. Again. Once more, the mildew and dust of the Cellar must have gotten to her.

As usual, the two of them were in their typical reading alcove in the stacks down below the main floors for the Library of Ashoka. It was a place they had learned to loathe. It was dim, dismal, and claustrophobic encased as it was by stacks of manuscripts and books. It felt like a cave.

Mira didn't answer at first, but he noticed her flash of annoyance, which was answer enough.

"Yes," she eventually admitted, her voice muffled as she wiped her nose with a handkerchief. "And I don't want to hear another word about it."

"Wouldn't think of it," Jaresh said, hiding a grin.

"I see you smiling," Mira accused.

Jaresh coughed into his hand, trying to suppress a chuckle. "What do you mean?"

"Very funny," Mira said. "Why does it amuse you so much when I sneeze?"

"It's not the sneezing," Jaresh said. "I just think it's funny how you always forget to take your medicine. I'd have figured it would be a priority by now given how miserable you are without it."

"Oh, shut up." Mira said with a disgruntled glare.

Jaresh was wise enough to do as Mira asked, especially since she looked as unhappy as a cat with a sore paw. He could tell she was doing her best to studiously ignore him, and he felt bad for mocking her. She really did look pretty pathetic as she sniffled and rubbed at the tip of her nose. "I'm sorry I laughed at you," he said.

"You mean you don't find it oh so amusing to taunt me," she asked, caustically.

"Well, making fun of you is fun," Jaresh said, "but I am sorry about your allergies." He pulled a small apothecary bottle from a pocket in his pants. "Consider this a peace offering."

He passed her the bottle, and she took it, eyeing him suspiciously. "What is this?"

"Your allergy medicine," Jaresh replied. "You've forgotten to take it so many times that I had another vial made up. I figured some day you were going to need it."

Mira's eyes widened in surprise and appreciation. "Thank you," she said. "And here I was about to curse you as an uncaring brute. This was sweet of you."

"Let's not get carried away," Jaresh said with a smile.

After Mira took her medicine, they got back to work.

For the past several days, Jaresh had been reading through a logbook dating back to before the fall of Rock. It had been written by Garth Vole, a Rahail caravan master and a known associate of the Sil Lor Kum. He had been executed in Ashoka in 1703 AF, three hundred fifty-nine years ago when his membership in the cult had been discovered. The book was fragile, and Jaresh handled it as carefully as possible. Most of what Vole described was prosaic stuff: information about the number of wagons, guards, materials transported...boring details really. But every once in awhile, Jaresh came across a series of numbers and symbols, randomly scattered throughout the log, only one or two of them at a time. He would find them in the middle of an account of guard shifts or descriptions of the land in which they traveled or the goods they carried. Their presence made no sense, but Jaresh's interest had been piqued, so he had transcribed them onto a fresh piece of parchment. Right away, he noticed there wasn't an obvious pattern, but there did appear to be what looked like a hidden cipher when the numbers and symbols were written down in sequence.

What was Mr. Vole trying to say without anyone else knowing? It was a puzzle, and Jaresh loved puzzles. As he worked the numbers, he realized if this *was* a cipher, it was most likely to be a substitution encryption with multiple characters in the code equivalent to a real world letter. Jaresh had already tried a simple pattern of matching the most commonly occurring numbers and symbols to common letters, but Mr. Vole had been clever enough not to make his code so simple. As a result, Jaresh hadn't made any progress, but he wasn't daunted. Not by a long stretch. He'd crack Vole's code yet. In fact, just this morning a thought had occurred to him: what if the numbers were one or more steps removed from the letter they were meant to represent?

He had already tried one step, then two, and now was on three…

He smiled in triumph. He'd broken the code. Each number was three steps above the letter they were meant to represent with multiple numbers indicating the same letter. As for the symbols, they had been a clever ruse. They represented nothing and had only been included to make the code more complex. Clever but not clever enough.

Jaresh quickly transcribed Vole's hidden message with a dawning sense of realization and excitement.

"Mira, take a look at this," he said, eagerly.

"What is it?" she asked.

"It's from a logbook that belonged to a Rahail caravan master out of Ashoka by the name of Garth Vole. He also happened to be a member of the Sil Lor Kum." Jaresh explained Vole's history and subsequent execution as well as the clever code hidden within the text of the logbook. "I only deciphered it just now."

"Ingenious," Mira said admiringly.

"I don't know what other reasons he might have had for writing down what he did, but you need to hear this:

In my dreams, the Queen commands, and Her wishes are not to be forgotten with the rising of the sun. Deep and grim punishments await any who fail Her.

The Knife was given into my hand by the very SarpanKum of Her Red Hand of Justice. The Bael, a fell creature by the name of Li-Slake, was as dark as a nightmare with a voice like rustling, aged leaves.

He said to me, "Take the Knife to your brother, the SuDin of accursed Rock, so the city may be purified within our Holy Mother's cleansing fire."

I was brave, and I asked the purpose of the Knife.

The Bael smiled and suggested I kill someone and find out.

Long was I troubled by his words, but there came to pass a battle, and one of our guards, a Kumma by the name of Hewter Steer was injured. We had no means to Heal him, so I offered to end his suffering.

When I slipped the Knife into his flesh, Steer arched as though in great pain. His mouth gaped silently, and the water seemed to evaporate from his body. Suddenly, I was connected to him. For a time, I knew all he knew; all his memories and all his Talents were mine. As was his Jivatma.

I was filled to blazing with the power of it, and where once was Hewter Steer, now only a dried out husk of corpse remained. I quickly added the Kumma's body to the purifying fire the warriors had built before any could see what had become of their brother.

As the days passed, Steer's memories and Talents slowly faded from my mind, but his Jivatma remained with me. And I remained stronger and faster than I could ever recall being. Thus, it was late one night when a treasonous thought came to me: why give over the power of the Knife to another when it could raise me to heights undreamt?

A day short of Rock, once again the Queen visited me in my dreams. Somehow, She knew of my plan. She described what would befall me should I betray Her. She even gave me a long taste of the torment She would visit upon me should I prove faithless.

I awoke in sodden sweat; the pain of Her torture sending waves of fire through my very bones while the sound of Her maniacal laughter rang in my ears like the cries of some monstrously large hyena. On the morning the caravan entered Rock, I made homage to the Council of Rule. Seven were there, one for each Caste, and they wished to know the meaning of my presence, but only to the SuDin would I speak. I wordlessly passed the Knife unto him, never to see it again.

Mira was silent, her mouth agape. "We did it," she breathed after a moment. "We did it!" she shouted, excited. "We found it!"

Overcome by emotion, she actually hugged Jaresh before immediately releasing him.

"Sorry," she quickly apologized, reddening with embarrassment.

"It's fine," Jaresh said, equally self-conscious and trying to hide how much he liked the feel of her arms around him.

Affection was fine between men and women of different Castes, so long as it was limited to friendship. Anything more, especially physical displays of affection, was an unacceptable breach of etiquette. Given all the time he and Mira had spent together in the past two-and-a-half months, it was the last thing they needed someone to witness. The gossip would be nasty and reputation ruining.

"I must have gotten carried away," Mira added. "It's just that after nearly three months of searching, we finally have confirmation. Dar'El was right all along."

"He usually is," Jaresh said.

"We need to meet with your nanna and let him know about this. Everyone needs to hear it."

Jaresh laughed. "Just think how relieved my sister will be when she realizes she won't have to get her hands dirty anymore poring through mildewy books."

"Especially since she's been stuck with Rector Bryce all these weeks."

"Rector isn't so bad," Jaresh said.

Mira shrugged. "He's honorable and decent enough," she allowed. "He's just so fragging stodgy."

"Mira!" Jaresh said, shocked by her vulgarity.

"Oh, don't 'Mira' me. Women curse, too. And it's true what I said about Rector."

"Maybe so, but don't let him hear you say it."

Mira gave him a withering look. "And here I was planning on going straight up to him and telling him what a jackhole I think he is."

Jaresh burst out in laughter. "You're incorrigible."

"Takes one to know one."

CHAPTER NINETEEN
DÉTENTE ACHIEVED

Returning home from a Trial is the sweetness of salvation.
Nothing else compares.

~From the journal of Durmer Volk, AF 2019

Jessira shivered.

The wind blew cool in the high hills west of Ashoka where they had set up camp for the night. Far away and down to the south, the Hunters Flats still sweltered in the summer sun, but here in the higher elevations the air was as crisp as an early autumn evening.

Their campsite was less than a day's march from Ashoka in a beautiful mountain meadow next to a crystal-clear stream stocked with trout. The water gurgled over and around large boulders jutting from the brook's bed as well as stones made round and smooth by time's endless passage. The sun had not yet set, and the sky was painted in dark reds and oranges with a few sunbeams punching through the low hanging clouds. A colony of blue and yellow butterflies flitted in the last of the light and amongst the velvety antlers of a surprised deer. He bounded away. The world felt as fresh and vibrant as the perfume of a nearby honeysuckle bush.

Jessira closed her eyes and inhaled the peace, treasuring the simple fact of being alive and able to witness such a lovely evening. Being clean for the first time in weeks also helped her appreciate her great, good fortune. As soon as they had made camp, she had taken the unforeseen yet greatly prized opportunity to bathe in the frigid water, washing away weeks of sweat, grit, and caked-on dirt. It was like shedding a second skin and left her feeling tingly clean.

Her pants and jacket were still sodden, so rather than put them back on, she had left them to dry on several large boulders that still held the warmth of the noonday sun. Protected only by a camisole and her torn shirt wrapped around her waist, her recently scrubbed skin was nipped by the mountain air.

At least the fire was warm.

She glanced toward the sound of water splashing.

Rukh was also cleaning up, hidden by the same boulders on which her clothes lay.

Although…her eyes narrowed in musing thought. Despite his long unkempt hair and scraggly beard from weeks on the road, Rukh Shektan was still easy on the eyes.

Too bad the rocks were in the way.

She stifled her laughter when she imagined how Rukh would react if he ever learned of her speculative interest in what he looked like without clothes. He'd probably blush red as a virgin maiden.

Jessira smiled.

Despite being a Pureblood prude, Rukh was a good man.

The manner in which he had saved her life still caused her consternation, though. Jessira could easily accept how he had Healed her using *Jivatma* – she always knew he could if he just tried – but it was the other thing which gave her pause. A kind, warm Shylow, who spoke mind-to-mind and could pass on knowledge from one person to another? Had it really happened the way Rukh said? It sounded like a children's story: *Here then is the fable of the good Shylow, the only one of her kind who will teach her cruel father and brothers of kindness.* It sounded too fantastical to believe, and yet, Rukh insisted it had happened.

The fact she was still alive was proof of it. She shook her head in disbelief. Wait until Stronghold learned of this. On the night she had collapsed, almost a week ago now, her last coherent thought had been the disappointed certainty that she would not live to see the next sunrise. And yet, she had, and in the morning, she had listened with wide-eyed incredulity as Rukh explained what had happened while she lay unconscious.

She was broken from her reveries by the sound of sizzling trout on a skillet, and she quickly returned her attention back to the fire. After setting up camp, Rukh had caught some fish. He had even cleaned them before handing them over to Jessira. Her job was to cook them, which she didn't mind since Rukh was a terrible cook. In his hands, the fish would have ended up as cinders and ashes.

Speaking of…she flipped the trout. One side was now gently blackened. Wouldn't do to burn them.

Unconsciously, she flexed her left shoulder. While it was still stiff and sore as well as being weak, it felt infinitely better than it had the night she had collapsed. She glanced at the wounds left by the Shylow. They were pink and scabbed over without any obvious signs of infection, but Jessira knew she wasn't out of the woods yet. Somewhere in her shoulder there was still a small nidus of contagion. It was one Rukh could hold in check, but one he couldn't completely eradicate. Neither of them had the knowledge on how to do so, but even if Jessira had been home in Stronghold, she likely would have still ended up losing the arm. She worried about the possibility. Rukh didn't think it would come to that. He was certain one of Ashoka's famed Shiyen physicians could cure her and save the arm as well. Jessira hoped he was right, but she also did her best to hold down her prayerful longing. She didn't want to be too disappointed if Rukh was wrong.

Beyond her own personal concerns, Jessira also worried what Rukh's actions would mean for him. She'd hate for his people to turn him out on her account or because he could Heal. Hadn't he said he might be declared Tainted for learning to Blend? What would the other Purebloods say when they found out he could also Heal? If they did tell him to leave, would he agree to come with her to Stronghold? She would definitely take him if he wanted. She owed him too much not to, and she knew he couldn't be turned away by the OutCastes. Long ago, the founders of Stronghold had decided that any stranger who came to the city would be offered sanctuary. Even though no one had ever actually come to her home in all the time since its founding, she was certain her people would accept Rukh with open arms.

He would be fine.

However, she might not be.

How would she ever explain her relationship with Rukh to Disbar Merdant, the man her parents had chosen as her husband? Their marriage was to take place in the spring, and he would not be happy to learn she had spent so much unchaperoned time in the company of a man who wasn't family. Would he believe nothing sinful had occurred between Jessira and Rukh? She hoped he would, but men could be so irrational about the supposed purity of their brides. Disbar had gruffly accepted her long assignments beyond Stronghold as a scout, but in those cases, he had known she would always be with her brothers and family. Rukh was neither, and Disbar would not be happy.

"Food smells good," Rukh said, interrupting her thoughts. His beard and shaggy hair dripped water, and he'd dressed in his sodden clothes rather than parade around naked. He glanced at her attire. "I hope you're planning on wearing something more when we get to Ashoka," he said.

Jessira glanced down at her camisole and the shirt tied around her waist. She wasn't exactly indecent, but a lot of flesh was certainly visible. She'd look like a right proper prostitute parading around in her current outfit. She inanely wondered if Ashoka had whores since Stronghold did not. She suddenly realized her nipples were taut from the cold, mountain air. Rukh seemed to notice as well. Jessira crossed her arms over her chest, cursing silently.

"Stop staring," she said.

"I wasn't staring. There's nothing to stare at."

She felt a brief stab of disappointment at his words. There was nothing to stare at because she was so flat-chested? Or had he meant it was because she was a ghrina? Probably the latter, an attitude she'd have to get used to when they arrived in his city. "I guess in Ashoka, people would only see the abomination and not even notice the woman, right? They probably wouldn't care if I walked around dressed the way I am right now."

"Try it and find out," Rukh said as he leaned against a nearby boulder, looking smug. "You'd only embarrass yourself."

Jessira stood. She'd had enough. Sitting around half-naked before a man who wasn't her fiancé was *not* acceptable decorum. She meant to walk to the boulders and reclaim her clothes no matter how wet, but Rukh's widened eyes let her know what had happened. The fire had backlit the full length of her legs through the fabric of the shirt.

She reddened with embarrassment and darted behind the boulders. The moment she was hidden from view, she pulled her clothes down from the rocks. Her nose wrinkled. Her pants remained soaked and they still stank, but she donned them anyway. The shirt and jacket could wait, though. With her shoulder still hurting, they were hard to slip on without Rukh's help, something she really didn't want right now.

"What did I do?" Rukh asked, sounding affronted when she emerged a moment later.

361

"What do you think?" she snapped.

"All I said was you'd embarrass yourself if you pranced around Ashoka wearing a tied-off shirt around your waist and camisole."

"I wouldn't be embarrassed but your people would. I know how priggish you Kummas are."

"I never thought of my Caste as being priggish," Rukh replied, "but even if we are, I've had to take care of those cuts on your back and chest, remember? Can't be a prude after seeing you all undressed like that." He smirked.

Jessira wanted to smack the smug look off his face. He didn't have to remind her of what he'd seen. She glowered, staring into the fire before glancing back at him, seeing his smug grin. Fine. He'd seen her wearing hardly any clothing. He didn't have to be an ass about it. She turned her attention back to the fish, idly moving them about.

"Why don't you let me help you with your shirt?" Rukh suggested a moment later.

Jessira glanced his way, but he wasn't looking at her. He appeared unsettled as he stared off into the distance. "Not right now," she said with a frown. The trout were a few moments from burning. She could figure out what had him so bothered after she saw to their supper. "Let me take care of this first."

Jessira lifted the skillet out of the fire, and doled out the trout. It was only then that she realized why Rukh was so discomfited. Every time she leaned forward, her camisole had fallen forward. Her gaze snapped around to Rukh's. He was beet-red and looked on the verge of standing up and walking away from her.

For a moment, she froze in embarrassment before quickly snatching the camisole back to her chest. "You jackhole! Stop looking!" she snapped as she stood up and glared at him.

He wore a look of affronted innocence. "What did I do wrong?"

"You should have looked away, pervert."

"I did look away," he reminded her, "and I also suggested you put on your shirt so the whole world can't see your nipples, remember?"

Nipples? Holy Mother! He'd seen that far down? She closed her eyes and silently mouthed a prayer for patience. "Can we forget this ever happened?"

"Fine by me," Rukh said, looking annoyed rather than angry. "I don't see why you're acting so offended. I didn't do anything wrong."

"You didn't do anything wrong? You all but mentally undressed me." She flushed when she realized how stupid that sounded.

She was grateful he didn't call her on it.

"I only looked once," he replied, "and that was on accident. I would bet the men of Stronghold would stare much more than I did – unless of course, they're blind."

"What's that supposed to mean?" she shouted, incensed. How dare he insult her kind!

"All I did was appreciate an attractive woman. As far as I'm concerned, you're the one who should apologize to me for yelling. Like I said, I *did* warn you. It's not my fault you didn't listen."

She paused in mid-tirade, replaying his words in her mind. Did he really think her attractive? She studied his face. He looked at her with puzzlement. He didn't seem to realize what he had just said. It was as if he had only spoken out loud what was obvious in his mind. She still wanted to be angry with him, but she couldn't hold onto the feeling, not after his words. Her disgust with him dissolved. Five weeks ago, he only saw her as a ghrina, but now, he actually saw her as a person, even as a woman. She would have never believed such growth possible for a Pureblood.

Rukh Shektan surprised her again and again. Whatever the faults of his culture, he was a good and generous man. Even if he was horrible sometimes.

And tomorrow, she would have to enter a whole city of people who thought as Rukh once had. She shuddered.

"I won't lie. Most people will hate you," Rukh said, speaking softly and somehow guessing – as he so often did – what she was thinking. "But you won't be alone. I'll be with you. And anyone who insults you will be picking their teeth up off the bricks."

"You against a whole city?"

Rukh smiled. "Bad odds?"

She laughed. "Even for you."

He shrugged. "I'll take them on one at a time then. I can handle it."

The worst thing was that Rukh actually sounded confident, as if he thought he *could* take on anyone in Ashoka.

Ah yes. The arrogance of young men the world over, the ones who were inexperienced enough to still believe themselves invincible. Eventually life intervened, and they either learned wisdom or they died.

Rukh was good – the best Jessira had ever seen – but he couldn't be *that* good, not when he was barely older than she was, and younger in some very important ways. After all, this was his first trip into the Wildness, and these past few weeks had likely marked his first true battles. Back in Ashoka, there were bound to be many warriors who were far cannier and deadlier than Rukh, which was in its own way an even more troubling thought.

She said as much.

Rukh grinned. "You're probably right," he said. "But a man can pretend, right?"

"As long as you don't do anything reckless," she said, cautioning him one last time. He obviously wasn't taking her warning very seriously, but she wanted to be able to say she'd done her best to get through to him.

"I won't," he said, making it sound like a promise he didn't plan on keeping.

She mentally sighed. Oh well. She'd tried. It looked like he'd have to learn his lesson the hard way. She only hoped it was an instruction he survived without receiving too many bruises in the process.

"But if it happens…" he shrugged, "…you'd be worth it."

Despite her frustration with his carefree attitude, his words made her oddly happy.

T wo swords were leveled at their throats while another scout had an arrow drawn and aimed.

Rukh kept his hands clear of his weapons. Taking on Chims at odds of ten-to-one was one thing, but taking on two Kummas and a Rahail with a bow at the ready? It was a death wish. Even taking on two Kummas alone would have been suicidal.

"You're a long way from home warrior," the lead scout said, his sword not wavering. "How is it we find you wandering alone in the Wildness?" He turned to Jessira. "And who is this Muran woman with you?"

Rukh had expected both their discovery by Ashoka's scouts and the questions directed at Jessira. The rough trail upon which they stood was the very same one he had taken on leaving Ashoka almost four months earlier. The High Army routinely patrolled it and all other routes leading to the city, as well as all the borderlands within a day's travel. Rukh would have been horrified if he and Jessira hadn't been challenged before approaching the city's Outer Wall.

The scouts – Rukh vaguely recognized them as being from Houses distant to his own – waited for an answer, each wearing expressions of polite interest. Their relaxed curiosity would change in a heartbeat if they guessed an OutCaste, a ghrina, stood in their presence. They might even go so far as to kill Jessira on sight if they knew what she was.

As a result, Rukh had decided the safest way to gain entry into Ashoka would be to hide the truth of Jessira's origins. Her emerald green eyes for which nothing could be done were clearly of Caste Muran, and so her other features would have to match them. They had dirtied her skin – this only hours after she had just washed off week's worth of road grime and sweat – dulling its natural red-gold Cherid hue until it resembled the golden-brown color of the Muran. Nothing could be done about her fine Cherid features or her honey-brown hair – a color seen only amongst the Rahail – so instead; they had wrapped a rough shawl around her head, draping it over her face. Their explanation was she had disfiguring scars so hideous that no man had offered to marry her, and the emotional pain from such rejection had led her to quit the city's safety for the dangers of the Wildness. It wasn't an unknown means of suicide among the city's destitute or desperate, although few spoke about it. Rukh's plan was to then describe how he had found her a few miles from Ashoka, sick and alone. Jessira, of course, would say nothing. Her accent would mark her as being from somewhere other than Ashoka.

"I was with the caravan to Nestle," Rukh answered. "I came across this woman while making my way home." He explained finding Jessira alone in the hills west of Ashoka.

"No point in life if I can't find a husband," Jessira said in a passable Muran drawl, sounding dull and broken.

"Why are you dressed in camouflage clothing," the lead scout asked, flicking a glance at her torn clothing.

"I figured it was the best way to survive the Wildness," Jesssira drawled.

The lead scout flicked her a final cursory examination before turning back to Rukh. "What happened to the caravan?" he asked.

"Nothing good, warrior," Rukh replied.

The scout's eyes narrowed. "Was it…"

Rukh shook his head. "I can't tell you; not until the Magisterium hears of it."

"That bad."

"Worse." Rukh hesitated. "Can you send one of your men ahead to the gate commander and tell him to expect our arrival. I don't want to be unnecessarily delayed."

"I'll see to it," the lead scout said. He nodded to the other Kumma, who took off at a dead sprint.

Just as he and Jessira were about to depart, the Rahail spoke. "Rukh Shektan," the man said with a grin. "It is you beneath all that hair, isn't it?"

Rukh nodded, working to hide his wariness as the lead scout studied him through suddenly narrowed eyes. He sensed Jessira tense up next to him.

"I lost a lot of money on you," the Rahail said, amiably. "Never thought I'd see a Virgin win the Tournament, especially against Kinsu Makren. He was the best I ever faced."

Rukh grinned. "If I was a gambling man, I wouldn't have bet on me either."

The lead scout smiled. "Travel safely, Champion," he said, stepping aside for Rukh and Jessira.

Rukh nodded as he and Jessira went on their way, continuing along the rough trail to Ashoka.

Once out of earshot, Jessira lowered her scarf and turned to him. "What Tournament?"

"The Tournament of Hume," Rukh said, distractedly. "Why?" He glanced at her, only then noticing her expression of open amazement.

Jessira frowned in puzzlement. "Is it some kind of competition?"

"It's a contest," Rukh said. "Every three years, those Ashokan warriors who wish to test themselves face one another in single combat to determine who has the swiftest blade."

"And you won?" Jessira asked sounding as though she couldn't believe what she was hearing. "We have something similar in Stronghold. We call it the Trials of Hume."

Rukh smiled, bemused as he wondered why the OutCastes would also develop such a similar martial competition. "Strange that our two cultures would both honor a Kumma like we have," he said.

"Not as strange as someone winning it on his first entry and without ever having faced battle in the Wildness," she said, appearing both incredulous and exasperated.

Rukh nodded, not sure what had her upset. For him, it felt like ancient history, unimportant given everything he'd been through since.

"So there really isn't anyone in Ashoka to challenge you?" Jessira mused, looking annoyed with him.

"Well I wouldn't go that far. All I said was that I could handle myself," Rukh replied, not sure why she was mad at him.

She shook her head in obvious disgust. "Men."

I ronically, it was twilight by the time they arrived at the Twilight Gate guardhouse. Twilight was one of the three major gates of the Outer Wall, and at all times it was heavily garrisoned by the High Army – the first line of defense into the city.

As they approached the gate's gaping maw, Rukh saw a line of warriors waiting for them.

"You Purebloods sure build them big," Jessira noted as they approached the Outer Wall.

Rukh could tell she was impressed and trying not to show it. He smiled. "It's about sixty feet tall and thirty deep," he said.

"And how many miles long?"

"Fifty."

"You have enough warriors to defend such a length?" she asked.

"No. The Outer Wall is only meant to slow down the Chims. The Inner Wall is Ashoka's true bulwark."

"But all your fields are between the Inner and Outer Walls," Jessira remarked. "If there is a siege, how do you plan on feeding the populace?"

"There's enough food and water stored within the city proper to feed Ashoka for six months. Add in the fishing fleet and the arable land inside the Inner Wall and the city should be able to last a year or more."

"If what we heard on the Flats is true, and the Queen comes for Ashoka, you might find those claims put to the test by next spring," Jessira said. Just then, she stumbled, and Rukh moved to steady her. It had been a long day, and her shoulder was bothering her again.

"We're almost there," Rukh encouraged.

Jessira nodded. "I can make it."

The warriors manning Twilight's entrance were led by Marshall Vol Lumer, a man Rukh knew from the House of Fire and Mirrors as a Martial Master. Before his time as an instructor, the Marshall had been a famous and decorated veteran of six Trials, captaining the final two. Now, he was a senior commander in Ashoka's High Army.

Rukh came to a halt and saluted.

"At ease, warrior," Marshall Lumer ordered. He studied him, taking in his ragged appearance before his eyes briefly lighted on Jessira, dismissing her out of hand. He turned back to Rukh. "Rukh Shektan," he said. "I didn't think I'd see you again so soon."

"Devesh has plans none of us can fathom," Rukh replied.

"And is it Devesh who impels your travels?" the Marshall asked. "You never struck me as a particularly religious man."

"The Wildness teaches us humility," Rukh said, repeating one of the Marshall's favorite aphorisms.

Marshall Lumer's lips quirked into a brief smile. "Rumor has it something happened to the Nestle caravan," he said. "Two other survivors made it back a few weeks ago, but they were nearly dead when we found them. The Shiyens aren't sure if they'll ever wake up." He paused and studied Rukh's studiously bland expression. "So what's the real story about what happened out there?"

Rukh shook his head. "I don't want to say. The Magisterium needs to hear of it first."

"Was it Chims?" the Marshall persisted.

Rukh hesitated. "I don't want to spread false rumors. It's best if I say nothing for now."

The Marshall studied him through narrowed eyes before nodding approval. "So be it," he said. "I'll make sure you have a horse and send word to the Inner Gate so you aren't delayed further. One of my men will see to the Muran. She looks in need of a physician."

Jessira shifted uncomfortably next to him.

"I appreciate the offer, but I promised her I would personally see her home. She made me swear on my honor before agreeing to come back to the city."

"Who is she to you?"

"Someone I found on my way home. She was alone in the Wildness."

"I see," Marshall Lumer said, understanding the implications of Rukh's statement.

"I was waiting to die," Jessira added in her slow drawl. "When the Kumma showed up, he told me to come back with him to Ashoka. I figured him being there and all, maybe Devesh wasn't done with me yet in this world."

"Then I leave her to your hands," the Marshall said. "Good luck." He signaled to one of his men, nodded to Rukh, and swiftly marched away.

Their horse turned out to be a placid old gray gelding of far better temperament than the stallion Rukh had ridden on the Trial. The animal took their weight without complaint and ambled along with a slow, steady pace best described as a plodding walk.

After passing without significant challenge through Kubar Gate and the Inner Wall, they stopped at a nearby Shiyen hospice. It was located just south of the Inner Wall in Stone Cavern, a neighborhood which was home to many Duriahs. No matter how careful, the life of a craftsmen often resulted in small injuries from time-to-time. To care for the frequently injured, the hospice here had been built large and was well staffed, with many physicians available. Even this late, just before dusk, it was still brightly lit with radiant, white firefly lanterns reflecting off the smooth, pale-yellow tiled floors. There was a smell about a hospice, a mix of blood, antiseptic, and putrification, and this one was no different.

Rukh wasn't bothered by the odor. He was more concerned with making sure to find a physician able to treat the infection still present in Jessira' shoulder. Also, while the claw marks themselves were no longer infected, they'd heal with heavy scars without a Shiyen's help. Jessira hadn't complained about it, but Rukh could tell it bothered her.

Thankfully, several physicians were still present, and it only took a few minutes to get in to see one. She was an older Shiyen, all brusque business, not even caring to listen to Rukh's story about finding Jessira out in the Wildness and essentially waiting to die. The physician led them into a small room with a narrow, wooden table and a couple of stools. Several shelves hung from the walls, most of them empty except for packets of bandages. A small sink crouched in a corner and bright, white firefly lanterns flooded the room with light.

The Shiyen asked what they needed, heard them out, briefly questioned them about the shawl wrapped around Jessira' face, and then got to work. She wetted some bandages with water from the sink and wiped the dirt from Jessira's shoulder. She paused as she took in the scars. "What mauled you?" she asked.

"A mountain lion," Jessira lied.

"Well, that mountain lion must have claws as long as my fingers," the physician said. "Never knew they got so big."

Jessira shuddered, wearing an expression of remembered terror. It was a bit over the top, Rukh thought. "It was a monster."

"Well, it got you good, and if you don't want thick scars on your shoulder and back, we'll have to put in some stitches." The Shiyen had no further questions as she pulled down another bandage and soaked it in a tincture of iodine. She gave Jessira's shoulder a thorough cleaning before Healing the infection in the bone and sewing the stitches.

"There," the physician said after finishing. "Now the scars will be thin and fine. Hardly noticeable." She looked pleased with her work, which Rukh took as a good sign. "Even with your Cherid skin, they shouldn't show all that much." Suddenly, her eyes widened as she whipped her focus on Rukh. "I thought you said she was Muran. She has the eyes for it, but her skin says she's Cherid."

Rukh felt Jessira tense. "She has a rare condition…" he quickly explained.

The Shiyen waved him to silence. "I don't want to hear it. You're Rukh Shektan. I recognize you from the Tournament. People say your nanna is a sensible man. I assume you are as well. Whatever's going on here is none of my concern. I Heal." She glanced at Jessira. "Whoever or *whatever* they might be." She gestured for them to leave with a flick of her hands. "Be on your way now."

Rukh and Jessira quickly gathered their meager belongings, paid for the services, and left. They didn't say a word until they were mounted and several streets away.

"She knew what I was, but she didn't say anything," Jessira exclaimed, sounding amazed.

Rukh couldn't believe it either. "I wouldn't expect it from anyone else," he said, glancing nervously at the crowded streets. "Now quiet down before your accent gives us away."

They remained silent for the next hour or so, passing through the busy streets of Ashoka, travelling east from Stone Cavern to the Plaza of the Martyrs before cutting southeast so as to bypass the madness of the Semaphore Walk. Soon enough, they reached the borders of Jubilee Hills.

"Just a few more miles," Rukh said, trying to rein in his excitement as they moved ever closer to his home.

He grinned when he saw more and more familiar sights: houses belonging to family and friends; stores and restaurants he used to frequent; and even the parks in which he had played as a child. It had been almost four months since he had left home, but it seemed like so much longer. The world had changed so much since then. He had changed. The smile left his face. How would his family react to him? He was a Kumma who could Blend and Heal. Many would think Rukh hopelessly Tainted by his newly acquired Talents. Would his family be amongst those who felt that way? He honestly didn't know.

Then there was the information he brought concerning the Chims and the Baels. The news would set the city afire. Suwraith had marked Ashoka for death, and the Queen might be planning on raising three Plagues of Chimeras to see Her will done. But what of the Baels? Would anyone believe him when he told of their role in possibly, or even probably, sabotaging the Queen's plans? Or of their claim of brotherhood with Humanity, a concept they insisted had been taught to them by Hume himself?

Rukh still had trouble believing the last. Given the fact he had witnessed all of this and *still* doubted, how could he expect anyone else to believe the Baels?

Of course, he would also have to describe what he'd learned of the Shylows and how he had learned it. No one suspected the cats could speak mind-to-mind, and who would believe him when he made such an outlandish statement?

And finally, there was Jessira. If Farn's reaction was any gauge, her time in Ashoka would be difficult. Most would be struck with horror at her very existence and what she represented: an adult ghrina from an entire city of ghrinas living their lives free and unhindered somewhere out in the Wildness. For many it would be a horrifying heresy. Jessira would face anger and abuse merely for being alive, and Rukh could do nothing to soften the blow. She would leave as soon as she was fit and able, and no one would be sad to see her go.

Except him. The five weeks he had spent with Jessira – traveling and getting to know her, really understand who she was as a person – had changed him. He didn't think of her as a ghrina. He thought of her as a woman…a beautiful and capable woman.

His worries dissolved somewhat when they left the heavier traffic of Cinnamon Road and turned onto the quietness of Hickory Place Avenue. Up the hill they went, their gelding slowly plodding along despite Rukh's urging. The beast just wouldn't go any faster. They passed a number of houses, but by now it was night, and all that could be seen were the firefly lanterns hanging beside their front gates and the lights shining through the windows. Eventually, they crested the hill, and there, with gates wide open and the grounds brightly lit was his home.

"There it is." He pointed. "Straight ahead." Jessira shivered, and Rukh reached back and squeezed her knee in reassurance. "It won't be as bad as you think," he said. "I won't let it."

The gate guards, old men who had served the House for decades in many different capacities called them to halt. At first, they didn't recognize Rukh but as soon as he spoke, they knew him. Their jaws gaped in shock.

"But how are you back so soon, Rukh?" one of them asked.

"We've heard something bad happened to the caravan," the other one whispered. "The 'El won't show it, but he's worried for you. So is your amma."

Rukh smiled. "I've got a long story to tell," he said.

One of the guards glanced at Jessira, still bundled up in her shawl. "Who is she?"

"A friend," Rukh replied. "I'm sure Nanna will explain it all after I've spoken with him."

"Of course," one of the guards said, hustling him along and letting them pass. "Should I inform him of your presence? He is meeting with the House Council."

Rukh considered the offer but decided against it. "Perhaps this one time, I will be the one to surprise him."

The gate guard smiled. "I'm sure you will."

As they rode up the drive leading to the seat of House Shektan, the gelding broke out into a lumbering canter. Perhaps he sensed the end of his journey. Rukh tugged the reins, turning the horse to the left and toward the large red barn, a looming presence in the dark. Shortly after they dismounted, a young groom, one Rukh didn't recognize, opened the barn doors, spilling golden light out onto the driveway and beyond. He offered to stable the gelding, for which Rukh was grateful.

Rukh and Jessira collected their meager belongings before entering the main house through the side entrance. They passed through the narrow hallway of the servants' quarters, but luckily none of the help was out and about. One less complication avoided. The firefly lanterns lighting these areas were turned low, and with the dark walnut paneling, the hallway was dimly lit. They soon came upon the main living quarters, arriving at the rear foyer with its large elliptical staircase. Nanna's study was just ahead.

At the doorway, Rukh paused, taking a deep, steadying breath. Time to find out if he was still welcome in House Shektan.

Something in his face must have clued Jessira. She gave his hand a reassuring squeeze. "They're your family," she whispered. "I'm sure they'll still love you even if you've changed."

Rukh managed a weak smile. "We'll find out soon enough."

He knocked on the door and without waiting for a response, entered the room. Inside were a number of people, including Nanna, Amma, and Sophy. There was also his brother and sister, Jaresh and Bree, along with Mira Terrell – Sophy's daughter. Rector Bryce was present as well. What was he doing here? From what he remembered, Rector was a fine warrior and a member of the City Watch and Ashokan Guard, but not someone who was also part of Nanna's inner circle. Rukh thought the man too much of a reactionary. And where were Durmer and Garnet?

Those questions would have to wait, though, as everyone turned to stare at him.

"Rukh?" Amma said, after a moment's hesitation.

Her question opened the floodgates, and his family enveloped him in their love, hugging and kissing him. It took some time to convince everyone he was really there and that he was fine. Shouted questions of what had happened and where he had been were snuffed out like a candle by Nanna's loud bellow for everyone to be silent.

After everyone settled down, Nanna pointed to Jessira. "And who is this?" he asked.

Jessira still had her face wrapped in the shawl, and her back was pressed to the door. Her posture was tense, and she looked ready to flee at a moment's notice.

Rukh moved to stand next to her. "A good friend," he said.

He nodded encouragement, and Jessira slowly removed her shawl.

Everyone recognized what she was immediately.

Sophy snarled in disgust. "What is the meaning of this?" she hissed.

Rector erupted to his feet, hand on his sword and an expression of loathing on his face. "A ghrina," he cried.

Rukh took a protective stance in front of Jessira. He had feared just this reaction. If only they would listen...Bryce had unsheathed a foot of his blade. The man looked ready to fully draw and attack. "Remove your hand from your sword," Rukh ordered.

"How could you dishonor our House like this?" Rector demanded. "You of all people, the Hume Champion. You are supposed to represent all that Hume held dear."

"There is more going on here than you know."

"She is not..."

"He's family, Rector," Jaresh said. "Be silent and let him speak."

"And you will be the one to silence me?" Rector snarled.

Rukh had heard enough, He took a threatening step forward. No one spoke to his family like that. Bryce's hard-headed stupidity made him want to punch the man. Swifter than thought, Rukh's sword was in his hands. "Be very careful, Rector Bryce. Jaresh is my brother, and this is the Seat of House Shektan, of which our nanna is the ruling 'El. Who are you to make demands here?"

"Enough. Rector, take your hand off your weapon," Nanna said.

Rector slammed home the foot of blade he'd exposed. "As you wish, my 'El."

Rukh sheathed his sword as well, working to calm himself.

Once he had his anger under control, he began his story of the past four months and everything he had witnessed.

"The caravan was betrayed and completely destroyed," he began. "I think the Sil Lor Kum had a hand in it."

"Their reach has grown so far then," Nanna murmured.

Rukh shot him a look of confusion.

"I'll explain later," Nanna said. "Continue."

"About a week ago, two men, a Muran and a Kumma were discovered near death no more than a day's ride from the city," Bree interrupted. "It's said they were from your caravan. One died this morning, and the other isn't expected to last much longer. What happened?"

"They must have been the men we discovered buried under a rock pile after the caravan was over-run," Rukh said. "There should have also been a Rahail with them. Something happened to them."

They listened as Rukh explained the attack on the caravan and Brand's remarkable joining of the Quad.

"A non-Kumma joined with you?" Jaresh asked, astonished and with a hopeful note to his voice. His brother had the will of a warrior, but his body was lacking.

"Yes, but there's more. Enough for all of you to think of me as poorly as you think of Jessira." He pointed to the young Strongholder woman, who was remarkably poised considering the hostility aimed at her. "While in the Quad, somehow Brand's Talent as a Rahail passed to us and our Talents to him. I can Blend now."

Silence greeted his words.

"Are you sure," Amma asked.

Rukh Blended, disappearing from their vision.

"Oh, Devesh, what have you become," Amma asked, looking horrified.

Rukh instantly let go of the Blend. His heart tightened with fear at her words and expression. Would his own mother disown him?

Something in his face must have given her insight into what he was thinking. Amma stood and hugged him. "I will always love you," she said. "No matter what happens. Your abilities caught me by surprise, but I will never stop being your amma."

"We all love you," Nanna said. "You might be different in some ways, but what your amma means is we will always see you as our son. Nothing can change how we feel."

"You're still my brother," Jaresh said.

"And mine as well," Bree vowed.

Rukh felt his heart unclench as his fears melted away. His family still loved him. They always would. He gave a great shuddering sigh of relief. But then again, how would they react to the rest of what he had to say?

"There's more." Rukh said.

"How can there be more?" Rector asked. "Isn't your Tainting…" He noticed the angry glares shot his way. "Fine. Isn't this *change* in you more than enough for one person to experience?"

"I wish it was," Rukh said, going on to explain how he and the other Ashokans had tracked the Chimeras to the plains of the Hunters Flats. "We had them all in our sight," Rukh explained. "The senior commanders of the Fan Lor Kum. I was about to order a strike on them…"

"Just the four of you," Rector asked, sounding dubious.

Rukh wished the man would shut up. "Yes, just the four of us," Rukh answered. "We had the element of surprise. It would have been a hit and run." He stared Rector in the eyes. "And we could all Blend," he said, willing the Watcher to acknowledge the tactical advantage of such an ability. "We could have completely decimated the command and control of the Fan Lor Kum. They would have been set back for years."

"What stopped you," Mira asked.

"The Queen arrived. Suwraith Herself."

"The Sorrow Bringer was out there with you?" Amma asked, her eyes large. "What were you thinking? You should have run."

"Run where? How? She's faster than any horse ever born," Rukh said. "Besides, we were Blended. She couldn't see us. And learning Her orders seemed worth the risk."

"And what did you learn?" Nanna asked, his voice smooth as a silken throw.

"She has plans for Ashoka. The Baels were ordered to breed up the Chim ranks. She wants three Plagues ready by next spring to march on the city."

"Devesh help us," Mira breathed.

"And this is where it becomes confusing and unbelievable."

"As if what you've already told us isn't?" Rector asked.

Rukh sighed. "Believe me. It becomes much stranger." He explained what happened later, after Suwraith left.

"The Baels plan on betraying Her?" Sophy asked in disbelief. "How do you know this wasn't some elaborate ruse on their part?"

"The Baels don't *plan* on betraying Her," Rukh corrected. "They've already done so. They have been actively undermining Her will ever since the fall of Hammer. I know this because of what happened next."

Bree mock-shivered. "I'm not sure I can take anymore."

Rukh smiled. "You'll have to, Princess," he said, calling her by the old nickname he and Jaresh used to tease her with when they were children.

She stuck her tongue out at him.

Rukh grinned at the moment of levity before going on to describe all he had heard and learned after Suwraith left; all of it from Jessira's appearance, to the battle with the Tigons, and the discovery of other ghrinas. "They call themselves OutCastes, by the way," Rukh said. "They don't call themselves ghrinas or abominations." And finally, he described the Queen's return.

"Somehow She learned the actions of the Baels. It must have made Her even angrier than usual. She ended up pouring Her madness into the Fan Lor Kum – all but the Baels. We could hear the cries of Chimeras from ten miles away as they murdered one another. During all of it, the Queen was sane. She knew the Baels had betrayed Her, and when She returned to where we had come across them, She killed them all. They were just gone. It was like a giant fist had punched a hole in the ground."

Nanna's face was ashen. "Suwraith is sane?" he asked in dismay.

Rukh shrugged. "I don't know," he said. "She was when She killed the Baels, but afterward, maybe not."

He continued his review of the prior four months, going over how the Ashokans and the OutCastes had saved the two Baels at the request of the SarpanKum, and how immediately afterward, the Shylows had attacked.

"Keemo and Brand died," Rukh said, forcing himself to speak past the catch in his throat and the tears in his eyes. "And the rest of us were scattered. The Chimeras were everywhere. I was lucky just to escape. Afterward, Li-Choke – one of the Baels we saved – said the Queen couldn't use the Fan Lor Kum as a vessel for all of Her madness. They would have kept on killing one another until they were all dead, and She would have become insane again."

"I don't see anything wrong with that," Jaresh replied.

"Neither do I," Mira added.

"Anyway, Choke thinks She is still insane, but less so than before. He wasn't able to say what it might mean long term, though," Rukh said.

"And that's everything, right?" Bree asked.

Rukh hesitated.

Amma noticed. "There's more?" she asked in disbelief. "What else could have happened to you out there?"

"Jessira got clawed pretty badly during the Shylow's attack. The wounds got infected, and she was dying. We were a few days from Ashoka, an area northeast of the Flats when one of the cats, a young female by the name of Aia, walked into our camp. She taught me to Heal. They call themselves Kesarins."

Rector barked laughter. "What cats? A Shylow? And they call themselves Kesarins and know how to Heal?" He sounded relieved. "This has all been some kind of joke then. Is that it?"

"Devesh save him, but he doesn't look like he's joking," Sophy said with a grimace. "Just tell us the rest."

Rukh described everything Aia had taught him about the Kesarins. "They speak with their minds, but only a few like Aia can speak with other sentient creatures. She took Jessira's knowledge of Healing and passed it to me. It's how I saved her."

Amma muttered a curse under her breath, while Jaresh studied Rukh, an expression of disbelief on his face.

"And that's everything?" Nanna asked, sounding hopeful, as if he couldn't take any more surprises.

Rukh nodded.

Nanna leaned back in his chair looking stunned. They all did.

The room was silent as the others tried to make sense of what Rukh had just explained. His words overthrew just about everything they knew of the Fan Lor Kum, the Queen, the Baels, and the Kesarins, not to mention the existence of the OutCastes. It was a lot to digest.

"All this really happened?" Jaresh asked him.

"Since I experienced it, then obviously, yes."

"And her role?" Mira asked, gesturing to Jessira.

"As I said, she was injured when the Kesarins attacked. She is from a city of OutCastes, a place called Stronghold. I think it's hidden somewhere in the Privation Mountains. Her brother risked his life to save Farn's. I couldn't do any less."

"And Brand and Keemo are dead. You're sure of it?" Nanna asked.

Rukh nodded.

Nanna sighed. "We have a lot to discuss," he said. "You and the…girl look worn out. Get some rest, both of you."

Rector stiffened. "She has been Healed," he said. "We owe her nothing more. The law is clear on this matter. She should be removed from the city immediately. Morality demands it."

Rukh wanted to level him. Sanctimonious prick.

Nanna rubbed his eyes. "The law is clear, but the survival of our city is not," he said. "The Magisterium needs to hear of all of this, from Rukh's lips as well as hers."

"But…"

"But nothing, Bryce! This is too important a decision for me to make on my own," Nanna said, his voice rising, and Nanna rarely shouted. "The Magistrates will decide her fate."

Rector looked like he wanted to continue to press his point, but Bree whispered urgently in his ear and eventually he nodded agreement with whatever she said, albeit reluctantly.

Rukh wondered what might be going on between his sister and the Watch captain. He prayed the two of them weren't in a relationship because right now, Rector Bryce was one of his least favorite people in the world. And it looked like his feelings for the Watch captain were shared by at least one other person. He had noticed the expression of distaste Mira had directed Rector's way on more than one occasion. At least Sophy's daughter showed some good sense.

Amma stood and came to him. "The girl needs fresh clothes. She can borrow some of Bree's. The two of them are about the same height."

His sister frowned, looking less than pleased, but nevertheless, she agreed. "Fine," she said, sounding irritated by the matter. "I'll take her to my room and she can try on a few things."

"Make sure to burn them afterward," Rector muttered. At the looks of annoyance shot his way from Amma and Nanna, he threw his hands in the air. "Fine. Treat her as if she were a real person," he said. "But the First Mother and First Father tell us what her kind truly are. As it is said in *The Word and Deed*: *Suffer not those who have lineage from two Castes. Know them for the truth. They are Ghrinas, abominations.*"

Jessira stepped out from behind Rukh, glaring with revulsion and fury at Bryce. "And *The Book of All Souls* tells us this: *Across the world, the Lord stretched forth His hand and caused Life. And those whom he gave understanding, He named as brothers and sisters.* I have knowledge, and I speak. According to Devesh's own words, I am a sister to everyone here," Jessira said, glancing around before focusing her attention back on Rector. "Or will you disobey the Lord Himself?" she challenged.

Bryce had no answer. He turned away, his teeth clenched in anger.

Bree rolled her eyes as she turned to Jessira. "Thank you for the philosophy lesson," she said. "Now cover your face. None of the servants can know who you are yet."

"You mean *what* I am," Jessira snapped before turning to the others. "I don't care if you approve or disapprove of me. Label me an abomination, a ghrina if you want to. My people long ago gave up any hope that the Purebloods would show us even the smallest amount of charity. Say the word, and I'll be gone from this fragging city before sunrise."

Someone, Mira maybe, inhaled sharply at Jessira's words, no doubt scandalized by her use of vulgarity. It was considered undignified for a woman to speak like that. But Rukh was secretly proud of Jessira.

Rector was about to retort angrily, but Nanna merely glanced at him in warning, and he subsided.

"The girl certainly has courage," Amma murmured.

Bree snorted. "If she wasn't what she was, I think I might like her."

———— • ————

Later in the evening, after a long soak in a bathtub and a change into fresh, clean clothes, Jessira felt better than she had in weeks. The Shiyen had cured her of most of the weakness and stiffness in her shoulder. Even the aching was gone and it was no longer infected– a minor miracle. Rukh's boasts about the Shiyens had proven to be true. The cranky old physician had Healed her up and had even managed to save her arm. She was more grateful than words could express.

Her one concern – and it was a major one – was the city in which she found herself.

Ashoka. From what she had seen so far, it was lovely enough; far larger than Stronghold with wide streets and beautiful, expansive parks. None of it mattered, though. Not for her. The nature of the place couldn't be hidden away beneath a patina of loveliness. In the end, Ashoka was still a city of Purebloods. For Jessira, it meant the place was a cesspool.

And then there were the attitudes of the people here. The Shiyen physician hadn't seemed to care about Jessira's background, but Rector Bryce and Sophy Terrell certainly had, and it had been in a hateful way. And apparently Rukh's sister, Bree, shared their attitude. The clothes she had offered to Jessira had been given over without any pretense at good manners or courtesy. The woman had rummaged around in her wardrobe for a bit and pulled out a pair of pants, a shirt, and an undershirt, throwing them in Jessira's direction with a haughty warning not to dirty them. Only for Rukh's sake had Jessira held back from punching the girl.

How could two people share the same parents but come out so differently? Rukh was open and curious, and despite his obvious intelligence, humble. Meanwhile, Bree struck her as being the opposite: haughty, arrogant, and close-minded. She seemed the type of person who was certain of their own cleverness and everyone else's stupidity.

Bitch.

Jessira flopped in the soft bed and tried to find a comfortable position. She sighed in annoyance. Her body must have grown used to the hard ground. She lay there for a while, hoping to get some sleep, but despite her fatigue, it stubbornly eluded her. She sat up with a frown. If she couldn't fall asleep, she might as well talk to someone. But the only person she knew was Rukh. She wondered if he was still up. His room was near hers – she'd passed it on the way to the guest quarters – and it wouldn't hurt to check.

She crept from her room. It was late at night and the house was quiet. All the servants were asleep, even Rukh's parents, who apparently had stayed up late into the evening, discussing the information their son had brought home before finally retiring themselves.

She hesitated at his door. If anyone saw her, this could appear most inappropriate. She was about to slip away when she heard voices from within. Good. He wasn't alone. She tapped lightly on Rukh's door.

"Come in, Jessira," he said.

She muttered a curse. How did he know it was her? She eased the door open. Inside, Rukh was sitting on the lip of his bed. Sitting on several chairs near him were Jaresh and Bree.

Great.

Jessira was about to back right out. "If I'm disturbing you…"

Surprisingly, it was Bree who called her back in. "Stay," she said. "You don't need to go."

"What are you doing here so late?" Jaresh asked, suspicion tinging his voice.

Jessira shrugged, feeling self-conscious before their scrutiny. Stopping by Rukh's room had been a mistake. "I couldn't sleep, and I heard voices, so…"

"Well Rukh was just telling us all about you," Bree said.

"There isn't much to tell," Jessira said. "I'm a scout. I got caught. I was injured. Your brother saved my life. The end."

"That's plenty more than I could say about myself," Bree replied. "In Ashoka, women aren't allowed to fight. We're considered too important for Humanity's survival." She snorted in derision. "We're animate wombs if you ask me."

Jessira wasn't sure how to respond. Did Rukh's sister expect her pity? Not fragging likely. If Kumma women didn't like their role in this world, then they should stop whining about it and change it. They were as much a part of Ashoka's culture as the men, and they had it in them to decide what was in their best interests. Nothing was stopping them except their own fear and laziness. Or were Bree's words supposed to help the two of them form some kind of sisterly bond? Again, not very likely, especially after Bree's earlier boorish behavior.

Jessira shrugged and was about to turn away when Bree spoke again.

"I know I wasn't kind to you earlier, and I'm sorry about my poor manners," she said. "I'm sure you know how we view ghrinas – I mean OutCastes – and your sudden appearance...it had me off-balance. I'm not at my best when I'm surprised, but Rukh straightened me out."

The words gave Jessira pause. She faced Rukh's sister, and studied her, wondering if she had misread the woman. The apology had sounded genuine, and Bree's expression was one of regret. Jessira had learned to trust her instincts about a person, but they had failed her with Rukh. Perhaps they had failed her in this instance as well.

"You're forgiven," Jessira said to Bree. "And don't feel too bad. Your brother wasn't much kinder when he and I first met. He wanted to kill me on sight."

Bree startled and turned to Rukh. "Is this true?"

Rukh shrugged uncomfortably.

"Rukh!"

"I wasn't really going to," he said. "At the time, I was just thinking about what was said about ghrinas in *The Word and the Deed*."

Jaresh chuckled. "And this is what we have to put up with," he said to Jessira. "A stickler for rules is our brother."

"But he has his uses," Bree added.

Despite their teasing tones, the love and affection was evident in both their voices.

Jessira smiled. "Yes he does." She glanced at Rukh. "For the most part, he's worth keeping around," she said, surprising herself by the fond tone in her voice.

She noticed the look of speculative concern shared by Rukh's brother and sister. They were probably wondering if their brother had sullied himself with an OutCaste. He hadn't, and he never would, but if Jaresh and Bree could wonder about it, then others would as well. Jackholes like Rector Bryce, and what they might say, could be ruinous to Rukh's good name. After all he had done for her, it was the last thing she wanted.

There *was* something she could say to help quell any sudden rumors, though. She could tell the truth. "When I get home, I imagine my fiancé will be grateful for all his help," she said.

"You're engaged?" Jaresh asked.

Jessira didn't miss the look of relief he shared with Bree.

Rukh laughed. "Five weeks travelling with her, and this is the first I'm hearing of it."

"His name is Disbar Merdant," Jessira said. "We were engaged over the winter, and our marriage is to take place next spring."

"Congratulations," Rukh said, sounding sincere. "But why did you decide to stop by my room so late in the night? I know it isn't for my sparkling wit or dazzling company."

Jessira wasn't sure herself. She had gotten used to Rukh's presence next to her after their time in the Wildness. He was comforting somehow.

"Like I said: I couldn't sleep," she said. "I think it's being here, in this house and this city, so I thought I'd come by and see if you were awake." She shrugged. "Besides you haven't told me how you won the Tournament of Hume."

Rukh groaned. "That again."

"How did it happen?" she asked. "I mean, how does someone so young defeat a city full of battle-hardened Kummas?"

"You know of the Tournament?" Jaresh asked, surprised.

"Stronghold also holds a martial contest," Jessira explained. "Only we call it the Trials of Hume." She nodded. "We honor him just like you do."

"His influence stretches far and wide, from Purebloods to OutCastes to even the Baels," Rukh added.

"You didn't answer my question," Jessira said to him.

Rukh sighed. "Fine. Come in and have a seat, and I'll tell you what you want to know. Prepare to be underwhelmed. I won the final contest by luck more than anything..."

"Start with the first one," Jessira interrupted. She settled into a chair, hoping Rukh's stories about the Tournament would take her mind off her worries.

CHAPTER TWENTY
A MORNING'S REVELATIONS

Foolish is the man who turns aside from the woman who might complete him.
He deserves our contempt.

~Sooths and Small Sayings by Tramed Billow, AF 1387

The next morning, Jessira woke much later than usual. Her sleep had been restless and filled with nightmarish visions of Rector Bryce chasing her through a dark alley, laughing maniacally even as he hurled vulgar promises of how he would brutalize her. In other dreams, rampaging crowds, their faces distorted with blind hatred, raced amongst the streets of an Ashoka destroyed by fire and ruin. Rukh had been amongst the rioters, and the mob had been baying for her blood. She shuddered in remembrance.

Perhaps sunlight would help her forget the nightmares.

She went to the double-doors leading out to the balcony. They were paneled with small, rectangular windows and curtained with thin, white diaphanous drapes, yet still thick enough to keep hidden the view outside. She unlocked the doors and drew them open, pausing on the threshold. Holy Father...this was Ashoka? She gripped the door handles tightly, and her mouth opened in stunned surprise. She had to force herself to breathe. She had seen some of the city yesterday, but it had been late when Jessira and Rukh had arrived. She'd also been in pain and hadn't noticed much more than cursory details. She had thought the city attractive enough, but when seen like this, in the morning...

The city was huge. Much, much larger than Stronghold. And so loud. There were so many sounds. Everything from people shouting to animals bellowing and the noises of traffic competing with lovely voices and instruments raised in song and music from several nearby buskers. It was a cacophony, but not an unpleasant one. Then came the aromas: the wonderful, delicious smells of various foods and spices drifting on the clean salty air.

But what took her breath away were the sights greeting her. Jessira found her gaze darting around as she tried to take it all in at once.

Steep, verdant hills – upon which were perched lovely homes in colors of salmon-pink, lavender, sky blue, or sunny yellow – tumbled down to the blue water, only to re-emerge here and there as rocky, green outcroppings far out in the deep bay. She had never seen the Sickle Sea before. How could so much water exist in one place at the same time? Throughout Ashoka were ornate buildings with lintels and columns carved into fanciful figures. They fronted or surrounded numerous courtyards or large private gardens where families and couples gathered for meals or a stroll. Jessira saw lines of wide, paved streets with medians of palm trees as they crisscrossed the city. Where the boulevards intersected were busy traffic circles. Somehow the ox-drawn wagons, mounted horsemen, rickshaws, and pedestrians managed to get through the tumult without anyone getting hurt. She traced one street until it ended at a large plaza with numerous fountains spraying water in the air. Near it was a giant stadium, larger than any building in Stronghold. She faintly remembered they had passed it last night. Jessira wondered if it was where Rukh had won the Tournament of Hume. To the south of her balcony was a park taking up most of the valley floor where several hills met. It was open and spacious, filled with trees, grassy fields, meadows, and even several small ponds. The park ran up to a rocky cliff and offered a glorious view of the bay.

Ashoka was stunning, and for an instant, Jessira was flooded with intense jealousy. It seemed so unfair for the Purebloods to have a place of such beauty and safety while the OutCastes were forced to squat in what amounted to caves. Would there ever come a time when her kind could walk the wide, lovely boulevards of Ashoka without fear of harassment or harm?

Jessira doubted it…at least not in her lifetime. But Holy Mother, she wished it could be so.

Eventually, she went back inside and donned her scarf. Couldn't scandalize the servants with her shabby OutCaste self.

She smiled at the thought.

Stronghold had no servants, at least not like the ones here. Her city was young and poor. Other than communal meals and bathhouses, which were maintained by a cadre of people whose job it was to service those areas, everyone was expected to do for themselves. If her family could see her now, they might have laughed at her worries about avoiding servants.

The smile slipped away.

She wished she could see her family now. She missed them. She prayed Cedar was safe. She hoped he had made it home and warned the city.

He would have so many events to relate to the city Elders. The world was far different than they thought. Until Rukh had described it all last night, she hadn't realized how many changes her people would have to confront. It was staggering. Who could have imagined all the sights Jessira Viola Grey would see since that eventful night on the Hunters Flats when the SarpanKum had offered Humanity the peace of fraternity?

It was surreal, and if she hadn't been witness to all of those events, she wouldn't have believed them possible.

There was a knock at her door, and when she opened it, she found Jaresh standing outside.

"Nanna would like you to join us downstairs," he said. "The Council is meeting."

She nodded acknowledgement, but before stepping outside, she made sure her hands were hidden within the folds of her shirt. Her Cherid skin did not match her Muran eyes. She shook her head in disbelief. The stupid lengths to which the Purebloods insisted people bend their features.

Jaresh led her down an elliptical staircase, through the rear foyer, and to his father's study, the same room in which they had all gathered last night. Waiting inside was Rukh. He looked relaxed and comfortable with a fresh shave and even a haircut. When had he found the time for either? It must be later than she realized. She silently scolded herself for sleeping in.

She also noticed Rukh's amma and nanna, as well as his sister and Mira Terrell. There were also two older men, both of whom gave her appraising and curious glances. She hid a grimace when she saw Rector Bryce and Sophy Terrell. Those two despised her and probably always would. Not that she cared. She'd be gone from Ashoka as soon as her shoulder was healed enough for travel. As far as she was concerned, it might as well be today.

"Are you one of the so-called OutCastes?" one of the older men asked.

Rukh's nanna, Dar'El chuckled. "Pardon Durmer's directness. At his age, he believes the accepted rules of decorum no longer apply to him."

"No reason to waste time on frippery," Durmer said. "Well, girl...are you?"

Rather than speak, Jessira simply unwrapped the shawl, letting them see the mixed heritage so obvious in her skin, her hair, and her eyes.

Durmer glanced at Sophy, a puzzled expression on his face. "The way you described her, I figured her to be as ugly as a Bael turd. The girl is lovely."

The other old man laughed. "Lovely is the correct description for a spring day. The *woman* is beautiful."

Durmer rolled his eyes. "Speaking like a poet won't get you anywhere with this one, Garnet, you lecherous old goat."

Jessira looked to Rukh in confusion, but he looked just as confused as she did. Had those two old men actually offered her a compliment? She would have wagered the sun stood a better chance of rising in the west than for a Kumma to call her beautiful or lovely.

Durmer must have noticed her surprise because he started laughing. "We're old, girl, but not cold."

"And as Dar'El says: at our age, the general rules of society aren't so important anymore. We've lived long enough to find the circumstances of a person's birth less important than the character of their heart."

Jaresh stirred and coughed into his hand. "Bullshit," he muttered into his hand, clear and loud enough for everyone to hear.

"Other than when a Sentya is adopted into a Kumma House as the son of the ruling 'El and wants to train as a warrior," Durmer said somewhat caustically. "We may have had trouble with that situation, but we all know how it turned out, don't we?"

Garnet chuckled dryly. "Jaresh can't fight as one of us, but his heart is Kumma. I've said it for years now."

Jaresh rolled his eyes, but he didn't have a chance to respond because just then Rukh's nanna spoke. "Sit down," Dar'El said, gesturing for Jessira to take a seat.

She had planned on sitting next to Rukh, but Bree patted the empty space beside her on the divan. Jessira hesitated, but Rukh wasn't paying her any attention, so she sat next to his sister.

"Everyone here knows your status and knows what you and my son told us last night," Dar'El began. "This information must be relayed to the Magisterium. They will meet with you in a few hours."

"And after that?" Jessira asked. "Will my presence still be required?"

"Surely you aren't considering leaving us so soon after your arrival?" Garnet asked. "Rukh says you were clawed by a Shylow, and you had to have stitches placed last night. Wouldn't it be better to have one of the Shiyens make sure the infection isn't lingering and have one of them take the stitches out for you?"

Again Jessira was surprised. She would not have expected such hospitality from House Shektan, not based on how they had treated her last night. "I'm honored by the offer," she said, "but I know none of you really want me here." She looked at Rukh. "Your House has already done more for me than I could ever hope to repay."

"If it is for our sake you wish to leave, then put it out of your mind," Dar'El said. "We will not have it said that House Shektan dismisses those in need."

Before she could respond, Durmer spoke. "Our world is changed. You are simply the most obvious and *lovely*..." he glared at Garnet, daring him to contradict him..."manifestation of the transformations we face."

"It would have been shocking enough to learn of your people," Garnet said, "but then to hear of the Baels and the Shylows..."

"Kesarins," Rukh corrected.

"Shylows. Kesarins. Who cares? I'm too old to learn new things," Garnet declared. "The point is this: the information you've brought home has the potential to overturn Ashoka. Much of what we once believed may be false," he said, an echo of Jessira's earlier sentiments about her own people.

"Rukh believes the Baels might be our allies," Rector Bryce said, his tone openly mocking of the idea.

Jessira's jaw clenched. The prig just had to talk, didn't he?

"Maintaining a scoffing and sneering pose won't lead a person to the truth," Garnet said. "You would do well to remember this, Rector Bryce."

"Neither does giving serious consideration to fables," Rector countered. "Or the fabulist who speaks them," he said, looking straight to Jessira.

Jessira found herself standing, heart pounding and full of a cold fury. She'd had enough of this arrogant bastard. Her thoughts were crystalline. "Am I a liar now?" she demanded, taking a step toward Rector. Bree tugged on her arm. Jessira yanked herself free. "You weren't there, Bryce. You were here, safe and snug in Ashoka while better men died."

Rector roared to his feet. "If you were a man, you would face my challenge for such an insult."

"And if *you* were a man, I would accept," Jessira shot back. "I was there. I've been out in the Wildness since I was sixteen. I've spent months in the field. I've survived ten of your so-called Trials. I know what I'm talking about. I heard everything the Baels said. I saw their commander, Li-Dirge, fight alongside your Ashokans against his own Tigons. I was there when Suwraith discovered the treachery of the Baels and killed them for it. I saw the Bael survivors fight with us against the Shylows. One even sacrificed his life so my brother could live. And another carried me to safety.

"Stronghold doesn't have an Oasis, so we *have* to be more cautious than you. I believe what I saw. I am no longer so sure the Baels aren't telling the truth. I think perhaps they have done their best to protect Humanity, even at the cost of their own lives, for centuries, ever since the fall of Hammer. We shouldn't dismiss their work out of hand."

"Please sit, Rector," Bree urged.

He glanced at her, an unfathomable expression on his face. "This is wrong," he muttered. "*She* is wrong," he said as he resumed his seat.

"Rukh said much the same thing as you," Mira said. "It's just so hard to believe. It sounds impossible."

"No different than Rukh Blending or Healing," Jaresh said.

"Yet he can do both," said Rukh's amma, turning to Jessira. "In the eyes of those without wisdom, he would be considered as Tainted as you." She graced Rector with a brief glance, leaving no doubt as to whom she was referencing.

"I have done nothing wrong," Rector declared. "Before yesterday, all of us would have thrown her out of Ashoka. As well as any Kumma who can Blend *or* Heal, much less both."

We need to see past what we've always been taught. If we don't our small-mindedness will doom us," Jaresh said.

"So now I'm small minded!"

"In this instance, yes," Jaresh said, refusing to back down. "And take your hand off your sword. Matters in this room aren't decided by whoever is the finer warrior."

"Leave it be, Rector," Bree urged. "These issues of philosophy are beside the point right now. We can deal with them later. Right now, Ashoka is threatened. Next spring, Suwraith might be leading three Plagues against us."

"Unless we strike first," Rukh said.

Jessira inhaled sharply. She knew what Rukh meant. He'd briefly spoken of it on the way back to Ashoka. "You mean to go after their breeding caverns," she said. "You'd need five thousand or more for such an attack to be effective."

"Five thousand Strongholders. Fifteen hundred Kummas with enough Murans and Rahails to Blend them could do it," Rukh said. "Two thousand would be better."

"What caverns? Durmer asked.

"Before the Queen killed him, Li-Dirge told me where the Chimeras breed. It's a cave system near the headwaters of the Slave River, where the water carves a steep canyon a few miles north of the Tripwire Falls. A fast moving strike force could kill their breeders and set them back for years."

"I am not sure we can afford to risk so many of our warriors on such a questionable cause," Garnet said.

"I think it's a risk worth taking. Face them now or maybe face them in the spring. This would be the first time we could do some real damage to their numbers." Rukh shrugged. "The other Castes wouldn't even be needed if the Kummas could Blend for themselves," he joked half-heartedly.

Silence greeted Rukh's flip statement. Jessira could tell everyone in the room was actually taking his jesting proposal seriously.

Dar'El was the first to break the quiet. "Can it be done?" he asked, softly. "Can you teach them?"

Rukh looked taken aback. "No," he replied without hesitation. "The only reason *I* learned was because I was Annexed with Brand Wall. It was a moment of desperation."

Bree and Sophy looked disturbed while Durmer and Garnet merely looked thoughtful.

"A pity," Dar'El murmured.

Rector looked like he would be sick. "I want no part of this," he said. "For the other matter I will give all I have, but for this…I must step aside." His final words spoken, Bryce stood and walked out of the study.

Jessira was privately glad the man had decided to leave. What a pain in the backside. He was worse than a needle in one's undergarments.

The room remained silent until Bryce had shut the door behind him.

"Many will feel as Rector," Jaresh warned.

"The man is trouble," Rukh's amma warned.

"He only follows what is in his heart," Bree said, defensively.

"And he never questions whether his heart is leading him astray or whether there is more to this world than what he has been taught," her amma replied. "Our feelings do not produce the sum of our existence. We were also meant to reason."

"There are several other issues we need to discuss with you," Dar'El said, turning to Jessira and interrupting the conversation between his wife and daughter. "First, I wish to apologize for how you were treated yesterday by those in my House." He looked meaningfully at Bree and Sophy.

"I've already apologized," Bree complained.

"I also offer my apology for my initial reaction to your presence," Sophy said, her words perfunctory.

Durmer chuckled. "And people say we're tied to old ways."

Dar'El looked disappointed with Sophy, but he said nothing more.

"What do you know of the Sil Lor Kum?" Rukh's amma asked.

"Only that they are vile and traitorous worshippers of Suwraith," Jessira said with a curl to her lip. "Is there anything else *to* know?"

"Are you sure you want to tell her this?" Bree asked.

"She needs to hear it. Her people need to know," Dar'El answered. He turned back to Jessira. "Several months ago, shortly after the caravan for Nestle left, we learned the Sil Lor Kum have been active once more here in Ashoka. There have been murders."

Jessira stiffened. "And you haven't found them yet."

"If we had, they would have already been hung, drawn, and quartered with their bodies left to rot on the Isle of the Crows," Durmer said, all humor gone from his voice. "I still don't understand why you didn't let me and Garnet know of your concerns from the beginning."

"I've already explained why," Dar'El said. "Both of you were suspects until we could clear up your whereabouts on the nights in question."

"Our bad luck to have dinner in Sunpalm on the evening of the first murder," Durmer said. "I still think you should have…"

"It's over, Volk. Let it be," Garnet interrupted.

"Unfortunately, there is more to tell," Dar'El warned. "The weapon used in the killings is something called the Withering Knife. Legend says it's tied to the Sorrow Bringer Herself. She is said to have used it on the Night of Sorrows. It also seems to appear whenever the Queen has targeted a city for destruction. The Sil Lor Kum kill with the Knife, and through the use of it, they somehow undermine a city."

"They betray us, the Plagues attack us, and Suwraith destroys us," Mira said.

"Your city will want to watch for their presence as well," Dar'El added.

"You'll need to leave if you don't want to be late," Jaresh reminded everyone. "The meeting with the Magisterium…"

With his prompt, everyone stood to leave.

Jessira wanted to talk things over with Rukh, but he walked past her, seemingly caught up in a conversation with Jaresh and ignored her completely. This time it was purposeful.

She paused, upset by his avoidance of her. An instant later, she cursed her own stupidity. How could she have been so naïve? Of course Rukh wouldn't want to be seen with her. Not now when he was home. He probably wanted as little to do with her as possible. No reason to sully his good name any further than it already was. She understood the reason for his behavior, but it still hurt.

◆

Rector sat at a table near the central fountain of the Martyr's Plaza looking out over the large square fashioned in honor of Ashoka's greatest heroes. This was the true heart of the city. It was located in an area relatively central to the many hills upon which Ashoka was built, and all along the perimeter, statues of men and women stood boldly, holding swords or hammers or musical instruments at the ready. But many, if not most of the figures, were Kumma, their swords held high and a defiant cry upon their lips. It simply reflected the unacknowledged truth as far as Rector was concerned: just as the Plaza was the heart of Ashoka, so too were Kummas the heart of Humanity. Even the Union Fountain, the large sculpture at the center of the Plaza, mirrored this fact. Standing atop stylized figurines in poses meant to emulate the best works of the other six Castes stood a Kumma, and it wasn't just any Kumma, either. This was the only statue of someone who was not of Ashoka. This was the greatest of Kummas, Hume Telrest.

The sculptor had chosen to give Hume's statue a stooped appearance, with head bent and shoulders hunched. But despite his world-weary pose, there was no denying the man's courage or his centrality to Kumma life and heritage. He was what all Kummas strove to be. And to hear the Baels supposedly honored him as well…Rector gritted his teeth. Some things should never be mocked or befouled. Baels as brothers to Kummas…the very idea was insulting.

A series of sharp calls drew his gaze. Small groups of children raced about the Plaza, and the ever-present pigeons scattered at their approach. He watched the young ones for a moment longer and wondered if Bree would show. They had agreed to meet here after this morning's council session and discuss the unsettling events of the past day. After the scene he had made in Dar'El's study he doubted if she would come. If she chose to stay away he understood what it meant, and he would regret it. He had come to like and respect Bree Shektan. She was bright and warm with a vibrancy lacking in most beautiful women. More enchanting, she seemed utterly unaware of the effect she had on others. And she certainly wasn't mannish like the ghrina woman her brother had brought home.

Despite how he felt for Bree, and the risk he had taken by speaking out as he had, he knew it had been the right thing to do. He wouldn't have been able to live with himself if he hadn't. He had said something all of the others needed to hear. Surely none of them could believe this wild tale of Rukh Shektan. The events Dar'El's son claimed to have witnessed and the Talents he now possessed…it was beyond nonsensical. It was blasphemous. If Rukh spoke the truth, and could Blend *and* Heal, then Bree's brother had been Tainted beyond all redemption. The only proper judgment for the evil he represented was the Slash of Iniquity. It didn't make Rector happy to say so, but he knew others needed to learn of this, even if it cost him his place in House Shektan and the heart of Dar'El's daughter.

His grim mood lightened slightly when he saw Bree. She wouldn't see the recent events, especially those regarding Rukh, the same way Rector did. He waited to hear how she would chide him.

Bree sat down beside him. "You embarrassed yourself today," she said without preamble.

Rector bristled. "I only spoke what was in my heart and the truth as I see it," he replied. "It's what I thought all of us had once been taught."

"Maybe," Bree said. "But your delivery left much to be desired."

"You think the ghrina woman should be allowed to stay?" Rector asked, stunned.

"Of course not," Bree replied. "She has to go, but while she is here, there is no reason to call her names or treat her so cruelly."

"She is what she is. Her very existence is an affront to everything we hold to be good and moral."

"Regardless, for Rukh's sake, I plan to treat her with kindness. And even if anyone wanted her to stay and she were offered the opportunity, she wouldn't take it. She wants to go back to her own home as badly as we want her out of *our* home."

"Good riddance," Rector muttered. He glanced at Bree. "Why did you apologize to her?"

"For treating her so rudely, and for the sake of good manners," Bree replied with a shrug. "Besides, she isn't at all what I expected."

"She is everything I feared," Rector said. "She is attractive…" At Bree's look of surprise, he laughed. "I despise her, but I am not blind. Even though she's built like a man, she's pretty enough – or at least she would be if she weren't so haggard and unkempt. She also seems to be quite capable as well as being smart and brave. So yes, she would be attractive to some. And she is dangerous because of all of those things. The Magistrates may see a person rather than a ghrina."

"I doubt it," Bree said.

"If half of what your brother says is true, why would such a decision be so hard to believe?"

"Because the Magistrates aren't fools."

"No. Not all of them."

Their conversation lapsed, and Rector watched the happy people around him, none of them aware of the evil lurking in the heart of his House's seat.

Bree smiled and turned to him. "Rukh had quite an eventful Trial," she said.

"You believe him?" Rector asked, wondering if her loyalty would blind her to the unreality of her brother's claims.

"I do," Bree said.

"And his Talents?"

"Are real enough. He demonstrated them after all. More importantly, Rukh is and always will be my brother. I will never go against him."

Her words were expected, but they still disappointed. "What of Jaresh then?"

"What about him?"

"He spoke rather rudely to me. I would caution him if I were you. His careless mouth will get him in trouble some day."

"Are you threatening him?" Bree asked, with a challenging lift of her eyebrows.

"Not at all. I respect Jaresh, but many Kummas don't, and if he continues to speak to us in this way, he's going to find the truth of the truism: if you bait the Bael, you'll get the horns."

"Jaresh can handle himself," Bree said. "And he also spoke the truth and showed courage as he always has."

"So you think I'm wrong?"

"You acted like an ass today. Yes," Bree said.

He had no response for her. How could she say something so crass to him. He worked hard to hide his anger.

A moment later she sighed. "What you said had merit, but you were so blunt about it. No one wants to listen to a scold."

"I spoke what was in my heart," Rector repeated.

"And you've never wondered if your heart might need...tempering?" Bree stood up. She surprised him when she paused next to his chair and squeezed his shoulder. "I like you Rector, but in this, I will always be with my family. You should remember that."

He spent the rest of the morning at the Martyr's Plaza and replayed their conversation, but the soft press of her hand on his shoulder was what stayed with him.

———⊷●⊶———

"**F**igured you'd be here," Mira said with a smile.

Jaresh was exactly where she had expected to find him: eating breakfast in the sunroom. It was a large, brightly lit space just off the kitchen with windows taking up an entire wall. Views beyond extended to Satha Shektan's pride and joy: her flower gardens, bursting in full bloom now. The windows were thrown open, and Mira tied off the curtains, which were billowing in the playful breeze. With it came the salty tang of the sea.

"I fixed you some food," Jaresh said, gesturing to a plate of eggs with several thick slabs of bacon. He grinned. "I figured you'd be hungry. You complain about it often enough."

"I don't complain," Mira explained in the overly patient tone she knew he hated. "I just don't think there's anything to be learned by being hungry all the time."

"Uh huh," Jaresh replied.

"And here I was going to fetch you some juice."

Jaresh glanced up from his food, a hopeful look on his face.

Mira laughed. "Don't get used to it," she said. "Kummas are meant to command. We don't serve."

"How could I ever forget?"

Cook Heltin already had two glasses of juice poured and ready when Mira went into the kitchen. She mutely passed them to her. Somehow the old Sentya always knew what everyone needed. It must be a gift.

When Mira returned to the sunroom, she plopped Jaresh's drink down in front of him. "There," she said. "Don't say I've never done anything for you."

"Wouldn't dream of it," Jaresh replied.

Mira silently studied him for a moment, not sure if she should tell him how proud she was of him and the way he had stood up for himself in the council meeting. Rector Bryce was a jackhole of blunt force stupidity, and she was glad her mother no longer brought up any talk of a potential match between the two of them.

Jaresh, on the other hand, had so many admirable qualities. It was a shame more Kummas couldn't see it. They saw the flash and bang of his brother – and Rukh was impressive, there was no doubting his abilities. Not anymore. Especially not after what he'd been through and survived. But Jaresh had a quiet competence to him as well, one which wasn't as bright and showy as Rukh's, but effective nonetheless.

She said as much.

Jaresh flushed, looking uncomfortable.

Mira smiled, recognizing she had embarrassed him. Jaresh was the kind of man who went about his work, did it well, and preferred to skip the accolades. His humility was sweet.

"Rector needed to be put in his place," Mira added. "I'm glad you were the one to do it."

Jaresh shrugged. "I only wanted to keep the meeting going. We don't have time for crises of conscience."

"No we don't," Mira said. "Rukh only came home last night, and I already feel as though weeks have passed. There is so much we have to digest, to reassess."

Jaresh smiled. "Rukh always was one to overturn the apple cart," he said, the warmth evident in his voice.

Mira frowned. When it came to Rukh, Jaresh never questioned anything his brother said. "And you don't have any second thoughts about what he told us?" she asked.

Jaresh shook his head. "No. Do you?"

"I might have some doubts, but, yes, overall I tend to believe him."

"I see no reason to *dis*believe him, now or ever. He's my brother. I grew up with him," Jaresh said.

"And now he is a Kumma who can Blend and Heal," Mira said. "There are those who will say he is no Kumma at all."

"Men like Rector Bryce, you mean." Jaresh snorted in derision. "I have no idea what Bree sees in him."

"Bree is interested in Rector?" Mira said, surprised.

"You haven't noticed?"

"I tend to ignore the man whenever possible."

"You don't think we're being a little harsh?"

Mira gave him a measuring look.

"I guess not," Jaresh said.

"He's a hidebound idiot, always so sure he's the only person who can tell right from wrong," Mira said with a grimace of disdain.

"In some ways, he sort of reminds me of your mother," Jaresh said. "No offense intended."

"None taken," Mira replied. "And I know what you mean. He *is* like Amma," she said. "It is strange, but sometimes I feel closer to *your* amma."

Jaresh grinned. "Then we would have been brother and sister."

Mira nodded, wondering what that would have been like. At least they would have gotten to know one another far earlier than they had. It would have been nice.

"You never told me what you think of Rukh's new Talents," Mira reminded Jaresh after a moment of quiet.

"There's nothing to think about. He never wanted any of those Talents, and if we can't have compassion for those who have been damaged through no fault of their own, how can we claim to be a good and merciful people?"

"Some might say the same about the OutCastes," she said.

Jaresh nodded. "I know. I've thought about it."

"And?"

"And I don't know," Jaresh said. "Why don't *you* answer some questions for once?"

Mira had no response to his challenge, and they fell into a comfortable silence.

A few minutes later, Mira spoke again. "Have you thought about Rukh's plan?" she asked.

Jaresh groaned. "You can't help it, can you?"

"Help what?"

"Help asking me a thousand questions."

Mira shrugged. "I value your opinion?"

Jaresh smirked. "Is that another question?"

Mira grinned. "You didn't answer the first one."

Jaresh sighed. "Fine. I think Rukh is right. If we strike now, we can cripple the Fan Lor Kum."

"And the rest? The Baels."

"It would change everything, wouldn't it?" Jaresh asked.

"Only if it's true."

"Rukh thinks so, and he is no fool. Jessira believes it too, and she has a way about her…" Jaresh smiled. "She's like a force of nature."

Mira felt something like a twinge of jealousy, which she quickly snuffed. "You like her."

"Well, she *is* likeable. And the way she stood up to Rector…I'll feel warmth toward anyone who does that."

"And I'm sure it doesn't hurt that she's beautiful," Mira said.

Jaresh shrugged. "She is attractive enough – or might be if she wasn't so worn out from being sick – but it doesn't change the facts about her: she is and always will be OutCaste. But, yes, I like her."

Mira nodded. "I like her, too," she said. "Or I suppose I might if she weren't what she is." The truth was Mira found Jessira refreshing. She was so bold and unafraid, so different than Kumma women, who weren't weaklings or cowards, but none of them would have thought to physically confront a man and challenge him to a duel. Jessira's actions were the stuff of bedtime fables. Secretly, she had cheered Jessira on during her confrontation with Bryce.

Another silence fell and once more, Mira was the one to break it.

"I hope the Magisterium agrees with us," she said. "I hope they believe your brother. He is far more than I ever gave him credit for being."

Jaresh leaned back in his chair, a look of surprise on his face. "Your opinion of Rukh certainly has changed," he said.

Mira shrugged. "I was wrong about him. He's a great warrior, but he's also much more patient and cunning than I expected. Imagine waiting to listen in on the Baels instead of just killing them."

"It was wise," Jaresh said. "I only hope he's wise enough."

"What do you mean?"

Jaresh looked conflicted, like he didn't want to say anymore, but eventually, he explained himself. "I worry for him. As I said, I like Jessira, but Rukh thinks of Jessira as a good friend. He doesn't see that she is first and foremost a ghrina."

Mira was vaguely disappointed by Jaresh's attitude. It was true: Jessira was a ghrina, but she was also a woman Mira found herself admiring. She couldn't even begin to imagine the amount of courage it must have taken for Jessira to enter the lion's den of Ashoka. More impressive, the OutCaste woman hadn't simply hidden herself away like a mouse hoping to go unnoticed but had instead loudly and boldly demanded respect. Mira doubted she had such bravery herself.

"I would have thought you of all people could see past our prejudices," Mira said. "Jessira might very well be a good friend to your brother."

"She is what she is," Jaresh said, stubbornly.

"Durmer and Garnet don't seem to care. Why should we?"

"That's because they are old and crotchety. They can get away with just about anything."

"Then maybe we should emulate them," Mira said. "I don't know how I feel about *all* the OutCastes, but I like Jessira, and I find I'm no longer so willing to see them snuffed out. Maybe the old men are right: we need to think more deeply about who we are as a people."

Jaresh frowned. "And maybe that's a bridge too far."

"Or not far enough."

CHAPTER TWENTY-ONE
HIDING IN PLAIN SIGHT

*Live your life as you see fit. Only remember morality
and don't bend yourself to the will of another.*

~The Word and the Deed

"I'm tired of wearing this ridiculous scarf," Jessira growled.

Rukh, walking nearby, remained silent and so did Nanna.

He understood what Jessira was really trying to say. Jessira wasn't complaining about the scarf. She was upset by what the scarf represented: fear and shame. It was the fear others would feel if they knew her true identity, and the shame Ashokan society felt she should bear for her mere existence as a ghrina. And Jessira would never be ashamed of who she was. She was a strong, proud woman who cared very little for the opinions or worries of the people of Ashoka. And while her current situation – huddled and hidden beneath a scarf – made her uncomfortable, it was a discomfort she would have to handle on her own. Rukh couldn't think of anything to ease her mind or make her feel better.

Besides, he had other things to worry about, such as the upcoming meeting. The Magistrates needed to know everything he had learned during his time in the Wildness, but he feared what they would say when they learned of his new abilities. Almost certainly, they would deny him any chance to marry, concerned his newfound Talents might pass on to his children. They might even go so far as to exile him. Who knew what the Magistrates might decide?

"Say nothing about the Knife," Nanna ordered, speaking into the silence as they neared the Magisterium.

"Why?" Rukh asked. "Are you worried one of the Magistrates might be a part of the Sil Lor Kum?"

"Or even the murderer. We know the killer has a limp, and Krain Linshok, the Kumma Magistrate was injured in his final Trial. He came home with a limp."

Rukh swore softly. "Anything else?"

Nanna hesitated. "Keep your new Talents private for now."

Rukh breathed a sigh of relief. "Thank you," he said. He didn't like lying or omitting the truth, but he also didn't want to be punished for something he didn't think was wrong. Over the long journey home, he had come to believe there was nothing wrong with a Kumma who could Blend. If anything, it made him a more effective fighter.

"We're here," Nanna said. "Remember what I said about the Knife."

The Magisterium was a large, round building built of a dark, chocolate-colored granite veined in white. A colonnade stretched all around its circumference, and the entablature contained friezes depicting idyllic scenes of Ashokan life from the viewpoint of all seven Castes. A Kumma held a raised sword at the ready; a faceless Duriah held a hammer and tongs; and a Muran stood behind a plow. Working with an abacus was a Sentya, while a Rahail held a rod through which he refreshed the Oasis. A close-eyed Shiyen had his hand raised as he prepared to Heal, and a Cherid received the supplicating hands of a multitude as he brought them together as one.

Rukh nodded to the pair of honor guards – both Kummas – who were dressed in bright red uniforms filigreed in gold thread as they stood at parade rest and faced out toward the Plaza of Toll and Toil, which fronted the Magisterium.

The doors were already open, and the three of them walked inside, entering a long hallway which was dim after the bright morning light. Upon the walls of the passage were hung portraits of some of Ashoka's greatest Magistrates. Rukh recognized a few of the Kummas.

Two more guards, dressed identically to the ones outside, flanked a pair of closed mahogany doors embossed with the seal of the Magisterium: a golden eagle clasping a sword and a scythe. The guards silently opened the doors and ushered them inside. Within was a large, round chamber and an open and airy dome whose ceiling rose thirty feet or more above them. Hanging from the fine mahogany paneling that stretched a few feet higher than Rukh could reach were more portraits, also of famous Magistrates, most of whom looked down with stern judgment upon those in the room. Higher up the wall, the paneling gave way to mullioned windows separated from one another by blocks of pale, green marble. Centered in the arching dome itself was a stained glass motif of the First Father breaking the WellStone and gaining entrance to the fortress of the First Mother. Firefly lanterns were mounted throughout the room, lit to full brightness, chasing away all shadows. A number of benches lined both sides of a central walkway leading to an attestation stand facing the seven raised seats upon which the Magistrates sat.

Nanna led them forward. At the lectern, he and Rukh bowed, followed belatedly by Jessira.

All of the Magistrates were present and seated. Some of them appeared irritated, while a few looked bored. Others wore expressions of polite interest.

Rukh racked his thoughts, trying to remember all he knew of the Magistrates. Fol Nacket, the Cherid Magistrate, was first among equals, and he was in charge, as was the usual custom. Krain Linshok, the Kumma, was of House Flood, a once prosperous House recently fallen on hard times. Rukh didn't know much about him. The Muran was Dos Martel, a singer of great repute, and although her voice had lost some of its rich timbre, just last year she had sold out a series of twenty concerts at the Opriana, Ashoka's largest concert hall. Brit Hule was the Rahail and the youngest Patriarch in memory. He still taught at the Shield where he terrified his students with his uncompromising standards and intolerance for even the slightest of mistakes. Poque Belt was of Caste Sentya, and he had started a private forensic financial service, hired by those who suspected their accountants had somehow cheated them. Rumors said the elders of Caste Sentya had elected him Magistrate simply so he would no longer have the time to run his business and cause them trouble. Jone Drent, the Duriah, was built like all of his kind: a brick outhouse. He was thick and powerful, but his hands were as delicate and skilled as his visage was coarse and ugly. He had the rare Talent to DeCohese, to cause an object or structure to come undone, which made him one of the finest sculptors in Ashoka. The final Magistrate was tiny Gren Vos, the Shiyen. She was elderly, appearing frail and grandmotherly, but it was said her cutting sarcasm could filet a side of beef and her biting bluntness could pound that same filet into scaloppini.

"Let us try to hold this meeting in as sensible a fashion as possible," Fol Nacket began. "Magistrate Belt, as the secretary, please make certain all present here are listed in the accounts. If the other Magistrates could state their names?"

"Oh, piss on that," Gren Vos said. "You know who we are."

Nacket was about to respond, but the Sentya Magistrate, Poque Belt, spoke first. "I know everyone here," he said. He pointed his pen at Jessira. "Except her."

Nacket turned to Jessira. "Who are you…ah, miss?" he asked, obviously put off by Jessira's covered face.

"And why is she all wrapped up? It's hot as a fever in here," Vos said. "Her thyroid hasn't failed, has it?"

"Her name is Jessira Viola Grey," Nanna said.

"An interesting name," Dos Martel, the Muran, commented.

"By interesting, I assume you mean odd," Krain Linshok said

"What Caste?" Magistrate Belt asked.

"We will explain her reason for being here later," Nanna said.

"That's not what I asked," Poque Belt said. "I asked her Caste."

"The reason for my reluctance will soon be made clear," Nanna replied. "I'm sure you'll agree with my decision once you understand the reason for it."

Magistrate Belt shrugged. "We'll see. It certainly adds to the mystery anyway," he said. "I'll include her as Jessira Viola Grey, a woman without a Caste for now."

"I don't like it," Fol Nacket growled.

"Oh, let it be, Fol," Gren Vos said. "We'll have our answers soon enough."

Magistrate Nacket grumbled something under his breath but settled back into his chair.

Gren Vos turned her gaze to Rukh. "What's going on, boy?" she asked. "There's all kinds of crazy rumors floating around ever since you made your unexpected return to Ashoka."

"The meeting hasn't been called to order," Fol Nacket said, looking irritated. "Strike her question," he instructed Belt.

"Then call it to order," Vos replied.

"Besides, you're only going to ask the same question she did," Poque Belt added.

Magistrate Nacket, who was about to speak, closed his mouth with a snap. He glared at Belt and Vos before turning back to Rukh and the others.

"If there aren't any further interruptions, we will begin. Call to order. This is an emergency meeting of the Magisterium in the twelfth day of the seventh month of year 2062 since the Fall of the First World. The meeting has been called in order to answer public interest and allay the fears of those we represent regarding the sudden return of Rukh Shektan from the Trial to Nestle and the accompanying rumors thereof."

Gren Vos snorted, and Rukh thought he heard her say something about a 'windbag'.

"Now then," Magistrate Nacket said. "What is going on *Dar'El* Shektan?" he asked, glaring at Gren Vos and daring her to laugh. Rukh had to bite his own lip to keep from chuckling at Poque Belt's eyeroll. "All sorts of rumors swirl through Ashoka ever since your son returned to us."

"With the Magistrate's permission, perhaps I can speak on my own behalf," Rukh said, stepping forward and taking the lectern from his nanna.

Nacket agreed with a brief nod.

Rukh took a moment to clear his throat before recounting the events he had experienced over the past four months. He started with the sudden destruction of the caravan in the hills directly north of the Hunters Flats. When he described his suspicions regarding the caravan master, Jared Randall, and his possible affiliation with the Sil Lor Kum, the room exploded into shouted questions. It took Fol Nacket several minutes to restore order.

"Explain yourself," the Cherid Magistrate said, steel in his voice. The foppish, self-important persona he usually demonstrated was completely absent.

Rukh described the last moments of the caravan and Randall's strange behavior.

Krain Linshok snorted. "And because a Rahail grew fearful, you would besmirch his name and legacy with such a vile allegation?"

416

"The Chims knew where we were," Rukh said. "We were surrounded before our scouts could warn us. Someone betrayed us. And the final words Randall spoke…it makes sense."

Magistrate Drent grunted, disbelief evident on his face. "I think you're jumping at shadows. I would have thought you had better sense."

Rukh ignored the insult. It wasn't worth his time to argue the point. There were still more important details to relate.

"You said four of you survived," Magistrate Drent continue. "Where are the other three?"

Rukh felt his throat momentarily tighten. He still hadn't mourned for Keemo and Brand, and after this meeting, he promised himself he would find the time. "Two of them are dead," he answered. "I don't know about the third."

It took hours to relay everything he had witnessed after the caravan's destruction. Every few sentences, one of the Magistrates would interrupt, demanding clarification. They all wore expressions of stunned amazement when they heard his account of Suwraith Herself raging in the sky. All were troubled by the conversation he had held with the Baels and their claims of brotherhood to Humanity. The meeting dragged on, and the Magistrates began arguing loudly amongst themselves, discussing Rukh's actions and the events he had witnessed. There was still more to tell though, and Rukh had to shout to be heard.

"With all due respect, my account is not yet complete!" Rukh yelled.

The Magistrates all stared at him with varying aspects of annoyance, but at least they had ceased their loud arguments. They settled into a restless quiet with muttered words still buzzing about now and then as they gazed at him with impatience. They had a lot of decisions to make.

"Go on," Magistrate Nacket said.

"She…" he pointed to Jessira "…represents maybe more of a challenge to who we are than anything else I've told you," Rukh said. He gestured, and Jessira unwrapped her shawl. Her appearance was like lightning in the room, stunning everyone into echoing silence. The Magistrates instantly knew what she was and what Rukh had meant when they saw her features. They listened, most with mingled expressions of fear and loathing, as they learned of the existence of an entire city of ghrinas, hidden and removed from the rest of Humanity.

Only Gren Vos appeared unphased by Jessira's presence. The old Magistrate studied her with keen interest. "She looks like a young woman, pretty if she weren't so emaciated and worn-out," the Shiyen Magistrate said into the silence.

"It is repugnant," Magistrate Drent said with feeling.

Rukh stiffened, his mouth forming a thin line of anger. He was tired of the dehumanizing attacks aimed at Jessira. *They* were what was repugnant. He could only imagine what Jessira thought of them.

"There is more, isn't there?" Fol Nacket asked, before Rukh or Jessira could respond to Magistrate Drent.

Rukh nodded. He described the attack of the Shylows, the death of Keemo and Brand, the separation from Farn, and the long march back to Ashoka, including the meeting with Aia.

"Rukh Shektan, you have undone us," Drent said. The Duriah had his head bowed, and he appeared to be trembling. "Our way of life is changed forever."

"He has saved us," Magistrate Martel said, her liquid voice soaring. "Change is part of life. We Murans know this better than any. We see it every day in our farms and our fields."

"This…tale," Linshok said. "Can you prove it?"

"Am I not proof enough?" Jessira asked, stepping forward and speaking for the first time.

Vos smiled thinly. "She has you there."

"He brought us warning of what we face," Magistrate Belt said. "Suwraith is sane."

"Worse, we face three Plagues. Devesh save us," Jone Drent said. "We are lost." He looked to Krain Linshok for confirmation.

The Kumma Magistrate looked unhappy and worried. "The battle will be bloody and hard," he said grimly.

"First, Li-Choke isn't sure how sane the Queen truly is. And second, the battle next spring doesn't need to happen. Not if we strike first," Rukh said into the morbid silence left by Linshoks's words. "I know the location of their birthing caverns." That got their attention. "The SarpanKum told me where it is and even described the make up of the defending force of Chimeras." He related everything Li-Dirge had told him that night before Suwraith had exterminated the Baels. "Based on what he said, I think a combined force of fifteen hundred-to-two thousand Kummas along with five hundred Murans and Rahails should be able to get there undetected and get the job done. We can kill every last one of their breeders and set the Queen back for decades. She won't have the three Plagues she wants."

"You believe this Li-Dirge enough to risk our warriors in such a way?" Linshok asked.

Rukh considered how best to answer the Kumma Magistrate. It wouldn't do to appear over-eager or trusting. "I don't like the Baels," he began. "I hate what they've done to us, but I've thought a lot about what Li-Dirge told me. Many of us have studied the military histories before Hammer's fall and how the Fan Lor Kum has fought ever since. We've all noticed their incompetence, but we never knew why it happened. Now, I think we do. Prior to Hammer, Humanity had seemed headed straight for extinction, but afterward...it's the only explanation that makes sense. I believe Li-Dirge when he said the Baels worked to protect us as best they could. And I believe Li-Choke, the Bael we saved. The Levner confirmed the words of his SarpanKum."

"You have given us much to think about, Rukh Shektan," Magistrate Nacket said. "It is time you three departed so the Magisterium may discuss how best Ashoka can deal with these...crises."

Rukh didn't miss the plural. By crises, Nacket wasn't only talking about the three Plagues possibly heading to Ashoka next spring. He was also talking about the Baels, but what he was especially referring to was the existence of the ghrinas, the OutCastes surviving and thriving in the vast Wildness.

Rukh and Nanna bowed as they prepared to exit. Jessira did not, and Rukh couldn't blame her. She hadn't missed the looks of loathing thrown her way or the words spoken by Magistrate Drent.

"And cover yourself," Magistrate Linshok said in a waspish tone to Jessira as she was about to turn and leave. "Your appearance will cause a riot."

Rukh heard her mutter in stifled irritation, but she did as she was ordered. He wanted to offer her support, but he didn't think doing so in public would go over very well.

They walked back in silence to the Seat of House Shektan and waited on the decision of the Magisterium.

It came quickly enough. Later in the afternoon, word arrived in the form of a specially printed bulletin, freely distributed at every major boulevard. It described the recent findings of the Magisterium. Everything Rukh had told them was included; the possibility of the Sil Lor Kum, the claims made by the Baels, Suwraith's presence, the Plagues, the OutCastes, the Shylows...all of it was explained in full detail.

The news set the city afire as people from all walks of life argued over what it meant for Ashoka. For the Kumma Houses, though, the most important detail was the last one: a strike against the Chimera breeding grounds was being planned. Volunteers were needed, and every able-bodied Kumma warrior answered the call, almost twenty thousand in all.

The only discordant notes as far as Rukh was concerned were twofold. First, the Magisterium was only willing to approve fifteen hundred Kummas and five hundred Murans and Rahails rather than the higher number he thought might be needed. And second, according to the bulletin, the man chosen to lead the expedition was Marshal Ruenip Tanhue of House Redwine, close ally and friend to Hal'El Wrestiva, father to Suge Wrestiva.

———•———

The Council of Rule, the highest body of the Sil Lor Kum gathered once again, as was their custom, in a non-descript room in the back of a non-descript place of business. Their meetings were never held in the same place twice in a row. One could never be too careful. This time they convened in the back of a tailor's shop, owned by an unskilled fool who had chosen to serve the Sil Lor Kum rather than face indentured servitude given his inability to sew a straight line.

The room was unremarkable, which was just how the Sil Lor Kum liked things. It contained a single, rectangular worktable. It was sturdy, and only an hour ago had been piled high with bolts of fabric and work orders, which the tailor farmed out to others. Above the table hung a series of firefly lanterns, and had they all been lit, the room would have been bright. However, this was a meeting of the Council of Rule, and their work required darkness. As a result, the lanterns were kept dim.

The SuDin studied the other members of the Council. They were all still here, in Ashoka, although all had their exits planned from the city. After all, none had forgotten Suwraith's promise as given to the SuDin in his dreams. She was coming. The Shektan whelp had simply confirmed it, and now the whole city knew.

Varesea tilted her head in slight acknowledgment when she caught his eye. He couldn't get enough of the woman. He caught himself dreaming of a night when he could cradle her in his arms as they fell asleep next to one another.

A foolish and impossible fantasy.

"Why have you called this meeting?" Pera Obbe, the pain-in-the-backside representing Caste Duriah demanded in her nasally whine. "Ashoka knows of the Sil Lor Kum. We should be cautious."

"Calm yourself," the SuDin said, speaking as condescendingly as possible, certain it would infuriate the arrogant Duriah. He hid a smile when he saw her stiffen in anger. "They merely know we exist. They do not know *who* we are."

"But now they will search for us," Obbe complained.

"They've known of our existence for the past two months," the SuDin replied. "Several Houses have inquired into the two sacrifices we've made, trying to ascertain how such deaths could have happened. The Shiyens are investigating as well."

Pera Obbe appeared appalled.

"And you saw fit to keep this to yourself?" Varesea demanded in her best hectoring tone.

The SuDin repressed a smile. The tenor of her accusation was strictly for the benefit of the other Councilors.

"There was nothing to tell," the SuDin replied. "I only know inquiries have been made by members of certain Houses regarding the two murders. Nothing more. It seemed unnecessary to reveal such vague information."

"And they have learned what exactly?" Yuthero Gaste, the physician of Caste Shiyen asked.

His question earned an exasperated exhalation. "I am not privy to what they know. They don't see fit to keep me abreast of their secret discussions," the SuDin replied. "But had we been found out, we would already be food for the crows."

"And what does the Queen have to say?" Mesa Reed, the Cherid asked in her languid manner. "Surely She has questioned our own loyalty given the betrayal by the Baels." Her drooping bodice allowed everyone a full view of her bosom.

Moke Urn, the Sentya, licked his lips and leaned forward, the desperate lust obvious on his face.

The SuDin watched Urn's reaction in amusement as he considered how best to answer Reed's question. "First, we do not know if the Baels have betrayed our Mistress. We only have the word of a Shektan brat…"

"And an OutCaste," Ular Sathin, the quiet, elderly Muran murmured.

The SuDin nodded acknowledgment. "And an OutCaste abomination," he added. "But in my estimation it is not enough to decide what truly happened to the Shektan or what he saw in the Wildness." He laughed. "Some of his tales, such as the one of the mind-speaking Shylow…it is utter folly. It is madness I tell you."

"Madness, eh? Do you then mock our Queen?" the piggish Pera Obbe challenged.

The SuDin openly rolled his eyes. "Only a fool would think so," he answered. Again, Obbe tensed with anger. The woman really needed to learn to control her temper if she ever wished to challenge the SuDin for his position. "Regardless, in answer to the Cherid's original question, the Queen has not yet made Her will known to me." In fact, it had been weeks since the Queen had visited his dreams, but there was no reason for the Council to know that. It would set them clucking like panicked hens. "But She was clear in Her most recent commands."

"Clear?" Varesea asked. "I don't believe I have ever heard Her described like that."

"She was *most* clear. Lucid, in fact."

"So Rukh Shektan wasn't mistaken. She is sane," Moke Urn said, the visible part of his face growing pale. "That is not good news."

"She was nothing of the sort," the SuDin said. "She was simply less insane." And it was true. Weeks ago, when the Queen had visited his dreams, She had been almost coherent, but the SuDin purposefully left vague his impression of the Queen's state of mind. It would leave the rest of the Council off balance as they tried to guess how best to plan for a somewhat less insane Suwraith,

"What did She command?" Varesea asked.

The SuDin glanced at her. "It is Her will that we do nothing for now. We are to await Her word."

"And the Knife?" Obbe asked. "Other than killing in a gruesome and spectacular fashion, have you been able to divine its purpose?"

"Of course," the SuDin announced. "It kills, and in doing so, it drains the victim's entire *Jivatma*, and I think it somehow channels it down into the crevices of the Oasis, eating at it like an acid." It was an utter fabrication but had the others learned the Knife channeled that stolen *Jivatma* directly into the murderer, they would have demanded use of the Knife themselves. It would vastly increase the risk of exposure for all of them, but the greedy fools wouldn't have cared. Their personal ambition was their true lodestar, whereas the SuDin did what he did for Ashoka. There might come a time when it was his strength and will alone that sheltered the city when the Sorrow Bringer came for them.

"Then is it wise for you to ever use it again?" Gaste asked. "If the Oasis crumbles before we are prepared to flee, the Queen might kill us all where we stand, especially if She is sane. She will think we secretly betray Her at every turn even as Her own Baels apparently have."

"She will not kill us," the SuDin said. "At least not all of us. We know the stories of the Sil Lor Kum from other cities. Men and women who escaped the destruction of their homes, washed ashore in a new place with their wealth intact. We will be fine. The Queen will honor Her compact with us."

"I hope you are right," Mesa Reed said with a sigh.

"There is one other thing," the SuDin said. "The Queen did demand I choose one last victim. I was loathe to fulfill her wishes until we convened, but now since all of you know, I feel compelled to carry out Her instructions."

"Perhaps this time you should choose a means by which the body cannot be found," Yuthero Gaste suggested.

"Do you have an idea?" Varesea asked.

Gaste nodded. "Burn it."

The SuDin smiled. "A splendid idea," he replied, knowing he would do no such thing. He enjoyed the fear the murders inspired. It was foolish, but as he'd once told Varesea, he didn't see a reason to deny himself of life's pleasures.

There were a few more items of business to address before the meeting was adjourned and the Council dispersed.

———•●•———

Several hours later, the SuDin stroked Varesea's bare back as she lay on her stomach. His hand drifted lower...

With an affectionate chuckle, she trapped his hand. "You are insatiable," she said, rolling to face him. She kissed his mouth but pulled back as his arms moved to enclose her. "But I am not as lusty as you seem to be."

"You can be," he said, his heart suddenly tripping faster. Should he tell her the truth about the Knife?

She frowned, clearly puzzled. "What do you mean?"

He changed his mind. "It's nothing."

She sat up, and the blanket slipped down. He drank in the sight of her naked breasts and bent his face toward them, but she lifted his chin, forcing him to look her in the eyes. "What is it you aren't telling me?" she asked. She eyed him as he remained mute. "You think I haven't noticed. Nowadays, you're as lusty as a young bull, and you don't limp like you used to."

She sat up further, and the blanket pooled at her waist.

The SuDin felt a stirring at the sight of her body. There were women far lovelier than Varesea that he could have chosen as a lover, but he wanted none of them. He only wanted *her*. With an almost painful start, he realized he loved her. He loved Varesea. In that singular moment of awareness, the SuDin made a decision: Varesea needed to know the truth. "The Knife drains *Jivatma*, just as I told the Council, but it does not send it against the Oasis. It transfers it to the wielder," he explained. "It is why I don't limp so much, and why I am able to…" he paused, a sly grin on his face, "…perform for you so frequently. And since there is a final victim to be killed, you can be the one who kills him. You can become like me."

"Him? You have chosen the next sacrifice?"

"Your husband. I have seen the bruises on your arms and stomach, and I know you didn't fall down some stairs or run into furniture."

She sighed, covering herself with the thin blanket, her arms folded. "He knows I share my bed with another. It infuriates him."

"Only your bed?" the SuDin asked, praying she would say something more, something to give him hope.

She did not. Instead, she looked him in the eyes and smiled sadly. "What do you think we are to one another?" she asked. "What do you think we can ever be?"

"I know what you are to me."

"And can we be together after my husband dies?" she gently scoffed.

"We already are in all the ways that matter," the SuDin said.

"You are a hopeless romantic, my SuDin," she replied, pulling him down to kiss her.

H is wife often chided Dar'El, saying he worried too much about the future and didn't pay enough attention to the moment. As in so many other things, she was right, but Dar'El didn't know any other way to live his life. He *had* to plan for the worst so when it didn't come to pass, everything that came after was a bright, happy surprise. And if disaster *did* occur, then he and those he loved would have been prepared. Right now, what had him worried was his son's future, specifically, Rukh's. The boy's first Trial had been extraordinary in ways no one could have predicted. Dar'El shook his head in disbelief. Words couldn't describe how eventful it had been. To experience so much so quickly...even a lifetime would seem too short for all Rukh had seen and accomplished.

But some of his accomplishments were dangerous, especially for the boy's future.

His ability to Blend and Heal, for instance. Dar'El wasn't ashamed of Rukh's new Talents, nor did he think of his son as a naaja, as Tainted. He would never feel that way about any of his children. Nevertheless, others did and would. Rector Bryce, for example. The Watcher would probably share his knowledge of Rukh's abilities with those who did not have Rukh's best interest at heart. His son might very well be found Unworthy because of his Talents.

Dar'El had long ago learned to gauge the currents and eddies of the Chamber of Lords. Amongst the 'Els of the older Houses, there was a growing sentiment to humble House Shektan. Dar'El's House had grown too powerful, too quickly. That jealousy had only grown more potent, gaining steady traction since the death of Suge Wrestiva and his father's humiliation at Dar'El's hands. What better way to punish House Shektan then by casting down their most visible, successful member. If the Chamber learned of Rukh's abilities, Dar'El felt certain, his eldest son would face ruin. And even if he avoided banishment, his life here would become unbearable. Rukh would be shunned and despised. He would never be allowed to marry and start a family. What was the point of such a miserable, stunted life?

So Dar'El worried. He couldn't see an easy path for Rukh's happiness, at least not here in Ashoka. But he and Satha both recognized the strong bond between their son and the OutCaste woman, Jessira. The two young people didn't share love, not yet anyway, but they did have a deep trust and friendship. If Rukh were found Unworthy, or his life here in Ashoka became a ruined wreck, then what about Stronghold? They would take him in. Dar'El had already confirmed it from Jessira.

Rukh would hate it, which is why he couldn't know of Dar'El's plans for him – plans to keep him safe and give him a chance at happiness.

Dar'El sighed. He hated manipulating others, but it was a skill he found came to him as easily as a bird took to flight.

He was walking back to his study, but he paused at the open, windowed doors leading out from the sunroom. He smiled. A perfect scenario could play out even now.

Rukh was alone in the courtyard out back, playing his mandolin. He sat upon a small bench with his back to Dar'El. As with all things outdoors, his wife had turned this area into a flower garden. It was her passion, and in another life she would have been a Muran. She had chosen ligustrum bushes to form a tall hedge that bordered the courtyard, and then shaped the flowerbeds with a winding path of chipped bricks. An arched passage opposite to where Dar'El stood led out into the rest of the grounds. Right now, some of the flowers – lilies – were in bloom with vibrant colors of bright orange, red, and purple. However, Dar'El's favorite plants were the large gardenias flanking the bench upon which Rukh sat. He'd always found their floral fragrance intoxicating, which was why Satha always wove them through her hair.

He smiled in remembrance, listening as Rukh played. His son obviously didn't have the sublime skill of a Sentya master, or even the average ability of someone like Jaresh, but his heart was in it. For a Kumma, he was actually quite good. The boy had always loved music, and Dar'El would have been just as proud if his son somehow ended up earning his living through the mandolin instead of the sword. He felt the same way about Bree and her fascination with medicine, or Jaresh and his love of history. Of his children, it seemed Jaresh would be the only one who would have a chance to follow his dream. For Bree and Rukh, those choices could never be, not so long as the Castes existed.

Perhaps Jessira's arrival and the presence of the OutCastes could allow Dar'El to achieve his long sought after impossible dream: the end of the Castes. It was a dream only Satha knew or shared.

From a purely pragmatic standpoint, it made sense. Dar'El imagined a Kumma warrior with the Talents of all the other Castes; not just able to Blend and Heal as Rukh could, but also with the ability to Cohese like a Duriah, achieve Lucency like a Sentya, and inspire and lead like a Cherid. Such a warrior would be all but undefeatable.

And even from a moral standpoint, it made sense. The words Jessira had spoken, the quote taken from *The Book of All Souls*: *Across the world, the Lord stretched forth His hand and caused Life. And those whom he gave understanding, He named as brothers and sisters.* It was a passage Dar'El had long considered, one that had resonated with him since he had first read it decades earlier.

Some philosophers claimed Humanity to be the seven spokes of an immeasurably large wheel, with each spoke representing a single Caste. But it was a metaphor Dar'El never understood. A wheel was a dead thing. It only moved if someone or something acted upon it. It was too passive to represent the vibrancy of Humanity.

Instead, Dar'El thought of Humanity as a single, great tree with seven majestic branches, alive and growing. It was hardy enough to survive even the strongest of storms. And was it not true that in most every type of tree, the limbs and leaves intermingled throughout the canopy such that from a distance, a person could rarely tell the main branch from which an individual leaf drew its sustenance? For Dar'El, Humanity was one family. It should act like one.

"It's good to hear you playing," Dar'El said as Rukh finished his song.

His son turned, a look of surprise on his face. "I didn't know you were there."

Dar'El smiled and took a seat next to Rukh on the bench. "You seemed so caught up in the music. I hated to interrupt you by announcing my presence."

Rukh cradled his mandolin. "It's something I missed when I was out in the Wildness," he said, a wistful longing in his voice.

"But since you can Blend, there's no reason you can't take your mandolin with you the next time you leave Ashoka. You can hide the sound of the music yourself and play to your heart's content."

Rukh grimaced. "I'd rather no one else know what I can do."

"You think it would make things hard on you? The other warriors would handle it badly?"

"Yes."

Dar'El nodded understanding even as he tried to figure out how to bring up the real reason he wanted to talk to Rukh in private. He chose the direct method. "I imagine your friend, Jessira, probably feels the same way," he said. "You know she wears a scarf over her face whenever she leaves the House Seat?"

Rukh nodded. He looked a bit guilty.

"It's a sad indictment of our culture, don't you think?" Dar'El asked.

"Yes it is."

"Can I ask you a question?" Dar'El didn't wait for Rukh's answer. "Why do you act ashamed of her?"

Rukh startled, looking uncomfortable. "Is it so obvious?"

"I've noticed. Amma's noticed. And Jessira is a bright, young woman. I'm sure she's noticed as well."

Rukh frowned sadly as he looked away. "I'm not ashamed of her," he began. "Jessira is a wonderful person, but it's just…" he shrugged. "I'm afraid."

"Afraid?" Dar'El's brows furrowed in confusion. "What are you afraid of?"

"Everything. I'm afraid for my future, my hopes, my dreams…all of it," Rukh answered. "I'm worried about my reputation and how it will suffer if I'm known to be too friendly with her. Especially if my new Talents also become common knowledge."

"Then you aren't a friend at all," Dar'El said. He was pleased to see his son flinch, but he was also disappointed in the boy. Dar'El couldn't tolerate cowardice.

"I'm sure she hasn't missed my presence," Rukh replied, sounding as if he was trying to convince himself. He was wrong, and he knew it, even if he wasn't ready to admit it yet.

Dar'El took a deep breath. Now came the manipulation. "A true friend would stand with her," he said.

"Is that what you would do?"

"It isn't for me to say," Dar'El replied. "This is your life, not mine. You have to find your own warrior's path."

"Then what would you *advise* me to do?" Rukh asked, looking slightly annoyed.

Good. He would be too focused on his irritation to see the true purpose of Dar'El's words.

"Friendship is a kind of love, and none of us should turn away from love. So you need to ask yourself this simple question: is Jessira your friend?" Dar'El answered, couching his words as carefully as possible, willing Rukh to take the correct lesson from them. "Think on it," he said, slapping Rukh's knee as he stood and went back into the house.

As he left, Dar'El was both pleased and sad at the same time. He hadn't missed his son's countenance. Rukh had worn a troubled expression. It was another manipulation complete, but it was one that left Dar'El wanting to cry. He would see his son safe, even if it meant he would never see him again. The boy would do what was needed.

Now if only his daughter would as well.

———— ● ————

The Martyr's Plaza was every bit as beautiful as Rukh had claimed it would be. There were the glistening, gray paving stones with flecks of crystals sparkling under the warm noonday sun; the nine fountains splashing water high into the air, the droplets glittering like diamonds; and the green hills of Ashoka, upon which elegant homes and wide boulevards subtly blended with the scenery rather than dominated it. Watching over the Plaza were the bronzed statues – turned green with time – of great men and women of the city's past. Especially gilded Union Fountain with Hume and all the heroes watching with proud attention over what they had wrought while happy, carefree children, ran and laughed under the warm gazes of their loving parents. Martyr's Plaza was a vibrant place of history and hope, much like the city itself.

Ashoka was as beautiful, warm, and safe a place as Jessira could have ever imagined. It was far lovelier than Stronghold. Her home was carved into a mountain fastness, in deep, dark caverns where even the Queen could hopefully not see or hear so well. Her home was quiet and utilitarian with everything designed for defense; they lacked the protective embrace of an Oasis and had no choice but to focus all their energies on making their city as impenetrable as possible. Safety was their only concern, not poetry or music or the oddity of theater. In Stronghold, the gentler arts had been left to lie fallow.

She sighed. But she wished it could be otherwise.

It had been three days since she had come to Ashoka and every day had been a revelation. The Purebloods had created a city of grace and loveliness but also of stern power, made manifest by the mighty Inner and Outer Walls and defended by the highly trained, highly disciplined army. She wondered if Ashoka's brilliance was cultural. The people here had decided to create a place where beauty and fine arts could thrive, and in order to protect their heritage, those born to the sword had taken it to be their holy duty to safeguard this home their forefathers had struggled so mightily to build. The other Castes worked just as faithfully to keep it beautiful and thriving.

Her own people could learn much from the Ashokans. In fact, they could learn from all of the Castes, but would the Purebloods share their learning? She didn't think so. Not with a city full of ghrinas.

"Are you ready to go?" Rukh asked, ending her reverie.

Jessira nodded. "I'm more than ready," she said, filled by an abrupt despondency.

"Are you alright?" he asked, noticing her sadness.

She grimaced, not wanting his sympathy. In the days since they'd arrived, he'd all but ignored her. She knew he was busy, having been chosen for the strike force aimed at the Chimera breeding caverns. The expeditionary legion was to be ready in ten days, a monumental undertaking, and one the entire city had thrown itself into with utter abandon. They might even make their departure date. So, yes, Rukh was busy, but why then, did he snub her even in the privacy of his home? It was obvious: he was embarrassed by his association with her. Their relationship was a stain lingering about him like a rotten stench – a description she had heard once while hidden in the anonymity of her cloak and scarf.

As a result, her days had generally been spent alone, wandering the city, wishing her shoulder would heal so she could go home.

However, for some reason, this morning Rukh had taken it upon himself to spend time with her. He had even offered to show her some of Ashoka's sights. It might have been meant as an apology for his poor treatment of her, but she wasn't in a generous mood. If he wanted to say he was sorry, he would have to say the words. She wouldn't make it easy on him simply to assuage his guilt.

"I'm fine," she said. "I'd like to go back now."

"Is it your shoulder?" he asked. "We can take a rickshaw if you want. You don't have to walk."

"I don't need a rickshaw," she said. "I can walk. The women of Stronghold don't require coddling."

Rukh remained quiet, and they made their way back toward the House Shektan Seat. They travelled along Bellary Road. Here the boulevard was wide and straight with bookstores, cafes, and restaurants along its length. In the near distance was the gloriously domed Magisterium and the inaptly named Plaza of Toll and Toil – on the occasions Jessira had been to the Plaza, entry had always been free and she had never seen anyone toiling. On they walked, nearing the border of Fragrance Wall, and large houses and manors with lush gardens began to appear. Summer blooms of jasmine and honeysuckle wreathed gatehouses in their green growth while their lovely aroma drifted on the breeze.

It would have been a nice, relaxing excursion, but throughout their walk, people had avoided both of them, and Jessira knew why. By now, her story was well known, and all knew the woman who walked Ashoka with her face covered was the ghrina, the OutCaste. She heard the muttered curses of the Purebloods as they crossed the street, shunning her. Her nostrils flared in anger. Jackholes.

Devesh help her, but she couldn't wait to leave this place. Ashoka confused her senses and her mind. The city left her loving and longing for its beauty and yet unable to fathom its people. How could a culture produce such grace and loveliness and be so hard-hearted to those whose only sin was to be born different. The Shiyen physician, the same old woman who had first stitched her up, was one of the few who could bear Jessira's presence without making an obvious show of her discomfort or disgust. It left her despondent.

Worse, the same physician also said it would take Jessira another two weeks to heal before she would be ready to go home. It was a frustratingly long wait, but at least Rukh's nanna had promised to provision her so she could make the journey home without too much hardship. He had even offered her a horse, which was a kind gesture, even if it had been made because he felt duty-bound to do so.

She glanced at Rukh and shook her head in disappointment. How could he be so great a coward in his own home? Or had he always secretly despised her, like the rest of his brethren?

An ugly voice inside spoke to her. *You know the truth. Admit it now. The Purebloods will never accept you.*

She knew the voice was right.

"I'm sorry," Rukh said, breaking the silence.

She was so lost in thought, she almost didn't hear him. "You're sorry," she repeated. "About what exactly?"

"For how I've behaved around you," he said, stopping to turn to face her. "For how I've treated you. I've...I've been a coward, and for that I am sorry. I can't even begin to imagine how hard this must all be for you, and then to have your only friend pretend like you don't exist. You deserve so much better, and I gave you so much less."

Some of Jessira's cold anger thawed. "*Am* I a friend?" she asked.

"Yes," he said. "A good friend."

"Then why have you treated me like this?" she cried, all the hurt, loneliness, and anger of the past three days coming out. "You're the only person I can trust here, the only one I thought might treat me like a real person."

"I don't know," he said. "I was scared, I guess. I'm scared of this coming expedition. I'm scared of who I've become and how I've changed. I'm scared of banishment if anyone learns what I can do, and I'm scared what people will think if they see me with you."

Jessira studied his face, seeing the confusion and unhappiness in his eyes. At that moment she felt very little sympathy for him. "You were right the first time. You are a coward."

He flinched as if she'd slapped him. He looked angry for a moment before he took a deep breath and seemed to set it aside. "Is there anything I can do or say to help you forgive me?" he asked.

She smirked. "Walk down this street with me hand-in-hand." She laughed in derision when she saw his comically aghast expression. "I wouldn't be so cruel," she said.

"Is there anything else?"

She considered. "I don't care how you behave in public, but in your home, act like I'm there. Talk to me and don't pretend I don't exist."

"I can do that," Rukh said with a nod, looking abashed and relieved at the same time.

"I'll hold you to it."

They began walking again, and after a moment of quiet, he looked at her. "How brave are you?"

"Braver than you."

"Brave enough to take off your scarf and walk uncovered in public?"

"Are you brave enough to walk next to a ghrina?"

"I can be," he said. He gently lifted the scarf from her face.

436

She smiled, feeling a warm breeze play on her hair. "You realize most Purebloods want to stone me, and they probably won't be too good with their aim. You'll likely get your share of rocks, too."

Rukh shrugged. "Let them try. I can take them. I'm the Hume Champion, you know." He grinned.

She rolled her eyes. "How could I forget?"

As they continued back to Jubilee Hills, she found she was wrong: no one tried to stone her. People still ran across the street when they noticed her, but many also glanced back in fascination, especially the men, some of whom might have even worn appreciative looks before catching her glance and hastily looking away.

Men.

"No one else treats you like a real person?" Rukh asked as they walked along a relatively quiet side street on the way to House Shektan. "Not even my sister or Mira?"

Jessira chuckled low. "Mira is civil, and Bree is polite, but neither is exactly friendly and neither will talk to me any longer than is absolutely necessary. In comparison, your nanna and those two old men of his, Garnet and Durmer, are warm and friendly, but they have no time for me either. They're too busy trying to save Ashoka."

"I promise I'll make this up to you," Rukh said.

"Don't make promises you can't and don't want to keep," Jessira warned. If he wanted to spend time with her, fine, but she didn't want his company if it was only because he felt sorry for her. She didn't need his sympathy, or the sympathy of any Pureblood.

"I want to."

"We'll see."

Rukh had no response, and soon, the seat of House Shektan came into view. Once inside, Rukh led her to his father's study. He always checked in with Dar'El as soon as he arrived home. While Rukh and his nanna spoke, Jessira perused the books lined along the shelves. At least Rector Bryce was rarely at the House seat anymore. His outburst on the morning after her arrival had been noted and judged unacceptable by Dar'El. As a result, Rector was no longer trusted as much. Or so Rukh said.

Minutes after their arrival, Jaresh burst in. "There's been a third murder," he exclaimed.

The Withering Knife.

"Send for Mira," Dar'El ordered. "Have her meet us there." Further orders were given, and Dar'El and Rukh were soon outside, quickly making their way down the drive.

Jessira accompanied them, face bare to the world. She had nothing better to do. At Rukh's questioning glance, she lifted an eyebrow in challenge, daring him to send her back. He shrugged.

"If you don't mind, I don't mind," Dar'El murmured, looking straight ahead. "But can she not cover her face?"

"*She* can but chooses not to," Jessira said, answering for herself.

Dar'El gave the two of them an inscrutable stare.

Rukh smiled in response. "You always told me never to pick a fight you can't win," he said. "Especially with a woman."

Dar'El flashed an answering smile. "At least you remembered my most important lesson."

Shortly before their arrival at East Vineyard Steep, home mostly to Sentyas and some Rahails, and the site of the third murder, Mira caught up with them.

East Vineyard Steep was an older part of Ashoka. The buildings there hadn't been refurbished in many years. They were a bit run down, in fact. The Sentyas were quite competent with both their own and other people's money, but they were also a tight-fisted, stingy Caste. Where others saw a somewhat drab and dreary area, the Sentyas saw a place that was practical and functioned well enough to suit their purposes. They saw no reason to spend currency to pretty up the buildings even if a few of them looked to be on the edge of falling down.

The City Watch had already cordoned off the area in question. Once again, the murder had taken place in an alley, this one bordered by several buildings that were obviously better maintained than most of the ones around them.

Rector Bryce had already arrived, and Jessira frowned. Wonderful.

He saw them and walked over, a look of disgust flashing across his face when he caught sight of her. He faced Dar'El, positioning himself so he wouldn't have to look directly at her. He began talking without preamble. "The victim was a Rahail Investigator by the name of Slathtril Apter. His wife found him this morning when she couldn't find him in the house. She's the woman screaming over there."

"What is an Investigator?" Jessira asked Rukh.

"The Rahails are the ones who maintain the Oasis. Their society is dictated by their work. The Investigators are the ones who inspect the work of other Rahails, making sure it's up to the expected standards. I'm told they can be pretty cruel and petty about it, too. No one likes them much," Rukh whispered.

"Then there's going to be a long list of potential suspects," she reasoned.

"There were no witnesses, obviously," Rector finished.

"Where was he found?" Jaresh asked.

Rector pointed to a body, shrouded in what looked like someone's cloak.

"We need to take a closer look," Dar'El said.

At a nod from Rector, the Watch let them through the barricades, even Jessira, although a few made the sign against evil as she passed.

Rukh bent low and uncovered the body, eliciting more cries of anguish from the woman Rector had pointed out as the wife. "Perhaps someone can see to her," Rukh suggested.

Dar'El glanced at Rector, who signed to one of his men to remove the wailing woman from the scene.

Jaresh and Dar'El bent to examine the corpse, while Rukh walked the alley, studying the ground, looking at the blood splatter and a few footprints. Jessira walked with him, wondering what he was looking for. She noticed something herself and bent closer. Bloody fingerprints left as streaks along the wall. She'd seen plenty of death, killing Chimeras when necessary over the course of her career as a scout, but the image of the bloody finger stains and what they represented…it was an unsettling image.

They returned to the others.

"Anything?" Dar'El asked.

"Lots of things," Rukh replied. "There were two killers, a man and a woman."

"I noticed that as well," Rector said.

"The man attacked first, and as Investigator Apter fled, he was hamstrung. It was a clean and quick strike, made within two strides. Our killer is skilled, and the limp you mentioned is hardly in evidence. It was the woman who killed the Investigator, though."

Dar'El frowned. "It doesn't make sense," he said. "Why go through the trouble? Why two of them?" He shook his head in frustration. "Anything else?"

"At the mouth of the alley, the killers stood still, as if they were waiting, and the Investigator went to them. In fact, he seemed to stop and stand no more than three feet from them."

"They knew him," Jessira guessed with sudden insight. "And he knew them. That's why he walked toward them. He wasn't afraid."

"If that's true, then the killers wanted the Investigator to know who they were," Mira said. "It's like they must have hated him or something."

"Are you saying it was personal?" Rector asked.

Mira shrugged. "I don't know. We're supposing quite a lot based on some footprints in the dirt."

"But look at all the cuts on the corpse. He was tortured first." Rector nodded. "I think Mira is right. They all knew one another."

Jessira saw the smile Jaresh shared with Mira. No one else seemed to notice.

"Why wouldn't anyone have heard him scream?" Jaresh asked.

"Because he had a canvas bag over his head," Dar'El said. "Look at that red band around his neck. It looks like a ligature mark."

"There is another thing," Rukh said. "The killer's movements – the man – the placement of his feet, and the angle of his strikes. There are only three Houses who train their warriors in such a way, and all are allied with one another: Houses Wrestiva, Bittermoon, and Sunflown."

"And all are on very unfriendly terms with our House," Jaresh said. "If we voice our suspicions, and we're wrong, it could cause a House war."

"It would be a disaster on so many fronts," Dar'El warned. "Civil discord amongst the Houses is the last thing we need if Suwraith plans on moving against Ashoka next spring." He sighed. "For now, we keep this quiet."

CHAPTER TWENTY-TWO
THE ART OF LEARNING

*Almost from the first, Hume taught us to appreciate the written word,
and we are grateful for his instruction. But of art, there is so much
more we wish we could have learned. We killed those who could have
instructed us, and perhaps that is our greatest regret.*

~From the journal of SarpanKum Li-Charn, AF 1754

Ashoka in the middle of summer was already hot, but it was not yet oppressive, especially with a cooling, stiff breeze blowing off the ocean to keep the city comfortable. These would be some of the final few weeks of temperate weather before summer's sultering heat hovered over the city like a miasma. Or so it had been explained to Jessira. As such, now would be a good time to take an early evening stroll, which is exactly what she was doing.

She walked in silence next to Rukh and Bree, but her mind wasn't focused upon the weather or the cool wind raising goosebumps on her skin. Instead, her thoughts were centered on the majesty she had just witnessed. Jessira had just been to her first play: *A Many Colored Shadow*. She hadn't wanted to go, but Rukh had been the one to ask her, saying he still felt guilty about how he had ignored her. When he learned Stronghold didn't have theater – her people didn't have time for such frivolity – he had insisted she come with him and Bree, telling her it was something she had to see at least once before leaving Ashoka. Given Rukh's impending departure in a few days for the Chimera breeding caverns, she had reluctantly agreed, certain she would find the experience dull and boring.

She had been more wrong than she could have ever imagined.

The play had been a revelation. Everything about it had touched her. The story, the music, the acting…all of it had been wondrous. From the moment the curtain had whispered open and for the following two hours, her heart had no longer been her own, and she had been happy to allow it. The play had figuratively transported her to a different place and time. She still had no idea how it had happened, nor did she want to know. It was part of the magic of theater, Rukh had explained. Afterward, she found herself replaying scene after scene, wanting to recapture and savor the emotions she had felt. There had been so many. It had been like a thick, hearty stew with many hidden flavors.

The play had begun simply enough: a social gathering where two young Kummas, Vare Kilan of House Listh and Ciliana Prien, daughter to the ruling 'El of her House, had shared a delightful afternoon with one another and soon after fell in love. But it was a love not meant to last for with the coming of his Trials, Vare was forced to leave his home and after his departure Ciliana was force to wed Kolth Renns, an older, ambitious member of her own House. Years passed in disappointment and grief for Ciliana's marriage proved to be cold and loveless. Nevertheless, she bore her husband three sons, her pride and joy. Fate, however, was to deal her further cruel blows, taking her two oldest in the Trials. Only her youngest child, Reva, survived his time in the Wildness.

Meanwhile Vare Kilan eventually made his way home, and when he did, it was to find the woman he had loved as a youth now married and with a family of her own. It was the way of the world, but it still pained Vare. He set aside his feelings and moved on with his own life, and in time, he wed as well. His wife, Shawl Kilan, was a woman he grew to love, although not with the passion he had shared with Ciliana. Vare and his wife had a daughter, a beautiful, happy girl named Calle, but it would be their only child. Several years after the birth of their child, Shawl died of an unexpected illness. Grief-stricken, it fell to Vare to raise the young girl on his own as he adamantly refused to ever marry again.

There came a time when Kolth Renns, Ciliana's husband, who bore a deep and abiding hatred for his wife's youthful lover, hatched a scheme, one meant to deceive Vare Kilan and leave him utterly ruined. The plan worked. Vare was rendered penniless with his only choice being to accept indentured servitude under Kolth Renns, and Renns would only absolve the debt if Vare – at an age when a Kumma should have lived out his days in peace – re-entered the Wildness for a final Trial.

Ironically, even as this was happening, Kolth Renns' son, Reva, met Calle Kilan during an afternoon social and the two young people fell in love. It was a love that did not sit well with Ciliana's husband, but he was powerless to do anything about it. Vare stayed in his city long enough to see his daughter married, and then he left home for the final time. With him went Ciliana. Over the decades that had passed, the two of them had never stopped loving one another, and so they left their city together, walking hand-in-hand in the early morning sunshine. They were never to be seen again.

Jessira had cried at the end of the play, and she wasn't ashamed to have done so. Bree had as well, and even Rukh had shed a few tears. For Jessira, *A Many Colored Shadow* had been like a summertime plunge into a shimmering pool of clear water. She was changed forever. It was truth made manifest on a stage, and she came to see the characters, not as Purebloods or OutCastes, but merely as people whose lives were marked by tragedy and pain, but ultimately, with love.

After the play, the three of them went to Masala Pull, one of Bree's favorite restaurants in the Semaphore Walk. It was a newer café and although it had only opened a few years ago, Bree already thought it served the finest fusion of Muran and Rahail cuisine to be found in Ashoka.

As they walked to the restaurant, Jessira realized she no longer received as many hostile stares as she once had only a few days earlier when she had first shed her scarf. The people of Ashoka must have become somewhat used to her presence. More often now, it seemed the glances thrown her way were curious rather than unfriendly. Of course, the looks given to Bree were more generally ones of approval and appreciation. Jessira smiled when several Kummas almost ran into a lamppost as they stared back at Rukh's sister.

Masala Pull proved to be warm and inviting with walls painted in a terra cotta wash. The ceiling was high and airy while a multitude of chandeliers with their firefly lamps provided plenty of light. The tabletops were made of brightly colored mosaic tiles arranged into various scenes of Ashokan life. The restaurant was already full with young, well-dressed couples and a few families, but luckily the three of them were able to be seated quickly. Delicious aromas filled the air, making Jessira's mouth water, and the food proved to be every bit as wonderful as it smelled.

The dinner tonight was cubed chunks of chicken in a spicy, buttery sauce served over a bed of rice and accompanied by a sweet, white wine. Jessira lost herself in the rich, flavorful meal. In Stronghold, food was just a fuel with taste a secondary consideration. It was nothing like this, or even what Cook Heltin provided at the Shektan House Seat on a daily basis. Delicious. Another aspect of Ashokan culture that Jessira admired: they had turned the simple act of cooking into an art.

She was so focused on her sumptuous meal that she failed to notice Rukh and Bree's open fascination as they watched her eat. Bree laughed and Jessira looked up from her food with a guilty start. "What?" she asked.

"I've just never seen anyone so in love with their food," Bree said.

"You made some…ah…interesting noises there," Rukh added. "A few matronly women were looking at you kind of funny."

"Be nice," Bree admonished as Jessira reddened in embarrassment. "No one looked over when you made those noises." She chuckled as Jessira reddened even further and glared ineffectually at the two of them.

Rukh grinned. "Don't be mad at us. We're just teasing…a little."

"Did I really, you know, make those kind of sounds?" Jessira asked, mortified.

"You didn't," Bree replied with a smile. "Ignore us, or at least Rukh. You should see him, or better yet, hear him when Cook Heltin makes sea bass tikka."

"I'm not that bad," Rukh protested.

"Yes. You are," Bree said. She made moaning noises.

Jessira burst out laughing. She was surprised by how much she was enjoying Bree's company. Until today, the two of them hadn't spent much time together. Bree was generally too busy or had other plans. But now, with the play and the early dinner afterwards, Jessira was finding Rukh's sister to be generous and…fun.

"Our last night in the Wildness, he made those exact same sounds when he ate some trout I had cooked."

Rukh laughed with them. "What can I say? I like fish."

"You can cook?" Bree asked, sounding surprised.

"Not like this," Jessira said, pointing to her plate, "but yes."

"I *might* be able to boil water, but don't ask for anything more," Bree said.

"So what did you think of the play?" Rukh asked, changing the topic.

Jessira took a moment to collect her thoughts. "I loved it. I never expected to, but how could I not? It was perfect and true."

Rukh grinned. "Didn't I say you'd like it?"

Jessira nodded. During the play, when Vare Kilan left Ciliana, she had wondered about something. She chewed her lower lip and glanced at Rukh, not sure how to phrase her question. "Was it..." she trailed off.

"Was it autobiographical?" Rukh asked, once more guessing what she was trying to ask. "No. But I did know someone like Vare Kilan." He gazed off into the distance and said no more.

"Who?" Jessira blurted out, realizing an instant too late that it might be a sensitive topic.

Rukh didn't answer, and a look of sorrow passed fleetingly across his face.

"It was Keemo," Bree said, speaking softly into the silence. Her eyes were wet with sudden tears.

Jessira wanted to melt into a puddle and crawl away. She felt terrible and apologized. "I didn't mean to bring up painful memories."

"I told you I'd grieve when I got back to Ashoka," Rukh reminded her.

"Keemo, Farn, and Rukh were all born within two months of each other. The three of them were raised together," Bree explained. "Keemo was from an allied House and Farn is our cousin. Our parents have been friends from back when they were our age."

"You were like brothers," Jessira guessed, speaking to Rukh.

"We were like brothers," he said softly.

"All of us were," Bree added. "Including Jaresh."

"I'm sorry," Jessira said.

"For what?" Rukh asked.

"For being so selfish after the Shylows attacked us. All I could think of was losing Lure. I never realized how much you were also hurting."

A sad half-smile stole over his face. "You have nothing to apologize for," he said. "Keemo would still have been dead. And I never thought you were being selfish."

"I could have made it easier on you…shown you some compassion," Jessira insisted. "Instead, all I saw was a Pureblood who wouldn't even shed a tear over a friend's death. I thought you were a monster, and I treated you like one."

"I think you know by now that I'm all too Human," Rukh said. "And it certainly wasn't easy having to tell Keemo's parents or Alia how he died. I cried plenty then."

"Alia?" Jessira asked.

"The woman Keemo loved," Bree answered.

Once more, Jessira remembered the play. She recalled Ciliana's grief after learning of the deaths of her two oldest sons. This was the knowledge Rukh had carried all the way home through their time in the Wildness. It was the message he knew he had to deliver, and he had never complained about it. He'd simply gone about his duty and kept her safe despite her frequent ingratitude. She silently cursed her behavior toward him. He had long since forgiven her, but it would take her far longer to forgive herself. Add in all the whining she'd done when he'd ignored her early on after their arrival in Ashoka, and she felt like an ungrateful prat. When had she become so selfish and demanding?

"What's wrong?" Rukh asked.

"I know you don't think so, but I still feel like I've wronged you. I judged you as a Kumma instead of a person. You deserve better."

"You mean OutCastes might be prejudiced against Purebloods?" Bree asked. "How ironic."

Jessira frowned, trying to find fault with the younger woman's logic, but the more she thought about it, the more she realized Bree was right. Jessira had been well-schooled in the bigotry her people felt toward Rukh's kind, and that bigotry had apparently taken firm root. She grimaced, finding it hard to accept a failing in herself and other OutCastes so similar to the one she hated in Purebloods. It was yet another reason to feel guilty.

Rukh looked her in the eyes, a sympathetic expression on his face. "It's not easy facing such an ugly truth about yourself. But maybe both our peoples need to grow some. Maybe we need to stop judging a person's worth based on their lineage but instead on who they are and what they've done."

"Blowhard," Bree murmured.

"Did you say something?" Rukh asked.

"I was just wondering when it was that you grew so wise, oh great Mahatma," Bree said in a falsely bright tone. She even batted her eyes and wore a rapt look of awe on her face as she gazed adoringly at her brother.

"I always have been," Rukh sniffed. "You just didn't and don't have the intellect to understand my stupendous wisdom."

Bree laughed. "Brother mine, I think you have things backwards between the two of us."

Jessira smiled as the tension broke.

They ate the rest of their meal without returning again to the topic of death or bigotry. Instead, they talked about *The Many Colored Shadow* and other plays Rukh and Bree loved. They even touched on music, literature, and history. Jessira already knew Stronghold had a very long road to travel before it could come close to approaching Ashoka's grandness in artistic accomplishments. Tonight had simply made her more aware of just how great that distance truly was.

Then came desert and all thoughts of bigotry, plays, and roads to travel left Jessira's mind. She drank a sweet, creamy, thick, luscious, and oh-so-heavenly concoction called hot cocoa. Jessira had never tasted anything so fine. When she finished, she was tempted to wipe her cup clean. She had to settle for licking her lips like a cat, finding every last delectable drop of cocoa.

"Well…I think we got our money's worth out of dinner tonight," Rukh said as he eyed her in bemused humor.

"I'll say," Bree agreed. "It's mesmerizing watching someone enjoy their food as much as you do," she said to Jessira.

"A woman has her needs," Jessira replied haughtily. "I just never realized good food was one of mine."

"Speaking of needs and desires, I'm supposed to have a report ready for Nanna by tomorrow," Bree said.

"Anything I can help with?" Rukh asked.

"Only if you can predict the price of hops and barley from Fearless compared to what we might get from Hanumun," Bree responded.

"Can't help you there," Rukh said.

"I didn't think so," Bree said as she stood up from the table. "I should get going if I want to have it done in time."

"Do you want us to walk you home?" Rukh asked.

"No. I'll be fine. You two stay. You should show her Dryad Park sometime before she leaves. Jessira's never been to the Adamantine Cliffs."

A flash of worry seemed to pass across Bree's face, so quickly that Jessira believed she must have imagined it. As she left the restaurant and headed home, Bree gave them a jaunty wave.

———●———

Soon after Bree's departure, Rukh and Jessira made to leave Masala Pull as well. They stopped to thank the owner, a slim, dignified Rahail, for their wonderful meals.

Jessira was especially complimentary about the hot cocoa. "That was without doubt the finest meal I've ever been fortunate enough to have," she said, her voice filled with enthusiasm.

Rukh wasn't sure if the owner actually heard any of her words. The man was too busy staring at Jessira in obvious fascination. It was an expression Rukh was growing used to seeing whenever Jessira came with him into the city. The eight days since Jessira had entered Ashoka weren't long enough to change the teachings and habits of a lifetime, and while most people still despised ghrinas and probably Jessira as well, there was also a sizeable minority who seemed entranced by the OutCaste woman. Looks of revulsion weren't as common as Rukh would have expected. And it certainly didn't hurt that Jessira had a confident, charismatic presence about her. She walked with the graceful movements of a trained warrior, so different from any other woman in Ashoka. Jessira was also beautiful in her own way, something Rukh had noticed on their first meeting. She wasn't as striking as Bree, but it didn't matter. There was an indefinable, compelling air to Jessira. People noticed, and Rukh wondered if Jessira even recognized half the admiring looks thrown her way when she walked down the street. He didn't think she did. She seemed oblivious to it all.

After they left Masala Pull, Rukh decided to take Bree's advice and lead Jessira to Dryad Park, an area fully as large as Semaphore Walk. It was surprising she had never seen it before. If Martyr's Plaza was Ashoka's heart, then Dryad Park was its soul. Centuries ago, the city's fathers had ordered its construction in a relatively empty part of Ashoka. It had been fashioned in a small valley and was surrounded on all sides by low-lying hills, except to the east where the two hundred foot sheer drop of the Adamantine Cliffs plunged straight into the Sickle Sea.

It was another short walk from the Semaphore to Dryad, and Rukh looked forward to seeing Jessira's expression when she saw the park. He guided her across Scythe Cut before leading her down a quiet residential drive of tall, stately townhouses, many with windows already lit, though it was only twilight. A median of grass and leafy elms split the road into two narrow lanes, and the broad branches of the trees arched over both sides of the street, providing both shade and a sense of security.

This was one of Rukh's favorite neighborhoods. So quiet and peaceful, especially since the drive ended at Dryad Park.

Rukh led Jessira into the green jewel which was Ashoka's soul. Rolling hills of grass and fields of wildflowers merged seamlessly with blue lakes and ponds. In the sunlight, the water sparkled like rainbows, but now, with the coming of night, it was a dull black and shimmered with the ivory light of the moon. A number of elderly men of every Caste played chess as they sat at a group of tables placed beneath a cluster of oaks. Firefly globes with muted hues of rose, gold, lavender, or violet hung above them, suspended from the broad branches of the thick trees. Beyond the collection of oaks, a scattering of black lampposts was the only source of light throughout the park. Further past the old men playing chess, a few people were still about this late in the day. Mostly they were young couples taking a final stroll along the winding gravel paths and lanes of Dryad before heading home, but no one else.

Rukh and Jessira walked deeper into the park, into places where it was empty. Their footsteps echoed as they passed over sturdy, wooden bridges arching over the numerous streams and rivulets that connected the various ponds. Rukh led her to the center of the park. They stopped at the crest of a small bridge spanning a gurgling stream. Its stone pillars were covered in lichen. Frogs croaked the coming of the night, and a cool wind carried a hint of sea and rain.

This was one of the most romantic spots in Ashoka, and Rukh worried what others would think if they saw him and Jessira alone out here, but he also figured most people wouldn't care. He wanted

Jessira to see all the beauty Ashoka had to offer.

Jessira leaned against the wooden railing. "It's like a dream," she whispered.

Rukh smiled. It had been the exact reaction he had been hoping for. "It took decades to make it look like this," he said, just as softly as he moved to stand at her side. He was aware of his arm sometimes brushing hers. She didn't move away, so Rukh held still as well. After their weeks together in the Wildness, he'd grown used to being near her. It was comforting somehow.

Jessira glanced at him. "And after all this time, you don't take it for granted?"

Rukh thought about her question and realized he had, in fact, taken it for granted, but not anymore. "Maybe before I left, but not now. It's too precious," he answered.

"My city...I love it, but it's so utilitarian. There aren't any soft edges. It's built for safety only." Her voice was filled with palpable longing and envy.

Rukh pitied her. "Maybe you aren't seeing your home for what it truly is," he suggested. "Your people refused to lay down and die when others decided their lives weren't worth bullshit on a boot heel. They were exiled and shouldn't have survived, but they did. And they built a home for themselves and made it strong enough for their children to grow up in safety. That kind of will, that kind of courage has a beauty all its own, don't you think?"

Jessira gave him a faint smile. "A nice sentiment," she said. "A few weeks ago, I would have thought you were being patronizing."

"A few weeks ago, I would have been."

Jessira laughed, and Rukh was glad to hear it. She had a nice laugh.

"You do like to get in the last word, don't you?" she asked.

"It's because mine are usually the only ones I find intelligent," Rukh said, deadpan.

Jessira arched an eyebrow. "You think so?" she asked. "Remind me to introduce you to my right cross. I think someone needs to knock the arrogance out of you."

"No thanks," Rukh said with a chuckle. "I think an introduction to your fists is one I'd do best to avoid."

"You *are* intelligent," Jessira noted.

"Sometimes."

"But not most times," Jessira replied. "Anyway, what I wanted to say before you got us sidetracked with your self-proclaimed genius…"

"Intelligence," Rukh interrupted. "I'm intelligent, not a genius." He grinned. "Humble, too."

"You've much to be humble about," Jessira said with a roll of her eyes. "*Anyway*, what I meant to say was this: maybe one day, instead of having only safety, my people can also live like you do: with art, literature, theater… and all the other glorious things Ashokans do so effortlessly."

"It's a good dream," Rukh said. From Jessira's description of Stronghold – it sounded like a grim, fear-filled fortress – he doubted such a change would happen in her lifetime, but he hoped he was wrong.

Jessira gazed at the wide expanse of Dryad Park and grew silent. She shuffled her feet, looking all the world like she was suddenly uncomfortable or nervous.

Rukh had learned to read her signs. Strangely enough, he often knew what Jessira meant to say long before she actually said it. It happened too frequently to be coincidence or luck, and while Rukh couldn't explain how he had developed such an intuition, he knew enough to trust it.

And right now, Jessira was nervous.

Rukh's jaw tightened, and he had to force himself to exhale and push out his sudden anxiety. Whatever was making her uneasy was affecting him also. It was going to be something he wouldn't want to know, but he had to hear her out. "You can tell me," Rukh said. "Whatever it is."

Jessira shot him a brief look of gratitude. "Remember those words after you hear what I have to say." She took a deep breath, as though preparing herself for battle. "I don't think there's anything going on between Mira and Jaresh, but they need to be careful. If they go on like they have been, I think something *could* happen."

Rukh worked to suppress the sudden rise of his hackles. Jessira was wrong. Dead wrong. He stepped away from her. There was nothing but friendship between his brother and Mira. To say or imply otherwise was more than scandalous; it could destroy both their lives. Rukh waited a moment, willing his anger to pass. He didn't want to say anything now, not while he wasn't in control of his emotions. "Do you understand what you're saying?" Rukh demanded. "What you're saying is a dangerous accusation. Some people might even take your words to mean that Mira and Jaresh already *have* an unnatural relationship." Despite his best intentions, the words came out in an angry rush, and his nails dug into the wood of the bridge.

Jessira noticed. She glanced at his hands, and her face grew hard. "By *some* people, I assume you mean yourself," she said.

"This isn't about me," Rukh protested, feeling his patience fraying.

"Isn't it? Why else would this get you so upset? And what's this about unnatural?"

Rukh sighed in irritation even as he tried to regain his composure. "Why do you get so prickly whenever I say the slightest thing which might be construed as a slur toward OutCastes? Are you searching for the insult?"

Jessira turned away from him, and he thought she wasn't going to answer. "I don't know," she finally said. "It's just the way I am."

"Well it's aggravating. And a bit childish."

"I know," Jessira snapped.

"Then stop doing it," Rukh snapped back.

Their conversation stumbled to a halt, and Rukh was left wondering how such a pleasant evening had ended in another argument between the two of them. They always seemed to find a reason to argue, and he couldn't understand why. Whatever it was, he was tired of it. He stewed over their spat as he stared out over the stream and the now darkened park. He could sense Jessira simmering like a hot skillet next to him.

"I'm sorry," she said into the angry silence. "I keep saying things, doing things…" She shook her head. "After all you've done for me, I keep acting like a jackhole."

Rukh didn't know what to say. It was true: she did often act like a jackhole, but pointing it out wouldn't help their situation right now.

"I'll try not to be so…sensitive about my people," she said. "Will you forgive me?"

Rukh didn't answer at first. Instead, he waited for his anger to fade away, and when it did, he reached for one of her hands, squeezing it briefly. At that moment, he didn't care about the prohibition between men and women of different Castes never physically touching one another. In the Wildness, he and Jessira had already broken that precept more times than he could count. "You're forgiven," Rukh said, glad to get their argument behind them. "Just stop doing it."

Jessira flickered a wan smile. "You're a good man to keep putting up with my tantrums."

"Someone in this city has to," Rukh replied with a slight smile of his own. "It's just my bad luck everyone chose me."

Jessira laughed softly, and the tension was gone as suddenly as it appeared.

"Let's head home," Rukh suggested.

"Let me just tell you *why* I said what I said about Mira and Jaresh.

Just hear me out, and then you can decide for yourself if I'm seeing smoke where there's no fire."

Rukh grimaced. He *really* didn't want to go over this right now, but he also knew Jessira would only keep pestering him if he didn't listen to her. "Go ahead," he growled.

"Mira and Jaresh spend a lot of time together," Jessira began. "We've all seen it, and as much as you Purebloods like to gossip, I'm sure others have noticed, too. It wouldn't be so bad, except for this: whenever one of them is around, the other is almost always close by. They don't always sit next to one another, but it's always near enough. And whenever they enter a room, they seek each other out before looking for anyone else. They share private smiles, and they always laugh at one another's jokes, even when they aren't funny. They…"

"Enough," Rukh said, interrupting her litany of observations. His eyes were closed, and he rubbed his temples. There was the beginning of a headache somewhere behind his eyes. He wanted to deny what she was saying, but her words had a horrible logic to them. "I think you've made your point," he said.

"I'm sorry I had to tell you this," Jessira said softly.

"I'm sorry, too," Rukh replied. *Oh, Jaresh, what have you done?* "I'll talk to my brother tomorrow."

———————◆———————

"T hought I'd find you here," Rukh said, sliding into a chair across from Jaresh.

He had found his brother in one of their favorite pubs, The Long Pull, sitting alone in a corner, a history book propped open on the table in front of him.

After Gris Holianth, the stocky owner, took Rukh's order – an order of samosas with a mint lassi – he looked his brother in the eye.

"I need to talk to you."

Jaresh took a sip of his beer. "About what."

"About Mira," Rukh said.

"What about her?" Jaresh asked, a testy edge to his voice.

Rukh had been dreading this conversation ever since last night when Jessira had told him her suspicions. Jaresh's obvious irritation only confirmed how carefully he would have to tread here. He took a deep, steadying breath. "People are starting to talk. The two of you spend too much time alone together. I don't think you should be seen with her anymore; not if it's just the two of you by yourselves."

As he feared, Jaresh bristled and looked outraged. "Why? Because people think I would dishonor myself or our House or *her*?" he whispered furiously. "I would never do that."

"I know you wouldn't. Others don't. And their opinions matter," Rukh said. "Now calm down. We're just talking here."

It was the wrong thing to say. If anything, his brother looked even angrier. "Don't tell me to calm down," Jaresh said. "Not when you come in here making those kind of vile accusations."

"I'm not accusing you of anything," Rukh said, trying to hold onto his own temper. "I'm only telling you what I've heard."

"Well it's bullshit."

"Bullshit or not, it's been noticed."

Jaresh snorted. "What's been noticed? There's nothing to notice. Nanna and Sophy asked us to search the Cellar for references to the Withering Knife. We did as we were told. That's it."

"And since then? Do you still see her?" Rukh asked, feeling like a hypocrite. After all, there was Jessira, and the same charges of inappropriate time spent with a woman not of his own Caste could also be made against him. And the two of them had been all alone in the Wildness for weeks on end.

"Of course I see her. Mira *is* a member of the House."

Rukh didn't answer, feeling sad and sickened. There had been an unvoiced note in Jaresh's voice when he had spoken Mira's name, only the smallest wisp of emotion, but it had been there. It was the sound of longing. Jessira was right. Just then, Rukh couldn't look at his brother. He turned away in disgust as he stared unseeing through the large streetfront windows at the passing crowd.

"What is it?" Jaresh asked. "Your face..." He sat back in amazement. "You don't believe this bilge water, do you?"

Rukh turned back to face him. "You curse most often whenever you're trying to hide something," he said, staring his brother in the eyes and smiling sadly. "It's why you're so lousy at poker."

Jaresh faltered. "That's not it at all," he said. "And I'm not falling for one of your word games right now. I'm cursing because I'm angry. I think I have a right to be after what you've just said."

Rukh waved aside his explanation. "Fine. I don't care. Curse all you want. It doesn't change what you have to do."

"I know my duty," Jaresh growled. "But if these rumors spread...I know what it's like to be ostracized. Mira doesn't. It's not right."

There was that hint of longing again. Rukh felt sorrow for the two of them and anger as well. How could Jaresh have been so damn stupid? How could Mira?

"She's a good person," Jaresh continued. "She deserves a happy life."

Rukh merely nodded, suddenly furious at Mira and Jaresh, but also with the entire situation. His idiot little brother. If only he had been born Kumma, none of this would matter.

"I'll do what honor demands," Jaresh said, "but none of this is true. You do believe me, don't you?" he implored, leaning forward.

"It doesn't matter what I think," Rukh said with a sigh, his anger draining away just as quickly as it had appeared and leaving him empty inside. "It only matters what *other* people think. And they are starting to think some very ugly thoughts. Like you said, Mira can't comprehend what it's like to be ostracized. You do. Do you want her to learn what you know all too well?"

Jaresh leaned back in his chair. "Suwraith's spit," he said softly. "No."

"Then do what's right."

They fell into silence until Rukh's food and drink arrived. Jaresh took a samosa and ate it as he stared out the streetfront windows, looking lost in thought. He turned to Rukh. "Just out of curiosity, who told you all this?"

Rukh shook his head. "Who cares? Let it be."

Jaresh grimaced and stared into his drink. "Whoever it was, they ought to mind their own business."

"That sounds dangerously close to an admission."

"I told you: I'm not playing your word games."

"You'll do what's needed?" Rukh asked.

Jaresh nodded. "I said I would. I'll make sure we're never alone anymore. I'll stop spending any time alone with her…" There again was the note of longing. "Our lives will go back to how they were before the murders." Jaresh took a long pull from his drink, still staring off into the distance, his face studiously blank.

Rukh wanted to comfort his brother, squeeze his shoulder. Anything. But he knew nothing he could say or do would help. It would only make it worse.

Jaresh waited for her within their favorite alcove in the Cellar. It had been almost a month since the two of them had confirmed the existence of the Withering Knife, and the place was just the way they had left it. The lighting was still dim and the bookshelves remained dusty and full of old manuscripts, scrolls, and books. It was quiet as a tomb, and the familiar smell of mold and musty papers filled the air. Not that he'd expected any changes. Why would he? Few people came down here anymore.

The high-pitched tapping of footsteps heralded her arrival. And here she was, standing at his side.

"I wasn't sure why you wanted to meet here again," Mira said with a smile. "Are we supposed to search for another legendary relic?"

Jaresh stilled the pleasure he felt at seeing her roguish grin or smelling the fresh, floral scent of her honeysuckle perfume. After his talk with Rukh, he understood now why Mira's presence filled him with such happiness. How could he have allowed such a sin to find a home in his heart? It wasn't something he had wanted to accept or believe, but he had never been good at lying, especially to himself. Jaresh knew what he felt for Mira. It was an unhealthy infatuation, and he had to end it. Now. He prayed it would be as easy to accomplish as his current resolve.

"It's not another quest," he said, answering her question and forcing a smile on his face. It was brittle, and Mira noticed.

"What is it then?" she asked, taking a seat next to him, not across the table as most people would have. Mira no longer smiled and her face was serious.

"It's about us," Jaresh began, disgusted he even had to have this conversation.

"What about us?" Mira asked, seeming to carefully sound out her words.

Jaresh hesitated, not sure what to tell her. He'd gone over what he wanted to say a hundred times, but the words had never come out sounding right. Now, with the moment on him, his tongue was glued to the roof of his mouth, tangled up in uncertainty. "I think we spend too much time together. People have noticed." He winced at the abrupt tone to his words.

"Have they?" Mira asked, her voice and expression grown stony. "And what are *they* saying? And more importantly, what do *you* think about us?"

Jaresh wiped the perspiration on his forehead. Speaking to her about this was harder than anything he could have imagined. What would she think of him if she knew the truth? About his feelings for her? He knew the answer without having to ask. She would be repulsed and despise him forever. He couldn't live with her contempt. Anything else, but not that. He decided she didn't need to know the truth. He could hide it, and that way they could at least still be friends. Or so he hoped.

"I'm sorry, but I think we need to limit how much time we spend with one another. We shouldn't be alone together, either." He said the words in a rush.

Mira didn't speak. Instead, she regarded him silently, her face inscrutable.

Jaresh couldn't look at her, and he gazed into the darkness of the Cellar.

He heard her chair scrape against the floor as she pushed away from the table. She walked the few steps to his side and paused. "I think I understand what you're saying," she said softly.

He glanced up and was caught as he found himself staring into her depthless eyes. Suddenly, her face was only inches away. His heart pounded. Her lips pressed against his, a soft butterfly's caress deepening for the merest of moments.

Jaresh was lost. He knew what they were doing was wrong, but he couldn't make himself care, not when it felt so right. But before he could pull her into his embrace, she stepped away from him.

"Goodbye, Jaresh," she said, a note of finality in her voice.

CHAPTER TWENTY-THREE
REPAYING DEBTS OWED

I am merely a warrior. I fight where I am told, and defeat those I must fight.
The means of my victory are for me to decide.

~The Sorrows of Hume, AF 1789

"**R**eport," Lieutenant Danslo ordered.

"We've run into a few of their patrols," Rukh said, standing stiffly at attention although his back and ass ached. The expedition had traveled one thousand miles, averaging thirty-five miles a day over the past four weeks, and scouting every day for hours on end was taking its toll. "Mostly a few traps of Braids, usually alone, but sometimes with Tigons."

"Still no Baels?"

"Like I said before, they're likely all dead," Rukh replied.

The lieutenant stroked his chin in thought. "It's what I've heard from our other scouts. The other lieutenants say the same thing." He frowned and shot Rukh a look of doubt. "What do you think they're up to?" he asked, his voice tinged with suspicion.

His expression was one Rukh had grown used to. Early on after leaving Ashoka, Rukh had spoken to the senior commanders of the expeditionary force and let them know of his ability to Blend. He had naively thought they needed to know all the skills their warriors could bring to bear. Every day since that ill-fated meeting, he wished he'd kept his fragging mouth shut. Marshall Ruenip Tanhue, along with his captains and lieutenants had greeted Rukh's announcement with thinly veiled disgust. It was a sentiment soon shared by the rest of the expeditionary force.

As a result, Rukh now found himself on permanent assignment with a unit of scouts, a mixed group of Kummas, Murans, and Rahails. The other warriors in his squad didn't like him, but it didn't stop them from making use of his unique Talents. They had offered him a grudging – if cold and resentful – respect. If there had been nothing more than the disdain of the other warriors, Rukh wouldn't have cared all that much. How the others treated him wasn't pleasant, but it was tolerable, and as far as he was concerned, his loneliness was a small price to pay if the expedition was successful in exterminating the Chimera breeding caverns. But then Aia had walked into their camp one night, and now Rukh was completely ostracized.

All told, there were two thousand warriors in the force, and somehow Aia had skirted past all of them and made her way untouched and unnoticed to Rukh's side. She had stood by his bedroll and nudged him awake with a cold, wet nose. His shout of fear at seeing her large face fill his entire field of view had awoken the other warriors. When they caught sight of a Shylow in their midst, they'd reacted with expected alarm. Within seconds, more than a dozen bows and spears and swords were leveled at Aia, with Rukh shouting for the other warriors not to shoot or attack. Eventually they had listened to him as Aia had simply sat on her haunches, not making any kind of aggressive move or gesture. She had watched the Ashokans with unblinking, mild interest. Her forehead rub against Rukh's chest, so like a housecat's, along with her insistent nudging for him to rub her chin had calmed them. Eventually the other warriors had put away their weapons.

Rukh had learned much from Aia that evening.

While everyone had been on edge as the expedition advanced deeper into the Hunters Flats, they had yet to suffer an attack by the Shylows. It was unexpected since the great cats were known to be very territorial.

Aia had apparently taken care of their concerns. She had spoken to her father, the Kezin to the Hungrove, and convinced him to allow the Humans to pass without troubling them. Word had been sent to the other glarings, and they had agreed as well. She had also consented to look into one other issue worrying Rukh, promising to find him again before the expedition reached the Slave River.

After she had left, Rukh had explained the situation to Marshall Tanhue. The commander had been relieved, but he and the rest of the warriors ended up viewing Rukh with even greater uncertainty and distrust. He had learned and done too much in his one Trial. Add in his friendship with a Shylow, and it was another plank on the pyre of his reputation; further proof of his Taint. In fact, it was the phrase most commonly used in describing him now: the Tainted One. Long gone was the glory he had earned by winning the Tournament of Hume. Most warriors who weren't of his unit ignored him or tried to pretend he didn't exist. A few even drew the sign against evil when he passed. His own squad barely tolerated him, and when they were out in the field, the others made sure his bedroll was furthest from the fire and separate from them.

Thank Devesh he hadn't mentioned his ability to Heal. The warriors would have run him off if he had.

"I don't think we'll find any Baels," Rukh said, tired of repeating his reasoning for why the Baels were absent from their troops. "They're all dead."

"Let's hope so," Lieutenant Danslo mused. "At least Devesh has finally gotten off his backside and helped with one of our problems."

"It's Suwraith you should thank for eliminating the Baels," Rukh replied. "I saw Her kill them." Immediately, he knew he shouldn't have spoken up.

His statement earned him a scowl of distaste. "I don't like you, Shektan. None of us do. You're all but a naaja as it is. If you don't want trouble, you'd best remember to keep those thoughts to yourself."

Rukh kept silent, his heart thick with anger, loneliness, and fear. It hit him just then: this would be his life from now on, shunned and hated by his fellow Kummas. When he returned to Ashoka, the knowledge of what he could do would spread, and the disgust and fear he currently faced would be a small taste of what he could expect back home. All the dreams he had once had of marriage, of family and children…all of it was gone. No one would allow their daughter to marry someone like him.

He was the Tainted One.

He grimaced. His life had turned out so differently than how he had expected. If it weren't so damn sad, it would have been comically karmic. A few months ago, he had been the honored and feted Hume Champion. Now – he scowled once again – now he was despised and the only place he might find acceptance would be in Stronghold, home to the hated ghrinas.

It was too bad Jessira would be gone when he arrived back in Ashoka. She might have taken him with her.

He stared the lieutenant in the eye, deeply resentful of how miserly and ignorant the man and everyone like him were. What had Rukh done other than survive what few others could have? He had lived through the destruction of his caravan and gained the ability to Blend. So what? He had witnessed Suwraith meeting with the Baels, and afterwards, he had spoken to Her commanders and found out about the breeding caverns. He had learned of the OutCastes and the Shylows. What he'd discovered might keep Ashoka safe for years or decades to come.

Rukh's anger burned slowly, but when it did, it burned white-hot. He wanted to wipe the smug look of superiority from the lieutenant's face. Right then, he hated Danslo and everything he represented, all the close-minded and judgmental bastards who thought themselves so much purer and better than him. The anger must have shown because the lieutenant's hand dropped to the hilt of his sword. Rukh glanced at Danslo's clenched fist and didn't bother hiding his sneer of derision. The lieutenant wouldn't stand a chance if Rukh wanted to take him. But he was also Rukh's superior officer, and – Devesh help them! – the expedition needed the jackhole.

Rukh suppressed his anger and instead leaned back on the habits of a lifetime of training, of how to respond when speaking to a superior officer. "I understand, sir," he replied, speaking in a clipped, even tone as he responded to the lieutenant's previous statement.

"Glad to see you still have some sense," Lieutenant Danslo said, his hand slowly lifting from the hilt of his sword. "I have new orders for you. We're still too far out from the caverns to be certain of the numbers we might face. We need to know the makeup of their defending force."

"Yes sir."

"This close to the caverns, we're not sending the scouts too far ahead of the main column. Only a few will be penetrating deep. You're one of them. Scout as far ahead as you can. Confirm the caverns are where we think they are. Get us numbers on who and what we'll be facing when we get there. Mark us a path to their doorstep."

Rukh smirked. Where *we* think the caverns are? Fragging hell. Did the dumbass even know how stupid he sounded? Where did he think the information came from anyway?

"The expedition will be right behind you," the lieutenant continued, apparently not caring about the expression of contempt on Rukh's face. "The Marshall wants us on the march through the night and most of tomorrow. If we're right, we…" there it was again, the 'we', "…should be in position to attack them tomorrow night. Kill them all in one fell swoop."

"How many should I take with me?"

"You're on your own. Less chance for the Chims to find us out that way."

"Understood," Rukh said, tonelessly. The lieutenant was sending him on a suicide mission. "Will I have time to eat before I head out?"

"Supper's on the pot," Danslo said uncaringly. "Have your fill."

Rukh grabbed a bite to eat and restocked his supplies. Given the cook's cool response when he had asked for food – the man looked like he wanted to spit in Rukh's stew – it was probably better he was on his own anyway. He'd rather be killed by the Chims then by one of his own.

He also wrangled a fresh mount out of the sour-faced supply sergeant. Too bad the one he was given farted constantly. Smelly bastard. It seemed an apt metaphor for his life as it was now.

***

Jessira tied off the last knot. There. Her rucksack and supplies were ready. Tomorrow morning, she'd be leaving Ashoka and heading for home. It would be a rough trip, but she was confident she could make it. She had plenty of supplies, and a new bow to replace the one she had lost in the Flats. She even had a sword – better than her old one – and a brace of throwing knives. Her shoulder still bothered her, but it felt good enough. It was long past time to get going.

Though she would have to sleep outdoors on the hard ground and make do with bland trail food, given the alternatives, she wouldn't have it any other way. She smiled. It would be good to feel the rough ground beneath her boots and see the stars of the unfiltered night sky. She looked forward to smelling something other than the press of Humanity. Rukh's home was too dense and populous. Jessira paused in the organization of her supplies. She thought about the city she would be leaving in the morning. She realized with a start that she would miss it. Ashoka's vibrancy, its life, not to mention the mouth-wateringly delicious food – all of it had been an eye-opening experience, and she was glad to have had it.

As she stacked her packs by the door to her room, she briefly wondered how Rukh and the expedition were doing. They'd left a few days ago, but before his departure, Rukh had still been angry with her. Or maybe not angry with her, but simply upset she had been so correct about Mira and Jaresh. Rukh hadn't said she'd been right, but Jaresh's sudden moodiness and general despondency as well as Mira's absence from the seat of House Shektan had told Jessira all she needed to know. As a result, on the last day before Rukh left, relations between the two of them had been tense, and she regretted they couldn't have departed from one another's lives on better terms.

A knock on her open door, and a servant poked his head in, letting her know Rukh's father wanted to talk to her in his study.

Jessira nodded acknowledgment and set aside her final pack. In the 'El's office, she found both Rukh's nanna and amma. Both looked distinctly unsettled and unhappy. Satha, Rukh's amma, had red eyes and her face was puffy, as if she had been crying.

"Can you delay your departure?" Dar'El asked without preamble.

Jessira closed the door to the study before answering. By their expressions, she knew something bad had occurred. She hoped it wasn't the expedition or something to do with Rukh. Her heart began thudding in her chest. "What happened?" she asked, managing to keep her voice calm and level.

"The Chamber of Lords has seen fit to banish Rukh," Satha Shektan spat, furious and anguished at the same time.

Jessira frowned, confused by what Rukh's mother was saying.

From her own perspective, she was actually relieved in a way. At least Rukh wasn't dead, but whatever this expulsion meant, it had to be something terrible judging by Satha's grief. Jessira looked to Dar'El for explanation.

"The Chamber of Lords is how the Houses decide what is best for Kumma society as a whole," he said. "An emergency session was called today. Somehow, one of the 'Els learned of Rukh's new Talents."

"It was that pig, Hal'El Wrestiva," Sophy growled. "He was the one who brought it up. When I find out who told him, I will wring that person's neck."

"The Chamber has found Rukh to be Unworthy…"

"We should be grateful they didn't mark him with the Slash of Iniquity," Satha broke in.

"At any rate," Dar'El said, continuing on as if he hadn't been interrupted. "The Chamber has decided Rukh can no longer be accepted in Kumma society."

"It wasn't their only reason," Satha muttered angrily. She flashed an unfathomable look at Jessira before turning to stare out the windows and fold her arms across her chest.

Dar'El shrugged. "It doesn't matter what their rationale," he said. "The point is when Rukh returns from the expedition, he will not be allowed to step foot within the Oasis or join one of our caravans. He can try to make his way to some other place and hope they will accept him there, but it won't happen. Once a man has been expelled, no other city will accept him."

"But Stronghold will," Jessira said, guessing the reason for this meeting. "That's why you asked if I could delay my departure."

Dar'El nodded. "How long can you wait before the snows close off the mountain passes to your city?"

"I can wait maybe another ten or eleven weeks, but it would be cutting it close."

"If all goes well, they should be back by then," Satha said. "Will you wait for him and take him with you?"

Jessira sat down. So much was coming at her at once. Something Satha had said, her expression…oh no. Jessira realized what Rukh's amma had meant when she said there had been another reason for the Chamber's decision. She felt sick. "It was because of me, wasn't it? You said his new Talents weren't the only reason for his expulsion. It's because of the time he spent with me."

Satha nodded. "Nothing was alleged but enough was implied."

Jessira covered her face, appalled by what had happened to Rukh and her role in it. "I should never have gone with him to that play."

"The play and dinner were fine since Bree was with you," Satha said. "It was what came after, when Bree left. Your romantic evening stroll through Dryad Park was noticed and remarked upon. If I wasn't so afraid for that stupid boy, I'd box his ears for what he's done. The brainless fool!"

Dar'El looked angry as well. "Rukh can be so stupid sometimes. He never sees how his actions can appear to others. He's blind to the obvious until it smacks him in his idiot face. The evening the two of you spent with one another could have been excused, but add in his Talents, and it became the final reason for the other 'Els to expel him."

Jessira slumped in her chair. Her head fell forward as she stared at the floor. This was all her fault. It was what Dar'El and Satha knew to be true, but for some reason were too kind to say so. Jessira had been so selfish, demanding Rukh's attention when she should have dealt with her loneliness on her own. If she had, tomorrow morning, she would have left Ashoka, and Rukh would have gone on to live his life as he would have wanted.

"I am furious with Rukh, but my anger doesn't matter, and neither does yours," Satha snapped at Dar'El. "We still need an answer from you, Jessira Viola Grey. Will you take our son to Stronghold?"

Jessira nodded. "Of course. I owe Rukh my life," she said. "But you're asking me to stay in Ashoka for the better part of three months. Where will I live?" She felt guilty thinking of herself at a time like this, but the question needed asking.

"Where else but here?" Dar'El asked, sounding surprised.

"What about Bree and Jaresh?"

"What about them?" Satha asked.

Jessira licked her lips in nervousness. "When they find out about Rukh's expulsion, especially my role in it, they won't be very happy. They'll blame me. I'm surprised the two of you don't."

Satha laughed bitterly. "I wish I *could* blame you for this disaster, but Rukh wasn't your responsibility. He was ours, and he's become a victim to our House politics."

"This is not House politics," Dar'El growled. "It is war, and if it is war House Wrestiva wants, it is war I will give them. When I'm finished, House Wrestiva will be liquidated, and their ruling 'El will be left impoverished and despised for his incompetence."

Just then, seeing the hard, cold determination on his face, Jessira was certain Dar'El Shektan would try to do exactly that. It was an expression mirrored on the face of Satha Shektan. Jessira was suddenly glad Rukh's parents weren't her enemy.

"We'll deal with Bree and Jaresh," Satha said. "And we'll make sure your time here won't be unbearable. But the House seat is the safest place for you to stay until Rukh returns."

Jessira nodded. "I'll wait for him," she said before leaving the study. Time to unpack. What a fool she had been. On her way up the stairs, she sent a silent prayer to Devesh. She prayed for Rukh's safety and also that he would find a way to forgive her once he learned what had happened.

After Jessira left the study, Dar'El walked to the door and closed it behind her.

"Are you certain of this path?" Satha asked. "What if she learns the truth?"

Dar'El glanced at his wife. "Which truth? How we just manipulated her, or the near-certainty that Rukh would have been found Unworthy regardless of their night time stroll through Dryad Park?"

"Either."

"Jessira will learn nothing, and even if she does, by then it will be too late. It's already too late. Our course is set."

Satha sighed. "I don't like lying, but we do what we must."

"Rukh's fate was sealed the moment Rector Bryce learned of his new Talents. I severely misjudged the man," Dar'El said with a grit of his teeth. He wasn't sure if he was angrier with himself or with Bryce.

Satha grimaced. "Speaking of the Watcher, what do you intend to do about him?"

"He will pay for what he has done. He will pay the harshest price I can devise."

"Bree?" Satha guessed. "He's already lost her. She knows Rector's actions in all this."

"No," Dar'El said. "Bryce will lose something he treasures far more deeply: his moral certitude."

Satha shrugged. "As long as he learns never to cross this House," she said. "And speaking of our daughter, has Bree forgiven you yet?"

Dar'El shook his head. "No. She hates her role in Rukh's banishment, and she blames me for it."

"Suggesting the walk in Dryad Park?"

"She immediately knew what would happen, but that's not why she's unhappy with me," Dar'El said. "She's convinced we should have told Rukh the truth."

"About the politics of the Chamber?" Satha barked in laughter. "And then *he* would have told Jessira…"

"Who we wouldn't then be able to guilt into taking him to Stronghold," Dar'El finished for her. "And Rukh likely would have refused to join the expedition to the caverns. He would have stayed here in Ashoka, determined to fight the charges and would have instead been branded a coward. Yet another reason for the Chamber to find him Unworthy."

"You still cling to that hope?" Satha asked, sounding surprised. "The possibility that Rukh's actions with the expedition might be so extraordinary that the Chamber rescinds their decision?"

"It's the only way I can see him one day returning home to us."

"And if he dies?"

"Death is always a possibility in the Wildness."

Satha didn't answer. It was an old argument between the two of them. Instead, she stood and paced the room. "What a mess," she said, rubbing her shoulders.

The room quieted.

"I'm going to tell him about the Book," Dar'El said into the silence.

"*The Book of First Movement?*" Satha rolled her eyes. "Ever since you joined that stupid society…"

"The Rajans were the ones who told us…"

"I know about the Rajans," Satha interrupted. "But we've manipulated our daughter, Jessira, and Rukh in order to grant him a future where he *might* be happy. And you want him to risk it all for some book no one has ever been able to read. Do you realize how dangerous such a journey will be?"

Dar'El suppressed his irritation. This was also an old argument. "The risks won't be as great as you think," he said. "Rukh is a Kumma who can Blend. If anyone can salvage the Book, it will be him."

Satha didn't reply. Instead, she seemed to scrutinize Dar'El. "You really think this Book is important enough to risk our son's life over?"

Dar'El stared out the window. Risk his son's life? Was anything worth such a price? The answer was obvious, but nevertheless, he hated voicing it. He hated having to make these decisions. Life would have been far easier if he could have remained a simple warrior, never becoming the ruling 'El of House Shektan or joining the Rajans. Then these soul-twisting choices would have never been required of him. "When the Book fell into Raja's hands two thousand years ago, he was opaque on so many items, but on the Book he was clear: it is our best hope to defeat Suwraith."

———————•———————

Night cloaked the column as it wended its way along the shingle beach marking the eastern bank of the Slave River. The water funneled through a long, narrow canyon, hammering and roiling across heavy boulders and rocks in a steep descent before finally thundering over the Tripwire Falls a mile or so to the south. High cliffs extended north and south, enclosing the gorge in gloomy shadow even under a noonday sun. At night the darkness was stygian, with water-slick gravel and stones creating a high risk for a turned ankle. The expedition had to proceed carefully and quietly, even though the sound of pounding water helped disguise any noise the warriors might have made.

So far they had avoided detection, swiftly silencing any Chimera scouts and warriors who might have given warning. It was surprising how lightly defended the breeding caverns were. Hardly any Chims whatsoever, but there had been enough to 'interrogate' – and a bloody, awful mess it had turned out to be. From them, the Ashokans had gained a fairly accurate picture of the cave system they planned on invading. According to the Chims, the breeders were housed in large caverns, widely dispersed throughout the cave system and guarded by roughly five thousand of their fellows, just as Li-Dirge had said.

Five thousand Chimeras... On an open field, two thousand Ashokans could have easily taken them, but in the tight quarters of the tunnels and caves, it would be a painful, deadly slog. Kumma speed and power would count for so much less in such narrow confines.

And since a man could easily get lost in the confusing warrens, the Marshall had insisted each warrior be given a map of the caverns and tunnels. If anyone got separated from their unit, they had to have a way of getting out of there.

As for the plan of attack, there were three entrances to the caverns, and the Ashokans already held them, having quickly overwhelmed the small defending force of Chimeras. Now it was time for the rest of the warriors to get in there and get the job done. Marshall Tanhue had split his command into three equal columns of just under seven hundred men each. Rukh had been assigned to the unit tasked with entering the southernmost entrance.

"I can't believe we're going into those caves," a warrior walking near Rukh murmured to a companion. "We have no idea what we'll find in there."

"We'll be fine," his friend replied. "That claw of Tigons and those traps of Braids we captured told us all we need to know."

"You think we can trust the word of a Chim?"

"No, but they only told us what we already figured to be true, like the Baels all being dead," the second warrior replied. "Or how the Sorrow Bringer killed all them horned bastards Herself and put the Tigons in charge. Just like the Shektan said."

"You mean the Hume Champion. Can't forget what a great

warrior he is," the first man said, a sneering tone to his voice. "Naaja bastard." He spit to the side.

Rukh clenched his fists. He was about to speak up, but almost immediately, he swallowed any harsh words he might have said. What was the point? Even if he put a beatdown on those two, nothing would change. The others wouldn't care. The casual slurs would continue.

At that moment, he wished he'd never been chosen for the expedition. As for the two men in question – a Muran and a Rahail – they had no idea who it was walking right next to them. It was the Tainted bastard himself. He supposed they thought he was just another Kumma.

"He is naaja," the second warrior said. "But I wouldn't rile him. Word is he's tough as nails." He glanced at his friend. "You hear how his lieutenant sent him scouting ahead without backup?"

"I heard," the first warrior said. "It was wrong if you ask me. The Shektan is Tainted, but it was a suicide mission. I say if you want to see a man dead, kill him in honorable combat."

"You want to be the one to take him on?" the second warrior scoffed.

"Who? The Shektan? No chance. I heard *he's* the one who took out most of the Chim scouts on our way in. Ten, twenty at a time…it didn't matter. He laid them all low. My lieutenant says all we did was follow his trail of dead Chims to their doorstep."

"I heard he took down three Balants by himself," the second warrior whispered. "Charged right in and cut them to mincemeat."

There was a whistle of appreciation. "His lieutenant better be careful to watch his back. A man like the Shektan might snap at any minute."

Rukh moved away. The men still didn't like him, but at least they feared him. It was something he supposed.

"Move out." The order came in a harsh whisper. "Double time."

The Ashokans marched into the cavern, quick and stealthy. Rukh glanced around. Dead Tigons and Braids littered the floor, about twenty of them, their bodies riddled with arrows. They had been killed only a few minutes earlier. Fresh blood still oozed from their wounds, and their bowels had emptied. It stank. Fluttering lanterns, evenly spaced on the relatively smooth walls of the tunnel, provided a disjointed light. It looked like he wouldn't need the dozen or so oil-soaked torches on his back. He shrugged. Who knew? Maybe the rest of the caves wouldn't be as well lit. Better to keep them.

The column reached a bifurcation, and Rukh took a look at his map. He was glad to see it showed the split where the column had halted. Maybe the information from the captured Chims would turn out to be accurate. The plan now was to further divide the forces at each junction of the tunnel until there were thirteen units of fifty warriors working their way through the cave system, with each group clearing a predetermined set of tunnels and caverns. It wasn't ideal, but with their force structure, it would have to do. Fifty warriors in cramped quarters should be large enough to handle whatever enemy forces they came across but also swift enough to get the job done: kill the breeders.

Their unit quickly divided into the predetermined thirteen units, and Rukh found himself assigned, as expected, toward the back of the squad. It was the most dangerous position to be in, but somebody had to do it. No surprise the lieutenant in command of the unit had chosen him for the job. It was just another punishment for being what he was. As a naaja, he was expendable.

They marched into the depths of the caves, and Rukh's stomach clenched as he imagined the shadows and adjoining tunnels hiding Chims waiting to leap and kill him. He was thinly supported. Would he even have time to get his sword and spear ready? He scanned behind the column constantly, especially the intersecting tunnels, looking and listening for danger.

It was a quarter mile before they finally came upon the enemy, a nest of Ur-Fels loping down a side passage and lumbering into the center of the unit. For a second, the Chims looked comically surprised to see their hated enemy marching through the very heart of their home. After they got over their shock, the Ur-Fels screamed their outrage and attacked. Most quickly died beneath the swords of the warriors, but one of them managed to escape, speeding away and howling warning to his brethren.

Rukh wiped sweaty palms on his pants. Suwraith's spit, but he wished he were somewhere else all of a sudden. Life was suddenly about to get much more interesting.

"Cavern coming up." The whispered word came down the line.

The pace quickened. They entered a wide, tall space. Within were strange creatures, like hairless, pasty versions of an Ur-Fel, chained at their necks to the walls. They were skeletal in appearance with protuberant abdomens and naked. Their mouths gaped when the Ashokans entered, revealing broken yellow teeth, and they took to howling. Their cries drew twenty Ur-Fels, who immediately threw themselves at the squad, but were swiftly cut down by a hail of arrows. The breeders were similarly killed.

"Move it. Take the tunnel to the right," the lieutenant whispered.

They traveled several hundred yards before coming to a jumbled halt.

"The hell are we?" Rukh heard the lieutenant growl. He and the first sergeant had their heads bent close to one another, furiously whispering as they studied their maps.

"We're supposed to be here," the first sarge whispered. His voice was loud enough to carry as he pointed at his map.

There was pause in their conversation as the lieutenant scratched his chin. "Suwraith's spit."

Rukh's head snapped up. He heard something. A scrabbling noise from behind them. He searched the tunnel leading back to the

Ur-Fel breeder's cavern, listening as closely as possible. They had passed a bend in the passage…his eyes narrowed as he concentrated. He heard it again. And something else. His eyes widened. He knew that sound. It was the growls of Tigons on the hunt. "Incoming," he hissed loudly, his heart pounding. "Tigons."

His words had the squad spun around and facing back in the direction they had come.

Before they could form up, fifty Tigons rounded the corner. With their prey in sight, the Chims eschewed their prior quietness. They bellowed in rage and charged.

Rukh threw two Fireballs into the faces of the lead Tigons. They stumbled and fell, tripping those behind them. It bought the Ashokans just enough time to form up. The front rank, three wide, quickly Shielded, while those behind them hurled Fireballs.

"More Tigons coming from up ahead!" someone shouted.

There were just as many as in the first group, trapping the squad in between.

"Second and third ranks, bows only. Front ranks, Shields and Fireballs!" the first sarge yelled out.

His words were hardly needed. The Ashokans knew their business. Fireballs screamed out, incinerating the charging Chims. The tunnel quickly filled with smoke and the stink of burning flesh. It didn't slow down the Tigons one bit. Thankfully, the damn cats, as they often did, threw their weapons aside in their unthinking fury and kept on attacking. It was a slaughter as arrows ripped through them. The few who managed to close were quickly hacked down. Bodies littered the ground, and blood splattered on the walls, soaking the floor and making footing slick.

Just as the Ashokans breathed a sigh of relief, another group of Chims charged in from a side passage, this time Balants. Twenty of them. They smashed into the center of the Ashokan column, separating a group of fifteen warriors from the main force.

Rukh was one of those cut off, and he had little room to maneuver, pressed on both sides by hooting Balants, who were busily laying about with their clubs. He launched a Fireball straight into the face of one of the elephant-sized, baboon-like Chims. The creature howled in pain, and Rukh took the sudden opening to fall back. The other Kummas had already planned for such a situation and fought in Triads and Duos. They were ably defending themselves, dispatching the Balants in a swift movement of sword and spear. No one had bothered to offer such an arrangement with Rukh. He fought alone.

His spear was knocked from his hands, and he was pushed further away from the column. Most of the Balants were swiftly put down, but of those still alive and fighting, a full five stood between Rukh and the rest of the squad. With a little luck, he might still be able to rejoin the unit, though.

He moved forward just as hissing cries arose from behind him.

Rukh spun around.

Suwraith's spit. Luck wasn't with him.

From beyond the bend in the tunnel and the mangled bodies of the Tigons, he heard the fast approaching sound of more Chims coming to join the battle. Braids judging by their cries.

Fragging unholy hell.

There was no way he could regroup with his column.

Time to run.

Rukh disengaged and took off down a side passage.

Four Balants gave chase. Rukh opened up some distance but not too much. He had a plan. He conducted *Jivatma*, letting it fill him, holding it until...He glanced back. Now. He let it out in a sudden burst. Fire Shower. The Balants didn't even have time to scream. And just as Rukh had hoped, their carcasses ended up blocking the tunnel, hindering the pursuing Braids.

Rukh paused, needing to get his bearings. He pulled out his map. He had a rough idea where he was. He also knew where the column was headed. So…if he cut down the tunnel over there, he might be able to reconnect with the squad. He put away the map and was about to set off when more Tigons appeared from up ahead.

Rukh ran, Shielding as he took a random intersecting tunnel. He unlimbered his bow as he went. He outdistanced the cats, but they followed close behind. At a bend in the passage, Rukh turned, aimed, and fired. One down. Two.

He flinched. Damn it! The Tigons were throwing spears. Hard. A few almost penetrated his Shield, causing it to compress against his chest. Time to go.

More spears and arrows peppered his back, but his Shield held. He drew on his Well, running faster. He took a turn at random, temporarily losing his pursuers and found himself in a large open cavern. His nose wrinkled in disgust. It smelled like cat piss. It had to be a Tigon breeder's cavern. Rukh paused for a moment, disturbed by what he saw. The creatures looked like deformed and stunted Shylows, with slack jaws and drool collecting on the ground. Suwraith's creations were all so damn ugly. The breeders howled at his presence, and he raced through the room, stabbing and cutting until the space was silent.

There were three entrances to the chamber. From two of them, a number of Tigons entered. The Chims saw Rukh standing amongst the mangled corpses of their breeders, and their eyes filled with crazed hatred. They screamed, a sound like a mill saw cutting bone.

By now Rukh had grown accustomed to his fear. It was like an old friend, not even hindering him anymore. He set it aside and took careful, steady aim with his bow and fired. An arrow in an eye. Another in a mouth. He smiled without humor. The Tigons were even more pissed off than before. Good. Sometimes, in their anger, they took the time to rip at their fur. They did so, and Rukh took advantage of their stupidity. He raced for the one unblocked exit. The Tigons moved to intercept. It would be tight getting out. His gut tightened involuntarily as two Tigons surged in front of him, flanking the passage he needed. He rolled under their sword swings, was through the doorway and out, before rising and sprinting away.

A short-lived surge of relief passed through him, but he wasn't out of the shithouse yet. The Tigons would give chase. The two in the lead were well ahead of the others. Their mistake. Rukh taunted them, keeping just out of their clawed reach. The Tigons ran harder, opening up even more distance between themselves and their fellow cats. The tunnel widened. It was the opening Rukh had been looking for. He spun around, sword at the ready, surprising the Chims. He slashed one Tigon across the throat before the cat even had time to raise a sword. The other one blocked a slash. Its return sweep caught empty air as Rukh twisted aside. A viper fast thrust took the creature through the heart. It gurgled its death even as it fell to the ground.

Six or so left. The others still chased after him, roaring their rage. Let them.

A cold malice had settled over his heart. Weeks of abuse at the hands of his fellow warriors, weeks of resentment at his mistreatment, at the fragging injustice of it all...someone would pay. It was just the Chimeras' bad luck that it would have to be them.

Rukh took a moment to quickly clean and sheathe his sword before running on. He had a plan. All he needed was the right opening. A few moments later, he had it as he came upon another large, round space, this one empty. No breeders. Maybe his luck was changing. There were two entrances, the one he had entered and one directly opposite. He briefly considered another Fire Shower, but it was overkill. He could handle the Tigons with sword and bow. Besides, he needed to save his *Jivatma* as best he could. Today was going to be hard as the unholy hells. He didn't want to waste his strength.

He ran to the opposite exit and crouched in the shadows, hidden and ready, ears straining for any flanking pursuit. He heard none, although he did pick out the distant sounds of battles echoing through the tunnels. He had no idea where the fighting was taking place or where his unit might be given the honeycomb nature of the caves.

His attention snapped back to the task at hand as a Tigon burst into the chamber. It ate an arrow. Another stumbled over his fallen brother, throwing off Rukh's aim, and his arrow sailed above it, but caught another Tigon in the chest, downing it. Three more entered the room. Time for one final arrow. Another one down.

Three of them then. He could handle it.

The Tigons closed, and Rukh dropped his bow and drew his sword, wiping sweaty palms on his pants before engaging. He conducted *Jivatma* and moved in a blur.

His training took over. No thought to it but muscle memory. He'd practiced these moves ten thousand times until they were as natural as breathing. He attacked right, ducking a slow, reckless slash at his face. A further slide to the right, and a kick crunched into the Tigon's knee. Something broke, and the cat went down, howling in pain. He parried a disemboweling thrust. *Step back, leap over the other two Chims, and surprise them.* Their backs were to him, and he pithed one, slamming his sword-tip through the back of its skull and into its brain. The other cat spun, and Rukh parried its thrust. He edged inside, hammering the pommel of his sword into the Tigon's chin. It bit its tongue in half and gurgled in pain. A kick to its gut brought it wheezing to its knees. A slice to the throat and the Chim was done. Take care of the injured Tigon, and it was finished.

Rukh cleaned his sword on the corpse of a Tigon and gathered his arrows, feeling oddly satisfied. Stupid Chims. Let them come. He'd kill any others he came across, too. And if he died here, on this night, he was determined to have it on his terms, doing what he'd trained all his life for. He was a Kumma. He was a warrior, and he had a mission to complete.

But first, he had to clean up. He stank. His face, hands, and clothes were covered with blood and bits of Tigon meat, leaving him wet and sticky. There were even chunks of flesh in his hair. Luckily, one of the cats had a canteen full of water, and Rukh used it to rinse off as much gore and blood as possible from his hands and weapons.

He knelt on one knee, leaning on his sheathed sword, and prayed. He wasn't sure what he wanted. All he knew was he was full of anger and terror, all alone in a cavern full of Chimeras. He didn't want to die here, not like this.

He sighed. Survive today and let tomorrow sort itself out.

For now, time to get back to work.

Once more, Rukh studied his map, trying to figure out where in the unholy hells he was. Fruitless minutes later, he still had no idea. Fragging hells. He'd eventually figure it out, or he'd be dead.

He exited the cavern full of dead Tigons, but in less than fifty yards, he almost ran headlong into a hooting herd of Balants. They hadn't caught sight of him yet. He was about to turn and run, but instead he decided to Blend.

He was hidden from sight – or so he hoped – as he hugged a corner of the passage, letting the Balants pass. They never saw nor heard nor smelled him. Except the last one, who turned and stared Rukh in the eyes. How had the fragging Chim seen through his Blend? Damn it. The Balant hooted his discovery, drawing the attention of his fellows.

Rukh sliced the beast's throat for its troubles and raced away. Fragging Balants.

The baboon-like beasts gave chase, but Rukh quickly lost them, taking a side passage easily missed in the gloom. His choice proved to be fortuitous. Good word, fortuitous. Jessira liked using important sounding words like that. He wondered where she was. Wherever it was, it had to be a damn sight better than where *he* was.

He entered a cavern full of what looked to be Balant breeders, judging by their size and appearance. Rukh's face scrunched up in disgust. They looked like a grotesque and tortured mix of simian, elephant, and ox, with the worst features of all three. The Balants he'd run into earlier were probably supposed to be here protecting them. Their mistake. He raced through the chamber like a wind of death. The breeders hooted and hollered as he took their lives. They didn't have his mercy, but they did have his pity. They looked to be nothing but dumb beasts.

He was about to leave the cavern when he noticed a small stack of barrels along one wall. He smelled oil, and a grim smile lit his face. He shucked the torches still on his back and grabbed a small barrel, strapping it to where the torches had been. It was hardly any weight at all, and it might prove very useful. For a moment he pondered how best to utilize the oil. The sound of clawed, running feet ended his speculation. By the howls, it was Ur-Fels. Lots of them.

Rukh turned and ran, planning to lead the dog-like Chimeras on a merry chase until he could figure out how to kill them. He took a side tunnel and briefly lost them. One of them must have caught his scent, though, finding him even through the Blend. Soon enough, he heard the Ur-Fels pursuing him once more.

Fine. Let them come.

He had an idea, and the Ur-Fels wouldn't like it.

He stopped where the tunnel narrowed and broke the cask of oil, quickly emptying it all over the ground, walls, and even the ceiling. The Ur-Fels were close, and Rukh sprinted for cover around a nearby bend. He peered around the corner, Blended, nearly invisible, and waiting.

The Ur-Fels didn't disappoint. They spilled into the tunnel, a howling mob of a hundred or so.

Rukh threw a Fireball. It screamed along the passage and ignited the spilled oil.

The tunnel went up like an inferno. The Ur-Fels screamed in

pain, and their column disintegrated. Rukh Shielded. Protected from the heat and fire, he attacked, leaping into the midst of the confused Ur-Fels. His sword ripped across throats and stomachs and into torsos. Blood and meat hissed and sizzled in the fire. Greasy smoke filled the air, and it became hard to see or breathe.

Rukh killed a dozen or more of the Ur-Fels before the rest got themselves free of the still burning oil and launched their counterattack. They attacked a ghost.

Rukh was already long gone.

He raced far ahead of the dog-like Chims, but this time he was unable to shake them, even Blended as he was. The Ur-Fels had his scent, and they weren't about to let him go. They kept after him. Rukh's lungs burned, and he took a different tunnel, this one wide and tall.

He should have realized why because a moment later, he stood in another Balant breeder cavern, this one occupied with Balants on guard, although a few were sleeping. They hadn't seen him yet, but they soon would, even with his Blend. He only had a few seconds before he would be discovered, and he put those seconds to good use.

He killed two breeders before the others knew what had happened. A Balant tried to corner him, and the dull creature reached to crush him in its massive paw. It hooted in pain when Rukh cut its hand off at the wrist. It swung a club. So slow. Rukh ducked the blow and stepped forward, thrusting up through the creature's slack-jawed mouth, piercing its brain.

The room was in an uproar.

Perfect.

The other Balants were enraged and pounded after him, trampling a few Ur-Fels, who had just emerged into the chamber. As Rukh had hoped, the baboon-like Chims ended up blocking in the quicker dog-like Chims.

Rukh ran, trying to ignore the stitch in his side. He needed speed and distance. He could lie down when it was time to die.

The tunnel narrowed further, and the Balants couldn't pass. Rukh glanced back, seeing one of them eyeing him hungrily as it hooted in anger. The thick-headed creature had the entire tunnel blocked and nothing could get past it. Rukh ran back, meaning to kill the stupid Chim. Somehow, the fragging creature blocked his blow with its club. A backswing smashed into his Shield, hurling him away as it almost crunched through his defenses. Rukh smashed into a wall, hitting his head hard. He stumbled to his feet and immediately fell to a knee. His vision blurred and his balance was off. He shook his head, trying to clear the cobwebs.

Suwraith's spit that hurt. His whole body ached, but at least nothing seemed to be broken.

Rukh glanced at the Balant, who was hooting in glee.

Laugh now, jackhole.

Rukh hurled a Fireball. The force of it punched clear through the creature, taking the Balant directly behind it as well.

He felt a momentary triumph but quickly realized maybe the Fireball hadn't been so wise. His *Jivatma* was growing thin. Blending took a lot out of him, and that Fireball...he should have just run. Worse, with his momentary distraction, he no longer knew where the fragging Ur-Fels were. He couldn't hear them. They must have taken a different route, and if he didn't get out of here, they would have him trapped against the corpse of the Balant filling the passageway.

Unless...

He slithered past the dead Balant and the one directly behind it. The tunnel beyond was empty, all the way back to the breeder's cavern.

He shook his head in disbelief at his luck. Dead-tired as he was, there was still one last thing he could do.

The Balant breeder's cavern was unprotected, and the beasts within were quickly silenced.

There. One more cavern cleared.

Afterward, he sheathed his sword and squatted, taking great gulps of air. His arms and legs were noodle-weak. Fighting, running, and conducting *Jivatma* non-stop took its toll.

Eventually some strength returned, and Rukh levered himself back to his feet. He leaned against a wall, resting as long as possible.

An arrow sliced across his right biceps, ripping open the skin. He Shielded. The next two arrows bounced harmlessly away. He looked for the source of the attack. The fragging Ur-Fels. They'd doubled back. They must have heard the Balant breeders' cries while Rukh was killing them.

Time to run again. This time, he couldn't risk drawing *Jivatma* to quicken his pace. He could maintain a Shield or increase his speed but not both. Not anymore. There wasn't enough *Jivatma* left in his Well.

He ran with only the speed of his weary legs to carry him forward. It felt like he was running in sand, like he'd been fighting for hours. Who knew? Maybe he had. He was tired, maybe too tired to win this race. The Ur-Fels pounded after him. They wouldn't give up. Not this time. Not after what he'd done to them. They wouldn't stop until either he was dead or they were.

He heard growls and hisses from up ahead.

Unholy hells.

Tigons and Braids.

Rukh took an adjoining passageway. This one was different. The walls were more roughly hewn, and it was dimmer. There were only a few lanterns mounted here, barely providing any light at all. The darkness might actually work to his advantage.

The Ur-Fels didn't need to see him to hunt him down. They had his scent, but the Tigons and Braids...they relied on their vision. They might overlook him in the dark passage. Maybe he'd even find a way to lose the Ur-Fels down here, too.

Rukh made his way down the tunnel as fast as he could. The sound of pursuit slowly faded. It was replaced by muttered growls and barks of fury. It sounded like the Tigons and the Ur-Fels were arguing about something.

Whatever it was, Rukh hoped it kept them occupied long enough for him to escape. Otherwise, he was well and truly fragged. He followed the rough tunnel, moving as quickly as he could given the gloom within it.

A large hand reached out from an unseen passage and grabbed him by the throat and slammed him against the wall. "You should not have delved so deep, foul creature," it growled.

Rukh grabbed the gripping arm, ready to break it…but…wait. He knew that voice. "Choke? Li-Choke? Is that you?"

He was abruptly dropped. "Devesh *does* have a sense of humor. Rukh Shektan?"

Rukh couldn't see in the dimness until several torches were lit. He stood in a cavern, much like the ones in which the breeders were housed, and standing before him was Li-Choke and a dozen or so Baels, ranging in age from a white hair to a young one barely up to Rukh's chest.

Rukh would have been afraid if he wasn't so damn tired. Choke might be a friend. He didn't know, but even if he was, the others didn't look particularly friendly. He couldn't take them all, and he couldn't run, not with his legs as rubbery as they were.

"It is a Human, covered in the blood of Tigons and Balants," said the old one. He sniffed again. "And Ur-Fels." He fixed Rukh with a glare. "What is your purpose here?"

"Surely you alone aren't the cause of all the noise and uproar taking place in the caverns?" another one asked.

Rukh had actually been hoping for just this particular moment, and with Aia's promise, he didn't intend to waste this opportunity.

"Ashoka has learned of the caverns here. We mean to disrupt

Suwraith's plans for the spring by killing all the breeders," Rukh said. "It was, Li-Dirge who told me of this place, and he named me his brother." While he had no real fraternal affection for the deceased SarpanKum, he had respected the commander. And more importantly, the Baels seemed to have a special love for the word 'brother'. Maybe they'd give him a chance to explain himself before gutting him.

"He named you his brother?" the old one asked, suspiciously.

"Choke must have told you what happened on the Flats," Rukh said.

"He spoke of it. And now, after centuries of slaughter, you consider the Baels to be your brothers?" the old one jeered.

"No," Rukh said. While a lie might have smoothed his way with the Baels, he suspected they would have detected it. Besides, the truth might serve far better. "But I came to believe in Dirge's vision. He spoke of a world at peace, and I hope that I might see it come to pass." Rukh's words caused a stir amongst the Baels. He took it as a good sign. Other than the old one, a few of the others didn't seem quite as hostile. He still gazed at Rukh with suspicion and distrust. "I don't think of the Baels as my brothers, but I wish I could. I wish I had a reason to," Rukh added.

"It is a start," Choke said. "The SarpanKum would have been overjoyed to hear this." He turned to the old one. "Leave it be, Li-Chant."

"The SarpanKum was a Bael of vision and wisdom," the old one said, "but how can we trust this man? He is Human. They hate us. They have always hated us."

"Trust begins as Li-Dirge taught, with a dropped weapon," Rukh said, letting his sheathed sword slip from his hand.

Another stir, and this time, even Li-Chant appeared impressed. The old Bael nodded. "So be it. Your life is yours," Chant said. "But what happens next?"

Rukh had a thousand questions, first and foremost: why were the Baels hiding down here? And it was clear they were hiding given the ragged and grimy state of their fur and clothing. And where were the rest of their kind? Did no more than this bare dozen here still live?

Questions would have to wait. Something more pressing took precedence.

"What happens next is we have to run," Rukh said, bending to retrieve his sword. "A couple nests of Ur-Fels and a claw of Tigons along with what sounds like two traps of Braids are on my tail. They'll be here any minute." Rukh listened and heard the unmistakable sound of pursuit. "Make that seconds."

"The Ur-Fels are still loyal to us," Li-Choke said, stepping out into the passageway, followed by the other Baels, who arranged themselves behind him, their tridents and whips at the ready.

Rukh was about to follow, but Li-Chant held him back. "Leave this to us. If the Ur-Fels see you, there will be no reasoning with them."

Rukh reluctantly agreed. He wasn't sure what the Baels had in mind, but he had to trust them.

After the old Bael left, taking his torch with him, the chamber was enclosed in darkness and Rukh was left to ponder his next move. One thing was for sure: there was no way he was going to wait inside this cave like a lamb waiting for the slaughter. Rukh Blended and edged outside, sliding behind the Baels. He drifted deeper into the passage, stopping once he was hidden in the darkness, well beyond the light of torches held by the Baels.

The Chimeras who had been pursuing him finally arrived. They stumbled to a confused halt when faced by the Baels.

"Your time past," a Tigon said, thrusting to the front. "The Queen kill you."

Li-Chant laughed in his face. He barked several commands, gesturing with his trident. The Ur-Fels ceased their growling and listened. Their attention infuriated the Tigons, who began laying into the dog-like Chims with sword and claw. It was the signal to set off a melee with the Baels and the Ur-Fels against the Tigons and the Braids.

Rukh could have helped, but Chant's words held him back. If he were seen, the Baels would lose the Ur-Fels as allies.

The battle was evenly matched, and it ended just as quickly as it began, with a final Tigon dying upon the prongs of Choke's trident. All the Ur-Fels and Braids were also dead as were several Baels. Rukh counted six of them still standing. The youngest of their number was amongst those who had fallen, and so was Li-Chant.

The passage echoed like the quiet after a storm.

Li-Choke shuddered when he saw Chant's body lying face up, a horrific, bloody rent tearing open his chest.

Rukh carefully stepped forward, passing by several Baels, who rumbled at him. He kept his hands from his sword. He didn't want any trouble. Not now when he might get all of them out of this mess with their skin intact. He stopped beside Choke. "I can't stay," he said. "I still have a mission."

Choke nodded.

Rukh knew what he had to do, but questions still burned in his mind. "What happened here?" he asked.

Choke frowned. "You mean why are the Baels hiding in these dark caves like frightened mice?" he asked. "Mother exterminated all the commanders at the Hunters Flats. You saw what She did. She intended the same here, but She couldn't do it Herself, not without also killing Her breeders. She is like a living hurricane. If She had entered the caverns, She would have erased all life from the tunnels. She cannot contain Her powers for the fine work needed to kill the Baels and leave the rest of Her Chimeras alive."

"She commanded the other Chimeras to kill you instead," Rukh guessed. "And you hid down here where they wouldn't find you."

Choke nodded. "The Ur-Fels remained loyal to us. They brought us food and water and did not reveal our location to the Tigons. The Ur-Fels and the Tigons have always hated one another."

"What will you do now?" Rukh asked. "If my people are able to defeat the Chimeras, they will find you eventually. They'll kill all of you."

Choke shrugged. "We will have to avoid them then."

"You could come with me," Rukh suggested. "I can Blend you and get you out of here."

"Where would we go?"

"If the Queen doesn't know you live, you could go anywhere."

"And where in this world would the Baels be safe?" Choke asked, bitterly. "The cities of men where we are rightfully reviled? Or the Wildness where Mother holds sway?"

"She doesn't bother with the Kesarins, the Shylows, very much."

"The great cats have little love for us, either."

"I spoke to one of them, a female named Aia. She's the daughter of one of the leaders of their glarings. Aia says she can ensure your safety."

Rukh quickly explained about the Shylows, and the conversations he had with Aia. When she had first invaded the expedition's camp, he had requested safe harbor for the Baels. At the time, he hadn't been sure why he had asked her for something so treasonous. While he had come to believe the Baels had truly done their best to protect Humanity over the centuries since Hammer's fall, he still wasn't sure what the one-time Chimera commanders were to him. Why should he protect them? All his life, he'd been taught extinction was their just reward. A part of him still believed that, even with what he now knew was probably the truth about their nature.

But, something that night, the loneliness of it all maybe, had sparked him to change his opinion. He wanted to see the Baels live. If Suwraith came for Ashoka next spring, a few of her former commanders wouldn't tip the balance one way or another. And Rukh didn't think they would be fighting alongside the other Chimeras of the Fan Lor Kum. Not if Dirge had been telling the truth, which Rukh believed to be the case. The Baels deserved life, not extermination, and Rukh wanted to help see it happen; even if doing so was considered wrong by everyone else, it *felt* right. Besides, he'd done enough killing today.

Aia had come back with her answer during the time when Rukh had been scouting ahead all alone.

"She says the Kesarins would allow the Baels entrance to the Flats and leave them undisturbed, so long as they kept to themselves," Rukh told the remaining Baels.

Choke blinked, and he looked surprised. "It is a generous offer," he said. "One I can scarce believe offered by a son of Humanity."

"Will you come?" Rukh asked. He hoped Choke would say 'yes'.

"We will come," the Bael replied.

The others gathered around, and Li-Choke explained Rukh's offer. The others murmured amongst themselves, sounding hopeful.

"We have to go," Rukh said, feeling a rush of pleasure and excitement over what he was about to do. "We need to get to the southernmost entrance before the warriors finish off the Chims. I don't think I can get you past them otherwise, not if they're blocking the way out."

They set off, and Rukh Blended all of them. The sound of conflict was dying off, and there were few Chimeras left to defend the caverns. The Ashokans still searched, looking for any final enemies to slay. Rukh avoided the squads of his fellow warriors even more carefully than he did the Chimeras. The Murans and Rahails could sense his Blend better than Ur-Fels, Braids, or Tigons. His shoulders were tight with tension the entire way.

Luck must have remained with him. Somehow, they made it unnoticed and unchallenged to the southern entrance; the one Rukh had entered hours before this night of blood and death. It was light outside, early morning. Rukh *had* been fighting and killing for hours. The Baels crowded behind him, and he glanced at them, seeing their anxious expressions. At least there was a chance he could save some lives today instead of only ending them.

Rukh pointed south along the banks of the Slave River. "Head past the Tripwire, then cut east. Aia says she'll find you there and lead you to safety."

Li-Choke took his hand, shaking it as a man might. It was an unnatural and awkward gesture for the Bael. "Thank you Rukh Shektan. We owe you our lives." The other Baels murmured similar words.

"Just remember what I told you and get moving. If anyone sees you out here, you're dead," Rukh said.

Li-Choke nodded and led his Baels away.

Rukh watched them swiftly march off into the distance, feeling an unexpected kinship with the Baels. They finally disappeared from view, and he breathed a sigh of relief. The entrance to the caverns was still empty. No one had seen the Baels leave or witnessed his role in their departure. If they had, Marshall Tanhue wouldn't have bothered with a tribunal back in Ashoka. He'd have ordered Rukh killed right there on the spot.

But Rukh figured his actions and the accompanying risk had been worth it.

As he had led the Baels through the caverns, it had become clear that the Ashokans had won a great victory here today. Rukh felt like he had won one as well, though a different kind. His life had been hard the past four or five weeks, but in the end, maybe he had found a way to redeem his pain. There had to be more to life than simply killing one's enemies. Maybe it had something to do with changing an enemy into a friend. And maybe he could change the hearts of the Ashokans as well. He hoped so.

He turned away and re-entered the gloom of the tunnel. Time to find out who was still alive.

* * *

"Do you have a moment," Jessira asked, closing the door to the House Library.

Jaresh was alone, reading a history or some such. It was how he typically spent his free time these days. Jaresh wasn't sulky or surly, but ever since Rukh had apparently spoken to him a few weeks back, warning his younger brother about his relationship with Mira, he had been distant. And after that meeting, Jaresh had thrown himself into his work, with hardly ever a free moment.

When Jessira did see him, there was always a hint of sadness to Jaresh's eyes, and she knew why. Jaresh was trying to keep himself busy so he wouldn't have time to think about Mira. He was dealing with heartbreak in the only way he knew how, but it left Jessira wondering what Mira was doing with *her* time. How was Mira keeping herself busy so *she* wouldn't have to think about Jaresh? It was a shame. Mira and Jaresh's relationship wouldn't have carried any stigma in Stronghold.

Jessira didn't regret speaking up and telling Rukh her concerns about Mira and Jaresh, but she did regret the pain it was causing the two of them. There was something she could do which might help. She doubted he would accept her offer, but she had to make it.

"What is it?" Jaresh asked.

"I need to confess something. *I'm* the one who told Rukh about you and Mira."

"You were?" Jaresh scowled. "I should have known," he said, his face cast along bitter lines. "You should have kept your mouth shut," he snarled.

Jessira had expected him to be upset, and she let his anger wash over her, holding tight to her patience. Let him berate her. As long as he heard her out, she didn't care. "And what would you have preferred? For me to keep quiet so you and Mira could go about your merry way and end up named ghrinas?"

"Nothing was going on between us," Jaresh snapped.

Jessira's eyebrows arched and she wore a look of disbelief. Who did Jaresh think he was fooling? "I'm not a Pureblood," she reminded him. "You don't have to lie to me about your feelings for Mira. Fall in love with her, get married, I don't care. In Stronghold, there would be no reason not to do any of it."

"Your point being...?" Jaresh asked curtly.

"You and Mira can come with me to Stronghold. I've seen how miserable you are. You think Mira is feeling any better?'

Jaresh settled back in his chair, his anger replaced by a look of startlement. "Go with you to Stronghold?" he repeated. "It's an interesting offer, but..."

"Before you say 'no', just think it over. I know it sounds ridiculous, but Rukh would be with you, and so would Mira."

"But my family is here. Ashoka is my home."

"And Mira is the woman you love."

Jaresh merely nodded, confirming what Jessira had already suspected to be true. "I'll think about it," he said. "But don't tell Mira. If I say 'yes', I should be the one who asks her."

"Just let me know as soon as you can," Jessira said. She left the library and closed the door on her way out, leaving Jaresh to consider her offer.

A few days later, she had her answer. She wasn't surprised that it was 'no'.

———— • ————

I n the tunnels and caves, it was chaos. It smelled like an abattoir, with the stink of burned flesh and blood hanging in the air. Bodies of dead Chims and far too many Ashokans were scattered throughout. A few final battles raged briefly and violently before the last of the Fan Lor Kum were killed. It had been as everyone had expected: the Chimeras of the breeding caverns had fought to the bloody end, never seeking to flee, and never seeking to surrender.

Eventually Rukh was able to reconnect with an Ashokan unit. It wasn't the one to which he had been assigned, but it was better than wandering the passages alone. They seemed glad enough for his help, undermanned as they were. They had taken horrific casualties, and all the warriors had the glassy-eyed look of utter fatigue. Many were injured with broken arms and ribs or worse. All of them were drenched in blood, both fresh and dried, and crusted pieces of flesh clung to their skin and clothes.

Shortly after Rukh joined them, they finished cleaning out their section of the caverns, and trickled outside where they were soon joined by a number of other squads. It soon became clear just how many men had perished within the tunnels. It was far too many, and those who had survived had all been injured in some way. Many would die before the day was done.

Duty was harsher than an icy winter gale, and Rukh knew his. Despite his fatigue, despite his desire to just lie down and rest, despite how reed thin his *Jivatma* was, he knew what had to be done. He had to Heal as many of these poor bastards as possible. While the demonstration of yet another Talent would only further widen the gulf that existed between himself and the other Ashokans, Rukh was indifferent to the possibility at this point. He knew many of the warriors here. He'd grown up with some of them, counted them as friends at one time. Despite how they had treated him, he couldn't ignore their suffering. Mercy – a taskmaster no less harsh than duty – demanded it.

Rukh looked for and eventually found his lieutenant. Although Danslo was an ass, and Rukh didn't respect or trust the man, he was still Rukh's commanding officer. Right now, the lieutenant was hip deep in injured men who were moaning in pain.

"Well miracles never cease," Danslo said. "You're still alive. I guess the Chims didn't want to kill one of their own."

The lieutenant paled as soon as the words were out of his mouth. Those words couldn't be taken back. Those words demanded satisfaction.

Rukh had wanted to do what was right. He had approached the lieutenant with charity in his heart. His generous spirit vanished, replaced by an all-consuming rage and need for vengeance. A red haze filled Rukh's vision. All the other men had heard Danslo, and they quieted, sensing Rukh's deadly menace.

"Pray now. You have one minute to make your peace with this world before I send you to the next," Rukh said, unsheathing his sword.

"Worry about your own," Danslo said, drawing as well but looking far from happy at having to do so.

Captain Regus, one of Marshall Tanhue's subcommanders, must have seen the two of them facing off. The captain stormed over and intercepted their impending duel, stepping between them. He looked furious. "What is the meaning of this?" he roared at Rukh and Danslo. "You would dare draw swords on a brother with our dead not yet even cold? Here and now? You dishonor all they fought for!"

Rukh stepped back and tersely explained to the captain the words spoken by the lieutenant. If the captain ordered them to cease and desist, Rukh would...for now. But even then, this wouldn't be over. Danslo would answer for his insults.

Regus' mouth gaped. "Is this true?" he demanded of Danslo.

Danslo's jaw clenched, and he nodded, short and curt. "I've said nothing to this...person that I regret."

The captain looked disgusted. "Then you are a Devesh damned fool. Apologize and pray he accepts it and doesn't gut you where you stand."

"Are you giving me an order?" Danslo growled.

"If that's what it takes to keep your fragging head attached to your fragging body, then yes."

Danslo scowled, but in the end, he acquiesced, sheathing his sword. "Please understand, my words were rash and inspired by the death and injury of the men entrusted to my care. I am sorry if what I said offended you," he said. It was a weasel-worded unapologetic apology and everyone knew it.

Rukh glared. He was about to let Danslo know where he could shove his worthless confession, but Regus gripped his arm, keeping him from attacking the lieutenant.

"It is the best you can expect," the captain hissed in Rukh's ear. "Or do you wish to spill the blood of your brother on a day when so many of our warriors have already died? Death hovers over us. There is no need for you to aid his swift sickle."

Rukh jerked his arm free. Danslo was definitely *not* his brother, but the captain was right. They had lost enough warriors today, and so many more would likely perish from their wounds before the sun had set. And hadn't he sought the lieutenant in order to help save those men? He gave a frustrated growl. Danslo would live.

Rukh slammed his sword home and stepped forward, staring the lieutenant in the eyes. The man carried not a hint of remorse for his words. Jackhole bastard. Rukh fired a *Jivatma* powered liver shot, lifting Danslo off his feet and landing him on his ass. It would be painful as hell, but not debilitating. "You are a coward to hide behind your rank and your orders. The men call me the Tainted One, but I know who I am and what I am worth. I am a warrior of Ashoka, and I won't kill you, *brother*."

He turned to the captain. "I can Heal, not as well as a Shiyen, but maybe enough to save some lives," he said. Upon hearing his claim, the warriors sitting, squatting, or standing behind him began murmuring in fear and consternation. "It's another Talent I picked up on the Trial. Give me a chance, and a few of the warriors who should otherwise die might actually live." The Ashokans wouldn't appreciate his help, but what they thought of him didn't matter to him any more. He was a Kumma, a warrior and a supreme killer, but he was determined to be more than that, even if no one else saw or cared.

The captain stared at him, confused and appalled at the same time. "What are you?" he whispered.

Rukh smirked. It was the reaction he had expected, and one he'd see again and again on the faces of the other Ashokans. "The only person who might be able to save many who have no hope."

The captain nodded. "Come," he ordered. "The Marshall will need to hear this."

Marshall Tanhue was hip deep in reports as captains reported their findings and passed on the lists of the dead and injured. A hastily thrown up command tent marked his position. Upon seeing Rukh, the Marshall frowned in distaste. "Whatever it is, I don't have time for it," he said.

Captain Regus quickly told the Marshall what Rukh claimed he was able to do, and the scorn left the commander's face, replaced by sudden hope. "Is this true?"

Rukh suppressed a surge of resentment at the Marshall's words and tone. "Like I told the captain, I'm not a Shiyen, but I might be able to do some good."

"I'll take help wherever I can get it," the Marshall said. He called for his aide. "Get the injured organized. Arrange them least injured to worst. Figure out who isn't going to make it even if Gelan Criatus himself was present to help them. Make those warriors as comfortable as you can. The ones who can get by without immediate help will have to do for themselves. There's no helping them right now. It's the men in the middle, the ones who would make it if they had a physician looking out for them who we need to focus on. This man..." he pointed at Rukh, "...may be able to Heal them. And make sure he sees my nephew."

Rukh followed the Marshall's aide, who had already set up a triage center. Injured men lay on blankets, moaning in pain, but it was those who made no sound at all who worried Rukh the most. They were either dying or had suffered some kind of head injury. Neither was a good sign. The final tally in the assault on the caverns had left a little over a thousand men dead and the rest injured in some way. Very few had escaped unscathed. Many had broken bones waiting to be set, or deep cuts that had already been bound and sutured. There were also two hundred and fifty men, so severely injured, they would die before the day was done, and another two hundred who might live if a physician could see to their Healing. It was these men to whom Rukh went first. He had to keep them alive until they returned to Ashoka; once there, the Shiyens could take over.

Even though he was stone-cold tired, Rukh got to work straight away. At first, he tried to Heal everything wrong with the men brought to him. It was a mistake. Working like that left him drained and hardly able to Heal anyone else. It made more sense to do only the bare minimum to keep a man alive. It meant those he sought to help remained on death's door, but at least they still lived, which was better than the alternative. The problem with Healing in this manner quickly became apparent: the warriors in his care never fully recovered, and they ended up needing his constant attention. Some emergency would always crop up, maybe a new problem, or maybe one he'd already dealt with would suddenly get worse again, like a torn blood vessel ripping open once more. It was a never-ending flood of injuries. He pushed well past his limits on the day after the battle; well past the point where common sense told him to get some rest, but he couldn't. The warriors might die if he did. Rukh wanted nothing more than to lie down and sleep, but as day turned to night, he slogged on, working to keep alive as many as he could.

The expedition stayed near the caverns for three days, cleaning out the caves and setting their dead to rest on shared funeral pyres before heading home. The passage from Ashoka had taken about four weeks, but the trip back took more than five. It was a journey Rukh barely remembered. He was exhausted all the time; lost in a fog of fatigue, hardly ever sleeping. He was awoken frequently on most nights, charged with caring for the sick and the dying. His new mission was worth it, though. Because of him, one hundred and nine men who might have otherwise died still lived.

Since he was too busy to perform his previous tasks, such as scouting or preparing his own camp, the other warriors were asked to help him out. They even brought him his meals while he worked on keeping their brothers alive. He figured they resented having to do so much for him, but he didn't much care what they thought.

"You push too hard, brother," a warrior said.

Rukh stood with a groan, hardly hearing whoever it was who had brought him supper. He'd been crouched for too long and his back ached as if someone had been beating on it with a club. He had been fixing the same fragging blood vessel in a warrior's leg he'd already Healed five times now. The damn thing kept coming undone. Hopefully, the Shiyens would be able to fix it. The expedition couldn't be too far from Ashoka by now. Surely, messages had been sent to the city requesting immediate help. He hoped so.

He didn't have much left to give. He'd caught sight of his face a few days back in a mirror. It wasn't good. He was haggard and had lost a lot of weight. He felt sick all the time, nauseated from sleep deprivation. His *Jivatma* was a translucent wisp, flowing so slowly from his Well. If he pushed any harder, he might rip his *Jivatma* to shreds and never regain it. He'd only ever read of something like that happening on rare occasions – the Unliving Death was what it was called – but it was also a risk Rukh believed he had to take. He would get his much needed rest when the brothers in his care didn't need him. Until then, he'd keep plugging away.

It was with these thoughts in mind that Rukh stretched and reached for the plate of food the warrior held. Only then did he realize who had brought his evening meal.

"Lieutenant," Rukh said, feeling stupid and suddenly unsure. What did Danslo want? He couldn't be here on his own. One of the commanders must have either ordered him to bring Rukh his meal, or the man had lost a bet or something. Either way, he fleetingly wondered if the food would even be safe to eat. Poisoning was dishonorable, but so was sending someone on a suicide mission. But even Danslo – untrustworthy though he was – wouldn't do something so insane. He had to know that Rukh was the only person standing between life and death for so many of the brothers.

"Your supper grows cold, warrior," the lieutenant said. "You should eat. Our brothers need your strength."

Rukh reached for the plate and canteen of water, not sure of Danslo's motive.

"I asked for the opportunity to bring you your evening meal so I could speak with you," the lieutenant said. "I was wrong about you, and I guess I wasn't alone, either. All of the warriors have treated you poorly, but we've also watched you. You fought through in the caverns, never giving up on your mission. And afterward, you've nearly killed yourself keeping our brothers alive. You've shamed us, and I'm speaking for all the men when I tell you this."

Rukh took a swallow of water, confused by the unreality of the whole situation. Danslo sounded surprisingly sincere. What could have changed the man's opinion of him so completely?

He was about to answer when the lieutenant spoke again. "For myself, I wish to apologize to you. The way I've treated you and spoken to you has been Unworthy and unforgiveable. But I have to ask: will you accept my most humble apology for all the ways I've wronged you? Will you allow me to stand with you once again as your brother, as all men should when we are on Trial?"

Rukh didn't know what to say. He knew what he wished he could tell the lieutenant, but the hurt was too near, and touched as he was by the lieutenant's words, he didn't have it in him to forgive what had been done. "Thank you for the food, lieutenant," he said, unable to muster up anything kinder.

"I understand," Danslo said with a sad nod. "And thank *you*, Rukh Shektan. Devesh protect you." The lieutenant stood, bowed briefly, and left.

After the meeting, Rukh took a more careful note of the warriors and saw the respect in their eyes when they met his glance. He'd grown so used to their contempt and dislike that he never expected to see such an approving emotion on their faces when they looked at him. For the first time in weeks, he smiled.

Perhaps there might be hope for him in Ashoka after all.

The next morning, he learned just how fleeting his hope would prove to be.

———————⊷•⊷———————

"Have you heard the news?" Varesea asked,

The SuDin glanced up. He had been waiting for her in a new meeting place, the back room of a restaurant. Neither were masked. "What news?" he asked, wondering what could have Varesea looking so happy.

"The expedition has returned. They were successful. The Chimera breeding caverns were exterminated. Not a single one of them escaped. It turns out the young Shektan was right."

The SuDin smiled broadly. "That *is* excellent news." His plans, so delicately balanced, were now on much firmer footing and could thus proceed forward.

"It is a shame about the Shektan," Varesea said. "Everyone is singing his praises, even the Marshall. They say he was the reason the Shylows didn't attack our warriors. Apparently, his story of befriending one of the great cats turned out to be true. They also say that during the battle, he was separated from his unit and had to fight his way out all alone, and when they searched the caves he had travelled, hundreds of Chimeras lay dead. And if that wasn't courageous enough, after the battle, he was like a Shiyen. He apparently Healed the injured warriors, saving scores of them. They're calling him a hero."

The SuDin sneered. "And I'm sure his father was the one to spread such rumors. The people will be led astray by any man with a sad and heroic seeming tale."

"You don't think the Shektan is heroic?"

"Of course he was heroic, but it doesn't change the facts of the situation. The man is Kumma who can Blend and Heal. Even worse, he brought an adult ghrina to our city, a woman with whom he may have had an illegitimate relationship…"

Varesea laughed. "Listen to yourself. Illegitimate. What are we then? We are ghrina just as much as him."

The SuDin scowled in irritation. "The point being, he still falls under society's rules. The Shektan was properly judged. We, on the other hand, have chosen a different path, and our *relationship* is the least of the reasons for which we would be condemned." Varesea said nothing, but he could feel her study him as he read the daily newssheet. "What?" he asked.

"You fear him."

The SuDin smiled. Varesea could see the heart of the matter as no one else did. It was why he loved her. "I feared his blade. I saw the Tournament. A few more years and a little more seasoning, and he could have bested me even when I was young."

"Even as you are now?"

"My power is far greater than it ever was, but, yes, even now, the Shektan would make a deadly opponent."

"Then it is good he can no longer threaten us."

"Indeed. And if the people cry out for Rukh Shektan's return, let them," he sneered. "Their petty wants and desires no longer concern us."

"Petty? How grand is your vision then?"

The SuDin smiled again, this time more broadly. "With the destruction of the caverns, the Queen's plans for Ashoka will have been set back by years, if not decades," he said.

"And we have the Withering Knife," Varesea said, smiling in return. "We will have all the time we need to kill and kill again, until we are potent enough to challenge even Her."

"You see my plan then. For two millennia the world has lacked a First Father and First Mother. I plan on rectifying that mistake," said Hal'El Wrestiva, SuDin of the Sil Lor Kum.

———— •• ————

E arly in the morning, a day out from Ashoka, Rukh was ordered to see the Marshall. He was feeling happy and grateful because the scouts had just now brought back a score of Shiyen physicians along with enough wagons to transport the most severely injured warriors back to the city. The Shiyens had done quick triage on all the injured, clucking in amazement at some of the injuries the warriors had sustained and survived. When they learned it had been Rukh who had Healed the men, they gave him troubled glances and sidelong looks of uncertainty. Their reactions were actually pretty mild given how the warriors of the expedition had responded early on to his Talents.

After the physicians left, Rukh wanted to slump over into an exhausted sleep, but he had to remain at parade rest. He was still in the presence of the Marshall.

Tanhue poured two drinks, passing one to Rukh. It smelled like whiskey. "There's something else I need to discuss with you, warrior," the Marshall said, sitting down, suddenly looking weary and bitter. "You must have powerful enemies, son. They've been busy while we've been out in the Wildness." He took a swig of his drink and sighed, looking saddened.

Rukh stared into his glass of whiskey. Based on the Marshall's words and attitude, it sounded like he would need the stiff drink. Their commander wasn't the sort who was easily rattled. Rukh downed the whiskey, holding back a gasp at its fiery burn. He braced himself, prepared to hear what the Marshall had to say.

"Suwraith's spit. There's no easy way to say this. Based on your new Talents and your association with a ghrina, the Chamber of Lords has deemed you Unworthy. You've been stripped of all rank and are hereby exiled from Ashoka and her Oasis, never to return on pain of death. None of her warriors can shelter you," the Marshall said. "I'm so sorry about this," he added a moment later.

Rukh's legs buckled, and he almost fell to the ground. He stared unseeing past the Marshall. Only yesterday evening, after speaking with Lieutenant Danslo, hope – thin and uncertain – had blossomed in his heart. For a few, brief hours, he had thought his life might not become the miserable wreck he had assumed it was doomed to be. He had allowed himself to believe he could reclaim his dignity.

The Marshall stared him in the eye. "For what it's worth, I wholeheartedly disagree with the Chamber," he said. "I find you Worthy, Rukh Shektan. Without you, many good men would have died. I saw you work. I saw you give everything you had even after we gave you nothing but a heaping pile of shit. It shames me how you were treated, and I hope someday you can find it in your heart to forgive us."

"Yes, sir," Rukh said, not really listening, but dimly appreciating the Marshall's words. What would he do now? Where would he go? Once a man was exiled, no other city would take him in. A death sentence had been handed out, and Rukh never even had a chance to speak up on his own behalf.

"There is someone here for you," said the Marshall. "You can talk to her here, but afterward, I'm afraid you'll have to gather your belongings and leave."

"Her?"

The Marshall stood. "I'll give the two of you some privacy," he said, coming around the worktable and leaving the tent.

Rukh wondered who Marshall Tanhue was talking about. Had Amma come out here to see him off? Or was it Bree? Whoever it was, she shouldn't have left the safety of the city. Not for someone Unworthy like him. He stared at the back of the tent, not seeing or noticing anything, stunned by the finality of it.

"You look terrible," a voice said. He turned. Jessira. Rukh's heart unclenched a little at the sight of her. At least he'd have a place to go. She gave him a tight-lipped smile of sympathy.

"I feel terrible," he said. He briefly wondered why she wasn't already back in Stronghold. She should have been, but here she was standing in front of him.

She must have understood his confusion. "You were exiled a few days after the expedition left. Your nanna asked me to wait for your return. I agreed."

"And will you take me to Stronghold?"

She nodded. "That was the plan. I have supplies and mounts for both of us," she said. "Your nanna was generous with his provisions. Are you ready?"

Rukh nodded, still unable to believe the terrible turn his life had taken. He would never again see Nanna or Amma. Or Jaresh or Bree or any of his other family and friends. He was dead to them. Even

Ashoka herself was forever off-limits. He'd never get to walk her beautiful hills and wide streets or witness her soul-inspiring culture and arts. He numbly gathered his belongings and followed Jessira to the outskirts of the camp where she had four horses waiting for them: two saddled and others with bulging packs. Nanna *had* been generous. Rukh tied off his gear and mounted up. He looked back toward the camp where the warriors of the expedition had gathered. They stared in his direction, and with a start, he realized they were there to see him off. He found Danslo, who nodded silent acknowledgement.

The lieutenant, so long his enemy, raised a fist to the sky and shouted, "Rukh Sai!"

His words were repeated by the rest of the warriors. "Rukh Sai! Rukh Sai!" they shouted.

"What are they saying?" Jessira asked.

"They are offering me the title bestowed upon the winner of the Tournament of Hume," Rukh said, his eyes wet with tears.

"I thought you won the Tournament months ago," Jessira said.

"I did," Rukh said. "I told them my Talents on the way to the caverns. They didn't take it well."

"Oh." Jessira didn't need him to spell it all out. She understood what he meant.

"What they're doing now…it's their way of apologizing," Rukh said. He stifled a sob. Warriors didn't cry in public. "After what the Chamber decided, this is the most they can do. Some of the ruling 'Els won't like it. They might even make trouble for these men."

"It's not your concern anymore, Rukh," Jessira said, softly. "They made their choices. They'll have to live with them." She paused. "And we have to live with ours. It's time to go."

Rukh waved to his brothers one last time before turning his horse so he could face her. "Why didn't Nanna come out with you?"

"He couldn't. The House Council decided it wouldn't be safe, and *he* wouldn't let your amma, brother, or sister leave the Oasis either. I'm all you've got. I hope you're not too disappointed." She reached into a satchel. "Your family sent you letters. Here." She handed them over.

Rukh took them numbly as he gently stroked the paper. His mother's handwriting was elegant and perfect as was Bree's. Jaresh's was so like Nanna's: an inelegant, squared off scribbling. He put the letters away. He'd read them later. "Will we make it to Stronghold before the snows?" he asked.

"We might get caught in a few storms, but the snows usually melt in a day or two this time of year. We should be fine if we hustle."

"Then we better get moving."

———————●———————

"You need to know something," Jessira said, speaking into the silence that had settled over them within minutes of leaving the camp. It was still early in the morning, and they had a long ways to go.

Rukh glanced over at her, but she kept her eyes locked forward, unwilling to meet his gaze. He shrugged, distantly wondering what had her so stiff. Was he forever riding away from Ashoka? It was still so surreal. How could this have happened? He vacillated between grief and a hollow emptiness, and he didn't know which was worse. The grief let him know he was alive, but right now, he wasn't sure it was worth it. The emptiness, though…it was what he imagined it would be like to die, to finally set aside all his burdens. It was seductive, the idea of giving up and letting it all end.

He grimaced. It was also a coward's death.

"The real reason you were found Unworthy is because of me,"

Jessira began hesitantly.

With a visible effort, Rukh pulled himself out from the terrible hurt of his loss and made himself listen to her words. "What are you saying?" he asked.

Jessira's countenance and bearing were those of guilt and regret. "The extra Talents might have been forgiven…"

"How did the Chamber find out about them anyway?" Rukh interrupted her, suddenly focused in on a question which had plagued him since he'd learned of his banishment. "Who told them?"

"Rector Bryce," Jessira answered. "He came out and admitted it. Your nanna was all set to Expel him from House Shektan – I understand it would have marked him as a traitor for all time."

"He would have become a ronin, an unHoused warrior. Scum. No other House would have accepted his membership, not with a stain like that," Rukh said.

"Like I said, Dar'El was all set to do just that, but for some reason, he didn't. The two of them had a private meeting, and your nanna let Bryce resign instead. Bryce is now a member of House Wrestiva."

Rukh grunted. "It's where he belonged all along."

They rode in silence as Rukh considered what Rector Bryce's betrayal and departure from House Shektan might mean. It was no longer his responsibility, but old habits died hard.

"What I was saying earlier," Jessira said, breaking into his thoughts. "You were found Unworthy because of Dryad Park. People claimed we had an illicit relationship."

"Dryad Park? Our walk at night after the play?" Rukh realized what Jessira meant. His jaw clenched in anger, and he had to stifle an urge to scream at himself. Fragging arrogant idiot! He had airily dismissed his own worries about how others would view his time with Jessira. Why hadn't he listened to that warning voice?

Jessira must have noticed his anger. She reined her horse to a halt, forcing Rukh to stop as well. "It's my fault," she said. "If I hadn't been so needy, none of this would have happened."

Rukh's teeth ground together, and he had to force himself to unclench his jaw. He was angry with himself, but there was no need to crack his own teeth. He rubbed his temples and sighed. Suddenly, the fury emptied out of him, gone as quickly as it had come. Nothing he said or felt or did would change what had happened. What was done was done. He had acted as he thought a friend should, and for his gross lack of judgment, he'd been found Unworthy.

"It wasn't your fault," Rukh said in a flat, lifeless tone, willing himself to believe his words. "I made those choices. Not you. It was my own stupidity that caused this mess." His eyes welled with sudden tears. Damn it! He hated crying.

Somehow, he found himself held within the circle of Jessira's embrace. He clutched at her, hugging her hard. He let the tears fall.

"I'm so sorry," she whispered into his ear.

He turned his head, meaning to say something to her. Instead, his lips found hers, a brief touch. It was a soft kiss that deepened. She cupped his face, and pulled him closer. All thoughts were gone. All he knew was the feel of her in his arms, and the soft press of her lips against his.

She trailed her fingers along the line of his jaw before pulling away. "We should go," she said, her voice sounding husky.

Rukh nodded, his emotions in turmoil: sorrow, pain, and a deep sense of loss. He followed after her as he left behind everything he loved. He followed her west.

THE END

A Note From the Author

I hope you've enjoyed Book 1 of *The Castes and the OutCastes*. If you have, I would very much appreciate it if you tell all your friends and family to purchase the book as well. Should you do so, all your wildest dreams will come true. Oh, wait. I mean all *my* wildest dreams will come true. Er…maybe that's asking for too much. Could you leave a review then?

GLOSSARY

Note: Most Arisan scholars use a dating
system based on the fall of the First World. Thus:
BF: Before the Fall of the First World.
AF: After the Fall of the First World.

Adamantine Cliffs: White cliffs, about two hundred feet tall that form the southern border of Dryad Park.

Ahura Temple, the: One of the schools of song in Ashoka. Open only to Sentyas.

Aia: A young Shylow/Kesarin.

Alminius College of Medicine: One of the two Shiyen schools of medicine in Ashoka.

Arbiter, the: The administrive judge of the Chamber of Lords, interpreting the various rules and points of etiquette. Typically, he is an older Kumma chosen by the 'Els for his wisdom and knowledge. Upon his election, he gives up his House name and takes on the surname of 'Kumma'. The position is ceremonial one, and his vote is only offered in the case of a tie. His social standing is that of a ruling 'El. Current Arbiter is Lin'El Kumma.

Ashok: Caste Unknown. Historical figure who is the reputed author of the <u>Compact and Binding</u>, the constitutional basis of all governments in Arisa.

Ashokan Guard, the: A reserve unit of about 25,000 warriors meant to support the High Army in times of crisis. It is composed of veteran Kummas, Murans, and Rahails. A few Duriahs have also joined the Guard over the years.

Baels: The commanders of the Fan Lor Kum. They are feared for their intelligence and unwavering commitment to Humanity's destruction as well as their imposing size, chained whips, and tridents. By convention, they are always given a hyphenated name in which Li- makes the first part.

Book of All Souls, the: Sacred text dating from the First World. Author unknown, but said to be Devesh Himself. Over time since the fall of the First World, it has taken on secondary importance to *The Word and the Deed* in the religious life of most people.

Brand Wall: Caste Rahail. Born AF 2041 to Trudire and Simala Wall. Twenty-one years old at the time of his first Trial.

Bree Shektan: Caste Kumma. House Shektan. Born AF 2044 to Dar'El and Satha Shektan.

Brit Hule: Caste Rahail. Born 2027. He is the youngest Patriarch in living memory as well as the youngest Magistrate in the Magisterium.

Caravan: Trade expedition meant to maintain contact between the cities. Protection of the caravan — a Trial — has come to be seen as a holy duty, for only through the free exchange of knowledge can Humanity hope to survive the Suwraith's unending madness.

Castes, the: The social, moral, and economic organization of all cities on Arisa.

There are seven Castes:

> **Kumma**: The warrior Caste. They are involved in all aspects of defense, supplying the vast majority of warriors to the Ashokan military and the caravans. Their Talents are especially suited for battle.

> **Sentya**: Known for their accounting acumen and their skill

with musical instruments and compositions. The finest musicians and composers are always Sentya. They possess the Talent of Lucency, which allows them to think with near utter clarity. In such a state, emotions are distant. They can also project this ability onto others.

Duriah: Born to build, they are thick and stocky. Their Talent is to Cohese: the ability to take various **objects and substances and from them forge something different and more useful. Rare individuals can DeCohese, which is the ability to break any object down to its basic components. A master craftsman is known as a Cohesor.**

Rahail: They maintain the Oasis, sensing where it is growing thin and working to repair and renew it. It is done through their Talent of Sharing wherein they literally give their *Jivatma*, letting it seep into an Oasis and keep it strong. It is an ability they can use but don't really understand, even two thousand years after it first manifested. Their Caste is structured entirely around this Talent, although some join the caravans or the Ashokan Guard.

Muran: Traditionally, they are farmers, although some join the caravans or the Ashokan Guard. Their Talent allows them to bring even a desert to flower. However, the pride of the Caste are their singers.

Cherid: Physically they are the smallest of all the Castes, but Cherids are generally the leaders of a city. It is through their natural intelligence and cunning, as well as their Talent. They possess the ability of Synthesis: they can combine *Jivatmas* and share it out amongst others. Thus, a Rahail can maintain the city's Oasis, not simply with the strength of his own Caste, but that of all Castes if need be.

Shiyen: They all possess the ability to Heal to a certain extent, but only the most gifted amongst them are chosen for one of Ashoka's two medical colleges. The rest are generally craftsmen and merchants.

Cedar Grey: OutCaste. Born AF 2039 to Sateesh and Crena Grey. Lieutenant in the Stronghold Home Guard as member of the Silver Sun Scouts.

Chamber of Lords: Kumma ruling council. It is made of all the ruling 'Els and presided over by the Arbiter. It is involved in decision-making that will affect the Caste as a whole. The Chamber also renders judgment for those charged with being Unworthy or thought to be traitors.

Chimeras, the: Suwraith's created forces who comprise the Fan Lor Kum. There are seven species of Chimeras: Baels, Tigons, Braids, Ur-Fels, Bovars, Balants, and Pheds. All species of Chimeras have some degree of intelligence except for Pheds and Bovars. Pheds are simply a meat source, grown only to feed the Fan Lor Kum. Bovars are beasts of burden, much like oxen, but it is from them that the most intelligent of all Chimeras were birthed: the Baels. The Chimeras are marsupial and born in groups of five, what they label a crèche, and mature to full adulthood within a few years, although the Baels take slightly longer.

City Watch, the: Peacekeeping unit of about three hundred warriors, called upon to maintain the peace and investigate crime in Ashoka.

Compact and Binding: The constitution by which all cities on Arisa are organized. Dated to just after the Night of Sorrows.

Conn Mercur: Caste Shiyen. He is the dean of Verchow College of Medicine.

Constrainers: Leather vambraces used in training or tournaments as a means to suppress the expression of an individual's *Jivatma*.

Council of Rule: Ruling council of the Sil Lor Kum. It is comprised of the SuDin and the six MalDin.

Dar'El Shektan: Caste Kumma. House Shektan. Born AF 2006 as Darjuth Sulle to Jarned and Tune Sulle of House Ranthor. Completed four Trials before retiring at age thirty-one. He transferred to House Shektan upon his return to Ashoka after his fourth and final Trial. Married Satha nee Aybar in AF 2039. Later, in AF 2050, he became the ruling 'El of his House.

Days of Desolation: A period of decades where the light of civilization was almost put out. Suwraith raged unchecked throughout the world, and Humanity lay huddled within its cities, hoping to ride out the storm.

Dos Martel: Caste Muran. Born AF 1998. As well as being the Magistrate representative of her Caste, she is also a singer of great repute.

Dryad Park: A large, public park known variously as 'the Soul of Ashoka' or 'the green jewel of Ashoka'. It was developed under the auspices of the Magisterium in AF 1363 on an area of boggy, impoverished land full of rundown homes and apartments. The park has gone through several transitions, including a disastrous period of time in the 1600's where the fashion of the day was to return public land to its natural state. The park quickly became a bog once again with swamp gases regularly polluting the air. Thankfully, this idea of 'natural' spaces was swiftly abandoned. In addition, during times of emergency, the park can be converted into arable land.

Durmer Volk: Caste Kumma. House Shektan. Born AF 1990 to Hurum and Kiran Volk. Completed six Trials before retiring at age thirty-five. He is charged with the early training of young Shektans and known as the 'Great Rahail' for how seriously he takes his duties. Member of the House Council.

East Vineyard Steep: An area of relatively rundown homes and buildings, which barely stand erect. However, the main denizens, the Sentyas, prefer it this way. They would rather not waste money to maintain their homes beyond what's absolutely needed.

Fan and the Reed, the: All-female Kumma academy in Ashoka. Founded AF 343.

Fan Lor Kum: The Red Hand of Justice. Suwraith's forces in the Wildness. Their soul purpose is to kill Humans wherever they find them. They are organized into Plagues, and the commander of each Plague is titled the SarpanKum, a Bael of great cunning and skill. The Fan Lor Kum are sometimes referred to simply as the Chimeras.

Organization of the Fan Lor Kum:

100 Chimeras form a Smash and the commander is labeled a Jut
10 Smashes form a Fracture and the commander is labeled a Levner
15 Fractures form a Shatter and the commander is labeled a Vorsan
8 Shatters form a Dread and the commander is labeled a Sarpan
2 Dreads form a Plague and the commander is titled the SarpanKum

> *All commanders at every level are Baels. Of note is the SarpanKi, who does not fit into this hierarchy. The SarpanKi is the special adjunct to the SarpanKum, almost always from his crèche, and outranks the Sarpans.

Farn Arnicep: Caste Kumma. House Shektan. Born AF 2041 to Evam and Midre Arnicep. He is twenty-one years old at the time of his first Trial.

First Father: Along with the First Mother, He was the ruler of the First World, greatly responsible for the peace and fortune of that time. Legends say that the First Father broke the WellStone and was thereby able to gain entrance to the fortress of the First Mother, and together, they were able to bring life to a dead and desolate land. The Baels claim it was the First Father's own Daughter, Lienna, who murdered both of her Parents.

First Mother: Along with the First Father, She was the ruler of the First World, greatly responsible for the peace and fortune of that time. The Baels claim it was the First Mother's own Daughter, Lienna, who murdered both of her Parents.

First World: Legendary time of peace and prosperity prior to the arrival of Suwraith. With the death of the First Mother and the First Father, the First World ended with the Night of Sorrows.

Fol Nacket: Caste Cherid. Born AF 2006. He is the Cherid Magistrate and head of the Magisterium.

Fort and the Sword, the: All-male martial academy in Ashoka. Only open to Kummas. Established AF 121.

Fragrance Wall: An area of manses and estates. It is the home to most Cherids.

Garnet Bosde: Caste Kumma. House Shektan. Born AF 1985 to Reoten and Preema Bosde. Completed five Trials before retiring at age thirty-four. One of Dar'El Shektan's earliest supporters and a member of the House Council.

Gelan Criatus: Caste Shiyen. Born AF 435 in Hammer. Widely considered the father of modern medicine.

Glory Stadium: Ashoka's main stadium where the Tournament of Hume and other city-wide events take place.

Gren Vos: Caste Shiyen. Born AF 1975. She was a highly respected physician in her day, and is currently the longest serving Magistrate, having first been elected in AF 2021.

Gris Holianth: Caste Shiyen. Born AF 2011. Owner of the Long Pull, a pub.

Hal'El Wrestiva: Caste Kumma. House Wrestiva. Born AF 2000 as Halthin Bramer to Suge and Bryni Bramer of House Wrestiva. Completed eight Trials before retiring at age 36. Married to Kilwen nee Asthan in AF 2038 and widowed in AF 2049. Became the ruling 'El of his House Wrestiva in 2046.

High Army of Ashoka: Professional army of Ashoka made entirely of veterans of the Trials. Most of their ranks are filled out by Kummas, including the post of Liege-Marshall. Currently composed of two legions and a total of approximately 11,000 warriors.

Hold Cavern: A quiet neighborhood of small homes and shops. It is home to many Rahails.

House of Fire and Mirrors, the: All-male martial academy in Ashoka. Generally for Kummas but open to other Castes. Founded AF 216.

Hume Telrest: Caste Kumma. Born AF 1702. He is universally regarded as the finest warrior in the history of Arisa, having completed twenty Trials. It is in his honor that the Tournament of Hume is held in every city throughout the world.

Hungrove, the: A glaring of Shylows/Kesarin led by Aia's father.

Insufi **blade**: The sword given to a warrior during his *upanayana* ceremony.

Ironwood: A fast growing tree known for its lightweight, hardy wood, which has properties similar to iron and is similarly fire resistant.

Isle of the Crows: An island infamous for its black crows in Bar Try Bay. It is where the remains of traitors are left to rot. With the lack of a purifying pyre, such individuals are thought to lose Devesh's grace, and are either punished within the unholy hells or shackled again to the wheel of life to be re-born in a position of impoverishment and suffering.

Jared Randall: Caste Rahail. Born AF 2025. Completed three Trials. Caravan master of the caravan to Nestle. Suspected member of the Sil Lor Kum, although the proof is rather sparse.

Jaresh Shektan: Caste Sentya. House Shektan. Born AF 2042 to Bresh and Shari Konias. His birth parents died in an apartment fire, and he was adopted by Darjuth (later to be Dar'El) and Satha Sulle. He is the only such individual ever adopted into a Kumma House who is himself not a Kumma.

Jessira Viola Grey: OutCaste. Born AF 2042 to Sateesh and Crena Grey. Warrior of the Stronghold Home Army and a member of the Silversun scouts.

Jivatma: Some believe this to be the body's soul. It springs from a person's Well like a waterfall and can be made richer and more vibrant through discipline and hard work.

Jone Drent: Caste Duriah. Born AF 2005. He has the rare ability to both Cohese and DeCohese. He is the Duriah Magistrate.

Jubilee Hills: An expansive area of rolling hills. It is home to Kummas.

Keemo Chalwin: Caste Kumma. House Dravidia. Born AF 2041 to Loriad and Mishal Chalwin. He is twenty-one years old at the time of his first Trial.

Kesarin, the: See Shylows.

Kezin: See Slayer.

Krain Linshok: Caste Kumma. House Flood. Born AF 2003 to Halsith and Jennis Linshok. He has completed five Trials. He is the Kumma Magistrate.

Kuldige Prayvar: Caste Kumma. Born AF 1825. Originally of House Trektim, he went on to found House Shektan in AF 1872. He was thereafter known as Kul'El Shektan. He is also a self-confessed member of the Sil Lor Kum, ruling them for a time as the SuDin.

Larina, the: The only school of singing in Ashoka. Open only to Murans.

Layfind Fish Market: A raucous area of stores and booths near Trell Rue.

Li-Charn: SarpanKum of the Fan Lor Kum at the time of Hammer's fall.

Li-Dirge: SarpanKum of the Fan Lor Kum during the destruction of the caravan to Nestle.

Li-Reg: SarpanKi to Li-Dirge and his crèche brother.

Lighted Candle, the: Sentya academy given over entirely to the study of finance and accounting.

Lin'El Kumma: Caste Kumma. Born into House Therbal on AF 1980. Completed six Trials and retired at age 34. Elected as the Arbiter of the Chamber of Lords on AF 2051, and thereafter took the surname 'Kumma'.

Lure Grey: OutCaste. Born AF 2044 to Sateesh and Crena Grey. Warrior of the Stronghold Home Army and a member of the Silversun Scouts.

MalDin: The Servants of the Voice. The leaders of the Sil Lor Kum. Along with the SuDin, the six MalDin comprise the Council of Rule.

Mesa Reed: Caste Cherid. Born AF 2017. She is one of the wealthiest women in the city, having earned her money through a combination of inheritance from her deceased husband and her own investments. She is a MalDin of the Sil Lor Kum.

Mira Terrell: Caste Kumma. House Shektan. Born AF 2042 to Janos and Sophy Terrell. She has recently completed her year-long internship with House Suzay.

Moon Quarter: Area of wharves, docks, and factories. By law, all manufacturing or industry, which might result in malodorous pollution must be placed in the Moon Quarter. As such, it is an undesirable residential area.

Moke Urn: Caste Sentya. Born AF 2020. He was born in relative poverty and obscurity but is brilliant when it comes to finances. He was given an opportunity to demonstrate his skills as a member of the Sil Lor Kum of which he is now a MalDin.

Night of Sorrows: The night when Suwraith was born and killed nearly half of all people living at the time.

Nine Hills of Ashoka:
Mount Creolite
Mount Walnut
Mount Channel
Mount Crone
Mount Cyan
Mount Bright
Mount Auburn
Mount Equine
Mount Style

Oasis: A powerful manifestation, supposedly of *Jivatma*, which appearedly suddenly and unexpectedly around certain cities of the First World just prior to Suwraith's arrival. Over the ensuing two millennia, they have proven nearly impervious to Suwraith's power. Rahails maintain the Oasis of a city through their Talent of Sharing, but how they manage this is a mystery even to them.

Plaza of the Martyr: The largest public plaza in Ashoka. Also known as the 'Heart of Ashoka'. It is famous for the Union Fountain.

Plaza of Toll and Toil: The large plaza into which the Magisterium opens. Historically, it was where the contracts of indentured servants were auctioned.

Poque Belt: Caste Sentya. Born AF 2018. He founded a forensic accounting service. Rumor has it he was elected Magistrate for his Caste simply so he could no longer audit the work of other Sentyas.

Rector Bryce: Caste Kumma. House Shektan. Born AF 2029 to Garnet and Maris Bryce. His parents divorced when he was twelve. Completed four Trials before retiring at age thirty-two. Member of Ashokan Guard as a lieutenant of the **Fifth Platoon, Third Company, Second Brigade, Third Legion,** and also a lieutenant in the City Watch.

Rose and the Thorn, the: One of the schools of song in Ashoka. Open only to Sentyas.

Rukh Shektan: Caste Kumma. House Shektan. Born AF 2041 to Dar'El and Satha Shektan. He is twenty-one years old at the time of his first Trial. He is the first Virgin to win the Tournament of Hume.

Sarath, the: Rahail academy in Ashoka. Students are instructed in both the maintenance of the Oasis and also trained as warriors.

Satha Shektan: Caste Kumma. House Shektan. Born AF 2019 to Mira and Rukh Aybar of House Shektan. Married Darjuth Sulle (later to be Dar'El) in AF 2039. She is as responsible for House Shektan's rise in wealth and prestige as her husband. She is admired and loathed in equal measure by the other ruling 'Els.

School of Water, the: All-female Kumma academy in Ashoka. Established AF 153.

Semaphore Walk: Ashoka's theater district.

Shield, the: Rahail academy in Ashoka. Focus is on the training of those sufficiently gifted to maintain the Oasis.

Shir'Fen, the: Rahail miltary academy in Ashoka. Rigorous admission standards and instructors are a mix of Kummas and Rahails.

Shoke: A wooden blade used in training and tournaments. It is blunted and possesses properties that allow it to produce as true a representation as possible of the damage inflicted by an edged weapon without actually causing permanent injury or death.

Shylows: The great cats of the Hunters Flats. They grow to be over seven feet in height and twenty-five feet from nose-to-tail. They are feared for their great speed, power, and ability to see through Blends. The cats are extremely territorial and hunt in glarings, packs of forty-to-fifty. They name themselves the Kesarins.

Sil Lor Kum: The Hidden Hand of Justice. They are the Human agents of Suwraith and are universally hated and despised. Many consider their existence to be a myth, although inexplicable setbacks are often attributed to the Sil Lor Kum.

Slash of Iniquity: A judgment by the Kumma Chamber of Lords in which an individual is found to be deviant and traitorous. Such an individual is either executed with his remains left on the Isle of the Crows or in some instances, merely banished forthwith.

Slayer, the: Leader of a glaring of Shylows. Also known as the Kezin.

Sophy Terrell: Caste Kumma. House Shektan. Born AF 2014 to Kolt and Versana Drathe of House Primase. Married Odonis Terrell of House Shektan in AF 2035. Member of the House Council.

Sorrows of Hume, the: Aphorisms attributed to Hume Telrest.

Spidergrass: A type of plant that grows best in temperate climates. It is used in the fashioning of items once made with metal. Duriah smiths claim it has tensile properties identical to the finest steel.

Stone Cavern: A neighborhood of craft shops and manufacturing. It is where most Duriahs live.

Styrd Bosna: Caste Kumma. House Andthra. Born AF 2032 to Darjuth and Selese Bosna. Completed four Trials. He is the Captain of the caravan to Nestle.

SuDin: The Voice who Commands. The leader of the Sil Lor Kum.

Suge Wrestiva: Caste Kumma. House Wrestiva. Born AF 2040 to Hal'El and Kilwen Wrestiva. He has yet to be chosen for his first Trial. He remains a Virgin at the age of twenty-two. It is somewhat scandalous.

Sunpalm Orchard: A wealthy, quiet neighborhood of stately townhomes and small craft shops. It is home to many Shiyens.

Suwraith: A murderous being of wind and storm who suddenly exploded into existence two thousand years ago. Her only desire seems to be the extinction of Humanity. Her origin is a mystery, although the Baels claim that She was the Daughter of the First

Mother and First Father, murdering them on the Night of Sorrows. The Fan Lor Kum name Her Mother Lienna. Humanity also names her the Bringer of Sorrows or the Queen of Madness.

Talents: Skills possessed by individuals of various Castes, each one unique to a Caste.

Tanner's School of Animal Husbandry: Shiyen school of veterinary medicine.

Trial: The holy duty in which warriors leave the safety of an Oasis and enter the Wildness in order to defend a caravan, even if it costs them their lives.

Trell Rue: A fashionable neighborhood of artisan shops and restaurants.

Triumph Court: Plaza surrounding the Glory Stadium.

Ular Sathin: Caste Muran. Clan Balm. Born AF 1989. Completed two Trials before retiring at age twenty-eight. He was a well-to-do farmer before selling his property to other members of his Clan. He is a MalDin of the Sil Lor Kum.

Unworthy: A designation by which a Kumma is felt to be a coward and/or morally compromised. Such an individual is banished from the city.

Upanayana ceremony: Ceremony that consecrates a boy to his duties as a man. It involves two days and two nights of fasting and praying in solitude and silence. In the case of Kummas and other warriors, it is followed by the granting of the *Insufi* blade at dawn.

Varesea Apter: Caste Rahail. Born AF 2019. Married to **Slathtril Apter. She is a member of the Sil Lor Kum.**

Verchow College of Medicine: One of the two Shiyen medical colleges in Ashoka.

Well: The place within an individual wherin *Jivatma* resides. Some believe the Well is simply another word for consciousness, and from consciousness, *Jivatma* springs forth.

Wildness, the: The vast area beyond the borders of the cities and their Oases.

Word and the Deed, the: Author unknown. It is a sacred text written prior to the fall of the First World. Over time, it has supplanted *The Book of All Souls* as the main source of religious scripture within the world.

Yuthero Gaste: Caste Shiyen. Born AF 2025. He is one of the youngest professors of Surgery at Alminius School of Medicine. He is also a MalDin of the Sil Lor Kum.

ABOUT THE AUTHOR

Davis Ashura is a legend...in his own mind. He resides in North Carolina, sharing a house with his wonderful wife who somehow overlooked Davis' eccentricities and married him anyway. As proper recompense for her sacrifice, Davis then unwittingly turned his wonderful wife into a nerd-girl. To her sad and utter humiliation, she knows *exactly* what is meant by 'Kronos'. Living with them are their two rambunctious boys, both of whom have at various times helped turn Davis' once lustrous, raven-black hair prematurely white (it sure sounds prettier than the dirty gray it actually is). And of course, there is the obligatory strange, calico cat (all authors have cats – it's required by the union). She is the world's finest hunter of socks, be they dirty or clean. When not working – nay laboring – in the creation of works of fiction so grand that hardly anyone has read a single word of them, Davis practices medicine, but only when the insurance companies tell him he can.

Visit him at www.DavisAshura.com and be appalled by the banality of a writer's life.